W9-AQC-041

Also by Karen Quinn

Wife in the Fast Lane
The Ivy Chronicles

HOLLY *would* DREAM

Karen Quinn

A Touchstone Book
Published by Simon & Schuster
New York London Toronto Sydney

Touchstone
A Division of Simon & Schuster, Inc.
1230 Avenue of the Americas
New York, NY 10020

This book is a work of fiction. Names, characters, places, and incidents either are products of the author's imagination or are used fictitiously. Any resemblance to actual events or locales or persons, living or dead, is entirely coincidental.

First Touchstone trade paperback edition June 2008

TOUCHSTONE and colophon are registered trademarks of Simon & Schuster, Inc.

For information about special discounts for bulk purchases, please contact Simon & Schuster Special Sales at 1-800-456-6798 or business@simonandschuster.com.

Designed by Jamie Kerner

Manufactured in the United States of America

10 9 8 7 6 5 4 3 2 1

Library of Congress Cataloging-in-Publication Data
Quinn, Karen.
Holly would dream / by Karen Quinn.
p. cm.
"A Touchstone Book."
1. Hepburn, Audrey, 1929–1993—Fiction. 2. Fashion design—Museums—Fiction. 3. New York (N.Y.)—Fiction. I. Title.
PS3617.U575 H65 2008
813'.6—dc22 2007042717

ISBN-13: 978-1-4165-7312-8
ISBN-10: 1-4165-7312-7

To Mark, Schuyler, Sam, Mom, Dad, Michael, and Don—the seven wonders of my world

Acknowledgments

If I COULD THANK every one of my readers and booksellers here by name, I would. Your support is such a gift. Please contact me anytime through my website—www.karenquinn.net or at www.myspace.com/authorkarenquinn. I am the author who always writes back.

I am grateful to my agent, Robin Straus, who has been an amazing champion from the beginning, along with my international agent, Sarah Nundy at Andrew Nurnberg Associates.

Special thanks to my wonderful editors, Trish Todd, Susanne Baboneau, and Kate Lyall-Grant, and future editorial star Libby Vernon. I am so lucky to work with you.

To my husband, Mark Quinn, thank you for supporting my writing habit and not making me get a real job. Kisses and hugs to my teenagers, Schuyler and Sam Quinn, even though you no longer want to be seen with me.

To Regena Thomashauer, the inner circle, the Palace staff, and all the goddesses at Mama Gena's School of Womanly Arts for their encouragement, inspiration, and sisterhood.

Thank you to my early readers for your brilliant notes and boundless enthusiasm: Shari Nedler (Mom—who willingly read the novel seven times), Kathleen Stowers (whose generosity knows no bounds), Kathleen Smith (who also provided invaluable counsel on ball gown construction), Judith Levy, Brooke Stachyra, Tatiana Boncompagni, Stan Zimmerman, Jim Berg, and George Wilman.

Special gratitude to Dr. Valerie Steele, director of the Museum at Fashion Institute of Technology in New York City, for your expertise and willingness to teach me just enough to be dangerous. Let the record reflect that the shenanigans that happen at the fictitious museum in *Holly Would Dream* would never take place at FIT.

Thank you to the crew and passengers I met on the *Silver Whisper*, the *Crystal Symphony*, and the *Emerald Princess*. You provided me with more inspiration than you'll ever know. A quick disclaimer: Captains on cruise ships do not have romantic liaisons with passengers (I'm told it's against the rules), and every cruise ship has a working morgue on board in the unlikely event that one is needed.

Grazie to Vivian Barsanti from the Hassler Hotel in Roma for showing me your sumptuous suites and for sharing stories about Audrey Hepburn's stay there while making *Roman Holiday*. And to the staff of Il Palazzetto, I will never forget the nights spent at your lovely terrace bar overlooking the Spanish Steps. *Grazie* for the hospitality.

Thank you to Dr. Jonathan Goldenthal.

To Tiffany Cammarano, for one of the funniest bits that made it into this novel. To Julie Nelson, for her resplendent Santorini opera debut. To She She Walker, who, in the spirit of the great courtesan Cora Pearl, served herself for dessert and gave Holly the perfect way to demonstrate her own newfound cheek.

The spark for this book came from my love of romantic comedies of the 1950s—*Roman Holiday*, *Sabrina*, *An Affair to Remember*, just to name a few. There are so many stars of that time who served as muses for this novel: Cary Grant; Deborah Kerr; Doris Day; Grace Kelly; Gregory Peck; and of course the lovely, talented, and graceful Audrey Hepburn. I would like to recognize the following writers and directors for making these classics that brought joy to so many people, including myself: Claude Anet, George Axelrod, Philip Barry, Marc Behm, George Bradshaw, Truman Capote, T.E.B. Clarke, Mildred Cram, George Cukor, Delmer Daves, I.A.L. Diamond, John Dighton, David Dodge, Stanley Donen, Julien Duvivier, Blake Edwards, Leonard Gershe, John Michael Hayes, Alfred Hitchcock, Ian McLellan Hunter, Henri Jeanson, Harry Kurnitz, Ernest Lehman, Alan Jay Lerner, Delbert Mann, Leo McCarey, Nate Monaster, Richard Quine, Stanley Shapiro, George Bernard Shaw, Donald Ogden Stewart, Peter Stone, Samuel A. Taylor, Dalton Trumbo, Billy Wilder, and William Wyler.

And finally, I am grateful to my friends and family who have extended a hand as I've journeyed down this most extraordinary writing path: Amy Aho; Theresa Attwell; Carol Becker; Anna Bidwell; Beth Blair; Meris Blumstein; Scott Bond; Ellen Bregman; Candice Broom; George and Betty Buckley; Marcia Burch; Athena Burke; Stuart Calderwood; Nichole Cannon; Claire Chasnoff; Jane Cleland; Jennifer Cohen; Claire Cook; Stacey Creamer; Laura Cunningham; Katherine Cusset; Robin Daas; Charlene Dupray; Randy Dwenger; Beverly Erskin; Amanda Filipacchi; Judy Finnigan; Kathleen Frazier; Danielle Friedman; Robyn Spizman Friedman; Bonnie Fuller; Lorenza Galella; Emily Giffin; Victoria Goldman; Ken Gomez; Phyllis Goodman; Heather Graham; Stacey Green; Shelly Griffin; Richard Hine; Ron Hogan; Scottie Iverson; Tracey Jackson; Benjamin Jones; Caimin Jones; Judith Kahn; Jill Kargman; Pam Keogh; Chris Lloreda; Richard Madeley; Jamie McDonald; Murray Miller; Nancy Moon; Don Nedler; Michael Nedler; Ben Neihert; Quen Anne Sherwood Nicholas; Elizabeth Noble; Benny Ochman; B. L. Ochman; Eva Okada; Candice Olson; Beth Phoenix; Joanne Porzio; Lynne, Vic, Wendy, Janet, and Ted Quinn; Erica Recordan; Alessandro Ricciarelli; Elvira Ryder; Nancy Salz; Leslie Schnur; Linda Spector; Dame Lori Sutherland; Joanne Tombrakos; Linda Warner; Amanda Weil; and Jamie Wells.

My own life has been much more than a fairy tale. I've had my share of difficult moments, but whatever difficulties I've gone through, I've always gotten the prize at the end.

—AUDREY HEPBURN

Prologue

Once upon a time, on the Upper East Side of Manhattan, there lived a brown-haired girl in a spacious apartment on Park Avenue, in the most desirable building in New York City, if not the world.

The apartment was enormous indeed, and had many servants. There was a maid to dust the Picassos, a chef to cook ten-course dinners, two pilots to fly the his-and-hers jets, and a landscape architect to tend to the terrace and roof gardens.

There were workers to service the indoor pool, the indoor racquetball court, the rooftop pool, and the rooftop tennis court.

There was a chauffeur of dubious distinction who had been imported from England to drive the family and care for their six shiny automobiles.

Also among the staff was a man of no particular title who took care of the family's toy poodle named Noodle.

This man of no particular title was father to the brown-haired girl who was called Holly. The two of them lived in the servants' wing of the grand apartment on Park Avenue.

As it happened, the mistress of the mansion, a woman of considerable taste, had a deep admiration for romance films of the 1950s, and most especially, for a certain actress by the name of Audrey. For her viewing pleasure, she had assembled a collection of Hepburn films, along with her other favorite classics from the golden age of cinema.

When her father was off brushing, bathing, or exercising the dog, Holly was allowed to amuse herself by watching any movie she desired. Every day after school, she would eagerly visit the media room, where she would lose herself in a simpler time when the clothes were beautiful, the men debonair, and the women unforgettable.

There was Sabrina, the awkward daughter of a chauffeur, who after going off to Europe and returning an elegant and sophisticated woman, was pursued by two brothers of great wealth and charm.

There was a shy, funny-faced book clerk in New York named Jo who became the toast of Paris, where she was transformed from caterpillar to butterfly by discovering her gift in the world of high fashion.

There was a princess called Ann who rebelled against the duties of her station by escaping her luxurious shackles for a Roman holiday with a newspaperman whose true motives were less than pure.

For the little girl who lived with her father in the sprawling apartment on Park Avenue, life was as close to heaven as one could get on the island of Manhattan.

Then one day, everything changed. Holly's father, the chef, the maid, the pilots, the landscape architect, and the chauffeur of dubious distinction were all told to pack their bags and leave, for the owner of the apartment had suffered a reversal of monumental proportion and would no longer be able to keep the staff in the style to which they had become accustomed.

With great sadness, Holly and her father gathered their belongings and journeyed to another place. In time, Holly's father secured a home for himself and his little girl in a one-room studio with a window facing a brick wall in Astoria, Queens, some ten miles from the Upper East Side of Manhattan. Her father drove a cab and played piano in jazz clubs, while Holly went to school, then came home to cook, clean, sew, and manage the tiny household.

Holly's father rarely got to see his little girl anymore. Their life had gone from blissful and gay to bleak and gloomy. To remind them both that life could be as wondrous as a fairy tale, Holly's father assembled his own collection of Audrey Hepburn's most endearing films. Each night, after finishing her chores, Holly would play one and transport herself on a marvelous cloud of romance and style to an enchanted world where endings were happily ever after and dreams almost always came true.

New York City

The Look of Love

I HAD ONE FOOT OUT the door, late as usual.

"You should see yourself right now," Alessandro said. He wore loose cotton yoga pants and no shirt.

"Why? What's the matter?"

"I should have said something before," he started. "But—*and don't take this the wrong way*—that skirt's too short. It makes you look cheap. If you want to be a curator, you've got to dress up more."

I took a deep, centering breath. "How cheap? Hooker cheap?"

Alessandro cocked his head thoughtfully. "I'd say—"

I interrupted him mid-cock. "Never mind, I'm changing."

Alessandro followed as I scurried to the bedroom, leaving a trail of clothes in my wake, throwing on the Versace linen suit I'd snagged for sixty bucks at the Lucky Shops charity sale last year. "There, *now* what do you think?"

He reached out and pulled me toward him until his head rested on my shoulder. "*Mmm, pretty!* You know, the only reason I told you is because I love you and I want you to get that promotion."

"I know."

Alessandro moved his hands up my back and then around the front, cupping my breasts in his palms.

My organs went all aflutter. Sex on a school day?

He stroked my breasts, let out a sort of moan-sigh, and pressed his morning protuberance into my groin. "Do you remember when we first met?"

"Mmmm," I murmured, meaning, *Yes, of course I do, my love.*

"That was before your boobs drooped."

I pushed him away.

"Holly, I'm just saying. If you don't wear a bra, your tits will be to your knees by the time you're fifty."

I whipped off my jacket and shirt. Glancing at my boyish figure, I knew my boobs wouldn't sag if I hung clothespins from my nipples. Still, I put on a bra to make Alessandro happy.

Alessandro Vercelli was my knight in shining armor, kind of. Six feet tall, slim, messy black hair, dark brooding eyes, he resembled a Latin Gregory Peck, one of my favorite actors. If I scrunched my eyes just right, he looked *exactly* like Gregory Peck, and like Gregory, Alessandro was a solid, dependable guy. He was always by my side whether I wanted him to be or not.

Unlike other boyfriends I'd had, Alessandro cared deeply about my professional success. Clothing had forever been my passion. Growing up, I'd first been inspired by the sumptuous costumes created by designers during the glamour years of Hollywood—Givenchy for Audrey Hepburn, Valentino for Marlene Dietrich, Coco Chanel for Katharine Hepburn. Later, I discovered a knack for making my own clothes.

Fashion awakened my senses like nothing else. Anytime I felt stressed, I'd jump on the subway and go to Bergdorf's. It calmed me right down. In the hallowed reverence of the store, I'd take in the aroma of designer gowns and unapologetic overpricing. It felt like nothing bad could happen to you there. With Alessandro's encouragement (and savings), I enrolled in the Fashion Institute of Technology, majoring in history and museum studies. When I needed him, Alessandro was there.

Last year, after spending nine months as Motel the tailor in an off-Broadway revival of *Fiddler on the Roof*, Alessandro was cast as the beast in Disney's *Beauty and the Beast*. It was a huge step up for him and I brought all our friends to the opening night to cheer him on.

After five years of living in his East Village rent-controlled apartment, Alessandro proposed. Like many rent-controlled tenants, he was there illegally, but who was I to judge? The place was small, yet comfortable: pressed-tin ceilings, a marble fireplace, plank wood floors, and a toilet that flushed at random.

Wait, where was I? Oh yes, Alessandro's proposal. It was time. At thirty-five, the expiration date on my egg carton was nearly past. Marrying him made sense.

A famous Hollywood writer once said that in the 1950s you wrote your scripts for Cary Grant, but you ended up with Rock Hudson. Truth be told, I wrote my script for Gregory Peck, but ended up with Alessandro Vercelli.

After replacing my jacket and shirt, I slipped my headgear over my face and inserted the protraction hooks into the molar grips. Last Valentine's Day Alessandro had surprised me with an orthodontic gift certificate to move my canines back. Romantic, yet practical. That's my Alessandro! The doctor told me if I wanted my teeth perfect by the time I walked down the aisle, I should wear it twelve hours a day, so I commuted in it.

"Have you seen my glasses?" I asked, squinting.

"Try the fridge."

"The fridge?" I thought, worried for my sanity.

"Why aren't you wearing your contacts?"

"I need solution. I'll get some on the way to work. Oh, and don't eat too much at lunch. We're meeting the caterers at six-thirty. Remember, they're giving us a tasting of everything I picked for the wedding.

Alessandro frowned. "I completely forgot. I'm sorry. It's too close to my call time. But go without me; whatever you choose will be fine," he said, retrieving the glasses. "Here, and take this. It'll bring you luck." He handed me his two-dollar bill, the one he credited with getting him the part in *Beauty and the Beast*.

I folded the money into my bra. "Oh, but how sweet. Thank you. You won't need it?"

"Nope," he said. "Today's *your* day." He kissed me on the lips (well, really on the metal face-bow of my headgear).

I looked around for Kitty, the three-legged Maine coon I'd rescued from the Con Edison softball fields.

"There you are, you sneak," I said, picking him up, holding him to my face where I could feel the vibration of his purring.

"I made you lunch," Alessandro said, handing me a turkey sandwich wrapped in foil.

"Thanks," I said, admiring his face, so handsome and rugged.

"Why are you scrunching your eyes like that?" he asked.

"Was I scrunching again? Sorry, bad habit. Break a leg tonight," I said, flitting out the door into the muggy air.

"No, *you* break a leg at the meeting," he yelled. "I love you."

A Foggy Day

Hustling down Avenue A, I stopped to pick up breakfast for my father (better known as Pops), and coffee for me. I love Dunkin' Donuts, especially those chocolate glazed munchkins, but boy do I take issue with them (the company, not the doughnuts). Every time a local store goes out of business in Manhattan, a bank or a Dunkin' Donuts shop takes its place. It's ruining the character of our neighborhoods.

I spotted Pops, with his naturally curly beard, wavy silver

locks, clear blue eyes, and weathered face. He was puffing away on a cigarette clenched between two knobby fingers. Part Jed Clampett, part Cary Grant, he presided over the stoop in front of Muttropolis Groom and Board, next to his shopping cart full of street treasures. Pops was a jazz musician slash panhandler who had driven a taxi until he was fired last year. It was a blessing, really—these days he barely made enough to lease his cab and cover gas. Plus, he always got lost, even on the way to places he'd been to a thousand times.

Six months ago, he was evicted from the one-room apartment in Queens where he'd raised me. It was a rent issue (as in he'd stopped paying it). I helped him arrange temporary quarters in Muttropolis' basement as a trade for walking the dogs. My friend Bobbie Liberty "BL" Ochman owns the shop. She had been looking for someone to mind the furry guests staying at her "Club Bow-wow" and Pops had always had a knack with animals. A scruffy, quasi-homeless dog minder wouldn't go over so well uptown, but East Village liberals loved the idea.

"You look fetching today, princess," Pops said. Raindrops were starting to *plink* on the sidewalk and the air was ripe with the scent of rotting trash.

"I do? You're not just saying that?" I handed him a cup of black coffee and an egg-and-cheese bagel sandwich with a side of Munchkins.

"Are you kidding?" He gave me the once-over. "Darlin', you may be skinny, but you got all the right curves for a woman. And that messy hairdo makes you look like a French shop girl."

"Oh, Pops," I said, blushing. Since I was a kid, I'd worn my hair cropped, like my favorite film star, Audrey Hepburn. Some people said we looked alike—both brunette, tall and thin, big eyes, swan necks. But our faces were entirely different. My nose was thinner, my lips fuller, my brown eyes darker than hers. Audrey's features combined to make her a dazzling beauty. My features combined to make me, well, let's just say my face was slightly funny. Alessandro said it'd be gorgeous when the orthodontist got through with me.

"Holly, you're a vision," he said, stubbing his cigarette out on the step. "Don't let anyone tell you otherwise."

Ha! Take that, Alessandro. Pops thinks I'm a vision. Of course, he was wearing plastic garbage bags tied around his shoes.

"If you'd take that Martian wire and those Coke bottles off your face, you'd be even lovelier."

Touching my headgear, I giggled. "It all comes off at work."

"Nice suit," he said. "Something special today?"

"Remember, I told you. My promotion's being announced. Send good thoughts my way."

Pops smiled, baring his tobacco-stained teeth. "*I'll say a little prayer for you,*" he sang. "*Forever, and ever, you'll stay in my heart . . .*"

"That's good, Pops. You should sing professionally. Oh yeah, you do." I noticed his crumpled brown suit and thin white dress shirt. "Why are *you* so fancy?"

"Job interview at Whole Foods on Houston Street. They pay benefits."

I chucked his arm lightly. "Knock 'em dead."

"If I do, breakfast is on *me* tomorrow, from Whole Foods. You think they'll make me wear one of those beard hairnets?"

"Shave it off," I suggested.

Pops rubbed his chin and then dismissed the idea. "Facial hair increases panhandling proceeds by at least twenty percent. Learned that the hard way last time I tried to clean up my act."

The gentle spit suddenly morphed into pelting rain. We scrambled up the stairs, beneath the green awning. Pops threw a dirty yellow poncho over his head.

"Shoot," I said, glaring at the black sky.

"You need an umbrella?" Pops said.

"You got one?"

"No."

A steady stream of cabs whizzed by, all with their headlights on, all full. I checked my watch: 8:25. Thirty-five minutes until the staff meeting. I dug around in my purse. "Rats, I left my cell at work."

"Use mine," Pops offered.

"You have a cell phone?" I said. "Not that you shouldn't, it's just . . ."

"Darlin'," Pops said, handing me the phone, "what do you think I do with the money I earn? Buy booze?"

"Pops, of *course* not," I said, in my most offended voice, although I'd seen him chugging the cheap stuff more times than I could count. The rain was hammering down like we were in a car wash. We huddled next to the doorway as sheets of water poured from the sky. Pops' poncho billowed in the wind.

"Tanya, I'm stuck downtown, but I'll get there as fast as I can," I said to my boss's voice mail. I couldn't afford to be late. Not today.

"Your shoes are getting wet," Pops said.

I jumped back, then stuffed the shoes in my purse. These were my real Jimmy Choos, the ones I kept meaning to return to HBO after the Fashionistas in Pop Culture exhibition we'd held at the museum where I worked. Sarah Jessica Parker wore them in the episode where Carrie tells Big she loves him and then he gives her an ugly Judith Leiber bag.

"You can't go barefoot. Here." Pops knelt down and held open a double grocery bag he pulled out of his cart. I stepped into it and he wrapped a rubber band around my ankle. "Give me your other foot, Cinderella," he said, grinning. "Hold this over your head for an umbrella." He handed me a black Hefty bag. I was good to go.

"Thanks," I said. "Do great on your interview. Oh, I almost forgot. I'm going to a tasting tonight of all the food they're serving at our wedding. Want to come?"

"Me, turn down a free meal? Oh, wait, I can't," Pops said, slapping his craggy forehead. "It's Monday. I'm busy." On Sundays and Mondays, he played piano at the Jazz Factory with Bongo Herrera's Latin fusion big band. It was his one steady job. The pay sucked, but the regular gig was its own reward. Pops was fond of saying, "Jazz, the gift that keeps on taking."

"That's okay; I'll reschedule," I said, taking a deep breath, holding my Hefty bag overhead, and stepping into the deluge. "Love ya."

Autumn in New York

I MOVED UP THE STREET deliberately, head low, garbage bag high, plastic-covered feet squishing with each step. May nobody I know, and I mean *nobody*, see me like this. Alessandro would have a fit. My *boss would read me the riot act*, I thought.

A torrent of water swooshed down the street, flooding the corners where the drains always back up. Just as I traversed a pool at First and Fourteenth, an ivory Maybach sailed by, shooting a heavy stream in its wake—and *sploosh*! "Oh, crrrr-aaap shoot," I wailed, shaking the water off my jacket and skirt. Passersby regarded me with pity, but no one offered to help. Bastards.

A block ahead, the Maybach pulled over, stopped, then backed up when the traffic cleared, its motor whirring. The door swung open. A gentleman stuck his head out and shouted, "Are you all right?"

I looked down at my champagne-colored suit, which was now soaked with muddy water. "What do *you* think? Do I *look* all right?"

"Why don't you get in," he said. "I don't bite . . ."

I planted my grocery-bag-covered feet firmly on the sidewalk.

". . . unless it's called for."

Cute, I thought. *Mr. Fancy Car is a comedian.* I did an emergency assessment. Outside: rainy, sticky-hot, and blocks to go before a subway station. Inside: dry, air-conditioned, clean, well-heeled middle-aged guy with chauffeur. What were the odds that the car that happened to splash me contained a rapist or serial murderer? Infinitesimal. I dove in the backseat, but not before asking the man to produce identification.

He pulled out a slim Gucci wallet and showed me his driver's license. *Sweet Jeezus of Nantucket*, I thought, glancing at the ID and then him. It was Denis King.

Denis King was a fortysomething mogul, masculine in a dorky but appealing way. He wore a simple navy pin-striped suit, this season's Armani. His neck was red where he kept tugging at his French collar. His body was neither thin nor fat. He had a cleft in his chin, and dancing kohl eyes. It was the eyes that dominated his face—they were penetrating, with lines radiating from the corners that bespoke laughter, wisdom, and experience. His brows were thick and his wavy brown hair faded to gray at the temples. In front of him was a tray that came out of the seat (like in an airplane). A laptop with spreadsheets on the screen sat on it. I looked down, then glanced up beneath my batting eyelashes, giving him my shy Princess Diana smile.

He smiled back and there were dimples, deep adorable dimples. I don't know why I'd never noticed them before. I'd seen his picture in the paper a thousand times and we'd met more than once at the museum. Each time, he'd reintroduce himself. Sadly, the man didn't know I existed, although I was chummy with his assistant, Elvira.

Denis was the next big benefactor my boss was looking to bag. He was a major supporter of New York City opera, art, ballet, and symphony. Tanya was after some of his do-re-mi for our fashion museum. He was scheduled to underwrite our upcoming tiara show. That was how Tanya lured them in before capturing an even bigger pile of their net worth. First she invited them to join the board. Then she named them underwriters of an important exhibit. Finally, after they enjoyed the publicity and prestige associated with a high-profile retrospective, she went in for the kill. She had secured millions in pledges this way.

As I pulled the door shut, his chauffeur took off. Inside, the Maybach smelled like success. I wondered if Denis would let me borrow the car if we ever got married.

"Which way you going?" Denis asked, closing his computer.

"The subway station at Fourteenth. I'm headed to Eighty-fourth."

His chauffeur silently passed back a roll of paper towels. Denis tore off several squares and watched as I patted myself down. "Thanks," I said. "Oh, lordy, I'm getting water all over your fine Corinthian leather."

Denis smiled. "Lordy?" he said, raising one eyebrow in Jack Black fashion.

I could tell he thought I was cute.

Denis took a few more paper towels and dried the seat as best he could. "Don't worry. We'll drive you. We're going uptown."

The car made its way west, then turned north on Union Square as rain pounded the windshield, wipers whipping back and forth to little avail. The traffic was crawling and a cacophony of horns blared.

I took in his fancy set of wheels. There was enough room to set up a kiddie pool. "Wait a minute. Is this the kind of car where the seats turn into beds?"

"As a matter of fact, yes," Denis said. "Why, you tired?"

"Are you being fresh?"

He laughed. "I was kidding. Anyway, you're not my type."

I shot him a hurt look. "Just because I'm wearing grocery-bag shoes, you think you're too good for me?"

"No, not at all," he said, looking concerned.

Snapping the rubber bands off my ankles, I said, "I'll have you know, these are Manolo Bagnicks."

Denis laughed, revealing those twenty-four karat dimples once again. Handing me his business card, he said, "Let me pay to get your suit cleaned. Will you send me the bill?"

"That's okay," I said, stuffing his card in my bag anyway.

"Seriously, I want to take care of you."

drop me in front of the Fashion Museum. I wondered if Elvira would blow my cover if I sent him the cleaning bill.

"Take care of yourself," Denis said with a grin.

I wished I could stay with him longer. Forever would be nice.

Reaching behind the seat, Denis produced an enormous black umbrella, the kind doormen used, and escorted me to the drugstore. I could see the top of his head as we walked.

"Thanks," I said.

He nodded and silently retreated into the rainy mist.

For Sentimental Reasons

I HAULED MY WET DERRIERE inside the museum and up the grand staircase to Tanya Johnson's office. She's the director of the museum. I'm her assistant, though not for long. Nigel Calderwood, the museum's conservator, stood at the top of the landing. Euro-trash thin with a sleek, chiseled face, dark almond-shaped eyes, chocolate complexion, and a bald head that was as shiny as his Bruno Magli shoes, Nigel was so delectably gorgeous that everyone automatically assumed he was gay (which he was). His eyes widened when he saw me. "Holly, is that you?"

"Nigel, you're back," I said. "How was France?" He refused my offer of a hug.

"Sorry," I said. "I know; I'm a mess. Is Tanya here? I don't want her to see me like this."

"She has someone in her office," Nigel said. "The staff meeting's been moved to ten."

"Great," I said, dropping my bag. "I have to tell you about Denis King. He picked me up this morning after his car splashed me."

"*Our* Denis King?" Nigel said. "Ooh, sounds like *That Touch of Mink* with, who was in that?"

"Cary Grant and Doris Day. It was just like that, although he wasn't exactly Cary Grant."

"Too bad, because you're *so* Doris Day," Nigel said.

"Am not."

"Excuse me, you're sweet as a cupcake; you brighten up a room; I'll bet you even sing "Que Sera Sera" in the shower. Need I go on?"

"No, you needn't. But only because I'm in a hurry. Anyway, he drove me to work," I squealed.

"Was he cute?" Nigel asked.

"Uh, yeah-ah. Although he's shorter than me when I'm in heels."

"A man looks taller when he's standing on his money, luv."

"Does he, now? No, he was really quite attractive, even though he had a touch of geek," I giggled, checking my watch. "Oops, gotta go. I'm a mess."

"What a coincidence! I adore rich geeks," Nigel said. "You

know who I'd fancy seeing all naked and sweaty? Bill Gates . . ."

"Eawww!" I yelled as I scrambled down the back stairs, and ran smack into Gus, who was guarding the vault. Gus was a feeble man in his seventies who would probably have a massive heart attack if anyone actually tried to break in. His uniforms were always a size too big and he packed heat (not a gun, but those foot warmers that skiers use). All our guards were Gus-like: gray-haired, liver-spotted gentlemen living in the last lane, but they worked cheap, which is why Tanya hired them. "A necessary evil dictated by insurance companies," she'd say. "Like someone would ever steal from *us*."

"You look like a drowned Chihuahua," Gus said when he saw me.

"I know," I said. "Here. Two chocolate-glazed doughnuts with sprinkles; they were out of vanilla."

Gus took the bag, peeked inside, then gave me a polite bow. "You're the best, Holly."

"Can you open the vault?" I asked. Gus could get in trouble for doing that. Technically, only curators and conservators were supposed to have access.

Gus unlocked the door and made a gallant arm gesture for me to enter.

I kissed him on the cheek. "Thanks, I know you're sticking your neck out."

"Pish," he said, practically spitting. "What are rules to a man with one foot in the grave?"

"My, but we're feisty today," I teased.

The vault was a locked climate-controlled storage facility where we kept clothes that weren't on exhibit. We named it the vault so donors would feel extra secure lending us their pieces. I figured I could take something from Corny's collection and put it back tonight. Borrowing clothes from the museum was strictly prohibited, under penalty of death or worse, which was why I had to do it in secret. I'd never done it before, and vowed never to do it again, but this was a fashion emergency—a *real* one.

Cornelia "Corny" Von Aston LeClaire Peabody was the patron saint of our fledgling institute, The National Museum of Fashion. We weren't losers, exactly, but compared to the Met's Costume Institute or the Fashion Institute of Technology Museum, we weren't as well funded or as highly regarded. Tanya Johnson, my boss, was determined to change all that. I liked to think of us as the little fashion museum that could.

Corny, our founder, had been a glittering and dependable fixture at the Paris and New York shows, a wearer and collector of all things couture, and a muse for some of the world's most accomplished designers. She had bequeathed twenty million dollars, her entire collection, and her magnificent white limestone mansion to create this valentine to her life's passion. Tanya, who was a fund-raising genius, continually courted the city's wealthiest benefactors in hopes of raising another hundred million to ensure that the museum endured in perpetuity. She fantasized about having it named in her honor. No one was supposed to know that, but as her assistant, I saw her doodle "The Tanya Johnson Institute of Fashion" on more than one scrap of paper.

The stately mansion was perfect for us. It had ceiling frescoes of angels and nymphs, finely carved paneling that glittered with gold leaf, and a lavish ballroom on the top floor that easily accommodated six hundred, a vestige of Manhattan's gilded age when the Vanderbilts and the Astors ruled. Corny's sumptuous home also boasted multiple galleries and an imposing walnut-paneled banquet hall that was ideal for charity lunches. It was an elegant showcase for special exhibits curated by the museum staff, along with Corny's own priceless ensembles, which comprised a significant part of our permanent collection.

The vault was three thousand square feet of cedar-lined heaven, filled with scores of handmade creations by the most talented designers of their time. Corny's wardrobe was stored in its own private room, where each piece was photographed, hung on fiberglass hangers molded in the shape of Corny's torso, placed in a white garment bag, and hung in alphabetical and chronological order by couturier and year it was created. Beaded dresses were laid out on special shallow drawers after being carefully covered in acid-free tissue paper.

Corny's collection was enormous even by wealthy socialite standards. And though the Cornelia Peabody Gallery was the grandest room in the mansion (besides the ballroom), only a fraction of her iconic outfits could be displayed at any one time. Tanya spun this limitation into an advantage by creating special mini exhibits from the enormous selection—Givenchy in the Fifties, Twenty Designers Interpret the Little Black Dress, The Suits of Schiaparelli, The Fashions of 1980s Hedonism (that was my idea).

Our staff meeting was about to start, so I headed for the "Y"s—Yves Saint Laurent—and pulled a 1940s-inspired pale yellow silk tailored trouser suit from his 1966 collection, the year he first introduced masculine elements into women's wear (his greatest contribution to twentieth-century fashion history, if you ask me). I knew it would fit, having dressed the mannequins in the Cornelia Peabody Gallery more than a few times. The two of us had been close enough to the same size: She—five nine and one hundred fifteen pounds. Me—five eight and one hundred ten pounds. Corny had worked hard to maintain her stick-insect figure. Not me. I eat well, rarely exercise, and never put on weight. Alessandro says my metabolism is one of my best features.

Too Marvelous for Words

STUFFING MY DIRTY WET suit inside the black Hefty bag, I hid it in a corner, and headed for the conference room, giving Gus a wink as I zipped by in Corny's proud vintage suit. As a kid who grew up wearing homemade creations, couture gave me a feeling of worthiness that I rarely experienced, and I enjoyed it more than I cared to admit. My heart raced at the thought of my promotion being announced. Tanya promised she would do it today.

Speaking of which, Tanya floated in behind me, the picture of executive chic with her size-two charcoal Oscar de la Renta suit, geometric blunt-cut black hair, pale complexion, and lips so vehemently red they looked like a fresh wound. She had recently taken time off to have "work" done. Nigel was sure she'd had her ass tightened, but she claimed it was her eyelids. Naturally, she wore Chanel sunglasses. Tanya said her corneas couldn't take the light after surgery, but we all saw it for what it was—a convenient medical excuse to imitate Anna Wintour, editor of *Vogue* and Tanya's personal goddess. Designers fought to lend Tanya their clothes, as she was so often photographed in the society pages at museum events and charity balls. They arranged for celebrity hairdressers and makeup artists to style her so she would look even more striking in their creations.

"Nigel, how was your trip?" Tanya asked, her chin raised high.

As the museum's conservator, Nigel's job was to repair and stabilize garments that were damaged. If we lent clothing for a show, he would first examine it, with every irregularity and impairment noted. He would repeat the inspection when the costume was returned to be sure it had not been harmed while it was out of our care. We often exported shows to other museums, and whenever we did, Nigel made the arrangements. Then he would travel to the exhibit to dress the mannequins. Believe it or not, you have to be specially trained to fit delicate garments over fiberglass forms. As a reward for his excellent work this year, Tanya allowed him to speak as a fashion expert on a luxurious Mediterranean cruise, a privilege usually reserved for curators.

"It was *très magnifique*," he said. "I sailed the French Riviera on the *Silver Whisper*. We started in Paris, where I led a tour of the Musée de la Mode et du Textile; that's in the Palais du Louvre. They had a special shoe exhibition featuring all French designers: Christian Louboutin, Michel Vivien, Pierre Hardy . . ."

"Yes, yes," Tanya said, "we *all* know our French shoe designers."

"Right," Nigel said, momentarily flustered. "Anyway, the ladies loved it and I daresay it would be a good model for a show we could mount. The history of the couture shoe."

"Ooh, ooh," I said, practically bursting out of my seat. "What if we didn't limit ourselves to shoes, but included *all* couture accessories—faux jewels, witty bags, amusing hats. We could call it *les riens de couture*, you know, the 'little nothings' that posh ladies buy at designer boutiques."

"I *love* it," Nigel crowed. "Balenciaga pillbox hats, Christian Dior pocketbooks and gloves, Moschino hats—remember when he showed that airplane headdress . . ."

"1988," I said, "also the year of the Napoleonic coat-hanger hat."

"We could show Christian Lacroix bibbed necklaces," Cosima Fairchild added. "Chanel brooches and cuffs and necklaces . . ."

"Oh my," Nigel said.

"Sto-op! It would be so much fun to put together," I said.

"Cosima, why don't you take this one," Tanya said. While we were all encouraged to offer ideas for exhibits, it was the curator's job to write the proposal and "own" the show. First, she would outline the story she wanted to tell, and then list the objects she would need to bring the narrative to life, along with where she thought she might find them. I'd ghostwritten more than my share of exhibit proposals.

"Nigel, did you give any talks?" Cosima asked, her green eyes darting from Nigel to Tanya and back again.

"When?" he asked.

"On the cruise," she said, twirling her flame-colored curls with an index finger. Bright blotches appeared on her ivory face and neck. Cosima, who specialized in fine jewels and accessories, was one of our most innovative curators, but she was deathly afraid to speak in public, which was why she hadn't yet lectured on the cruise circuit. Tanya had warned her to overcome the phobia, or else. The top cruise ships were swarming with potential donors for our museum. We had already garnered hundreds of vintage ensembles, four million dollars in donations, and twenty-five million in promised bequests just by befriending and working this überwealthy crowd. I had to hand it to Tanya. It was another of her shrewd fund-raising strategies and none of our competitors had caught on.

"I gave the lectures that Holly wrote," Nigel said. "The Life and Times of Coco Chanel, The History of Oscar Fashions, and Hollywood Legends as Style Makers. They were well received. Thank you, Holly."

Oh, go on, I thought, but sadly he didn't.

"Let's go around the room for updates," Tanya said. "Elaina, what's the final word on the Audrey exhibit?"

Elaina Erskin, another senior curator, always reminded me of Marilyn Monroe. She had golden blond hair, a bright smile, and wore low-cut dresses that showcased her voluptuous breasts. Elaina was active in the human potential movement and often quoted *A Course in Miracles*.

"I'm happy to report that Tinsley Stachyra Presents: Audrey

Hepburn, Icon of Style was the most successful show in the history of the museum," Elaina trilled. "We spent half a million dollars to mount and market the exhibit, but ninety percent was covered by Tinsley's donation. Ticket sales were two-point-eight million over four months, net profit was two-point-six million, and the publicity and prestige the show brought us was priceless. We'll be dismantling over the next few days and shipping it to Italy for the fiftieth anniversary of *Roman Holiday*."

"I didn't realize *Roman Holiday* is only fifty," Nigel said.

"Fifty-five, but Italians aren't sticklers on time," Elaina explained.

"What's our cut?" Tanya asked.

"Ten percent of the gross," Elaina said.

Tanya led us all in a round of applause. "Excellent. Leveraging the fiftieth anniversary of *Roman Holiday* was one of my more brilliant notions," she said, taking a bow with a slight nod of head.

Tanya suffered from an acute case of high self-esteem.

It may have been Tanya's idea to send the Audrey show to Rome, but it was *my* idea to create the exhibit in the first place. I was sure the public would love it and naturally they did. As a little girl, I would watch *Sabrina* and daydream that my father would ship me off to Paris, where I'd learn to crack eggs properly and bake a soufflé. When I was a teenager and went to my first boy-girl party (where no one asked me to dance), I retreated to the world of *Roman Holiday*, and dreamed of waltzing in the arms of the oh-so-manly Gregory Peck. After I got my first job in a Greenwich Village bookstore, I would put on *Funny Face* and imagine Fred Astaire popping in to do a location shoot, discovering me, and putting me on the cover of *Vogue*. The Hepburn show was my way of honoring my favorite actress of the 1950s, the woman who never failed to raise me up when I was down. And the exhibit was a major success, thank you very much.

"Cosima, how's the new show coming along?" Tanya asked.

"We announce Denis King Presents: Tiaras through Time on Wednesday," she said.

My stomach did a somersault when she mentioned Denis' name.

"The press conference is set. Tomorrow, Lloyd's of London is installing the special safe they're requiring. Starting Thursday, they're providing their own security guards. They won't accept ours. I want to thank Holly, who has been instrumental in researching and writing the catalog and organizing the press conference."

Oh, please, no need to applaud, I thought, *unless you* really *want to.*

"Excellent updates, everyone. And now I want to announce a staff change," Tanya said.

Oooh, time for my close-up, I mentally squealed. I was scared. I was excited. I practically tinkled in anticipation.

"As you know, with Karolina Burden's departure, we've had an open senior curator position that I've been looking to fill for some time. I am happy to announce that Sammie Kittenplatt has been chosen for the spot."

They Can't Take That Away from Me

THE ROOM WENT SILENT. Jaws dropped. Eyes widened. For a minute I thought she said someone else was getting my job. But that wasn't possible. I'd worked years for this opportunity. Tanya told me I was indispensable, that the job was mine. Alessandro said "break a leg" this morning. Pops sang a little prayer for me. I shook my head. *Rewind. Delete. Do over.*

Tanya continued, oblivious to my mental meltdown. "Sammie

graduated from Bauder College. She has always had a passionate interest in our industry. Her mother, Tappy Kittenplatt, is a founding member of our board and her family has long been among our top contributors. After interviewing Sammie and listening to her innovative ideas, I am convinced that she is by far the best woman for the job. Let's all welcome our newest senior curator, Sammie Kittenplatt." Tanya gestured toward the side conference room door and, as if on cue, in walked a familiar fixture from the Manhattan social scene.

Wait, STOP! I wanted to shout. This was *my* job. It was promised to *me*. How could Tanya cast me aside for this interloper? My heart was thumping and I could barely catch my breath. *Objection*, *objection*, I thought. But I was momentarily paralyzed, which happens to me under stress. I sat there like a pile of discarded fabric on the dressmaker's floor.

You could tell that Sammie was one of those girls born with a Kmart exterior that had been attended to by the right dermatologists, hairdressers, trainers, and stylists. Now she was all Bergdorf's—legs that were long and lean, arms that were buff, shimmering peach skin, Aegean-blue eyes accenting her thick blond mane. Her heart-shaped face was punctuated by a short, wide pug nose that had not been fixed. All that perfection surrounding such a snout made Sammie ugly and pretty at the same time, prugly like Diana Vreeland had been. I envied her. Ugly beauty was all the rage this season.

"Hello, everybody," she chirped. "I'm Sammie Kittenplatt. It's an easy name to remember; think Sammie, only without the Davis Junior. And without the black skin or glass eye." She turned to Nigel, the only person of color in the room. "Not that

I have a problem with black skin or glass eyes, because I don't."

"Do I look like I have a glass eye?" Nigel whispered under his breath.

Now I remember, I thought. *She introduced herself the same way on* Project Runway *last season.*

But back to my rant. Miss Kittenplatt was dressed head-to-toe-to-purse in the same designer (Chanel), which simply isn't done by anyone who knows anything about fashion. And let me add that her entire ensemble was black, a look that went out in the late nineties, just two more good reasons why I (mentally) cried foul play.

Tanya led us in a round of applause for Sammie. I joined in. I'm such a weenie.

Sammie's face brightened and she fanned herself with one hand. "Thank you. Thank you. Tanya, I'm honored that you gave me this opportunity," she started. "Ever since I was a little girl, my dream was to be a fashion designer. But when I was bid *auf Wiedersehen* on *Project Runway*, it gave me the chance to rethink my career choice. And the more I thought about it, the more I realized that my talents would be better spent showcasing designers who were even *more* talented than I. So I talked to my mother, who's on the board here, and, well, the rest is history. Get it?" she chuckled. "*History?*"

Nobody laughed.

"History. See, we're a fashion museum that displays *historical* things. That's what makes it funny," she explained.

Silence.

"You know what they say," Sammie added, "those who *can't*, work in museums."

Tanya chose this comedy knucklehead over me?

Checking her watch, Tanya said, "Sammie, I'd like you to spend a week following each of our curators and Nigel, our conservator, so you'll have a better idea of your responsibilities. Holly'll put together a schedule for you. She'll brief you on everything about the museum. Holly knows more about what goes on here than anyone—next to me, of course."

Tanya stood and breezed out of the room, with her perky whack-job new hire in tow. Sammie was dragging a few squares of toilet paper on her heel. That was the only bright spot of the morning.

"I'm speechless," Nigel said. "That job was yours."

"What could you not accept if you but knew that everything that happens is gently planned by One Whose only purpose is your good?" Elaina said. "That's from *A Course in Miracles*."

"Are you saying this is for my good?"

"Tanya had no choice," said Martin, our ultrareligious Jewish audiovisual guy who always left early on Fridays. "Sammie's a Kittenplatt, of the *Cape Cod Kittenplatts*. Her parents are huge donors. *Res ipsa loquitur*."

"*Res* what? I said.

"It's Latin. 'The thing speaks for itself,'" Martin said. "Something I learned in law school before I dropped out."

"The girl's an A-list socialite," Cosima said. "She knows everyone who matters, serves on the right charity committees, goes to the right parties. She'll be pure gold when it comes to fund-raising."

"Silly society gadabout," I muttered.

"Yes, and you can't compete with that," Cosima said.

"I know, but do you think Tanya might make me a curator too? Not a senior curator," I said. "I'd settle for being a junior one."

My colleagues shook their heads. "This isn't the Met. We can only support so many curators," Elaina said.

So that's it? The end of the story for me? Suddenly, there was a lump in my throat the size of Sammie's schnoz. For once, I could not speak.

You Call It Madness

"Please, help me understand," I said, sitting across the desk from my boss.

Tanya spun her leather throne around and looked me in the eyes. "She came up at the last minute and was better for the role."

"But . . . but how can you *say* that?" I asked. "I have a master's in fashion history from FIT. She went to Bauder in Atlanta. I've assistant curated almost twenty shows. I wrote half the lectures anyone here has ever given. I researched eighty percent of our catalogs. I'm the only one here who knows how to write a foundation grant. I know more about what goes on at this museum than anyone; you said so yourself."

Tanya pursed her lips. Then she laced her fingers together and cracked her knuckles. "You have all the technical qualifications," she murmured. "I'll give you that. But there's more to being a curator than experience and education. Curators are the public face of the institution. And we're a *fashion* museum. Look at you—no makeup, no manicure. And the way you dress, Holly." She pointed to Corny's Yves Saint Laurent. "It's so pedestrian."

I glanced at the sleek, streamlined suit. It was from the 1966–67 couture collection, one of the earliest examples of "Le Smoking," which became a perennial style in Saint Laurent's future collections. A similar ensemble had sold at Sotheby's last winter for fifty-eight thousand dollars. Tanya had an MBA from Arizona State University. She knew her profits from her losses, but not her vintage Yves Saint Laurents from Loehmann's back-room specials.

"I earn forty thousand dollars a year. It's all I can do to shop thrift stores and rummage sales or sew my own stuff. If you promoted me to curator, I'd get a clothing allowance and invitations to private sample sales. Designers would lend me things."

"Holly, Holly, Holly," she said sadly. "It's not just your *clothes*. It's . . . it's your whole package. You lack style, polish, *je ne sais quoi*. These aren't qualities you can learn. No, you can acquire them only by moving in the right circles. Sammie was raised on the Upper East Side. She went to Spence. Her family is wealthy.

She knows the right people. She'll attract donors. You can't do that. You grew up, where? In Queens?"

I held my head high. "I lived on Park Avenue till I was twelve. *Then* I moved to Queens."

Tanya pursed her lips together. "Yes, well, living in servants' quarters on Park Avenue isn't the same thing. When Sammie became available, I had no choice but to take her over you. I'm sorry."

I swallowed hard. "So that's why I didn't get the job?" I said. "Because my father was the help?"

Tanya sighed. "Sammie's father is heir to a huge fortune. Who do you think will garner more respect from our patrons? You or—"

"Tanya, please," I said, holding up both hands. "I wasn't born yesterday. You gave Sammie the job because her parents promised a big donation. Why can't you be honest instead of blaming my clothes or my lack of pedigree?"

"That's another thing. You're always so negative," Tanya added.

What? I thought. *Now, that's unfair. Joy is my middle name. It really is. Holly Joy Ross.* "I'm not being negative. It's just . . . I'm trying to understand why you gave Sammie the job you promised to me."

"Okay, fine," Tanya said, spritzing herself with perfume, infusing the office with the subtle scent of roses. "There's truth to what you said. Sammie Kittenplatt will more than cover her salary with the donations she'll attract. The day you bring me a million-dollar check, we'll talk about making you a curator. Until then, I'm promoting you to *senior* assistant. How does that sound?"

I stared at her.

Tanya made an apologetic smile. "Holly, you're very talented and a hard worker and I love having you by my side. I'll even give you a five percent raise. That's two thousand more a year. What do you think of that?"

"Thanks," I grumbled. My career dreams were dead, at least for the moment.

Send for Me

THAT EVENING, AFTER GOING home to change, I met Nigel at the Coffee Shop. It was a retro-inspired joint on Union Square featuring stunning waiflike waitstaff, mostly young women biding their time before becoming models or actresses. I rarely went there, because hip places intimidate me as a rule. But Nigel was paying, so I made an exception. We sat at the bar.

Nigel regarded me with sympathy and I regarded him back.

With his drop-dead looks, he fit perfectly into this place. "How about we make me vice president in charge of cheering you up?" he said, tapping my chin with his finger.

"Leave me alone. Let me sulk."

"Maybe you should apply at the Met," Nigel suggested. "I'd hate to see you go, but it would serve the bitch right."

Being British, he pronounced right like "roit."

"I'm not going anywhere at the museum," I said. "She made *that* clear."

The bartender interrupted, uncorking a bottle of Cakebread chardonnay that Nigel had generously ordered. He poured a smidge into a glass so that I could test it. I sniffed, swirled it around, and acted like I knew what I was doing. Then I took a small swallow. "Mmm, yummy," I declared. "So, do you have contacts at the Met?"

"Sweetheart, do *I* have contacts at the Met?" Nigel asked. "Do goldfish piss in their bowls?"

"I don't know. Do I look like a marine biologist?"

"It's an expression, luv."

"Sorry," I said. "I'm just frustrated. I suppose it wouldn't hurt to talk to someone there," I said, sipping. "You know, tomorrow we're doing What's My Line? I should tell Tanya to take Sammie instead of me."

"Don't you dare. If you want to work at the Met, then you *must* sit in," Nigel pointed out. "I reckon they'll see how brilliant you are, won't they?"

I considered his point. What's My Line? was the fierce competition we held every year against the Costume Institute at the Metropolitan Museum. The Fashion Council–sponsored contest at Bryant Park featured vintage couture creations from top twentieth-century designers. Both museums were allowed to appoint two experts to name the line each outfit came from and the year of the collection. The winner received a fifty-thousand-dollar grant from the Fashion Council. Tanya always appointed herself for the visibility and me for the answers. We'd won the past two out of three years.

"You're right. It'd be good for me. But let's change the subject. I'm sick of talking about me. Did I tell you Denis King picked me up this morning?"

"I know, you said," Nigel said. "But you're about to be married. What are you doing fancying other boys?"

"I don't fancy him. He happened to pick me up . . . *in his chauffeur-driven Maybach.* Have you ever been in a Maybach? Oh, my God, it's soooo luxurious," I enthused. "Anyway, the thing about Denis was, for a powerful guy, he was really kind. You saw what a mess I was this morning, right? Well, he said I looked perfect. Why can't Alessandro say I look perfect when I don't? Whyyyy? Oh, lord, I'm slurring my words. Do you think I'm having a stroke?"

Nigel laughed. "Don't be daft. Why don't you order something to eat?" He topped off my glass and slid over a menu. Gesturing with his chin, he asked, "Is that bloke over there checking me out? Don't look."

I looked. "Yep, he is."

"Aren't you happy I'm one of those men who is blissfully unaware of how strikingly smashing he is?" Nigel said. "If I weren't, I'd be insufferable."

I punched his arm. "Oh, you . . ."

"So tell me, did you give King your number?"

I gasped. "Of course not."

"Why not?"

"I couldn't let him know who I was. Number one, I was a mess. Number two, what if he told Tanya he met one of her employees and she was wearing grocery-bag shoes? She'd kill me."

"The correct answer to that question was, you didn't give him your number because you're engaged," Nigel said.

"And number three, what you just said."

My cell phone rang and Alessandro's name appeared. "Speak of the devil . . ." I whispered. My stomach sank. He would be so disappointed when I told him I didn't get the job. "Alessandro, I have some bad news for you—"

"Honey, not now, I'm in a bit of a pickle," he said. His voice sounded strained.

"A pickle?" I said, sitting up straight.

"I'm in jail," he whimpered.

What? I thought. Not my Alessandro. My Alessandro was a staunch believer in the penal code, or so he had always led me to believe. "*You're in jail?* Why? What did you do?"

"Tell me. Tell me," Nigel urged.

I shushed him.

"Soliciting a minor," Alessandro said in a low tone.

"Soliciting *what* from a minor?" I asked. Honestly, I had no idea. Soliciting donations? Soliciting phone calls? Soliciting public comment?

"Soliciting sex," he groaned.

"*Sex?*" I said. "That's impossible."

"What's he charged with?" Nigel asked.

"Soliciting sex from a minor," I whispered.

Nigel's eyes grew wide. "Male or female?"

"Male or female?"

"Female, *of course*," Alessandro said. "Do you think I'm a perv?"

"Ah . . . ah . . . ah . . . how *could* you?" I was about to hang up on him, but he was screaming into the phone.

"She *said* she was eighteen!" Alessandro bellowed. "I swear! We were on her roof deck and a guy in the building next door recognized her and called her parents and the police. She turned out to be sixteen, but if you'd seen how she came on to me and the way she was dressed—"

"Jeezus, you're more than twice her age," I said. "What were you thinking? We're getting married next month."

"It might make the papers," Alessandro mumbled.

"*What?* Why? Who *is* this girl?"

"Not her. *Me*. I'm on Broadway now," Alessandro said. "In a *Disney* show. Fuck! Please call the theater and tell them I'm sick. Then call Suzy Hendrix. She'll know what to do."

"Suzy can't help. She's an entertainment lawyer," I said.

"Holly, *call her*. And don't worry. We'll beat the charges."

"Wait a minute, but did you say 'we'?"

"Please," Alessandro begged. "You're my fiancée. You *have* to stick with me."

"You should have thought of that before you stuck it to Lolita on the roof."

"Please" (whimper, whimper), "call Suzy and then come rescue me. I n-need you."

"Okay, okay, fine. I'll call her. We'll figure this out later."

"Holly," Alessandro said. "Be sure to wear something conservative, you know, in case we're photographed."

My jaw dropped. "Anything else?"

"Yes, don't wear red. It bleeds in pictures."

I snapped the phone shut. My eyes filled and I tried to blink the tears away.

Suddenly, my career worries that had seemed so important a few minutes ago faded. Poof! Gone. Jobs would come and go, but Alessandro was my fiancé. He might not be my Cary Grant, but he was the only leading man I had. Then it hit me. Of course, Alessandro wasn't my Cary Grant; he was my Hugh Grant.

In the Wee Small Hours of the Morning

Nothing personal, Hugh Grant. As a professional in the arts, I appreciate your body of work, and as a woman, I fantasize about your body. But you and I both know that, once upon a time, you did something dishonorable, shabby, and goatish. I have a new appreciation for Elizabeth Hurley and how she must have suffered. Knowing that you're both doing so well these many years later gives me hope. Of course, you did break up.

It was after midnight when Alessandro and I returned home on the night of his "incident." Apparently, after one is arrested in Manhattan, interminable waiting is the central theme of the experience.

"We need to talk," Alessandro said as we closed the front door and collapsed on the couch. Poor Alessandro. Normally so pulled together, tonight he was a mess. His black hair was stringy, his skin pasty, and he smelled like Pine-Sol with a vomit chaser.

"Holly, this will *never* happen again," Alessandro said in his most sincere voice, the same one he used as Motel when he tried to convince Tevye to let him marry Tzeitel in *Fiddler on the Roof*. "It was a terrible mistake on my part. I still want to get married and I hope you feel the same."

I picked up Kitty and hugged him. He purred as I stroked his head. "Do we have to do this now? I'm so tired."

"You know, Holly," Alessandro said, moving toward the kitchen, "I'm worried about you. You're young to be so lethargic. If you'd take a multivitamin you might have more energy. Wait, I'll get you one."

Was he kidding me? I thought as he walked to the kitchen. No, I guess not, I realized when he returned with a One-A-Day and some water.

"Alessandro, I am emotionally and physically exhausted after discovering that the man I'm supposed to marry next month was arrested for—"

"*Stop*. Please." He slammed the glass onto the table, splashing water everywhere. "If you saw the girl, you'd understand she looked eighteen."

"Okay," I said. "Maybe she did and you made an honest mistake.

Let me rephrase. I'm emotionally and physically exhausted after discovering that the man I'm supposed to marry *has been cheating on me*. You *cheated*, Alessandro. How *could* you? I thought we loved each other."

Alessandro screwed his lips into pout position. "I do love you. It was a mistake. You have to forgive me."

"I don't have to do anything." I tramped off to the kitchen, opened the freezer, grabbed a half gallon of rocky-road ice cream, stuck it in the microwave, and zapped it until it was soup. With the ice cream carton in one hand, Kitty in my arm, I marched to the bedroom and butt-slammed the door behind me.

Sitting up against my pillows, I clicked on the TV. There was Audrey Hepburn in the tennis pavilion waiting for William Holden. Have I mentioned I keep one of her movies loaded in my DVD player and watch scenes from them every day? Well, not every day. I rarely take them with me when I travel. I drank the chocolate soup out of the carton, but soon felt sick, like there was a tumor the size of Alessandro's head pressing against my lower intestines. My eyes filled, then tears sloshed down my face. Soon sobs came in hard, painful waves. "It's not fair. It's not fair!" I screamed. "Where's *my* happy ending?" I threw the ice cream carton at the television set and it made a big brown Rorschach stain on the screen. Kitty leaped out of bed and went over to lick up the drippings.

I was deep in alpha slumber when Alessandro shook me. "Huh? What? What time is it?"

Alessandro was wearing his boxers and his breath smelled like beer. "It's three thirty. Holly, I'm sorry to wake you, but I had a terrible nightmare."

"Huh, a night . . . ?" Then it came back to me. What a surprise. The cheater had a nightmare. "Go back to sleep."

"It was our wedding day. Your mother was there," he said. "It's like she came back from the dead to watch you get married."

"Go away, Alessandro."

"Please just listen. Your mother came to give us her blessing, but then suddenly you changed your mind. You *refused* to marry me."

"Was it because you're a child molester?"

Alessandro winced. "No, no, you *wanted* to stand by me, but you were afraid something like this could happen again."

"*Noooooo*, really?"

"Your mother came to *assure* you and then *warn* you," Alessandro said, his eyes wide, his voice dramatic.

"Of what?"

"She said if you married me as planned, I would be faithful to you for the rest of your life. But if you marry another, you and your husband and children will be *cursed*," he said. "You will know nothing but pain and misery. That was her message."

I rolled my *eyes*. "Jeezus, Alessandro, how many times did I see you in *Fiddler on the Roof*? That's the dream Tevye made up to convince Golde to let Tzeitel marry Motel instead of Lazar Wolf."

Alessandro cocked his head. "So it is. That must be the source of the dream, my having acted in the show so many times, but your mother was there; I swear it."

I buried my head in the covers and muffled a scream. "Go away."

"Please, give me another chance to love you," he begged, pulling down the blanket as he tried to kiss me.

It was awkward, because I was wearing my headgear.

"I'm so sorry; please, please Holly. I need you."

Alessandro ran his tongue down my neck, since the headgear made lip access impossible. Then he started to lift the T-shirt over my face and next thing you know, we were doing it. Don't ask me why. I was furious with him, but I was desperately afraid to let him go. Is it true what they say—better the asshole you know (than the asshole you don't)? I was completely flummoxed, so I let him screw me again.

Someone to Watch over Me

THE HOUSE WAS STILL when I snuck out the next morning. Alessandro was sleeping on the sofa. Empty beer cans were strewn about.

I'd hardly slept. It was early. There wasn't even a line at Dunkin' Donuts. Pops, unshaven and bedraggled, was manning his stoop, singing "Thank Heaven for Little Girls" to a white teacup Maltese in his lap. I sat down and set up breakfast between us. The smell of rotting trash wafted through the air, making the outdoor picnic less appetizing.

"Cute puppy," I said.

"Poor thing," Pops said, crushing out his cigarette stub. "She cried all night. She misses her human. We're waiting for him."

I took the white fuzz ball and cuddled her in my hands.

"Did you see the *Post*?" Pops said.

My face burned. "No, why?"

"Here. Someone dropped it in the trash."

My stomach sank when I saw it. The headline read "Babe and the Beast," accompanied by a picture of Alessandro and me fleeing the police station, story page six. I was wearing my red Jil Sander shift, the one I'd picked up at the Sloan-Kettering Thrift Shop. Alessandro was right. Red does bleed.

"Here's the *News*," Pops said.

"Oh, my God," I moaned. "This is so embarrassing."

"Broadway Hound," the headline shouted, accompanied by the same delightful photo of Alessandro and me midflight, story page five. They had an inset shot of the minor Alessandro was accused of violating. It was taken from her MySpace page. The blond nymph was making love to the camera with her striking eyes and a come-hither smile. She definitely looked older than sixteen.

I sunk my head. "A year ago," I said, "no one would have cared but me. He was just another no-name actor."

"In my experience these sorts of things can be blessings in disguise," Pops said. "You never wanted to marry that boy, Holly."

I held the warm puppy close to my eyes, stifling my tears in his soft fur. "What makes you say that?"

"The way you talked about him," Pops said. "Like you were trying to convince yourself he was the one." He stuffed his trash into the Dunkin' Donuts bag and then tossed the sack like a basketball to the can, missing. "I'm losing my touch." He got up and threw it in the garbage. A cement truck roared by, sending up a cloud of dust.

"There's my little Cookie Wookie," said a gaunt man with lacquered red hair dressed in jeans and a blue work shirt as he ambled up to the stoop. He wore a massive gold Rolex watch. I recognized him as Phillip Shayne, the manager of Old Time Records around the corner.

Pops stood and placed the fluffy Maltese in his arms.

"How'd my little baby girl do?" the big guy asked as Cookie furiously licked his nose.

"She was lonely and cried for you," Pops said. "So I let her sleep with me and gave her some extra TLC."

"Thanks, man," the guy said. He reached in his pocket and pulled out a ten. "Here you go, Pops. C'mon, Cookums."

Pops went back inside and soon came out holding a black-haired shih tzu with a pink bow in her hair. "Meet Orangy," he said.

"That's her name? Orangy?" I said. "Even though she's black?"

"It's ironic," Pops said, feeding her a chocolate Munchkin. "Her human is Fran Stevens, the rock singer. She's on her way over."

"Pops, I don't think chocolate is good for dogs."

"Really?" He seemed surprised. "Even with all the antioxidants? What about dark chocolate?"

"No chocolate, period," I said. "It's full of sugar and caffeine."

Not a minute later, a petite dynamo with a squidged-up face bounded up the block. She had a turned-up nose, freckles, jet-black hair, and a remarkable resemblance to the dog she had come to claim. "Orangy, Mommy's here," she sang.

Pops put the ecstatic, trembling dog in the woman's hands

while the pup emitted high-pitched squeals of joy and leaked urine. "She really missed you," he said. "But don't worry. I let her sleep with me and gave her extra TLC."

"Thanks, Pops." She reached into her pocket and pulled out a twenty. "We appreciate the special treatment," she said. "Don't we, Orangy? Yes, we do."

"That's quite a hustle you got going there," I said, after Orangy's owner disappeared down the block.

"Isn't it?" Pops said proudly. "I pick up an extra fifty a day making owners feel like I love their pets the most."

"You think that's okay?"

"I'm not lying. I treat 'em all the same—like royalty. And anyway, I need the money. Whole Foods wouldn't hire me. Said I was too old."

"They can't say that. It's against the law."

"Oh, they didn't use those words exactly," Pops explained. "They said I was overqualified. That's code for too old."

"Aw, sorry," I said, laying my head on his shoulder. "I didn't get the job I expected, either."

"Why not?" Pops asked.

"My boss said I wasn't good enough . . . didn't dress the part . . . couldn't bring in big donations like the Sammie-come-lately she hired."

Pops gave me a squeeze. "I'm awfully sorry about that, Holly. You had a rough day yesterday, didn't you?"

"Truer words have never been spoken, Pops."

Put Your Dreams Away

I WAS THE FIRST TO arrive at the office that day, except for Gus, of course, who had been minding the store all night. He was snoring and whistling, just like in a cartoon. I gently shook him awake. "Here, two vanilla-glazed doughnuts with sprinkles, the way you like 'em."

Gus yawned and stretched his arms. "Thanks, Holly. You are the brightest star at this museum."

"Awwww, shucks." I giggled, blushing. Gus always lifted my spirits. "You're too good to me."

"I'd do anything for you."

At least *somebody* appreciated me at work. Tanya's door was closed. I stepped into my cubicle, switched on the computer, and checked my e-mail.

"Oh, lord," I muttered, crumpling into my chair. Everyone I knew and scores I didn't must have seen the papers. My in-box was crammed with messages: "Are you okay?" "What happened?" "Call me!!!" "That shithead!"

I checked Gawker and PerezHilton. Photos of Alessandro and me fleeing the police station, along with snarky stories, topped the sites. Perfect. There was no way Tanya hadn't heard about it. I started to google Alessandro's name to read more press, but I couldn't bear it.

I pondered for a moment and then typed in newyorksocialdiary .com. If you want to read about the Manhattan blue bloods and observe them at play, this was a good place to start.

I entered Denis' name and pages of photos came up with him posing at various fetes with the same woman, a sapling, really, on his arm. With a click of my mouse, I scrolled through the photos. The human bauble by his side was Sydney Bass (of the Oyster Bay Basses). She was a beautiful girl if you liked perfectly proportioned designer-clad blondes with long, sinewy legs, translucent skin, piercing blue eyes, and sultry lips. You know the type—they don't burp, fart, poop, or take public transportation. I had read about her in the Style section of the *Times*, in an article about ambitious well-born daughters pursuing the new socialite game—the one in which they use their family names and contacts to become nationally recognized brands, like Aerin Lauder and Ivanka Trump. If you ask me, that was piggish. What, it's not enough for them to be rich and gorgeous? They want meaningful lives too?

Sydney Bass played a leading role in her family's real estate business. She had inherited twenty-five million square feet of office space on four continents from her father. While attending Harvard Business School, she along with her advisers parlayed her inheritance into the largest privately held portfolio in the city. The woman was smart, rich, beautiful, socially prominent, and twenty-six years old. I hated her on principle.

Scrolling through the photos, I noticed she looked the same in every picture—arched neck, pouty lips, a naughty little wink—which led me to believe she must have spent hours working with a smile consultant to fashion the perfect paparazzi face. Call me crazy, but anyone I've ever known with a rehearsed snapshot pose has turned out to be a liar and a fornicator (Alessandro immediately comes to mind).

I googled Denis and clicked on parkavenuepeerage.com. There I read that he was forty-eight, divorced, father of a ten-year-old girl, a real estate developer—well, that part I knew. Let's see, he had a yacht, a jet, houses in Southampton and Sun Valley, a two-floor penthouse on Fifth Avenue with a basketball court and paintings by Picasso, van Gogh, and Matisse. *Well la-di-da*, I thought. So he's the ninth-richest man in America under fifty (according to *Forbes*). Hrrmph! What's a billionaire his age doing squiring about a girl more than twenty years his junior? Because he could, I supposed. Still, my respect for him dropped a notch, as it always does for older gentlemen who pursue the taut flesh of youth.

Checking Denis' rating on famestat.com, the site run by catty society blogger Chessie Knickerbocker, I saw that he was one of two real estate moguls with high ratings, the other being Donald Trump. Three hundred and eighty parties, two hundred and seven pictures. Jeez, who would want to live like that? *I would! I would!* my less-evolved self squealed. Google revealed that Denis was part of the King real estate dynasty that had built some of the most celebrated buildings in New York. Their family's foundation had donated millions to the Metropolitan Museum, Lincoln Center, the New York City Opera, and Sloan-Kettering Hospital, just to name a few. No wonder Tanya was working him for a major gift.

I sighed. A woman could live happily ever after with a man like that. Any guy who would return to help the stranger his car splashed could be counted on to hold your hand when you walked down the street or your hair back when you puked. Not that I'm the kind of girl who expects some knight in a shining white Maybach to come along and sweep me off my feet. That only happens in the movies, and life isn't like that. Although I often wish it were.

The happy ending I had hoped to have with Alessandro was dangling by a silk thread. Apparently, the neighbor who spotted him on the roof videotaped the crime-in-progress as Alessandro did the deed. He only shot the perp's backside. Last night, the arresting cop played it and asked if the ass on top was Alessandro. I could tell by the way he . . . oh, never mind. What if the only reason he wanted to marry me was so I couldn't testify against him? There was a case like that on *Law & Order* once.

But back to Alessandro, the philandering perv. How could I say "I do" to a guy who would cheat a month before his own wedding? Sure, I'd had my doubts about us, but that was normal. On the other hand, what if he needed me now more than ever?

Was this craving to be with underage girls a sickness, a sort of pedophilic cancer? If I helped him get counseling, could we start over? That would be the right thing to do, the loving thing, the Buddhist thing. I'm not Buddhist, but I've read they're a forgiving people. I like to think of myself as forgiving, at least theoretically.

I pictured myself alone with Kitty in an empty studio apartment located multiple subway stops into Queens, eating Duncan Hines chocolate frosting out of a can, maybe starting some kind of spinster blog. A wave of sadness swept over me and I started to cry, then sob, right into my computer keyboard. Tears fell down my cheeks, alien sounds spilled out of my mouth, and a torrent of snot poured from my nose.

Tanya stuck her head out. "Holly, would you cease with the boo-hooing? How do you expect me to get any work done with you carrying on like that? Take it outside. Go on. Go." She waved her hand toward the staircase, and then retreated.

"I'm okay," I called, wiping my nose on my sleeve. "I'll sto-op." Bugger! Tanya Johnson was the last person on earth I wanted to see me cry.

All things considered, my circumstances had deteriorated so quickly that this was shaping up to be the worst twenty-four hours of my life so far. I didn't know what to be more upset about. Finding out I wouldn't be promoted? Discovering my fiancé was a cheater? Learning he was a pedophile? Seeing my stricken face and bleeding red suit on the front page of the *News* and the *Post*? Knowing that I might have to break my engagement and undo months of wedding plans? Realizing I may soon lose my home? At least things couldn't get worse. Of course, having thought that, I was certain it was only a matter of time before they did.

The Lady Is a Tramp

I RETIRED TO THE BATHROOM and checked the damage. Blotches of mascara framed my red and raw eyes. Lovely. Splashing my face with cold water, removing the hasty makeup job I'd attempted that morning, I looked at myself in the mirror. "Pull yourself together. You can do this."

Grabbing the folder for What's My Line? I hustled to Tanya's office. Martin Goldenblatt, our doughy-skinned audiovisual guy, stood by her desk sniffing the top of his hand. The lapdog (aka Sammie) was flipping through the *Post*.

I mustered a thin smile. "Ready to prep for What's My Line?" I asked Tanya.

"How *are* you?" Sammie said. "I read the paper. You are *so* brave. I can't imagine how you got out of bed today."

"I'm fine," I said. "And you know what they say . . ."

Yes, those who *can't*, work in museums," Sammie finished.

"I was going to say, the show must go on."

Tanya pursed her lips. Then she laced her fingers together and cracked her knuckles.

Oh, boy, I thought.

"Holly, these headlines are *humiliating* . . ." Tanya said.

"I know," I said, wondering if maybe she would show me some compassion.

". . . to the museum," she finished. "I think it would be best if you didn't appear in public with me today, or possibly forever," Tanya said. "You understand."

My stomach sank.

"But who's going to support you up there?" I didn't want to say it, but what Tanya knew about vintage couture could fit in a hummingbird's bladder.

"Well," Tanya declared conspiratorially, "Sammie will sit by my side. She's new and needs the visibility. But *you* will secretly feed us answers through hidden receivers. We're wearing them now. Can you tell?"

I checked their faces, hands, hair. Nothing. "You got me. Where is it?"

"It's built into our *earrings*," Tanya explained, pointing to the large gold balls clipped to her lobes and the matching pair that Sammie wore. "Martin made them. They're wireless and surprisingly chic. No one will ever know."

Tanya was asking me to cheat for her. That took brass ovaries. "But, Tanya," I said, "that's dishonest. You can't do that."

She turned to me. "Oh, really, Mother Teresa, and why not?"

"Yes, Mother Teresa," Sammie added. "Why not?"

"It *is*, uh, wrong," said spineless Martin.

"And *you* who leaves early on Fridays," I accused. "Is the fancy yarmulke for show? Does it mean nothing to you?"

"Tanya said I had to. She's the boss," he said. "It's an ingenious device. I should patent it."

"No, it belongs to the museum," Tanya said. "You made it on company time under my direction. Any profit it generates belongs to us."

Sometimes I think Tanya is psychotic, and I mean that clinically.

"I'll be able to answer the questions," Sammie said, smiling eagerly. "I *did* graduate from Bauder College."

Tanya gave her an incredulous look. "I'm not willing to stake my museum's reputation on your delusions of adequacy." Sammie's smile disappeared.

"Seriously, Tanya, what if you get caught?" I said. "There's a fifty-thousand-dollar prize at stake. If you win by fraud, that's a crime."

"I will *not* get caught," Tanya said. "The plan is foolproof." She handed me a microphone that Martin had hidden inside a cell phone shell. "Just speak into this and I'll hear you through my earring."

It occurred to me that when your boss insists that you cheat or commit a crime, the only way to say "no" is to resign. But I was about to lose my fiancé and his rent-controlled apartment. If I quit my job, I'd have nothing left but Kitty (and he only had three legs).

"It'll be our little secret," Sammie declared. "No one will ever know."

"Martin, if we get caught, you'll back me up in court, right?"

"Well, I, uh," Martin stammered, "whatever Tanya says."

I rolled my eyes. If I was going to be part of a criminal conspiracy, why did it have to be with Martin Goldenblatt? "I guess," I muttered, "but I'm acting under protest."

Answer Me, My Love

THAT AFTERNOON, I FOUND myself standing in the back of a white tent at the Bryant Park fashion shows. What's My Line? would be the warm-up act for last year's *Project Runway* wunderkind, who was showing his highly anticipated collection. It was a hot ticket and the room was buzzing with designers, buyers, movie stars, editors, socialites, and various and sundry jet-setters. Paparazzi snapped away at the audience. Billy Bush from *Access Hollywood* was interviewing Donald and

Melania Trump by the tent's French doors. Camera crews were setting up. Scarlett Johansson sauntered in with an unidentified hottie wearing a kilt. One of the Olsen twigs was gossiping with Heidi Klum, who was seated with Michael Kors. Anna Wintour and her Chanel sunglasses ruled sphinxlike in the front row. I would have enjoyed the whole juicy scene if I weren't about to soil myself from sheer terror over the dirty deed I was about to do. All my life I've been morally against breaking the law, especially when I'm afraid of getting caught.

Nichole Cannon, senior curator of the Costume Institute at the Met, and Candice Broom, another of their top dogs, were both being miked at the dais. Tanya made her way to the stage, stopping frequently to double and triple air kiss potential donors and well-wishers. Sammie followed a few steps behind, waving at the socialites she knew through family connections. *Maybe she is the better choice*, I thought. *She's so plugged in to the charity circuit. I don't know any of these people*.

Once Tanya and Sammie were settled and miked, I tried out Martin's nifty invention. "Testing, testing, one, two, three," I said into the cell phone. "Do you read me?"

Tanya turned and caught my eye, curling the corners of her mouth upward. That would be a yes.

I repositioned myself to the far side of the room, where I could see both my boss and the runway. At this point, I was sweating like a four-hundred-pound woman running for the crosstown bus.

Valentina de la Costa, director of the Fashion Council, welcomed everyone and introduced the players who would be vying for the fifty-thousand-dollar grant.

My real cell phone vibrated. I flipped it open. There was a text message from Alessandro:

H, the wedding is off. Pls return the ring ASAP.
Must sell it to pay lawyer. A

I gasped with disbelief. Alessandro was breaking up with ME? By text message? After *he* cheated with a minor? Isn't there a mandatory penis-cooling-off period before making such a drastic decision?

"How come you aren't up there?" asked Elaina, my coworker and curator of the Audrey Hepburn show. I hadn't noticed her next to me.

"Huh?" I said, snapping the cell phone shut. A lump was forming in my throat. *Alessandro's leaving* me? *Shouldn't I be leaving* him? *Stop it*. I took a deep breath. *Think about it later. Pull yourself together. You have laws to break, crimes to commit*.

"Why aren't you up there?" Elaina repeated.

"Um, you know Tanya," I said. "She wanted to give Sammie a try."

Elaina's eyes widened. "That's risky."

"She thinks I'm bad news with Alessandro getting arrested and all."

"Alessandro got arrested?" Elaina said, her eyes wide in horror. "What happ—"

Suddenly, "Puttin' on the Ritz" blasted from the speakers.

If you're blue and you don't know where to go . . .

Music blared and camera shutters clicked at deafening volume. A lightning storm of fluorescent flashes was followed by the sound of editors' notebooks snapping to attention. Out strutted a gazellelike brunette wearing a flirty red silk crepe number. This was so obviously Chanel's little black dress realized in red. The topstitching technique was unmistakable, visible even from where I stood. And of course, the fabric-covered buttons were signature. "Chanel, 1927," I said into phone/mike.

Onstage, Sammie had hit the bell before the Met team.

"Yes, Fashion Museum," Valentina said.

Tanya tilted her head so she could hear better and fixed her eyes on me as I said, "Chanel, 1927," over and over into the phone.

"Fashion Museum, we need your answer," Valentina said.

I put the phone aside and mouthed "Chanel" in an exaggerated but (hopefully) subtle way.

"Holly, what are you doing?" Elaina said, looking at me with the expression of a woman in the direct path of a speeding subway train.

"Edith Head, 1940," Sammie cried out.

Edith Head? I thought. *That girl is a blooming idiot* (Sammie, that is; not Edith).

Nichole Cannon hit her bell. "Chanel, 1927."

"That is correct," Valentina said.

The crowd applauded furiously.

Tanya made her shrew face, but then smiled and pulled her public self together.

The soundtrack switched to the Andrews Sisters singing "Boogie Woogie Bugle Boy."

He was a famous trumpet man from old Chicago way . . .

The music didn't seem as loud this time. An impossibly slim blonde emerged in a dramatic tailored black suit with three bold sequined mint-green leaves emblazoned across the jacket front, and an inverted velveteen shoe worn as a hat in her hair. She vamped across the stage and down the runway while the crowd clapped enthusiastically.

I was sure Tanya would know this one since we'd had a Schiaparelli exhibit less than a year ago. While we hadn't shown this particular piece, her style was unmistakable. She was known for overlaying sequined insects and other decontextualized designs on sharp-tailored suits. "Elsa Schiaparelli, 1934," I said into the phone. But from the puzzled expression on Tanya's face, she wasn't reading. *Think, dammit, think,* I psychically begged my boss. *You* know *this one.*

Candice Broom slammed the bell. "Schiaparelli, 1930," she declared.

"That is incorrect," Valentina said. "Fashion Museum?"

Tanya and Sammie scrutinized me. With my left hand, I scratched my head with three fingers, and with my right hand, I wiggled four fingers by my ear.

"Holly," Elaina stage-whispered, "stop. You're cheating. Wait. Only the self-accused condemn. That's from *A Course in Miracles.*" She shook her head. "I'm confused."

"I'm following orders," I told her.

"That's what the Nazis said."

"Schiaparelli, 1925," Sammie said.

Oh, come on, I thought. *Schiaparelli didn't do her first collection until twenty-nine, the year of the Great Depression. Everyone in fashion knows that. Except, perhaps, heiresses who secure their curator positions through nepotism.*

I gestured for Martin to come over.

"They can't hear me above the music," I whispered. "Can you increase the volume?"

"I'd need the earrings to do that," Martin said. "Just talk louder."

"No, I'll get caught," I said. By then Bobby Darin was singing "Mack the Knife" and a bag of bones with translucent skin and red hair glided down the catwalk swathed in a luminous navy cocktail dress. Its soft-shouldered, round-bosomed top was cinched at the waist in corsetlike fashion, topping a skirt of blue taffeta that poufed into a round hemline, giving the artful gown the shape of an upside-down wineglass. Any student of fashion would know this iconic piece. The designer's excessive use of rich, sumptuous fabric was the giveaway that it came from Christian Dior (about whom Coco Chanel famously said, "Dior? He doesn't dress women; he upholsters them").

Oh, the shark, babe, has such teeth, dear . . .

"Christian Dior, 1947," I said in as loud a voice as I could muster without calling attention to myself. "Christian Dior."

Sammie's blank stare told me she either hadn't paid attention in class or was a complete flibbertigibbet.

Tanya's nostrils flared like a bull about to charge. I could feel her glare from behind those sunglasses. She should have been glaring at Martin Goldenblatt, who'd invented the cockamamie device without considering the fact that *every fashion show on the planet* plays loud music.

Just end it now, I thought, *because the most vicious shark in the room is going to have me for lunch when this is over.*

Nichole Cannon slapped her bell. "Christian Dior, 1949."

"That is not correct," Valentina said. "Fashion Museum, it's your turn."

"Dior, '47, Dior, '47, Dior, '47," I repeated over and over again into the phone.

The blue vein in Tanya's neck was pulsating so hard it looked like it might pop. But sadly for me, it didn't. Sammie slammed down the bell. "Yves Saint Laurent, 1950?"

"That is incorrect," Valentina said. "The correct answer is Christian Dior, 1947."

Gwen Stefani's "Rich Girl" blasted from the sound system. Out floated a willowy blond angel wearing a sensational sleeveless yellow silk evening dress with a hem of black-and-white beaded flowers.

Sammie hit the bell.

Aha, I thought. *This was the trick piece.* Ever since the Met canceled their first planned Chanel show over Karl Lagerfeld's objection that the exhibit wasn't going to include contemporary pieces, the Fashion Council always slipped a new design into their contest.

"Oscar de la Renta, 2006," I mouthed, having given up completely on Martin's nifty but useless invention.

Sammie cocked her head and I could see that she was attempting to catch my drift.

"Oscar de la Renta, 2006. Oscar de la Renta, 2006," I mouthed.

Sammie's eyes bulged like a goldfish's; that's how hard she was trying to read me.

"Oscar de la Renta, 2006," exploded from my lips. "Yoinks!" I said, slapping my hand to my mouth. "Sorry. Accident."

Seemingly at once, the entire audience turned and gaped at me (except for the model, who stayed in character, as models do). Hands clapped mouths, heads cocked, jaws dropped, gasps sounded. *Holy mother of pearl*, I thought, *what do I do? RUN!* My inner voice shouted. *LIKE THE WIND!* But I didn't. I stood paralyzed, unable to act. I always choke in emergencies. It's a character flaw.

Gently, a security guard took my elbow and escorted me to the exit without even stopping at the goody bag table. I tossed the mike/phone to Martin, who was too busy sniffing his hand to make the catch. I prayed that Martin could pull a rabbit out of his yarmulke.

Isn't It a Pity

IT WAS FOUR P.M. when I was booted out of the What's My Line? tent. Tomorrow, Tanya would make me pay.

Feeling light-headed and lousy, I dragged myself home to Alessandro. What kind of jerk breaks off a serious relationship by text message? That's worse than a Dear John e-mail, which is harsh enough. *I'm well rid of the bum*, I thought. *But where will I live? What will I do? Dear God, I hope he paid the orthodontist in full.*

"Did you get my text message?" Alessandro asked as I trudged inside. He was lying on the couch in his yoga pants, shirtless, watching *Dr. Phil.* The air smelled of burned popcorn. There were silver Hershey's Kisses wrappers everywhere.

"Child molester," I muttered, tromping to the bedroom, throwing on a pair of sweats. "What, no theater tonight?" I said when I emerged, clicking off the television. I felt like hurting Alessandro.

"They put me on indefinite leave," he said. "Because of the headlines. My lawyer is going to fight it."

"Good luck with that." I rolled my eyes and sank into the sofa next to his feet, which reeked of toe jam, so I did a flying leap to the other side of the room.

Alessandro sat up. "It's an illness, you know. I need help."

"And I might have been willing to help you if you'd given me half a chance."

Alessandro nodded. "Dr. Blumstein be . . . she believes I was unconsciously sabotaging our relationship because I didn't want to get married."

My stomach dropped like a glass elevator in a Hyatt atrium. He was really breaking up with me. Right here. Right now. It was happening.

"Blumstein *gets* me," Alessandro said, not much louder than a whisper. He looked at me with those (formerly) irresistible eyes. "That's why I text messaged you."

"Classy, Alessandro, really classy."

"I was trying to show you mercy," he explained. "Blumstein said you'd need time to process the blow."

"But . . . but what about your nightmare? What about my

mother's message?" I pleaded, not knowing why I was trying to save us. Alessandro had done me a favor. It's what *I* should have done the moment I found out he was cheating. But I'd been afraid to let go. I'd been counting on Alessandro to be my happily ever after.

"My nightmare? I lied," Alessandro admitted. "Last night I was so freaked out, I wanted to hang on to you no matter what. Dr. Blumstein helped me see that I need to be on my own, to take time to get to know the real Alessandro Vercelli, whoever he may be."

"But we have a cat together," I implored, pacing. "What did Blumstein say about that?"

"Kitty is the least of my problems. Right now, I'm all about getting into detox," Alessandro said. "Blumstein's working on it."

"You're not an alcoholic."

"It's part of our legal strategy," Alessandro explained. "Break the law; go to detox; beg forgiveness: Mel Gibson, Kate Moss, the black dude from *Grey's Anatomy*, blah blah blah."

I plunked myself into a chair and looked around the apartment where I'd hoped to build a home for us. My eyes began to fill and an errant tear escaped. "Yesterday I thought I'd be getting married in a month," I said, wiping my face with my sleeve. "Now you're telling me it's over. This is not how my life is supposed to go."

Alessandro waxed philosophical. "Life isn't always what you like, you know."

How dare he tell me that! As if I didn't already know. "You are such an ass. First you cheat on me. Then it turns out to be with a minor . . ."

"Good, Blumstein says anger is good," Alessandro started.

"Then we get our pictures in the paper. Our friends saw that picture. My boss saw that picture. She refuses to be seen with me anymore . . ."

"Whoa there, Nelly! Is that all you can think about—*yourself*? How do you think *I* feel? I'm looking at jail time." Alessandro seemed incredulous that I could be so selfish.

I growled and wagged my finger at him. "Whoa, Nelly? What am I, a horse? You listen to me, Alessandro. You do *not* get to do the breaking up. If anyone gets broken up with, it's *you*."

"Fine," Alessandro said. "If it's that important to assuage your ego, we'll tell everyone *you* did the breaking up."

"Fine," I said.

"Fine," Alessandro answered.

"*Fine*," I said.

"But you and I will always know I'm the one who called it off."

Why did Alessandro always have to have the last word? *Why?*

"I need the ring back so I can sell it to pay for Suzy Hendrix and detox. Lawyers cost a fortune these days. And Promises in Malibu is eighteen hundred dollars a day."

I flashed him a look of disdain. "So go somewhere cheaper."

"All A-list actors go there," he said. "Suzy says if I don't do the right kind of damage control, I could spend the rest of my career in regional theater or reality TV. No, it *has* to be Promises. Besides, the contacts I'll make there will be invaluable for my future."

I glanced at the rock on my finger. It was a two-karat round cut that, if sold, could pay my rent for months to come. I marched over and stuck the ring in his face. "Can you not think of anyone besides yourself? *You're* putting *me* out on the street. Do you know how expensive it is to get an apartment in New York City? Selling this will be invaluable for *my* future."

Alessandro lunged for my finger. I jumped back, stuck my hand up my shirt, and slipped the diamond into my bra. Alessandro grabbed for it, but I pushed him away. "Don't you dare," I said in my take-no-prisoners snarl that scared even me. He backed off.

I knew I was supposed to return the ring. But *he* cheated on *me* and *he* broke the engagement. Right then I didn't want to give it back. I may never want to give it back. I may throw it in the East River rather than give it back. Alessandro deserved to suffer.

I plunged forward toward our bedroom, dizzy with rage, and pulled the roller suitcase out from under the bed. As I threw my clothes inside, Alessandro sat on the edge of the rocking chair we bought at the old Sixth Avenue flea market. He babbled on, asking why I didn't want him to have the best defense possible, and wouldn't it be tragic if he had to do reality TV, and what if he had to go to jail, and what kind of bitch doesn't return the engagement ring when her fiancé is facing prison, and then the capper—if he had to, he'd sue me for the ring.

The nerve! I looked him in the eye. "If you sue me, I'm calling the owner of the building and telling him you're here illegally. You can kiss your rent-controlled apartment goodbye." Was that *me* talking, the girl that Nigel had just yesterday compared to Doris Day? Would I sink that low? I wondered. Yes, I believe I would. A painful lump was forming in my throat, so I packed faster. If I didn't get out of there quickly, I would explode in tears.

I zipped my suitcase, which wasn't easy because it contained most of my wardrobe. Sidling over to the nightstand, I glimpsed our wedding binder under a stack of bridal magazines. I'd been so hopeful making plans for what I thought would be our dream day. The only blessing was that everything had been charged to Alessandro's American Express card. "Here, take this. It has all the contracts for our . . ." I choked. "The hotel, the band, the caterer, the florist, the photographer, anyone else we committed to. Right now I don't remember. I made the arrangements. *You* undo them."

Alessandro trailed me toward the front door. "Why should it fall into my lap?" he argued. "It was *your* wedding too."

I turned and faced my ex–significant other. "If it was *our* wedding, then why did you let *me* make all the arrangements?"

"I thought you *wanted* to."

"No, I wanted *us* to pick the band together, choose the food together, find the—"

"Yeah, whatever. Here, don't forget your headgear." He threw it at me. "It's so sexy," he spat. My canines meant nothing to him anymore.

I stuck the appliance in my pocket. "Where's Kitty? There you are, baby." He was asleep, curled up in his little bed. I picked him up. He was like a warm pillow. "You're coming with me."

"He's my cat too," Alessandro declared. "You can't just take him."

"Oh, really? I thought he was the least of your problems."

"I didn't mean . . ."

"Forget it. Kitty's mine. The dress, the veil, the tiara, they're in the hall closet, all paid for. I don't know if they'll take them back, but you can try."

"Holly, I *refuse* to do all this," Alessandro said, stamping his foot like a petulant child. "I'm going to be too busy mounting my defense."

At that moment I saw Alessandro, *really* saw him. He was appearing in the movie of his life and it was about to bomb. Why would I want to costar with such a loser? Was I *that* afraid to be alone? Well, not anymore, sister.

I grabbed the binder and stuck it in my purse. Opening the closet, I removed the Kleinfeld bag with my dress and veil, unzipped my already overpacked suitcase, and attempted to cram it inside. That wasn't going to happen. I pulled everything out, including the tiara, which I stuck on my head, and tried stuffing the dress and veil inside again. This time, I made it work. "Okay, Alessandro, I'll cancel what I can. Enjoy getting to know the *real* Alessandro Vercelli. If you ask me, he's an unconscionable trout."

Guess I'll Hang My Tears Out to Dry

THE SUN WAS SETTING as I made my way up Fourteenth Street. With my right arm, I lugged my bursting-at-the-seams suitcase. My bloated purse kept slipping down my shoulder, and I was using my left arm to restrain Kitty, who was squirming like a greased piglet. It was a delicate balancing act made all the more tenuous by the cars whizzing by. Where was Denis King and his fancy white Maybach when I really needed him?

Stop whining, I thought. *You can do this. You* have *to do this.* I imagined I was starring in the movie of *my* life and this was my dramatic flight from a shattered relationship that I was no longer willing to endure. *Oh, the pain, the heartache of it all. But I am strong. Wait, I don't feel strong. Shut up. I* will *make it . . . at least as far as Muttropolis. BL will lend me a cat-carrying bag. Or better yet, maybe she'll board Kitty until I find a place to live.*

Crossing Fourteenth Street, my right arm cramped so sharply from pulling the heavy case that I stopped to switch sides. That's when Kitty bolted.

"Kitty, STOP!" I screamed. Dropping the suitcase, I sprinted after him. He moved like a ball of tumbleweed, swift but rough because he was missing a leg. As he whizzed past Pops, who was playing chess near his stoop with Mr. Lim, the Korean flower guy, I yelled, "Grab the cat!"

Pops jumped up and tried to tackle him, but Kitty was too quick. He slipped right through his hands. Mr. Lim took off after the cat, but he wasn't even close. My heart pounded furiously. Please, God, don't let Kitty get run over.

A loud *bam!* sounded. I turned. "Noooooo," I shrieked. A city bus had plowed into the suitcase I had momentarily abandoned in the middle of Fourteenth Street, causing it to explode (the suitcase, not the bus). My clothes and makeup and shoes were raining from the sky, only to get smashed by moving taxis, cars, and minivans. The suitcase was demolished on impact.

It seemed surreal, as though it were a dream. Everything was happening in slow motion. I watched my wedding gown float through the air like an errant plastic grocery bag until it hit the ground just as the street cleaner rolled by. "Hhhhhhh," I gasped.

In a matter of seconds, my exquisite Carolina Herrera discount wedding dress was reduced to a wet, muddy blob of netting, satin, and lace. There was no way Kleinfeld would take it back now.

It felt like I'd gotten whacked in the solar plexus. "Pops, keep looking for Kitty!" I yelled. "I'll be right there!" I took a deep breath, and attempted to channel my anguish into saving what clothes I could. When the light turned red and there was a temporary lull in the traffic, I rushed into the street and grabbed the ravaged bits of fabric and leather lying in my reach.

It had taken me years of secondhand trolling to find each treasured article, painstakingly collected from the best charity thrift stores and private school rummage sales in the city, bought for a fraction of its original price. Many I had redesigned and updated myself. I'd never had much in the way of possessions, but I had my clothes, and each piece said something about me. I started back into traffic to rescue more when Pops grabbed me. "Forget it. They're just possessions."

"But . . . I'll be destitute."

"Better that than road kill," he said tenderly. "C'mon, Holly."

"Did you find Kitty?" I said.

"Not yet, but we will."

I glanced back at the street, sick over my loss. There was the canary-yellow Diane von Furstenberg I'd bought at the Nightingale-Bamford rummage sale for six dollars. Six dollars for a dress that originally retailed for six hundred dollars! Now it had black tire marks running down the center. My Christian Lacroix armadillo handbag with its armor of rhinestones, chain link, and crystals lay pulverized on the road, like a carcass on a busy Texas highway. I'd found it at a rummage sale benefiting the

Metropolitan Opera. Some society matron had to die for it to be donated. A rainbow of flouncy blouses, slim pants, and tailored jackets were being whooshed up Fourteenth Street by the cars to which they were affixed. Shoes were scattered, many thoroughly crushed, none with its mate. My vintage Venetian lace demi-bra was flying like a flag on the antenna of a shiny black Cadillac speeding west on Fourteenth.

"I can't look," I said, covering my eyes, collapsing on my hands and knees. The artifacts of my world were gone. How could I possibly start my search over—secondhand stores, flea markets, charity sales, eBay—I wasn't sure I had it in me. "I am strong," I muttered. "I can do this."

My father helped me up and led me away, shielding me from the crash site. Then he gasped. "It's a miracle!"

I opened my eyes. "Kitty?"

"No," he said, pointing to my priceless, one-of-a-kind cherry tree Choos that lay strewn on the sidewalk, no worse for wear. It was like a tornado victim finding one treasured photograph, completely unharmed, in the pile of lumber, bricks, and rubble that used to be her home. Seeing them gave me hope.

"Thank you, Lord," I cried. "Now please, help us find Kitty."

We searched everywhere, behind trash cans, inside courtyards, under parked cars, in every nook and cranny within a five-block radius. I prayed he was curled up in some tiny space somewhere, which was his favorite thing to do. Pops led me back to the stoop. "Oh, my God, he's go-o-one," I cried. Salty tears spilled down my cheeks and into my mouth. My whole life was unraveling before my eyes and there was nothing I could say or do to stop it. I wasn't sure which was worse—losing Alessandro or my precious Kitty.

Pick Yourself Up

Pops took me inside Muttropolis, offering a place to stay as long as I needed it. I could have called Nigel or BL, but no friend could take the place of my father. "Here you go, Holly," he said, gesturing to his bed. "It's all yours. Make yourself comfortable." BL had set aside a previously barren space for Pops, with an AeroBed next to a small night table and shadeless lamp. (Her paying canine guests slept in custom-made wrought-iron beds with Duxiana mattresses.) There was a small

TV, but no rug, plant, or picture to make his little corner of the basement feel like home. The room smelled like dog, but after a few minutes you didn't notice it.

Two Chocolate Labs, a poodle, and a Chihuahua kept us company that night, all resting in their "suites" near a couple of newly rescued cats.

"I'll ask BL to make lost signs for Kitty," I said. "She has his picture on her database from when I first found him."

"'Course," Pops said. "I'll post them around the neighborhood while you're at work. Don't worry, he'll come home."

Practically everything I had left in the world was in that basement—the ratty sweat suit I was wearing, my quasi-stolen Jimmy Choos, a rhinestone tiara, my headgear, and my engagement ring.

"Do you want to call someone?" Pops said, offering his cell phone. "A girlfriend, maybe?"

"No," I murmured. "Thanks for taking me in."

"That's what fathers are for, baby."

I crawled onto Pops' mattress, under his sheets. He made his blanket into a sleeping bag and set up camp at the foot of my bed. When we lived in Queens, Pops had given me the bed while he slept on the couch. He was generous that way.

Tears spilled down my face. I tried to stifle my crying noises, but the sniffling sounds were hard to disguise. "Maybe you should get a job as a driver for a rich family on Long Island, huh, huh, huh. Then we could move out of the doghouse."

"What?" Pops said. "So we can have an apartment above the garage and you can fall in love with one of the handsome sons who lives in the mansion? Remember how things turned out when we lived on Park Avenue? Life isn't like *Sabrina.*"

"Why can't it be?" I moaned. "Don't *we* deserve a happy ending?"

"I never should have let you watch those old films. They ruined you for real life."

"No, they didn't," I said, snorting up some phlegm. "They were my escape growing up. I really believed that someday you were gonna take me on a Roman holiday like you promised. Stupid, stupid me."

"C'mon, Holly, stop bellyaching," Pops said. "Do you see me mooning over my life? Right now, my entire net worth is in my pocket—twenty-seven fifty. Do you hear me groaning about it? Do you?"

"No," I admitted, "and that's nothing to write home about."

"You're damn right it isn't," Pops said. "But you know what? I feel like the richest man in the East Village. You know why?"

"Why?"

"Because I have you."

"Yeah, and look how brilliantly I've turned out," I groused.

"Now, stop. In every great life, there's angst," Pops said. "Think about it. The best movies are the ones that put you through the wringer before the happy ending. Rejoice! This is your wringer, kid."

"So, in other words, if the movie of my life was *An Affair to Remember,* this would be the part where I got run over and paralyzed and missed my rendezvous with Cary Grant on top of the Empire State Building?"

"You got it."

"How long do you think my wringer'll last?"

"It could be a while," he said. "Mine started over twenty years ago and shows no signs of letting up."

"That's encouraging."

He held out an apple. "Hungry?"

"Thanks." I sat on the floor by his side and took a bite.

"At least we have each other," Pops said. He got up and opened the cage door for a large chocolate-colored dog. "Have you met Benny yet?" he said. "He's sixth-generation Labradoodle. Stays with us a lot because his human is some kind of Internet guru who consults all over the world. BL always puts him in the Presidential Suite. Doesn't she, Benny? Yes, she does. You are so sweet, yes, you are," he said, kissing the dog right on the mouth.

"You shouldn't do that, Pops," I said. "He was just licking his balls."

Pops wiped his mouth with his sleeve. "Sorry, Benny, Holly's just jealous. C'mon, Benny. C'mon, boy." The dog curled up next to Pops. "Benny's a natural electric blanket. 'Night, Holly."

"'Night," I muttered. After washing my headgear in the canine bathtub, I slipped it over my face and inserted the metal prongs into their holders. Even as my life disintegrated around me, I remained committed to orthodontia.

I don't remember ever being so spent. As I fell into a despair-induced coma, I wondered how I could go on. The next thing I knew, sunshine was streaming in the window and Pops was headed out with five dogs on leashes, all agitating to do their morning business.

"Who let the dogs out? Who? Who?" he sang.

The world would keep spinning whether I liked it or not.

◆ ◆ ◆

Later that morning, I gave Gus his coffee and glazed doughnuts, and told him what happened the night before, sparing no details.

He looked me over and sighed. "Say no more, my dear. You'll need something from Corny's closet. Come."

I sighed. *What am I doing, wearing clothes that belong to the museum? It's unprofessional,* I thought. *But what choice do I have? My wardrobe was decimated. I should never have taken that first suit the other day. Borrowing from the vault is getting easier and easier. It's a slippery slope.*

"So what do you think?" Gus said, gesturing toward Corny's collection.

"Well, let's see. It should be newer, nothing too valuable. I suppose it has to be black and somber looking," I said. "I'm mourning the loss of my love."

"You mean Alessandro?" Gus said.

"Yes," I said.

"Wait. I'm confused. Is he dead?" Gus asked, eyes wide.

"To me he is."

A simple black cotton Prada dress circa 1990 would work fine. Corny had the perfect mesh veil that would have completed my grief-stricken widow look, but I passed on that. We were tearing down the Audrey Hepburn exhibit, so I needed to see what I was doing.

Unforgettable

The Audrey Hepburn retrospective at the National Fashion Museum is one of the most entertaining fashion exhibits ever produced in our city. —The New York Times

How can it miss with all the memorable roles Hepburn played in her life: Gigi, Holly Golightly, Sabrina Fairchild, Jo Stockton, Princess Ann, Eliza Doolittle, Reggie Lampert, Gabrielle Simpson, Maid Marion? It can't and it doesn't. —The Daily Post

TANYA WASN'T IN HER office when I got to my desk. Good. My plan was to answer e-mails quickly, then hide for the rest of the day. The phone rang.

"Get down here stat," Nigel ordered. "Tanya and Sammie are five minutes away."

"How do you know?"

"Tanya called Elaina to yell at her," he said. "They're at Starbucks. She's still fuming over yesterday."

"What about yesterday?" I said.

"You didn't see the *Post*? I'll tell you when you get here. Hurry. You'd best steer clear of her today."

My feelings exactly, I thought.

When I arrived, Nigel and Elaina were standing in the Funny Face area of the show. Nigel was wearing his surgical magnifying glasses, inspecting the midlength wedding gown that Audrey wore in the last scene of the movie where she and Fred Astaire floated into the sunset on a river barge singing "'S Wonderful."

"There's a slight worn spot on the bottom left side of the bodice," Nigel said. Elaina recorded it on the form. For insurance reasons, every piece had to be scrutinized and irregularities noted before it was shipped out. They would be reexamined when they arrived in Rome, and checked again after they were returned to us.

When I came up with the idea for the Audrey exhibit, I envisioned it as a series of separate mini black-box theaters, each featuring an original costume from one of Audrey's movies with the scene where she wore it playing in a continuous loop on a screen behind the mannequin. That's exactly how we set it up. Visitors could take a self-guided tour, wearing audio headphones, not only viewing the exquisite outfits Audrey wore but also watching the classic Hollywood moments in which they appeared. The videos added welcome sparks of life to the show without upstaging the costumes.

Oh, how I adored Audrey Hepburn. As a little girl, I lived for her enormous smile, that melodic voice, and the way she said "rotha" and "mahvelous" and "cross my heart and kiss my elbow, dahling." I still use her expressions anytime I can.

After I grew up, I identified with her characters (who didn't, right?)—Sabrina, the chauffeur's daughter who never felt good enough until she morphed into a new and improved version of herself. *When will that happen to me? When?* Holly Golightly, my namesake, a young lady trying to transcend her background and make it in the big city. *I live that struggle every day*. Jo Stockton, a girl who would have loved to travel to Paris but couldn't afford it. *Someday I want to go abroad too, but I can't afford it either.* Gabrielle Simpson, the assistant to screenwriter Richard Benson, who helps write the screenplay when she was only hired to type. *I'm so much more than an assistant too, but no one recognizes that.*

I probably shouldn't say this, but I've always wished my life would unfold like an Audrey Hepburn movie, the kind with the happy endings—*not* like *Roman Holiday* where the princess chose duty over Gregory Peck. Hello-oh! What woman in her right mind would do that? Nor would I want my own leading man to be as old as any of Audrey's on-screen lovers. Poor Audrey, having to kiss those liver-spotted geezers—Humphrey Bogart in *Sabrina*, Fred Astaire in *Funny Face*, Gary Cooper in *Love in the Afternoon*? Some things never change, I suppose. The same is true for salaries. It still peeves me that Audrey was paid $7,000 for *Roman Holiday* and $12,000 for *Sabrina*, while Gregory Peck earned $100,000 and Humphrey Bogart received $200,000. But I digress. The point is, I would rather be a character in an Audrey Hepburn movie more than anyone else in the world, including (especially!) myself.

Audrey Hepburn wasn't terribly famous when she was getting ready to make Sabrina. Roman Holiday *had not been released. Paramount sent her to Paris to see Hubert de Givenchy and ask him to create her French costumes for the movie. He had never heard of Audrey and presumed his meeting with* "Miss Hepburn" *was with Katharine.*

When Audrey arrived, Givenchy was too busy preparing his new collection to design for her, so Audrey convinced him to let her use pieces he had already completed. She selected three dresses: For the scene where she arrives at the Glen Cove station and is picked up by David Larrabee, who doesn't recognize her, she chose a gray wool suit with a cinched waist, double-breasted jacket, and calf-length skirt. This was accessorized with a light-gray turban hat, kid gloves, and a matching toy poodle. For the Larrabee ball, she selected a white strapless confection with an ankle-length skirt and detachable train. The bodice and skirt were embroidered with a floral design of black silk thread and shiny jet beads. Finally, for her date with Linus Larrabee, she picked a black cocktail number with a high boatneck, a calf-length ballerina skirt, and small bows on the shoulders.

The first meeting between Audrey and Hubert was the beginning of a lifelong friendship and professional collaboration. Givenchy designed Audrey's wardrobe for seven of her most memorable movies, including Funny Face *and* Breakfast at Tiffany's. *Here's a choice little tidbit that sent tongues wagging—Edith Head took credit for all the costumes in* Sabrina, *and Givenchy wasn't even given a screen mention. Later,* Sabrina *received six Oscar nominations and won but a single award—Edith Head for Best Costume Design. Even after that, she didn't share the glory. For an industry based on beauty, the fashion world can be one ugly place.*

—AUDREY HEPBURN, ICON OF STYLE
(SHOW CATALOG) BY HOLLY ROSS

"Get in here now," Nigel said, resting his magnifying glasses on top of his shiny head. "Tanya just arrived."

Yikes! I gently shut the door to the exhibit behind me until I heard it click. "So tell me, what happened after I left yesterday?"

Nigel and Elaina glanced at each other, and then looked around to be sure no one was listening.

"Well," Nigel said, "it's a good thing you got out when you did."

"It sure is," Elaina added. "Martin started mouthing the answers from the back of the room."

"And he got caught?" I said breathlessly.

"Not exactly. He got everything wrong," Elaina said. "What does Martin Goldenblatt know about fashion? Nothing. But Tanya and Sammie took him at his word and they kept losing. Tanya must have thought I was giving him the answers, but I wasn't."

"You're so honorable," I said.

"That wasn't always the case," she said. "I used to lie and cheat like everyone else, but *A Course in Miracles* showed me a better way."

"Wow," I said. "That must be some powerful course."

As Nigel finished his paperwork on the garment, Elaina

removed it from the mannequin. "It is. Give me a hand with this, would you?"

Gently, we lifted the wedding dress off the fiberglass form that had been custom-made in Audrey Hepburn's exact size. We laid the garment out flat on special tissue paper, wrapped it, and placed it inside an acid-free box.

"Tanya got caught," Nigel said. "Well, *she* didn't; Martin did. And we were disqualified."

"NO!" I said, wondering if Tanya would blame me even though I wasn't there. Yes, probably.

"Over here," Elaina said. She strolled over to the famous black dress Audrey wore as Holly Golightly. It had recently sold at auction to the house of Givenchy. They were kind enough to lend it to us for the exhibit, along with several other pieces.

"Heidi Klum caught him," Nigel said, as he began to inspect the iconic dress.

"Well, cross my heart and kiss my elbow!" I said, wondering if anyone but me knew that expression came from *Breakfast at Tiffany's*.

"Heidi was antsy for the next show to start and was looking around the room," Nigel said. "That's when she spotted him."

"She whispered something into Valentina's ear and Martin was busted. What's My Line? was O-V-E-R," Elaina said, signaling "cut" with her finger across her neck. "The Met's getting the prize and I'm sure the Fashion Council won't ever do it again."

"Not with us, anyway," I said.

"Martin got fired," Nigel said.

"*What?*" I said, outraged but not entirely surprised. "She *made* him do it, just like she made me do it."

"She told him *auf Wiedersehen* right there and then," he said.

"She fired a devout Jew in German?" I said. "That was cold."

"Tanya was trying to impress Heidi," Elaina theorized. "I still can't believe she cheated. I have to decide if I can continue working for someone like that. 'I will step back and let Him lead the way.'"

"*A Course in Miracles?*" I asked.

Elaina nodded as she gently lifted the black dress off the mannequin.

"Elaina, the basic trouble with you is you're *too* honest," Nigel said. "Anyway, the story's in all the papers. Tanya looks like a fool."

"It was a blessing I got kicked out early," I said. "Elaina, you've got to hide me today."

Elaina gestured at the enormous exhibit that needed to be inspected, dismantled, and packed. One thing about working in such a small museum was that everybody pitched in to help colleagues. "Your wish is my command."

I smiled at my friends, grateful for their support.

"Sooooo," Nigel said, "how did you make out with Alessandro?"

"We broke up." I told them how Alessandro had the nerve to dump me by text message (they were shocked and appalled), how a bus ran over my wardrobe, and how I was now homeless.

"But otherwise, Mrs. Lincoln, how'd you enjoy the play?" Elaina said with a giggle. "Come, let's do the *Sabrina* costumes. Those are already inspected, right, Nigel?"

"Right-oh," he said.

My phone vibrated, but I didn't answer it. Alessandro was cell phone stalking me, leaving message after message demanding his ring back. Plus, he kept asking if I'd canceled the wedding plans and gotten his deposits refunded. The calls were good therapy. His obnoxious behavior was softening the blow of being dumped.

We wandered over to the dresses Hepburn wore for *Sabrina.*

"You know what never ceases to amaze me?" Nigel said. "These are over fifty years old, but if you wore them tomorrow, you would be completely in fashion."

"That was the genius of Givenchy," I said. "His style was timeless."

"Oh, bloody hell!" Nigel shrieked. He had caught a glimpse of the ethereal gown Audrey had worn to the embassy ball in *My Fair Lady*. The dress, designed by Cecil Beaton, was a cream silk organza overlay with a ballet neckline, empire waist, and a matching silk crepe de chine underslip. It was embroidered with thousands of tiny silver and gold beads, along with fiery Swarovski crystals. Somehow it had suffered a four-inch tear on the side seam. A smattering of beads lay on the floor near the gown. "How did this happen?"

Elaina ran over and inspected the damage. "A visitor must have gotten too close," she said. "Mrs. Weidermeyer can fix it."

Nigel gasped. "Have you lost your senses?" Mrs. Weidermeyer was a highly skilled seamstress who worked on modern garments the museum needed stabilized. But only a certified conservator could restore vintage couture. In this case, Nigel would first contact Warner Brothers' costume archives to see if he could obtain thread from the spool that was used to sew the gown in the first place. Whoever repaired the gown would follow the original seam line, carefully placing his needle through the same holes left by Beaton's tailors when the dress was first created.

Each bead would have to be individually hand sewn and knotted back to its original position. This would all be done under intense magnification, without rush and with utter perfection. Sometimes Nigel repaired garments himself. Other times, he hired outside experts.

"I'm kidding," Elaina said. "I know Mrs. Weidermeyer can't do this."

"She just wanted to give you a heart attack," I said.

"Puh-lease," Nigel said, "we'll send it to Jacques Doucet."

"Can he fix it in time for Rome?" Elaina asked.

"Doubtful. We'll ship it late if we have to," Nigel said.

I gently ran my hand over the silk lace. The craftsmanship in the gown was impeccable, the material exquisite.

Nigel and Elaina gingerly removed the gown from the mannequin while I knelt on my hands and knees to gather up every bead I could find. We carefully folded the slip and lace overlay, wrapped it in tissue, and packed it into an oversize acid-free box. Then we set the tiara, Edwardian necklace, and earrings into custom cases that were placed in the container with the dress. For the movie, these pieces came from Cartier. However, we used copies made with cubic zirconia stones. For our upcoming Tiaras through Time show, only the real thing would do. But since the star of this exhibit was the clothing, costume jewels were acceptable. Even so, insurance required that each ensemble that was lent as a package stay together.

"I'll take the dress to Doucet tomorrow," Nigel said.

"Remember the Gina Lollobrigida bridal gown from the Hollywood Weddings show? All those seed pearls that fell off?" I said.

"These costumes are fragile to begin with," Nigel said, shaking his head sadly. "They can take only so much stress before they fall apart."

I sighed. "Like my heart."

"Don't be daft," Nigel said. "Your heart is mightier than you think. You'll get through this and there will be something better waiting for you, I promise."

"Thanks," I said weakly. "I hope you're right."

After Nigel inspected each costume, Elaina and I would carefully pack it into boxes that were placed in special wardrobe trunks that would be shipped to Rome shortly. Tanya never came looking for me. I later found out that she had been so stressed by the events of yesterday afternoon that three of those hard boulder zits erupted on her face. She had to be rushed to the dermatologist to have them professionally popped.

Don't Get Around Much Anymore

Pops' hair had arranged itself in seven different directions, his eyes were bloodshot, and his fly was open when I got home from work that evening, home being Muttropolis. He smelled like an ashtray. It was obvious he'd been drinking or crying, maybe both. He stood hunched over by the indoor doggie playground on the second floor where Irving the humping poodle was doing what he did best with Bartholomew the submissive bulldog.

"What's wrong?" I asked, grabbing his hand. "It's not Kitty? Did you find Kitty? Is he . . . ?"

"No." He shook his bowed head. "It's not Kitty. He's still out there somewhere."

I sighed with disappointment. "Did you panhandle today? Was your money stolen?"

"No."

"Oh, my God. You're sick? You're dying?" I cried. Oh, please, not that.

"No," Pops said, tossing an envelope toward me.

Inside was a handwritten note, something you don't see too often these days. "Can I read it?"

Pops shrugged. I took that as a yes.

Hey, Pops,

It finally happened. I'm selling the Jazz Factory. I was offered six mill for the real estate—too much bread to refuse. They're turning it into a bank. Can you believe it? And they say jazz doesn't pay. Our last show is next Monday. A bunch of cats are coming to play. After that, I'm retiring to Paris. See you Sunday. Invite friends and family. It'll be our final encore.

Bongo

The Jazz Factory was Pops' only regular job. Having that gig made him feel like he was a pianist in a big band at one of Manhattan's oldest jazz haunts. Losing it had to be a terrible blow.

"Oh, Pops," I said, "I'm so sorry. Maybe there's another regular act you can find. What about Arturo O'Farrell? Doesn't his band play at Birdland on Sunday nights?"

Pops shook his head. "Arturo's a pianist. There's no place for me. Face it, Holly, your old man's washed up. I'm a loser."

"Don't talk like that," I implored. "You're just going through the wringer so your happy ending will be that much sweeter. At least we're not eating out of trash cans anymore. That's something." After we moved to Queens, Pops would troll the garbage cans of the city's finest restaurants after his cab shift ended. Bouley was his favorite. Their dishwashers eventually got to know him so they wrapped leftovers in foil and put them out for Pops every night. Once he found a retainer inside a piece of pie and returned it but refused the reward.

"We ate damn well back then," Pops said. "In those days, I could put food on our table, *gourmet* food."

It was crummy that our lives had come to this. Somehow, someway, I would turn it around. "Look, things have been tough for us both. But they'll get better. I promise." I just wished I knew how.

I Still Get Jealous

SAMMIE AND TANYA WERE becoming like Eng and Chang, the famous Siamese twins. You never saw one without the other. Maybe they're lesbian lovers, I thought. That would explain why Tanya gave her such preferential treatment. That and the seven-figure donations her parents gave. I called them the Satan twins behind their backs—SAmmie and TANya—get it?

"Is the presentation ready?" Tanya said.

Sammie was peeking over Tanya's shoulder. A man with a

camera was filming our encounter, while another guy stuck a microphone boom in my face. "What's going on?"

"Just act natural," Tanya said. "These guys are filming Sammie for a segment on *Extra* about top socialites. Her publicist set it up."

I turned to Sammie. "You have a publicist?"

"Duh-uh," she said in a guttural tone.

I hoped they got that on tape, Sammie saying "duh-uh" from the bottom of her throat. It was extremely un-top-socialite-like.

"Are you finished with the presentation?" Tanya said.

"Sure, I was just about to proof it," I said. "Do you want to do a run-through?"

"No," Tanya answered. "E-mail it to Sammie, would you? I'm letting her do the honors."

My heart sank. I was counting on making that presentation to show Tanya how impressive I could be. "But this is *my* show with Cosima. She said I could speak to the press."

"And I'm Cosima's boss and I'm telling you that Sammie will do it. After the negative publicity over What's My Line? this press conference has to be perfect."

"But I wrote it. Don't you think it has a better chance to be perfect if I present it?"

"No, I don't. Sammie's new and needs the visibility. Plus, this way we'll get the press conference on *Extra*. And the girl *reeks* of good breeding. Who better to represent the museum?"

Obviously not me, I thought.

"Can you hurry?" Sammie added. "I need time to practice."

"Here," I groused, getting up from my desk and offering her my chair. "It needs spell-check and then you can print it. Finish it yourself."

THAT AFTERNOON, I SLIPPED into Corny's banquet hall, where the press had gathered to hear about the new exhibit we were launching at the end of September. The room was teeming with reporters from every important fashion publication, along with the *New York Times*, the *Wall Street Journal*, *Newsweek*, *Forbes*, the *Financial Times*—you name it, they were there. It helped that our press conferences were known for putting out spreads catered by the premier chefs of our time. Today it was bliss-enducing sushi from Masa, the most expensive restaurant in New York City, and obscenely luscious bonbons from South'n France, the finest chocolatier in the country. Reporters are vultures in more ways than one.

I caught a flash of Cosima's flame-colored hair across the room. She, Tanya, and Sammie were shaking hands with Denis King, our show's benefactor, who had just arrived. The team from *Extra* was filming the meeting, focusing mainly on Sammie, the socialite in her natural habitat.

Tanya, who made the policy that we could never, ever borrow a piece from any collection under penalty of death or worse, was wearing the diamond tiara of oak leaves and acorns that the fifteenth Duke of Norfolk gave to his bride, Gwendolen Maxwell, in 1904. It's an insult to the little people when those in power think the rules don't apply to them. That's why I didn't feel as guilty as I probably should have for borrowing Corny's dresses. It was my way of taking a stand in the fight for human equality. Naturally, it was a political statement I preferred to make in secret so I wouldn't get fired.

Denis was nattily attired in a charcoal pin-striped Brioni suit, crisp white shirt, and red silk tie. Trustees who had retrospectives named for them typically arrived with entourages, but not Denis. He came with one person, a little girl, his daughter most likely. I hung back so he wouldn't see me.

It was completely unfair. Cosima and I had spent two years working on this exhibit. We had compiled the greatest collection of tiaras ever to be assembled in one place—over three hundred bejeweled head ornaments. Each was priceless and irreplaceable, which is why Lloyd's of London installed its own safe and insisted on providing round-the-clock armed guards. With millions of dollars worth of diamond, emerald, sapphire, and ruby crowns on display, some from the personal collections of the royals, others from such renowned sources as Fabergé, Cartier, and Lalique, it would take more than our beloved Gus to keep the collection safe. Tanya had him stationed by the door to the banquet hall so he wouldn't feel bad about being replaced.

Cosima and I had worked side by side to track down the pieces we hoped to exhibit, obtain permission to borrow them, learn their unique history, and distill the wealth of information we uncovered for the show and for this very moment—when we would reveal to the world details of the mouth-dropping retrospective that would be unveiled in a few weeks. Cosima promised I could take center stage, mainly because she was deathly afraid to speak in public. This was supposed to be my moment. Instead, Sammie would get the glory.

I might as well eat the designer food, I thought. It would save me having to buy lunch. Each piece of sushi was a work of miniature art. Chef Masayoshi Takayama himself had prepared everything. This was as close as I'd get to dining at his ungodly priced restaurant.

I looked up and noticed Denis' little girl shaking hands with

Gus. Cosima was introducing them. She looked over and caught my eye. Next thing I knew, she was escorting Denis and the child over to me. Yikes! There was no place to hide.

"Holly, have you met Denis King?" Cosima asked.

Denis cocked his head. "I believe we've met, haven't we?"

The blood rushed to my face. "Yes, Holly Ross. We were introduced last time you were here."

Denis looked uncertain, but shook my hand. His grip was firm and his hand was dry. He smelled kind of musky with a touch of sweetness—very sexy and masculine.

"This is my daughter, Annie," he said with pride. "I wanted to show her what the old man's been up to."

Annie reached over and shook my hand. She was a dainty little niblet, about ten, freckle-faced with thick chestnut brown hair. "Daddy, can I wear one of the crowns?" she asked.

"I think it's against the rules," he said.

"But that lady over there is wearing one," she said, pointing at Tanya.

I leaned down to Annie and whispered in her ear, "Why don't you ask that lady if you can try on her tiara? Tell her you're Denis King's daughter and he said she should let you wear it for the rest of the press conference."

Annie giggled. "I'll be right back." She skipped off.

"Say excuse me," Denis called after her. When she didn't, he shrugged apologetically.

"Denis, Holly was my partner in putting this exhibit together," Cosima explained. "She's the brains behind it."

"And the beauty too, I see," Denis said, flashing dimples that could disarm a small army.

"Well, thank you. If you love the show, I accept tips," I joked. *Oh, that was lame.* "No, really, I was kidding. I don't accept tips. Although I *do* accept free vacations." *Someone, stop me. Please.*

Denis laughed. "And if I *don't* love it, can I blame you?"

"Of course," I said. "I'll do whatever I can to make you happy. With whatever you don't love about the exhibit, I mean. That's what I'll make you happy about."

"Then I will come to you with any complaints I have," Denis said. "Although I don't expect to have any."

Cosima touched his sleeve. "There are more people I want to introduce you to." She turned to me. "He wants to meet everyone who worked on the show."

"Yes, I want to thank them for their contribution. So thank *you*, Miss Ross."

"Call me Holly, please."

"Thank you, Holly. You did a brilliant job with the exhibit and I appreciate your hard work. *You* made *me* look good, and that means a lot, especially with my daughter here."

"Oh, go on," I said modestly.

"If you really want me to, I will."

I giggled like a schoolgirl. Cosima looked at me with an urgent expression. She wanted me to act more professional, at least that was my interpretation. I straightened up and cleared my throat.

He leaned in to me. "Can I ask you a personal question?"

"I was hoping you would," I said in a flirty tone. *Sorry, Cosima.*

"If you and Cosima are the brains behind my exhibit, why is

Sammie Kittenplatt making the presentation?" he whispered. "I watched that girl grow up. She's not the sharpest stiletto in the shoe box, if you know what I mean."

I tried to hide my smile. "Don't worry," I said, touching his arm. "Our boss, Tanya, has every confidence in Sammie."

"Ah, diplomatically put," he said.

We both looked over at Tanya, who had removed the 1904 Gwendolen Maxwell tiara from her head and had placed it on Annie's. The invisibly set diamonds on the gold acorns reflected fiery points of light throughout the room.

"Well, Holly, it was a pleasure," Denis said, shaking my hand goodbye.

"Yes, it was, wasn't it?" I murmured as they walked off toward Nigel.

"Did you try the white truffle tempura?" a gentleman from the *Post* asked.

"What? Huh?" I said.

"The truffle tempura," he said. "It's wonderful." His skin bore scars from a serious acne condition, but the look suited him.

"Not yet," I said, glancing at the spread. "My Lord, will you look at that tower of lobster."

"It's a fucking temple," the man said.

A sexually ambiguous person in jeans was piling his/her plate with sushi. "I'm going to take mine home with me," he/she confessed. "You should do the same."

I looked over and saw Denis laughing with Nigel and Elaina on the other side of the room. Sammie was walking toward them with her camera crew in tow.

"Excuse me," he/she said, "are you taking any of this home?"

"What? Oh, yes. I probably will," I said. "Can I help you put sushi in your bag?"

"How thoughtful," the androgynous person said. "And would you mind stuffing a few bonbons in my pocket? I'm Sloan Scott from the *Times*. Normally I cover science, but our fashion reporter was out sick today. She said I should come for the food. That why you're here?"

"Oh, yes, the food, of course," I said, taking a bite of a toro maki roll. "Mmmm, delish. Forget the tiaras, maybe you should write about the sushi."

Let's Call the Whole Thing Off

"Yoo-hoo, everyone," Tanya announced. "If you'll gather round, I'll introduce our newest senior curator, Sammie Kittenplatt, who will tell you about a breathtaking exhibit that will soon grace our humble institution."

The *Extra* crew situated themselves up front next to Annie, who was watching her father. All the other journalists pushed toward the stage and snapped open their notepads. Sammie stood with Denis King by her side. He was beaming as he gave a little wave to Annie.

Sammie hit a button on her laptop and a larger-than-life photo of the Oriental Circlet tiara designed by Prince Albert and worn by Queen Victoria and Queen Elizabeth the Queen Mother appeared on the big screen. "Ladies and gentlemen," Sammie started, "we are honored to announce the latest exhibit that is soon to open at the Fashion Museum—Denis King presents: Tiaras through Time. Thanks to loans from private collections, royal vaults, museums, and esteemed jewelers from around the world, this breathtaking exhibit will trace the evolution of the tiara from ancient Greece and Rome to the early eighteenth century to the present day, and it will provide an extraordinary look at the scintillating jewels themselves, their powerful owners, and intriguing histories . . ."

Those were *my* words that Sammie was speaking. I wondered if I could kill her while she was at the podium and make it look like an accident.

"But before we give you a sneak peek at the majestic tiaras that will soon dazzle and delight, we must first recognize the man whose generosity is making this retrospective possible, the man who has underwritten the show, the man of the hour. Members of the press I give you . . ." (reverent pause as the theme from *Rocky* was cued). Sammie hit a key on her laptop and Denis' picture appeared on the big screen. Henry VIII's crown had been Photoshopped onto his head. A bold headline hung over the image reading "Denis King—The Biggest Man in Town!" Sammie looked to the sky and held her arms high in a wide "V." It was dramatic but cheesy. Reporters chuckled, then guffawed that evolved into loud hoots and whistles. I thought they were laughing at Sammie's goofy pose, but then I saw what was up. The headline had a typo. Instead of "Denis King—The Biggest Man in Town" it said "Penis King—The Biggest Man in Town."

I gasped and grabbed a press kit, to see if the mistake had found its way into the handouts, and yes, there it was in black and white, right on the first page of the package: "Penis King—The Biggest Man in Town!" Flipping through, I saw that his name had been misspelled only once, on the cover page, but that was little comfort.

Denis stared bug-eyed at the screen. He pointed the typo out to Tanya, who clapped her hand to her mouth. She grabbed Sammie and swung her around (while she was still holding that ridiculous "V"). Sammie scrambled to hit the off switch on the computer, but it was too late. The damage had been done. I could see Annie's lower lip trembling dangerously from across the room. The pockmark-faced man from the *Post* was scribbling in his notebook, a cigarette of lobster dangling from his lips. I could already imagine tomorrow's headline.

Sammie's face went crimson and she held her hands up to silence the crowd. "Ladies and gentlemen, please, I'm *so* sorry. Mr. King, Annie, our deepest apologies. We meant no disrespect. My assistant, Holly, typed this for me and obviously she made an egregious error." Sammie pointed accusingly at me and all heads swung in my direction.

Oh, this was rich. All respect I ever had for Sammie Kittenplatt just vanished into thin air, not that I ever had any. *Hello!* I *told* her I hadn't proofed the document. Making my way to the front of the room, I could hear what everyone was thinking: "Dead Penis Walking."

The smirking crowd watched me expectantly. After Tanya had publicly fired Martin at What's My Line? I fully expected to suffer the same fate. Denis eyed me with a steely gaze, a far cry from the smile he'd offered just moments ago when we met and shared a few chuckles. *Humor. The man has a sense of humor,* I thought. *Use it.* "Hi, folks," I started. "Well, that's the last time I ever rely on spell-check to proof a page. This should be a good lesson for all of us."

The crowd chuckled as they realized how this mistake must have been made.

"You know," I said, "now I understand why the reporter from *Penthouse* showed up to cover the press conference. I couldn't figure it out before. But in all seriousness, I'm *really* sorry, Mr. King."

The room fell into laughter again with a smattering of applause. Denis leaned over and whispered in my ear, "I'm smiling and pretending to be joking with you, but I want you to know that I'm unhappy, *very* unhappy. This is inexcusable. You people humiliated me in front of . . . Forget it. After my exhibit is over, I will never give this two-bit museum another dime."

"Oh, Mr. King, you're so funny," I said, slapping his back while laughing knowingly (knowing I was about to be fired). Denis grinned at me really friendly, and then at the reporters.

I turned the laptop back on, and finished giving the presentation that Sammie had abandoned. The only glitch was a typo on the last slide thanking Denis for his "pubic service," instead of his "public service." Luckily, I caught it immediately and switched off the computer. At that point, I received a standing ovation. Well, there were no chairs in the room, but they would have stood, that's how much the audience liked me and appreciated my quick thinking and keen sense of humor. If only Denis felt the same way.

As soon as the applause died down, Denis leaped off the dais and said a few words to Tanya. As he and Annie dashed off, Tanya hastened after them and snatched the 1904 Gwendolen Maxwell tiara off the child's head.

"Ouch," she yelped. "You pulled my hair. Daddy, she pulled my ha-aaaair."

"I'm sorry," Tanya said, her hands clasped in front of her heart. "You forgot to give it back . . . Please forgive me. I never meant . . ."

Denis kissed his little girl's head, took her hand, and led her out the door.

As soon as the last reporter left, Tanya (with Sammie in tow) cornered me. The *Extra* camera crew continued filming, while the sound guy stuck a microphone boom in my face. "I don't know *what* to say to you," Tanya said.

"How about 'Thank you for taking the blame for Sammie's mistake.' I told her the presentation hadn't been proofed."

Sammie's jaw dropped. "This was my first week on the job. How am I supposed to know his name was Denis and not Penis?"

"You're kidding, right?" I said.

Tanya laid into me. "Your mistake made us look like fools, Holly."

Is this it? I wondered. *Am I to be finished off by an errant typo, now, on top of everything else?*

"You humiliated Denis King," Tanya continued. She was on auto-rant. "He made it clear we would see no more money from him after the tiara show ends. Do you know how long I've been courting him? Do you know how much your negligence is going to cost us? What were you thinking? No, never mind," she said, not letting me get a word in. "You weren't thinking at all."

"That's right, you weren't thinking at all," Sammie parroted as she stormed out of the room behind Tanya, with the *Extra* crew on her tail.

As I watched the Satan twins disappear, I crumpled to the floor and rested my head against the wall. In my mind, I went through a checklist of everything I'd lost. Promotion. Check. Wardrobe. Check. Kitty. Check. Apartment. Check. Alessandro. Check. Denis King's respect. Check. My dignity. Check.

Admittedly, not all had been perfect. Who wants to be a curator for a megalomaniac like Tanya? Who needs a cat with three legs when you could have one with four? Who wants to marry a hypercritical child-molesting lying rat fink like Alessandro Vercelli? Knowing what I know now about him, I see that my life had been no more than a facsimile of a cheap imitation of a sham. But still, it was my sham, my promotion, my beloved cat, and now they were gone.

"As God is my witness, I will reclaim my life," I declared aloud. Not my old life, a better one! It was all very Scarlett O'Hara without the dirt and turnips. But I meant it. I was sick of playing it safe. I chose Alessandro because he was safe, and look where it got me. From now on, I'm going for what I want, no more selling myself short or letting people walk all over me. For the first time in my life, I felt an inkling of my own power. I would have my happy ending. It was all up to me.

I've Got the World on a String

MY EAR WAS GLUED to the door, but I couldn't hear what Nigel was saying on the phone. Old mansions are so solidly built. Damn them.

Nigel whipped the door open, causing me to jump back.

"So? What did they say?" I asked, biting the inside of my lip. This was step one of my master plan to take my life back. Nigel was pitching me to speak on the *Tiffany Star*'s upcoming trip to Rome. He knew the booking agent from just having lectured on the French Riviera cruise.

He smiled. "There was good news and bad news, luv. They would be happy to have you speak, but not on *that* trip. You see, they've already scheduled a fashion expert."

"Shoot," I said, leaning against the wall. "It has to be *that* cruise. When Denis King picked me up, he specifically said he was taking the Athens to Rome trip."

"I told you there was good news, didn't I?" Nigel said. "The speaker they've booked is Cosima Fairchild. You know how she loathes public speaking."

I stood up. "Of course. Do you think she'd give me her spot?"

"It's done," he said. "I told them she has a conflict, but that we're sending the assistant director of the museum instead. They were thrilled."

"But I'm the assistant *to* the director."

"Semantics, my child," Nigel insisted. "Cosima's been going to a hypnotist for weeks trying to prepare for this. Last night she was in sackcloth and ashes over it. You've done her an enormous service."

"Thank you *so* much. And I can bring a companion?" This would be my chance to take Pops on the Roman holiday he'd always promised me.

"That's the arrangement. Every cabin is a suite, so your father can sleep in the living room while you're in the bedroom. Wait'll you see the ship. It's sooooo luxurious. And you get a butler."

"A butler! What do I do with a butler?"

"Whatever you want," Nigel said. "He'll help you unpack, iron your clothes, bring you tea, caviar, champagne, anything your charming little heart desires."

I started to skip around Nigel's office. "I'm getting champagne,

I'm getting caviar, I'm getting a butler, I get to live like a moo-vie star . . ."

"You have to give three talks," Nigel said. "Don't forget that."

"Pish," I said, waving my hands as though that were nothing. "I wrote the presentations." Then it hit me. "I haven't got a stitch to wear. Neither does Pops."

"Darling, you'll borrow some pieces from the vault."

"I don't know," I fretted.

"Relax. We'll choose dresses that can take the wear and tear."

"But what about Pops?" I asked. "He owns one suit, from the Salvation Army; he needs a serious bath, a haircut, a shave, a . . ."

"An extreme makeover, eh?" Nigel said, stroking his chin in Sigmund Freud–like fashion.

"The works."

"Well, you needn't fear, because I am queer," he said. "I have an eye for this sort of thing. It'll be fun."

"Right," I laughed. "The Queer Eye."

"Exactly," Nigel said. "And I have contacts at every men's fashion house in Manhattan. Your father will be the best-dressed passenger on the ship. Just get me his measurements."

"I'll take them tonight," I said, jumping up and hugging Nigel. "I love you so much. You're my guardian angel."

Nigel corrected me. "Puh-leaze, luv, I'm your fairy godmother."

It Ain't Necessarily So

SAMMIE AND I SAT in the visitor seats across from Tanya's desk. "Nice counterfeit purse you're carrying," she whispered. "If you ever want something real, I have some bags set aside for Goodwill."

"Thank you, no, I'd rather chew glass. You're brave to be seen in last season's Ferragamos," I muttered, nodding toward her shoes.

"Is that Dana Buchman you're wearing?" Sammie sneered. "Where'd you get it? Dress Barn?"

No, it's vintage Mary Quant from Corny's closet, I thought. Lucky for Sammie I could be fired for wearing it, otherwise I would have called her on her clueless remark.

Tanya swung her leather executive swivel chair around to face us. She shuffled a few piles on her desk, and then gazed at me with a stony expression.

Okay, sparring practice was over. Clearing my throat, I started, "I just wanted to tell to you both that I'm sorry about what happened earlier."

"You should be," Tanya said, straightening some papers. "That was unforgivable. I'm stripping you of your senior assistant status. You're back to being my regular assistant."

Sammie's lips curled in a triumphant smirk.

This was going to be harder than I thought. I took a sip of water. "Tanya, I've been under a lot of pressure lately. Alessandro was arrested. Then we broke up. It's no secret I was disappointed about not getting that promotion."

"After yesterday's performance, can you see that I made the right decision?" Tanya said. "This is a small museum. We needed Denis King. Your little mistake could cost us millions."

"I'm not sure we'll ever recover," Sammie said sadly. She looked as though she might cry. "Did you see *Extra* last night? The whole ugly mess was broadcast for the world to see. That story was supposed to be about *me* and my life as a top socialite, but instead it was about *you* and your stupid mistake."

"You're right," I said, "and I *never* want to screw up like that again. If I could just take time away, heal, I could come back fresh—"

"*Now.* You want time off?" Tanya said. "*Now?*"

"No, no. Not *time off*. I have an opportunity to sail on a cruise and speak on behalf of the museum starting September fifteenth. After all that's happened, it would be a break for me. I could come back rested, ready to pull my weight."

"Who said you could represent the museum like that?" Tanya demanded, her back stiffening. "*I* certainly didn't."

"And *wouldn't*." Sammie sniffed.

"It's an *opportunity*," I said. "I'm asking your permission. Yes, I messed up this week, but think of all the good work I've done for you and the museum in the past."

"What about Tiaras through Time? It's opening at the end of the month," Tanya said.

"You are stripped of that responsibility," Sammie declared. "After what you did, we don't want you anywhere near Denis King."

Tanya flashed a searing look at Sammie.

"You agree, don't you?" Sammie backpedaled. "Holly's done enough damage. I can be the liaison with Mr. King."

"Yes, you be the liaison," I agreed. "My work for the show is done. I'd be back by the twenty-fifth. The opening's the thirtieth, in case you want me to do anything. In the background, I mean."

"You'd be rewarding bad behavior," Sammie trilled.

"Okay, go," Tanya said, giving Sammie a frigid stare. "We could all use some space. Sammie, you can fill in for Holly while she's gone." She dismissed us with a wave.

"Oh, Tanya," I said, as though I just remembered something. "This cruise is on the Tiffany line. There'll be a boatload of wealthy passengers on board. If I can land the million-dollar donation that you said I never could, will you agree to make me a curator?"

Tanya burst out laughing. Sammie giggled. I didn't see what was so funny.

"Holly, you've *got* to be kidding," Tanya said, wiping a tear from her eye.

"Is she too much, or what?" Sammie said.

"I'm *serious*," I said. "I deserve this chance."

"Are you mad? You want me to promote you?" Tanya said.

"If I prove to be a rainmaker, yes."

Tanya gave me a look of pity. "Holly, these things take time and finesse. You don't just meet a big fish and waltz off with a check. It takes *years* to secure a seven-figure donation. If you were *of* this world, you'd know this."

"I've seen it with my parents," Sammie explained. "There's an art to separating a rich man from his pocketbook, a slow dance that takes place. The rich are a special breed. If you're not brought up in their milieu, you'll always be an outsider. To gain their trust for donation purposes, you must come from within, and you *never* will. That's why you can't be a curator. Do you get it now?"

Sammie looked at me expectantly, as though she was waiting for me to slap my forehead and say, "Thank you. Hearing you explain it to me *that* way makes me realize for the first time how crazy my desire was. Finally I see the light."

Ignoring Sammie, I turned to Tanya. "Please, I know it's a long shot, but humor me. Let's say I *do* come back with a seven-figure check. Would you promote me?"

"No way," Sammie said, rolling her eyes. She turned to Tanya.

"If you ask me, Holly has some nerve to make such a ridiculous request."

"I don't recall anyone asking you," I said.

Tanya regarded Sammie with cold speculation.

"You won't promote her, right?" Sammie said. "After her mistake? How can you ever trust her?"

"Sammie, when you saw the name Penis King in the presentation, didn't that raise a red flag?" Tanya asked.

"I just assumed . . ."

"What? You assumed that was his name?" Tanya said incredulously. "Thirteen years at Spence and you honestly believed a woman from a socially prominent family on the Upper East Side of Manhattan would name her son Penis?"

It was my turn to smirk, but I didn't because I'm too polite.

Tanya looked me in the eye and smiled wickedly. "You're on, Holly. You bring me a million-dollar check, I'll give you Sammie's job. I'll even double your salary."

Sammie bolted from her chair. "*What!*"

"Triple," I said. "You'd have to triple my salary if I brought in *that* much. I know what the curators make."

"Yes, I suppose I would," Tanya said thoughtfully.

"What? Huh, no! *Excuse me*, hello-oh!" Sammie was having a connipshit over this unexpected turn of events. "You can't do that. My mother is a trustee . . ."

"I giveth and I taketh," Tanya said. "You were hired over Holly because your mother *assured* me you could bring in donations. Well, we just lost a huge fish. Holly's to blame, but so are you. Whoever brings me a million-dollar check first is my new curator. The loser can be my assistant."

Sammie looked at me with loathing.

"But she can't get the money from her mother," I said. "That wouldn't be fair."

"Life isn't fair, Holly," Sammie said, "or haven't you noticed?"

Oh, I've noticed all right.

Tanya nodded. "Holly's right. Your mother's already a donor. Find someone else." She extended her hand. "Shake?"

"No," Sammie cried. "It's not fair. If I lose, I lose my job. If Holly loses, she keeps the job she already has."

"Life's not fair, Sammie," I said, "or haven't you noticed?"

Sammie screwed her face up like a cross child. Apparently she was not familiar with the concept of setbacks. It's so satisfying when things go badly for snot-brained she-devils like Sammie Kittenplatt, who have never had to struggle for anything in life besides staying a size two.

Finally, Sammie thrust her hand toward mine and shook.

"Trust me, you will fail," Sammie said as we left the office.

"Just you wait, Sammie Kittenplatt. Just you wait," I said.

Fools Rush In

I STUCK MY NOSE IN Nigel's office. He was finishing up a call. Closing the door behind me, I cried, "We have liftoff!" I jumped on his couch and danced the Tom Cruise. "Tanya said I could go. Yippee! She promised to make me a curator and triple my salary if I come back with a million-dollar check before Sammie does. Double yippee!" I told Nigel everything.

"That's brilliant!" Nigel said.

"Do you think I'll do it?" I cried.

"Not a bloody chance in hell."

"*Shut up*," I said, jumping off the sofa. "Really? You don't think I can? Oh, but I have to. I will! I'm gonna get that check from Denis King. Ooh, I can just imagine Tanya's face when I bring him back as a benefactor."

"There'll be lots of rich people on board. Why go after him?" Nigel said. "Didn't you see how ticked he was when he left?"

"He'll cool off," I said. "He was such a gentleman when he rescued me from the rain. And did you see how he insisted on meeting and thanking everyone at the museum before the presentation? Have you ever seen a named donor do that? I haven't. No, I intend to devote my not-inconsiderable talents to the immediate solicitation of a million-dollar donation from Mr. Denis King for our beloved museum. Tanya will be totally impressed."

"Don't count on it."

"You're so negative."

"All Sammie has to do is call a few wealthy relatives. You're screwed, my friend," Nigel said.

"Oh, ye of little faith," I said.

"You asked my opinion," Nigel said.

"So lie. Give me hope."

"Let's not fight, luv," Nigel said, tilting his head and curling his lower lip. "I know just what you need."

"What?"

"*Retail therapeeee!* We'll go shopping in the vault and select your wardrobe for the cruise."

"Not today, Nigel," I said. "I'm beat."

"Don't be a bore. C'mon," Nigel insisted. "It'll be a hoot. Besides, haven't you noticed all those pesky security guards from

Lloyd's of London that are starting to lurk about? This could be our last chance."

GUS OPENED THE DOOR to the vault and gave me a friendly wink. Seeing him, smelling the cedar-lined walls, surrounding myself with beautiful clothes, thinking about the trip—I immediately felt better. I could never have afforded to go to Europe on my own. After all I'd been through, a week on a luxury liner sounded heavenly.

Nigel scoped out the room, looking for outfit candidates. There were many to choose from. Besides the eighteen thousand costumes and accessories from Corny's collection, twenty-five thousand more ensembles had been donated or acquired at auction through the years. Compared to the Met's hundred thousand garments, our collection was small, but it dazzled. Most pieces came from society doyennes, so the size would be right. In New York, socialites wearing anything over a size four were pretty much considered cows.

Nigel stepped over to the trunks that were packed with costumes from the Audrey Hepburn show. "Holly, I've just had the most inspired idea."

"I'm listening," I said, eyeing him suspiciously.

Nigel put his index finger to his mouth and tapped his foot in thought. "The Hepburn show starts on the twenty-sixth, right? Why not take the reproduction costumes from that god-awful TV movie? You could wear any of them on the ship, display them for your talk, whatever you like, no harm, no foul."

I nodded slowly. When Sony Pictures produced the movie of Audrey Hepburn's life a few years back, they re-created the best-known dresses and gowns from Hepburn's pictures. These pieces were new, sturdy, and replaceable. For our opening gala, we had hired Audrey look-alikes to act as show guides and dressed them in the wardrobe from the TV film. The Istituto di Moda in Rome was using the same gimmick for their launch party.

"The cruise ends in Rome on the twenty-fourth," Nigel continued. "After you dock, take what you borrowed to the museum. This way, no one can fault you for traveling with the clothes. You're hand delivering the reproductions for the opening night party. It's perfect." He laughed like a mad scientist.

"I'm not sure," I mused. "Sony Pictures lent them to us. If I'm going to take this kind of risk, shouldn't it be with clothes from our own inventory, maybe some newer items?"

"Puh-leaze, these are Jennifer Love-Hewitt costumes, circa 2000," Nigel said. "If by some accident anyone catches on, we have a better cover story than if you borrowed original pieces from the museum."

My heart leapt into my throat. "You really don't think anyone would find out?"

Nigel knelt by the six brown leather trunks that were ready to ship. He examined the packing slips attached to each, and then slapped the side of the third container. "Here are the repros. We still have to box up the mannequins and call the art shippers. As soon as that's done, everything'll go out. I'll fill a dummy trunk with fabric and boxes, so six cases will still be dispatched. No one will know you borrowed a thing." Nigel's eyes took on a diabolical cast as he spoke.

"But what happens when the cases are delivered in Rome and the reproductions are missing? They'll flip out."

"Luv, with the timetable we're on, the whole lot won't get there until the last minute anyway. I'll call Rosa Di Giacinto the day everything arrives and tell her the guides' costumes will be hand delivered in time for the party. It's foolproof!"

"Let me get this straight. What you're really saying is, I wouldn't be taking them so much for myself, but I'd be taking them because it *could* be safer than shipping them."

"One might look at it that way," Nigel said.

"So this isn't a loss of integrity on my part, it's a means to an end, a service to the museum—I'm just making sure the dresses get where they're supposed to be on time."

"Of course."

"Okay, I'll do it."

"Marvelous!"

"Let's see what's inside," I said, my heart performing a swan dive into my stomach.

Nigel opened the trunk and began sorting through the garment boxes where the dresses had been securely wrapped and encased. Each had a snapshot of the costume it held taped to the front. "Perfect," he said. "You'll need three things for formal nights, and that's exactly how many gowns we have." He pulled out copies of the white strapless confection I loved so much from *Sabrina*, the red chiffon from *Funny Face*, and the cream-colored silk brocade gown from *Roman Holiday* with its matching tiara, collar, and earrings. The oversize trunk contained eight more suits and dresses, including an impeccable duplicate of the elegant black number Audrey wore in *Breakfast at Tiffany's*. I pulled it out of its box, stood in front of Corny's full-length mirror, and held the iconic piece to my body, imagining myself peering wistfully into the famous jewelry store window while munching on a croissant from a brown paper bag. *Maybe if I wear the same gowns as Audrey, I'll inherit some of her style and grace*, I thought. *Wouldn't that be something?*

"These will do for the other nights and for your speeches," Nigel declared. "During the day, you'll wear shorts. Those you can get on your own. The Mediterranean is positively sizzling this time of year. Now, what's your shoe size?"

"An eight," I said, my voice quivering. Even though these were copies and I was merely making sure they were safely delivered for the opening party, I still felt like a borderline criminal (or at least a bad seed) borrowing them. They were gorgeous, hand-made reproductions that belonged to Sony Pictures, not the museum. Of course, I would treat them as I would my own children. Then I remembered I didn't have children. Okay, I would treat them as I would my beloved cat. Then I remembered Kitty was lost. Oh, screw it; I would care for them as I do my headgear, which is in mint condition after six months of daily use. My orthodontist said that was practically unheard of.

Something fell in the back of the room, clattering when it hit the floor. "Gus?" I said.

"Sorry to scare you. It's me," Sammie trilled. "Is Nigel with you? Tanya's looking for him."

I glanced at Nigel, concerned that Sammie may have heard us. But he seemed unfazed as he excused himself to go look for our boss.

"Are you guys packing up the Hepburn show?" Sammie asked. "Can I help? I need to learn how to do that."

"Gosh. Darn it," I said. "You're too late. We just finished."

Just One of Those Things

When I arrived at my old apartment that night, I realized I'd forgotten the key.

I pressed my neighbor's buzzer since I wasn't sure Alessandro would let me in.

"Who is it?" Mrs. Levine said through the intercom.

"It's me, Holly. I lost my key. Can you let me in?"

"You do this all the time, Holly. You're disturbing Herman's nap."

"I'm sorry, but please be a dear and let me in."

The latch clicked and I entered the ancient vestibule and bounded up the stairs.

A door opened from two flights below. Looking down, I saw a cloud of brassy-colored hair attached to an old woman who was shaking her fist and yelling, "Holly, not so loud! You'll wake Herman. And get another key."

"I'm sorry, Mrs. Levine."

"Herman's an artist. He needs his rest. If it happens again, I won't let you in."

"Don't worry, Mrs. Levine, there won't be a next time."

Upstairs, I checked under the mat, where I had recently stashed my spare key. Bingo! To my great relief, Alessandro hadn't changed the locks. I opened the door and found him asleep on the couch wearing only his Simpsons boxers. His face was unshaven, but the Skid Row stubble didn't look cool on him like it did on Ryan Seacrest. His skin had taken on a chalky sheen. There were empty cans of soda and beer strewn around, a bong, and Twinkie wrappers on the couch. Dirty dishes and pots were stacked in the kitchen.

"Alessandro?"

Slowly, he emerged from what must have been a deep slumber. "What time is it?"

I checked my watch. "About seven fifteen."

"A.M. or P.M.?"

"Night."

He shook his head to wake himself. Then he sat up. "Why haven't you returned my calls? Have you canceled the wedding plans yet?"

I dropped the binder on the coffee table. "I'm leaving the country next week. You'll have to do it yourself."

Alessandro sat up. "I . . . wha . . . no . . . I don't have time."

I looked around, my eyebrows raised. "Yes, I can see how busy you are."

"You lost Kitty," Alessandro said.

"Who told you?"

"There are flyers all over the neighborhood."

"We'll find her. You're not back on Broadway."

"How'd you know?"

"You're here and it's after call time."

He frowned. "They cited the morals clause and fired me. Disney won't allow accused sex offenders to act in their plays. Bastards."

"Gee, what a surprise. Well, that'll give you incentive to work really hard to cancel these contracts," I said, pointing to the notebook. "The deposits are on your AmEx card. If I were you, I'd get right on it. You're on the line for upward of fifty grand."

Alessandro gulped. "*Shit!* How could you spend so much?"

I sat on the only chair I could find that was clear of Alessandro's debris. "That's what weddings cost these days. You agreed to everything. See." I opened the notebook and pointed to his signature on one of the contracts.

"Fu-uck," Alessandro said, falling back into prone position. "Why didn't *you* sign?"

I shrugged. "Because I only have a debit card and there's no money in my checking account. Anyway, they only needed one signature." Alessandro looked so lost that I almost felt sorry for him. Then I remembered that he cheated. He dumped me. By text message. I was not the villain here. "Oh, this is for you," I added, slapping a pink piece of paper on the table.

"What is it?"

"A pawn shop receipt. They gave me two thousand for the ring. You can buy it back anytime in the next ninety days for two grand plus interest."

Alessandro blew off the couch like a geyser. He grabbed my arms and shook them hard. "That ring cost twelve thousand dollars!" he screamed. "How could you do that to me?"

I pushed him away. "I can't go on a cruise without cash in my pocket."

"You're going on *vacation* while I'm facing criminal charges? While *I'm* out of work? While *I'm* trying to rescind God knows how many contracts for *our* wedding? While *I* have to pay two thousand dollars to get back the engagement ring that's rightfully *mine* out of hock? What kind of bitch are you?" he spat.

I smiled. "I'm the bitch you almost married, Alessandro. And don't expect me to feel sorry for you, because I don't. Good luck and good riddance."

My heart was beating so fast I could barely catch my breath as I raced the four flights downstairs and out the front door. Alessandro and I were so over. I couldn't remember what had made me love him. And that was just sad.

As I walked down the street where I lived for the last time, I inhaled deeply through my nose and chanted "oms" to calm myself. Alessandro broke up with *me*, I reasoned. *He* should clean up the mess. I kept two thousand dollars from the ring. Big deal. Alessandro could redeem it, sell it, and have ten thousand left over. That was more than fair. *I am not a bitch. I am not a bitch. Om, om, om. So what if I am a bitch? Who cares? I am sick of being Little Miss Doris Day Nicey-poo. Om, om, om.*

Anything Goes

ENTERING THE WORLD OF Muttropolis cheered me immensely. It was filled with my Lower East Side neighbors and their dogs enjoying yappy hour, a weekly favorite among customers and canines alike. The air smelled of freshly baked cookies mixed with dog odor. My friend BL was serving tea and pastries to the humans and homemade meat biscuits to the pups. I gave her a wave.

Irving the humping poodle quivered at the sight of me.

"Irving, no," I said, shaking the gray-haired pup off my leg, but he held tight.

"You excite him, heh, heh, heh," Irving's creepy owner said. He was a tall, skinny guy with stringy brown hair and a birdlike wattled face, not someone whose dog I wanted to hump in public.

I laughed politely and gave Irving a friendly kick so he'd find a new victim.

The room was hopping with Pops playing piano and singing "Fascinating Rhythm." His voice was a cross between Louis Armstrong and Frank Sinatra, croaky and deep from years of smoking and drinking, but also smooth and intimate. He had a way of expressing the meaning of a song with the sort of vocal storytelling that only the greats seemed to master. The plastic cup on top of the piano overflowed with dollar bills. Watching him, I was filled with love for the man who had taken me to my first day of school, told me the facts of life, and worked extra shifts to pay for my sewing lessons as a child. We never had much, but we had each other.

Benny, the chocolate-colored Labradoodle rubbed his head against my thigh, so I hugged him. When I tried to leave, he stood on his hind legs and offered me his paws.

"He wants to waltz with you," BL said. Her strawberry-blond hair was styled in an eighties shag she had cut herself with dog clippers. But it suited her perfectly. She wore a vintage Pucci hostess caftan with a white boa, and held her weenie-dog, Crookshank, who was dressed to match. "Dancing is Benny's thing."

Why not? Benny was male with a full head of hair. I held him close and we swayed back and forth to the music. He flashed me a big doggie smile as thick white slobber spilled out of his mouth. I laughed because I couldn't remember the last time a male had drooled over me. The glow of puppy love on Benny's face filled me with a joy I hadn't felt in ages. No wonder canine therapy is such a burgeoning field.

A dishy musician type in tight black jeans and a black T-shirt lifted the front paws of Chiquita, his German shepherd, and box-stepped with him next to us. Others took their small dogs in their arms and moved rhythmically to the beat. The room swelled with canine-human bliss.

When the song ended, I excused myself from Benny, excited to tell Pops the big news. We were going on a cruise! There was so much to do if we were going to be ready to leave in a week. This would be fantastic. It was just what he needed to cheer him up after losing his Jazz Factory gig. Plus, after I got the donation for the museum, I'd use my bigger salary to rent an apartment for the two of us. But before I could reach Pops through the sea of dogs and the humans who loved them, BL intercepted me.

"I have a surprise for you," she said, taking me by the hand and leading me to the basement.

"What is it?"

"Guess?"

"A new pony?"

"Oh, shut up," BL said. "Ta da!" She pointed to one of the cat suites that had been empty the night before.

I gasped. "Kitty!"

BL opened the cage and placed the three-legged fuzz ball into my waiting arms. Most of his right ear was missing and had been stitched up. Scratching his head and holding him close to my heart, I felt the warm hum of his purr. "Why, you poor no-name slob, where have you been? You're hurt."

Kitty meowed softly as I held him.

"He was found bleeding near Hudson and North Moore. A Good Samaritan took him to Bide-a-wee," BL said. "They got my address through the microchip the vet implanted when you first found him."

"What happened to his ear?"

"Doctor thinks he got into a fight somewhere."

"Where have you been wandering, you little drifter, you? Did you want to see the world? Look at what a mess you are," I said, "just like your human, yes you are." Smiling, I took BL into our hug. "How can I thank you?"

"After you and Kitty reunite, you can come upstairs and help me with yappy hour," she said. "We're about to play pin the tail on the human."

I giggled. Thoughts of Alessandro and work evaporated, at least for the moment.

Why Can't You Behave?

"HOLD STILL. WE'RE ALMOST done," Archie said. "I just have to rinse. Ten words. Two words. Two words . . ."

I clapped my hands twice. Archibald Carbunkle was the balding, rotund groomer at Muttropolis. He suffered from a type of obsessive-compulsive disorder that caused him to announce his word count anytime he spoke. It took two claps to get him to stop. That was his rule. If he miscalculated his word count (which I'd never seen him do), then he had to lick every lightbulb in the room. This was also his rule.

Pops had his head in the canine/feline bath while Archie washed his hair with Doctors Foster & Smith Flea and Tick Shampoo. I offered to run to Duane Reade and pick up people shampoo.

"No, no, dog shampoo's good enough for me," Pops insisted. "In fact, I cut my nails with canine clippers and brush my hair with Benny's brush."

"Lies and deceit," I cried. "Your hair hasn't been brushed in days."

"She's right," Archie said. "You look like a mutt. But I'm going to release your inner poodle and then I want to see some pride from you. Do you see how your hair's got a natural curl to it? Thirty-six words. Two words. Two words . . ."

I clapped twice. Archie counted hyphenated words as one.

"No girlie cuts," Pops insisted.

"How about something wavy and short like a King Charles spaniel?" Nigel suggested.

"If you're going spaniel, go cocker," I said, "like *Lady and the Tramp*."

"Cocker works for me," Archie said, reaching for his trimmer. "Does cocker work for you? Nine words. Two words. Two words . . ."

Clap. Clap.

"Yes, but don't touch the beard," Pops said, his hands protecting his face. "I need it for panhandling."

"Mr. Ross," Nigel said. "Are you planning to beg for change on the ship, hmm? I thought not. You can grow it back later."

"But it makes me look like a sea captain," he groused.

"Off with your beard," Archie declared. "Four words. Two words. Two words . . ."

Clap. Clap.

Pops closed his eyes as Archie shaved his face. I'd never seen my father without the beard (at least not that I could remember). Archie clipped his hair until half of it was on the floor. He styled the cut, which I'd describe as conservative cocker, then streaked his gray locks with a black Magic Marker to give him a more regal salt-and-pepper look. Finally, he added a touch of grooming spray to hold the cut.

"You look ten years younger," Nigel marveled, handing Pops a mirror.

"I do?" Pops said, grinning at the reflection of his popcorn kernel smile. "Yes, I do!"

I was proud. Pops was a new man, bearing little resemblance to the homeless dog minder slash jazz musician he really was.

"Take this with you," Archie said, handing Pops the black marker. "You can touch up the hair whenever you need to. Fourteen words. Two words . . ."

"Thanks," Pops said, clapping twice. "You, Archibald, are a true artist."

POPS STOOD IN FRONT of the mirror as Mrs. Weidermeyer, the museum's stooped Eastern European seamstress, pinned his Armani tuxedo sleeve. Mrs. Weidermeyer was all of four feet tall with the posture of a shrimp, which made hem pinning easy for her, since her head automatically faced down.

Nigel had called a few of his publicist friends at the top men's fashion houses, and a first-class wardrobe magically appeared the next day. Of course, it would all have to go back after the cruise, but for now, Pops was marveling at the sight of himself looking so dapper.

"Ouch!" Pops shouted. "You just stuck me with a pin."

"I'm sorry, Mr. Ross, but you need to stop squirming or we'll never get this done," Mrs. Weidermeyer said.

"Please, Mrs. Weidermeyer, call me by my Christian name, Sven. And can't you see that I don't want our time together to end?" Pops said in a playful voice.

"Sven, *don't*, I'm a married woman," Mrs. Weidermeyer said, waving him away. But the flush in her face said, *do, do*.

I'd never seen this side of my father. In the years since he lost his cat-minding job on Park Avenue, he had fallen into a state of dishevelment, adopting a grungy homeless look that didn't foster flirting. Seeing him dressed up like this, all proud and debonair, made me more determined than ever to get that promotion. With a better job, I could give Pops an apartment of his own, new clothes, a full refrigerator, an electric Rascal Powerchair to toot around on when he became old and infirm—a good life, a life where he wouldn't have to sleep with dogs. For now, he'd have to settle for a wonderful adventure at sea.

After Mrs. Weidermeyer pinned the last pair of pants, we cabbed over to the Elizabeth Arden Red Door Spa, where Nigel had arranged for the three of us to get manicures, pedicures, and facials. The museum had done a cross promotion with the spa at our last yearly benefit. They had donated hundred-dollar certificates for the gift bags and we had a pile of them left over.

Pops was not pedicure-friendly. Every time the technician rubbed his foot with the pumice sponge stones, he'd yelp and pull out of the water. "That tickles," he'd say. "Stop, I can't take it anymore."

"Contain yourself," I said to him. "If you can't, they'll have to put you to sleep."

"You're shittin' me, right?" he said, splashing his foot out again. "Ouch, how do you ladies stand it?"

"Honey, a girl must suffer for her beauty," Nigel said. "So what airline are you taking?"

"Lufthansa," I said. "We have to stop in Frankfurt in both directions."

"First class all the way, eh, luv?"

"Well, actually, I traded in our first-class seats for two in coach. We'll use the difference for spending money."

"Why, that's brilliant."

"But I couldn't get us seats together," I said to Pops. "You don't mind, do you?"

"'Course not," he said. "I plan to sleep on the way over."

"Don't forget," Nigel said, "you have to check the costumes at the special international courier counter. They'll x-ray the trunk, escort it and you to the gate, and let you watch them load it on the plane." Even though the dresses were only reproductions, we were transferring them as we would any precious cargo on loan to another museum. They were insured for eighty thousand dollars, too much to trust to a baggage handler's care.

"Do I get to ride on one of those electric carts?"

"Only if you're very polite," Nigel said.

"Aren't I always?" I said. "Will you arrange for me to watch them move the trunk to the plane we're catching in Frankfurt, and then pick it up at the gate when we land in Athens?"

"Of course, luv. You'll follow it every step of the way."

As our feet were being scrubbed and our fingernails buffed, we role-played Pops speaking to the other cruise passengers. He didn't want anyone to know his real circumstance. For this trip, Pops would be Sven Ross, concert pianist.

"So, do you enjoy classical music?" Pops inquired. "Maybe you've seen me perform with the New York Philharmonic."

"Don't mention any specific orchestras people might know," I suggested. "Here's an idea. When you're talking to people, pretend you're an actor *playing* a concert pianist and you're improvising scenes. Just answer their questions the way you think Leonard Bernstein would."

"Funny you should mention Len. I'm playing a duet with him in Brussels next summer," Pops said.

"Isn't he dead?" I asked.

"No," Pops said. "I had dinner with him last Sunday at the Quilted Giraffe."

"The Quilted Giraffe has closed and Bernstein's dead," Nigel said.

"So that's why he was so quiet," Pops mused.

I wagged my finger at him. "Oh, you-ou."

"Why don't you say you're a jazz pianist? Most people don't know the names of famous jazz players," Nigel said.

"I *am* a jazz pianist," Pops said.

"So it will be easy," Nigel declared. "Now, talk to Holly like she's an old biddy looking for action on the ship."

"Really, Nigel, you don't have to Henry Higgins me," Pops said.

"Ah, but I do," Nigel replied. "It has been ages since you've moved in such swell circles. Now, how would you talk to a smashing old bird you meet sitting at the bar?"

Pops cleared his throat. "So enough about me, tell me about you, gorgeous."

"Brilliant," Nigel said. "Everyone loves to talk about themselves. In fact, when you're with a woman, just keep repeating, 'Why, that's fascinating. Tell me more.' They'll love you for that. But don't call the ladies on this ship 'gorgeous.' That would be rude."

"That's right," I said. "This crowd requires a higher level of manners than you're used to."

"Holly," Pops said. "In life, it's not a question of good manners or bad manners. One must have the *same* manners for all humans, and dogs for that matter."

"Fine, then treat everyone the same—like a king," I said.

He let out a sigh. "I can't remember the last time I conversed with a bunch of rich geezers."

"It's like sex," Nigel explained. "Once you get started, it comes back to you."

Pops' face lit up. "Now you're talking my language. If I can't get laid in these new duds, with this fancy haircut, I may as well pack in the ol' pecker."

My stomach sank. "Pops, please. Don't embarrass me on the ship. And whatever you do, don't mention your 'pecker' to passengers. Remember, I'm on a mission. We *both* need me to get that donation."

"I *know* the difference between charm and smarm," he assured me.

The nail technician started to paint clear polish on Pops' pinkie.

"What're you doing?" Pops asked, jerking his hand away.

"You don't want?" the young Chinese woman asked. Then she covered her mouth and giggled.

"I believe I'm done here," he said.

Nigel raised his arms and snapped his fingers. "*Au contraire*, luv. Clarisse, he's ready to have his nose and ear hair trimmed."

Turkey and Greece

Come Fly with Me

By eleven New York time we had been airborne for two hours. Terminally bored passengers had long since devoured the dinner of brown meat with matching gravy, potatoes au paste, broccoli à la blech, and bruised fruit torte.

I wore my headgear, since the flight was long and I was behind in my hours, having developed a rash on my cheeks and chin from the face straps last week. The TSA Nazis confiscated my anti-fungal spray, claiming the can was too large. Do you know how hard it will be to find orthodontic anti-fungal spray in Europe? I prayed the ship stocked a decent medicated powder.

The lights had been turned down and everyone was snoring away, having ingested powerful sedatives on takeoff. But not me. I stayed awake so I could mentally fly the plane.

I watched the movie for a while, *Oceans Fourteen* or maybe *Eighteen.* It was hard to tell because the actors were speaking dubbed German. If there was a way to watch the film in English, I couldn't figure it out. So I pulled out my book on the history of the British monarchy. I'd grown fascinated with the royals when we were putting together the Tiaras through Time show.

The munchkin behind me whined to his mother, "I want a titty taste; I want a titty taste."

"That's not the proper way to ask for the breast, Morgan," his mom said.

"I want a titty taste . . . *please*."

"That's better, sweetheart."

Call me old-fashioned, but it seems to me that if a kid is old enough to ask for it in a full sentence, he's old enough to drink from a sippy cup.

A ruckus in the front of the cabin interrupted my reading. There was pounding on a wall or door, screaming, and people moving about. Just what a shaky flyer like me fears most—an "incident" at thirty-five thousand feet. I peered around the seat in front of me, but it was dark and I couldn't see what was happening.

A muscular, compact man a few rows ahead rushed to the action. Hopefully he was an air marshal packing heat. Soon the plane banked to the right until it made a midair U-turn. What the . . . ? Most people were asleep so they didn't witness the ensuing drama. A steward named Stewart (it said so on his name tag) came down the aisle to make sure everyone's seat belt was on.

"*What's happening?*" I asked. "Is there a problem?"

"There was an 'incident' up front," he said, making quotation marks with his fingers. "But not to worry, the instigators are in custody. Unfortunately, we have to circle back to Kennedy."

"Huh?" the man in the rumpled suit who had been sleeping next to me mumbled. "*What?*"

"We have to return," Stewart said. "I'm sorry."

The guy hit a button on his watch and the face lit up. "Jesus, we have to fly all the way back, then get the terrorists off the plane, and eight more hours to Frankfurt. What a waste of time."

"Terrorists," I said. "You think that's what this is?"

The man nodded knowingly. "If they think we're a threat to anyone on the ground, they'll send fighter jets to take us down."

Moaning, I was officially about to puke. I slunk into my seat, paralyzed with fear. In the face of danger, I am a worthless slug. I vowed to work on that if I lived.

Dear Lord, I prayed, *don't let this be the end of the story for me.* I wondered if the *New York Times* would run my death notice. Not likely, since I hadn't done anything noteworthy. My obit would have to go in the paid section, that is, if any of my friends would even pay for it, and who among them could afford it? None of them, that's who. *I'm soooo scared. What will it feel like to die? Will it hurt? Will it be fast? Will there be a ghost whisperer? For Pops' sake, I hope so. He loves that show . . . Wait, what about Pops? Excuse the interruption, Lord, but I need to tend to my earthly father.*

I unbuckled my seat belt and tentatively made my way to the front of the cabin where he was seated, but he wasn't there. I checked the bathroom, but both stalls were open. "Excuse me, ma'am," I said to an aging stewardess who was sitting down, reading *USA Today*. "I'm looking for my father. He's in ten-c. He's got grayish hair; he's wearing tan corduroy pants . . ."

"That's your father?" she said. "He's up front."

"Oh, you upgraded him?"

She gave me a slow, appraising glance. "Not exactly. Come."

We walked through the business class cabin. In the kitchen space, by the door, there was Pops sitting in one of the jump seats usually reserved for crew. Next to him was a leggy, highly made up bottle-blonde in a dress so tight her breasts were hiked up to her chin. Both had their hands in their laps; both were wearing handcuffs.

I Will Wait for You

I WAS FLABBERGASTED. WHY WAS my father under arrest? I knelt at his feet. "Pops? What did you do?"

"I just—I don't know. I met this nice lady here," he said, motioning his head toward the woman by his side.

"Hello," she said, her voice cracking. "I'm Elizabeth Blair, but you can call me Beth."

"Beth and me were getting to know each other," Pops continued. "One thing led to another and we decided to join the mile-high club."

"The *what?*"

"The mile-high club. We wanted to, you know, in the bathroom, a mile up in the air," he whispered. He made the international symbol for intercourse—a circle with his thumb and pointer finger, his other pointer finger jackhammering in and out. It was awkward with the cuffs, but I got the point.

"Oooh-kay," I said, glancing at Stewart the steward, who was situated in a jump seat across from Pops. He gave me one of those "hey, what can you do?" shrugs, although what I sensed he meant was, *What is wrong with that horny father of yours that he can't keep his pants zipped up for one lousy flight?*

"Did my father commit a crime?"

"The new rules state that two adults can't enter a bathroom stall at the same time. We worry about people coming together to make, oh, I don't know, a *bomb*," Stewart said, dropping the word like it *was* a bomb.

"But clearly these were two consenting adults . . ."

Stewart held up his hands. "That's not for us to decide. The Department of Homeland Security will meet them in New York to investigate."

"Oh, lordy," Beth said. "We're not going to one of those secret jails where they torture people, are we?"

"You want my opinion?" Stewart snarled.

Not if you're going to snarl, I thought.

"When the passengers wake up and find out we're back at Kennedy," he said, "you're gonna *hope* that's where you're going."

Several hours later, we landed in New York. Nobody was allowed to get up until the police came on board to arrest Pops and Beth Blair. The passengers were then told to deplane, but to stay near the gate because the flight would take off as soon as it had been refueled and serviced.

"I'm carrying a trunk with special cargo in the hold. Can I get it removed while I go look for my father?" I asked Stewart the steward who was saying his "bub-byes" at the door.

"Haven't you caused enough trouble?" he asked.

"I haven't caused any trouble," I said. Pops, on the other hand . . . "Do you know where they took my father?"

"There's a Homeland Security office next to the x-ray machines in Area B. They're taking them there," he said. "But don't go beyond the gate area. We could be reboarding at any time."

I shot him an incredulous look. "I'm not leaving, not without my father," I said. It was very Sally Field in *Not Without My Daughter*. But truthfully, I was torn. My first duty was to stay with the dresses I was carrying. But Pops was in trouble. I couldn't just leave him. "How much time before we take off?"

Stewart shrugged. "Forty minutes. An hour."

I checked my watch. "I'll be back in thirty minutes." As I made my way out, FBI agents were waiting to enter the plane with bomb-sniffing German shepherds. "You're wasting your time," I shouted, but not too loud for fear of getting arrested.

I rang the buzzer at the Department of Homeland Security's unmarked door, which a guard at the x-ray machines had pointed out. A NYC cop let me in. The waiting room was pure government office circa 1970—beige linoleum floors, pewter-colored folding chairs, water cooler with a Dixie cup dispenser, and a cheap black Formica table with several copies of *Counterterrorism News* strewn on top. There was a closed door marked "No Admittance." That's where they must have taken Pops and Beth Blair, I thought.

"You'll have to wait," the cop said.

"Does my father need an attorney?"

"Not if he's innocent," the officer said. He disappeared through the "No Admittance" door.

Swell, I thought. *That's what they say on* Law & Order *when they're trying to get someone to confess before lawyering up*.

I used my cell phone to call 1-800-lawyer. What do you know? There was such a place. The secretary transferred me to an attorney on staff who insisted on talking to Pops immediately, just as soon as he took my debit card number.

I opened the "No Admittance" door and shouted, "Hello-ow, Sven Ross, Pops, don't say a word. I need to speak to my father. His *lawyer* is on the line."

An ash-blond interrogator wearing a headset peeked out of a door. "Can I help you?"

I bolted down the hallway and slapped the phone in her hand. "Give this to my father *now*. It's his lawyer." I prayed it wasn't too late. Those interrogators can trick even the most innocent people into incriminating themselves, or so I've witnessed on countless police dramas. She closed the door behind her.

Five minutes later, as I perused an article on "Bomb Basics—What You Need to Know" in the September issue of *Counterterrorism News*, the blond officer came out and handed me the phone. "Your card was declined, so the lawyer hung up. Sorry."

I slumped back in my seat feeling helpless and alone. I checked my watch. Thirty minutes had passed since I'd deplaned.

I'd better go back, I thought. *If the plane takes off with those costumes, I'm screwed. But what about Pops? What if they drag him to Guantánamo Bay? Gowns? My father? My job? My father? I'll stay for five more minutes, ten at the most.* I went back to my magazine and tried to concentrate on what I needed to know about bomb-making basics, but I won't lie. My heart wasn't in it.

Fifteen minutes later, Pops and Beth came out the "No Admittance" door, shaking hands with their interrogators, apologizing for causing such a to-do.

"Are you okay?" I asked, glancing nervously at my watch.

"Yes, fine," he said. "I'm sorry."

"Me too," Beth Blair said. "Apparently this happens about once a week. They should really announce it's against the FAA regulations to fornicate in the bathroom. I don't understand why they don't say something during the safety demonstration."

I rolled my eyes. What a pair these two made. "C'mon, we have to hurry and make the plane." I was desperate to get back to the gate.

"We missed it," Pops said. "They're rebooking us now."

"Good thing," Beth Blair said. "Those passengers would have lynched us if we'd reboarded."

I slumped back into my folding chair and moaned.

Ten hours later, we boarded the same flight as yesterday (only now it was today) to Athens by way of Frankfurt. If there were no further delays, we would arrive two hours before the ship sailed. It would be tight, but we would make it.

We'd spent all day trying to reach the Lufthansa baggage office to be sure they took our suitcases off the earlier plane and locked them up until we arrived. They promised they had retrieved our bags, and that they were safe and secure just awaiting our arrival.

This turned out to be half true. When we finally got to Athens, exhausted, bedraggled, hungry (I could go on and on with adjectives, but I won't), Pops' suitcase was under lock and key. My luggage and its eighty-thousand-dollar contents were nowhere to be found.

Call Me Irresponsible

When it became painfully obvious that the search for my bags was destined to end badly, I sent my bleary-eyed father on to the Hotel Grande Bretagne on Constitution Square. He promised to behave. Had we arrived twenty-four hours earlier, we would have checked into the hotel and slept a few hours, then gone to the dinner at the Olive Garden. No, not the chain, the *real* Olive Garden. It's a quaint little restaurant located on top of the Titania Hotel with postcard views of the Acropolis, lit up in all its golden glory. The place is known far and wide for its fresh Mediterranean cuisine, at least according to Nigel, who insisted we dine there and made the reservation himself. Sadly, we would neither enjoy their fine fresh fish nor the spectacular views, as we were arriving a day late, thanks to Pops' inability to keep his pecker in his pants, not that I was angry about it.

The Grande Bretagne is an elegant hotel, one of Athens' finest, brimming with marble, chandeliers, and antiques at every turn. This was where the Tiffany Cruises Line sets up the exclusive holding pen for its newly embarking guests who have nothing to do until the ship opens for boarding at one P.M. At the hotel, passengers are treated to live folk music by a Greek violinist and served stuffed grapevine leaves, boiled octopus, cheese pastries, baked halva, and unlimited champagne until the ship has been thoroughly cleaned and readied for its new lucky load.

After one, the passengers are taken by bus (but *only* the finest buses) to the Port of Piraeus, where they are checked in and personally accompanied to their cabins to be reunited with their luggage. Guests don't even have to unpack, as they have butlers for that sort of thing. They can settle into their new digs and enjoy the wine and caviar snack that has been thoughtfully laid out on their veranda tables. Of course, I would not be reunited with my luggage, nor would I watch my butler unpack, as everything I had checked was now lost due to my father's midflight misbehavior, not that I was bitter about it.

Oh, who's fooling whom? I was bitter. How bitter? Let me count the ways. If the trunk containing the borrowed costumes wasn't found, I was in serious trouble. Tanya would probably fire me, and who could blame her? Those dresses were worth two years of my salary.

It isn't that I didn't *consider* carrying the clothes on board. I did. But eleven costumes would not squeeze into one suitcase that fit into the overhead compartment. The airlines are so strict these days about what size bags you can carry on board. So I went through the special courier check-in and literally witnessed the baggage handlers loading the trunk into the cargo hold. Had we transferred in Frankfurt and landed in Athens as planned, I would have watched them remove the trunk from the plane and taken custody of it right at the gate at both stops. But thanks to Pops, I had violated the cardinal rule of being a museum courier: Never separate yourself from the precious load you are carrying.

If Alexander Soros, the baggage complaint department manager, was to be believed, the luggage *did* make it to Athens. The costumes (along with my bras and undies) had been packed in the original brown leather trunk from the museum. All my other clothes, shoes, and makeup were in a smaller matching suitcase. Alexander was sure he remembered my trunk because it was identical to one he was still holding. A butler named Jorge from the *Golden Goddess* (another five-star ship cruising the Mediterranean) had come by and picked up what we think was my trunk and matching suitcase. Apparently, Jorge was assisting one of *his* passengers whose luggage had also not arrived. It would have been easy to confuse our bags had one not taken the time to check the name tags. How could a professional like Jorge be so negligent? It was an outrage to butlers everywhere.

Luckily, the *Golden Goddess* was cruising the same itinerary as the *Tiffany Star*, only they were a day ahead of us. Alexander suggested that if we could just get the passenger and/or his butler to check my bags at the next port, I could retrieve them there. I wrote down the passenger's name from his tags and prayed that Alexander was telling me the truth, and not sending me on a wild-goose chase to get me off his back.

Till There Was You

BY THE TIME I arrived at the Hotel Grande Bretagne, Pops was gone. There was a handful of people milling around the special Tiffany Cruises Line section, and hotel employees were dismantling the VIP setup. My heart leaped to my throat. Was I too late? Did I miss the ship?

Then I spotted a woman who *had* to be a *Tiffany Star* cruiser. She was in her late sixties or early seventies, but well maintained and über-rich. This I gathered from the ornate jewels that adorned her well-toned body, the crisp shopping bags she carried from Prada, Tod's, Bulgari, and Gucci, and the chic nature of her very person down to her astonishingly pink fingers and toenails. She wore her hair in a geometrically perfect silver pageboy. Her bright lips had that puffy artificial filler look and her eyes a permanent expression of surprise. In her arm, she carried a Yorkie with Mediterranean-blue highlights. Everything about her screamed, "Rich," "Social," "New Money." Naturally, I assumed her to be a snob. But then she caught my eye and sent me a smile that could light up an ocean liner. I was intrigued.

"Hi," I said, "I'm Holly Ross. Do you know the time? Please don't tell me I'm too late."

The woman flashed me the face of her bejeweled Cartier. It was six diamonds past an emerald, whatever that translated to in minutes and hours. "You're cutting it awfully close," she said in a Southern drawl. "See, they're closin' up. Ship sails in less than half an hour."

"What happens if you get there after it sails? Can you still board?"

The woman gave me a bewildered look.

I slapped my forehead. "Oh, duh. Sorry. I've been up for forty-eight hours. My brain is all mushy."

"Carleen Panthollow, Tulip, Texas," she said, holding out her hand. I was temporarily blinded by the enormous rock on her ring finger. "And this is Famous, my furry child."

I petted the Yorkie, who was alarmingly high-strung. She quivered and shook at the sight of me. I do that to dogs.

Carleen stood and grabbed her bags, dropping Famous inside one of them. "Come, darlin', time to go."

We boarded the ultrafancy bus, along with a few uniformed members of the crew and one other couple loaded down with new purchases. Carleen retrieved Famous, and then threw her packages in the empty row behind ours. The specially outfitted bus boasted extra-wide leather first-class seats and ample legroom. We lurched forward and soon were humming our way through Athens, toward the water. Maybe it was my imagination, but I could swear the exhaust fumes smelled like perfume.

"You a regular cruiser?" Carleen asked.

"It's my first. You?"

"Oh, Lord have mercy, no," she said. "I've been sailing for the past seventeen months and I don't expect to stop soon."

"Really?" I said. "You don't get tired of it?"

"Hay-ell no," she said. "I have one of the big two-story penthouses and that's plenty comfortable for Carleen Panthollow."

"You're so thin," I remarked. "How do you resist all the rich food?"

"Darlin', I've been on a diet since World War II. Gotta look good for the boys, not that I've gotten any lately," she said with a wink.

I laughed. "I hope you don't mind my asking, but why don't you go home, at least to visit? Seventeen months is a long time to stay on a ship."

"Some people have been on for years," she said. "It's the finest retirement community money can buy. The food is better, the service is divine, and there's dancing every night. Plus, if you fall and break your hip in a nursing home, they stick you in bed and turn you like a pig on a spit. If you fall and break your hip on a

Tiffany ship, you get a butler, a penthouse, and free spa services for the rest of your life."

"So you're retired to the ship?"

"Sort of," she said. "My husband died about five years ago. We did the world cruise together ten years in a row. In fact, he died the day after we got back from our tenth trip. I'll never forget. His bags weren't even unpacked." There were tears in Carleen's eyes.

"I'm sorry," I said. "Can I ask what happened?"

"His old ticker just gave out," she said. "We had a ball on that last cruise."

"You must have really loved him," I said, touching her hand.

"Oh, I did, darlin'. I did. I was his second wife, but we were married thirty years. He bequeathed me *beaucoup* bucks in trust, with the remainder going to the kids from his first family after I kick the bucket. Those children of his are as nasty as you are skinny. Do you know they challenged the will?"

"Nooo!" I said in my supportive, aghast voice.

"Yep," she said. "They hate me, always have. Resent the fact that I made their father happy. So, after his kids' lawsuit got thrown out of court, I booked the big penthouse indefinitely and I plan to cruise until I spend all their daddy's money. That'll show 'em."

"How long'll that take?" I asked.

"Two hundred years." She laughed. "My husband, Tex Panthollow—maybe you've heard of him—he invented the multiple-fold automated umbrella. You know, you see them everywhere? He left me more than the gross national product of California. I could cruise till eternity and never spend it all."

"So the kids'll get the money eventually, huh?"

"Oh, yes," she said, "but not before I put a dent the size of Texas in it."

I almost asked if she'd like to make a million-dollar donation to the Fashion Museum, but decided to wait until I knew her more than ten minutes. "Would you like to adopt me?" I said instead. I was kidding, of course. Okay, not really.

She laughed warmly. "You'll have to stand in line behind all the crew on the ship. What about you, darlin'? What brings you here? You're gonna be the youngest cruiser by a century. Excuse me," she said, hailing a steward who was offering champagne in Baccarat flutes. "I'll have one. You?"

"Not for me."

Carleen took a sip.

"I'm sure I'm not the *youngest* cruiser," I demurred.

"Honey, this ship is *Jurassic Park* at sea. What's your story? You married?"

"Heavens, no."

"Lesbian?"

I regarded her with curiosity. Was she asking me out? Couldn't she see that our age difference would always be a stumbling block?

"I was just going to say this isn't the right ship for that," Carleen said. "There are special cruises for that," she said, making air quotes around the word special. "So what gives? Why're you here by your little lonesome?"

I shook my head. "You don't want to know. I've had a tough run of luck." Then I proceeded to spill my guts after securing Carleen's solemn oath never, never, never to tell a soul, and

I meant never ever. I confided how Alessandro was caught in the act with a minor. How he dumped me. How I didn't get the promotion I so richly deserved. How a city bus destroyed my clothes. How my luggage was lost on the way over. How I was coming on board as a speaker with my father so I could heal my wounds (I made no mention of my ulterior motive—soliciting a donation—lest she think I was some kind of vulture, which I was, but preferred not to publicize).

As the bus pulled into a parking lot, I saw the ocean liner looming ahead.

"Whoa," I cried, pointing to the lustrous ship that glistened in the Greek sunlight. It was enormous, like a bobbing white skyscraper. "Is that ours?"

"Yes, that's her," Carleen said.

She patted my leg. "Don't feel bad about losing your fiancé like that, darlin'. Something worse happened to me."

"Not possible," I said.

She whistled. "Oh, but it is. You ever heard of Haroldson Lafayette Hunt?"

"Name doesn't ring a bell."

"Well, H. L. Hunt was one of the richest men in Texas, in the whole country at one time. That man was slicker than snot on a doorknob. When I graduated college, he proposed marriage and naturally I said yes."

"Was he your first husband?"

"Hay-ell no," she said. "The night before the rehearsal dinner, he dumped me for my maid of honor's second cousin, Lyda Bunker from Little Rock."

"That swine," I groused on Carleen's behalf.

"Come, off we go." Carleen stood and gathered up her pooch and packages. I followed her out of the bus. "The point is, darlin'," she said, "I made out much better, although it didn't seem like it at the time. For ten long years, I felt like the biggest loser in the Lone Star State. He and Lyda had kids and lived the good life. Spent their summers at Lake McQueenie. H. L. was so loaded, he'd buy a new boat every time his other one got wet. I was green with envy. But then H. L. married Fran something-or-other without even divorcing my poor cousin. Can you imagine? He had a second family with kids and pets and everything. I couldn't put up with that kind of bigamy bullshit, not me. So you see, in the end, what seemed like a tragedy turned out to be a blessing. Ten years later, I met my Tex, and I fell for him like an egg from a tall chicken. Same thing'll happen to you. Be patient."

"I hope you're right, but somehow I doubt it."

Carleen pointed to a small tent where two men in crisp white uniforms sat behind a table.

"Welcome to the *Tiffany Star*," an officer cheerfully piped. I gave my ticket to the one with the most ribbons on his pin, turned in my passport, had my picture taken for an ID card, and rinsed my hands with disinfectant gel. Apparently that was to stave off gastrointestinal outbreaks that plague so many cruise ships. Just before we started up the gangway, a photographer asked Carleen and I to smile for the camera. "Oh, I hate seeing pictures of myself," I said. "I've barely slept in two days. I must look a sight . . ."

"You're nothin' short of gorgeous, darlin'," Carleen said.

We stood under a huppahlike structure, posing in front of a fake ocean backdrop and a Bon Voyage sign while the photographer got off a few shots. Suddenly I felt very appreciative of this old woman who was taking me under her wing for no reason at all. I turned and gave her a hug. “Thanks, Carleen. You’re the first good thing that’s happened to me in two days.”

She smiled brightly. “Well, your life will get better from here on out, I promise you that. And if you need to borrow some clothes until they find your suitcase, just ask me.” She looked me up and down. “Lordy, you’re just a pair of tits on a stick. But I’m pretty sure you’ll fit into Lucille’s clothes.”

“Who is Lucille?” I asked.

“She’s been on board for eleven months. *Her* family built the Chrysler Building.”

Gee, Baby, Ain't I Good to You?

As soon as we stepped inside the ship, what little energy I had evaporated in a pouf. I was so wiped out that I could hardly appreciate the magnificence of the six-story lobby in which I was standing—its ice palace decor, the white marble floor, the three-story ceiling-to-floor waterfall, the staircase so grand and sweeping that Rhett Butler would have found it suitable for hauling Scarlett O'Hara up its steps were they alive and cruising today.

Waiters in black tuxedos offered champagne and hors d'oeuvres while passengers buzzed about with excitement. In the center of the room was a table filled with shrimp, crab, and lobster encircling a giant ice sculpture of a mermaid. A band made up of four men, one black, one Latino, one white, and one Asian—a pu-pu platter of nationalities—played "Hot, Hot, Hot." I looked for Pops, but he was somewhere else, in la-la land most likely.

"What do you think they do with the ice sculptures after they melt?" I mused. Did I just say that? Okay, now I was starting to scare myself. "Thanks for everything, Carleen. I'll meet up with you later. I need to catch some Z's."

Carleen handed Famous and her packages to a tuxedo-clad gentleman. "Oh, no you don't, darlin'. No one sleeps until they see the maître d', make their Il Valentino and Au Mandarin reservations, and set up their spa appointments. If you don't do it now, you'll be shut out. Follow me."

I felt like I was in a dream, but tagged behind Carleen nonetheless. As we floated up the grand stairway and down to the back of the ship (aft? port? I had no idea), we passed a Sotheby's showroom with artwork that would be auctioned on the ship. There were Monets, Picassos, da Vincis—surely they weren't real, or were they? This didn't seem like a reproduction-type crowd. An old but well-maintained woman ambled toward us. She was tall, grasshopper-thin, and green-eyed, with beauty-parlor-teased hair the color of wet sand. With the help of a walker, she shuffled steadily but slowly. The walker looked like it was gold-plated, but that would be ridiculous, or would it? She gave Carleen a nod and asked how she'd spent the day.

"Lucille, this is my new young friend, Holly. She's going to be speaking on the ship, but *really* she's here to nurse a broken heart. Do you know that her boyfriend was arrested for child molestation? And then *he* dumped *her*? Can you believe it?"

Lucille gasped and regarded me with pity. "You poor lamb," she said. "You must hate yourself."

"She's sick about it," Carleen said. "Practically suicidal."

So much for Carleen's sacred vow to never reveal my private business to a living soul.

"I've recently suffered a broken heart myself," Lucille confided.

"Really?" I said squeezing her bony, gnarled hand until the canary diamond on her finger made a ten-karat indentation in my palm.

"Don't let the age fool you," Lucille said under her breath. "There's a smoldering cauldron of sexuality bubbling under these liver spots."

I laughed. This old bird was a hoot.

"Do you think you can cool your flame long enough to lend Holly some clothes?" Carleen asked. "She lost her luggage and is going to need to borrow some things from you. I think they'll fit."

"Of course," Lucille said. "It would be my pleasure."

"So what do you think?" Carleen said. "Can you fix her up with your son?"

"He's on this leg of the trip with my granddaughter," Lucille explained. Then she leaned into me and whispered, "And his fiancée, whom he's marrying when we dock in Rome."

"That girl's as useful as goose shit on a pump handle," Carleen stage-whispered.

"Hush, Carleen," Lucille said, wagging her finger.

"She's colder than a witch's titty in a brass bra."

"Stop it," Lucille said. "You know this marriage is my raison d'être. It is the coming together of two of America's top industrial families, like a Rockefeller marrying an Astor."

"Lucille, it's the twenty-first century. People marry; they don't merge. Wouldn't you like your son to be happy? After dating a pedophile, don't you know that a wounded sparrow like poor, pathetic Holly here would appreciate what he has to offer and would treat him like a prince?"

"Carleen," I said, "I'm standing right here. I can hear you. I wish you wouldn't talk about me like that. My troubles are personal and you promised."

"Don't you fret, darlin'. The one person I'll tell is Lucille and only because we need her to lend you clothes. Tomorrow's a sea day and dinner's formal. She'll set you up. And, Lucille," she said, turning to her friend, "not a word to anyone about Holly's troubles, and I'll tell you all the rest later."

Lucille pretended to zip her lips. "I'll take your secrets to my grave."

The deep baritone whistle of the ship sounded. I looked out the window and realized we were sailing. It felt like we were standing still, but the shoreline was moving. That was my clue.

"We're off to see Bradley. We need to get Holly set up for dinner," Carleen said.

"Oh, fabulous," Lucille said. "You simply must be seated at the right table."

As we walked along the corridor and talked, Carleen pointed out the library, cigar, piano, and champagne bars. She told me where to find the various boutiques, the casino, the gym, the spa, the tennis and basketball courts, and the computer room.

"I'll bet you're dying to know Lucille's story," Carleen said with no prompting from me whatsoever. When it came to other passengers' personal affairs, Carleen was the human Google. "Well, she's been suffering a deep depression ever since May, when her favorite dance host died. Claude Chavasse—he was French. They were 'sinking the titanic'" (wink, wink).

"No!" I said. "He was on top of her when he died?"

"Yes!" Carleen said. "For weeks, she was so upset she didn't know daylight from dark. Claude was dumber than a toothbrush, but he was good-looking and a marvelous dancer. For the last three segments, he'd been pleasing the 'elder floozies,' and I include myself in that category."

"He wasn't just Lucille's lover?"

"Oh, no, darlin'. You get to be a certain age and there aren't enough eligible gentlemen to go around. So we shared. If you don't use the equipment, it rusts."

"Nobody minded?"

"For goodness' sake, no. With Viagra, every coot with a cock thinks he's Hugh Hefner. Who can keep up with that? But back to Lucille. Dance hosts are strictly prohibited from bedding the passengers. So it was a good thing Claude died because he would have been fired anyway."

"And that's why Lucille's family came on board?"

"Yes, to cheer her up," Carleen continued. "Not that the rest of us weren't sick over losing Claude, because we were, but since she's the one he died pokin', she gets to play the grieving widow. Anyway, her family's here and her son decided to get hitched in Rome since everyone would be together and it wasn't his first marriage anyway. They're having the ceremony at Palazzo Ferrajoli, an old mansion from the 1500s. They'll honeymoon at the Ritz in Paris. Lucille refuses to invite me to the wedding because she believes I'm against this union."

"Why does she think that?"

"Oh, I tell her every day."

Love for Sale

We arrived at the end of a long hallway where passengers sat patiently waiting their turn as if at a doctor's office. A computer-printed sign on the closed door said MAÎTRE D'.

"Why are we here?" I whispered to Carleen.

"Honey, getting seated at the right table can make or break your trip. And it's highly competitive. But luckily, you're with me."

I took a seat. Soon Carleen shook me awake. "It's our turn."

We entered what appeared to be a card room. Seated behind a table was Bradley, the maître d' (it said so on his name tag). He was thirtysomething, with a pink scalp fringed by wispy brown hair and searing blue eyes that lit up when he saw Carleen. "It's my favorite girl," he said, rising to hug her. I could see that with Carleen by my side, I had real juice on this ship.

Carleen asked Bradley to check my table assignment.

"Let's see, you're at a table for two in the south end of the dining room."

"Well, darlin', Holly can't sit in Siberia. She's one of the top fashionistas in New York City."

"Really?" Bradley said, his eyes wide. "Have I seen you in the papers?"

"Well I *was* on the front page of the *News* and the *Post* a few weeks ago," I demurred modestly, as though I was practically Catherine Zeta-Jones but didn't want special treatment.

"Bradley, be a dear and put Holly and her father with some nice people, would you?"

Bradley studied his online map of the dining room. Names of passengers were plugged into each seat. He shook his head. "Every table's full. Look." He turned the monitor around so we could see it.

I perked up, scanning the map for Denis King's name. "Oh, what about here? This looks like a better location," I said when I found him.

"Impossible," Bradley said. "That's the captain's table."

"Yes, that'll be perfect," Carleen said, "Move me there too."

"But, Carleen, I have the Kings there, along with Baron and Baroness DuLac. Every seat's taken."

"Move the DuLacs somewhere else," Carleen said, waving her hand. "Baroness DuLac's sat with the captain a hundred times. Between you and me, she says he's windier than a bag of assholes with all those goddamn sea stories he's always telling."

"But they're Tiffany Star Society Members," Bradley said.

"Bradley, darlin', Mommy will make it worth your while."

Bradley flinched ever so slightly, punched a few keys on his computer and the dirty deed was done. *Nya ah ah*, I thought. My dastardly plan had been set in motion. There was no turning back.

Next, Carleen whisked me over to Il Valentino and Au Mandarin, the two private restaurants on the ship, where I reserved a table for four at each place, but not on formal nights, as she instructed. We followed this with a trip to the spa and beauty salon, where massages and hair appointments were booked at Carleen's insistence, and at her expense.

"Oh, you really shouldn't," I said. But wait! How could I not assist my new best friend in her quest to deplete her bank account so it wouldn't fall into the hands of her evil stepchildren? I couldn't. I wouldn't. So I didn't.

I yawned. "Is there anything else, Carleen? Do we need to reserve deck chairs? Meet the social director? I'm exhausted."

Carleen checked her watch. "You really ought to sign up for some land trips. Come, we'll do that quickly."

"Do you have to get off the ship to take those?"

"Never mind, darlin'," Carleen said. "You'd best catch some sleep. I'll take care of your tours."

"Yes, g'night," I said. "Let's hope my room has an ocean view."

Too Marvelous for Words

A WHITE-JACKETED BUTLER NAMED JOHN Savoy showed me to our tenth-floor penthouse suite. John was exceptionally yummy-looking for a butler, at least compared to Mr. French on *Family Affair*, the only other butler I knew. Of course, there was also Cadbury, Richie Rich's butler, but he was a cartoon. John was in his early twenties, slim with coal-black hair, dark watery eyes, a deep tan, and lashes so thick they cast a shadow on his cheeks.

I asked if he could get me an outfit from one of the shops on board, plus clean underwear to last me through the cruise. "No problem," he whispered so as not to wake Pops, who was sacked out on a fold-out bed in the living room. "I'm at your service." He handed me a brochure that had been clipped outside my door. "Here's your *Tiffany Tattler*. It tells you what's happening tomorrow."

I could *so* get used to having a butler. John was from Italy (it said so on his name tag). "What city are you from?"

"Roma," he said. "My family is royalty."

My eyes widened. "What are you, like a prince?"

"I am cousin to the prince," he said, "named after American royalty, Mr. John Kennedy Jr. My sister is called Caroline."

"I didn't know Italians had a royal family," I said. "Why are you working on a ship as a butler? Shouldn't you be cavorting on a yacht in the South of France with William and Harry?"

John smiled. "I wanted to see the world and this has allowed me to do that. I'll be leaving when we dock in Roma and starting university in a few weeks."

So not only did I have a butler, I had a smart, educated, royal butler. This was good. I was going to need his help tracking down my lost bags. Sitting on the edge of the bed, I told John what had happened, gave him the luggage receipts and the name of the person traveling on the *Golden Goddess* whom I suspected of having my stuff, thanks to the inexcusable mixup by Jorge the butler.

"Do you know Jorge?"

"Yes, I do," John said. "Sometimes we run the same itinerary as the *Golden Goddess* and the butlers from the two ships meet and share best practices."

"Really?" I said, impressed.

"Oh, yes," he said. "We take our jobs seriously and constantly strive to find new ways to delight and astonish our guests. When I go to university, I plan to study Hospitality Science."

"Wow," I said. "If you could find my luggage for me, I would be delighted, astounded, astonished, and indebted to you for life. You have *no* idea."

John executed a modest bow and then backed out of the room the way subjects remove themselves from the presence of the Queen of England. I had the impression that with a conscientious butler like John Savoy taking care of me, nothing bad could happen.

Pops sat up. "There you are, Holly," he said, yawning. He donned his robe and joined me in the bedroom. "I was worried about you. Did you find the bags?"

I frowned. "No, not yet. Holy cannoli, would you look at that?" On my night table sat a brand-new box of cream-colored stationery with my name engraved in gold leaf, along with matching personalized Post-its. I stuck the Post-its in my purse since I'd never owned any that fancy and didn't want to leave them there.

"Good thinking," Pops said. "I packed my stickies already, along with stationery, soap, shampoo, cotton balls, toilet paper, a feather pillow . . ."

"Pops, that's stealing," I said.

"No, it's not," he said. "They *want* you take that stuff. They *expect* you to take it. They'd be disappointed if you *didn't* take it."

"I don't think so," I said, shaking my head.

"Can you believe it?" Pops said with a wide grin. "The two of us living in the lap of luxury? I *love* it!"

"Me too." I giggled. "It's a far cry from Muttropolis."

"Or eating out of trash cans," Pops said.

"Or panhandling in the subway," I added.

Pops whisked me into his arms and began twirling me around the room. *"Fairy tales may come true, it could happen to you . . ."* he crooned. When the song ended, he dipped me back most of the way to the floor, then dropped me on my butt. "Are you okay? I need to practice my dancing."

I laughed heartily. "It's okay. Just don't drop any old ladies. They have brittle hips." As I sat on the floor, I looked around, taking in the cabin for the first time. It was exquisitely appointed (and I say this not just because it said so in the brochure). Decorated in muted tones of tan and white, with walls sheathed in exotic bamboo, furniture straight off the pages of *Architectural Digest*, a flat-screen TV in both rooms. My queen-size bed was topped with a luscious feather-down duvet. Fresh orchids graced my nightstand. The butler had laid out a luxurious Frette bathrobe and plush slippers.

I pulled myself up from the floor, slipped on my robe, and padded to the bathroom, brushed my teeth, donned my headgear, and then got all comfy under the covers, resting my head on the cool goose-down pillow. It felt like heaven. "'Night, Pops. I'll see you in about eighteen hours."

"Wait," he said. "Someone from the cruise director's office called to say that your presentation is at ten A.M. tomorrow in the Galaxy Lounge. They wanted to know if you needed anything."

"No, I'm fine," I mumbled.

"One more thing. Don't fall asleep yet," Pops said. He was sitting on the edge of my bed. "We're supposed to muster for the safety drill at five."

"Take notes for me, will you?" I said.

"You're not missing dinner, are you?"

I opened one eye. Pops looked earnest, afraid, and slightly desperate. It had been years since he'd flexed his polite society muscles. Sure, I thought. I may as well "bump" into Denis King and get it over with. "Of course not," I said. "I'll meet you in the dining room at eight thirty. We're at the captain's table, by the way."

"How did that happen?"

"Long story, Pops. 'Night."

The Best Is Yet to Come

THE RING OF MY seven thirty wake-up call jolted me. It was still light outside. I'd only gotten two hours of sleep, but it would have to do. It occurred to me that something was very wrong, but I couldn't remember what. Then it hit me. The lost luggage. How could I have left those costumes unattended? What if Jorge from the *Golden Goddess* didn't take them and they were just randomly missing, misplaced by baggage handlers in Athens? How would I find them then? But there was nothing I could do about it now, so I tried to put it out of my mind.

I considered the donation I planned to solicit and wondered what Denis King would say when he saw the woman who had so publicly humiliated him seated at his table. My stomach flipped at the thought. I prayed to the Lord for forgiveness (from Denis, not the Lord).

What to wear? After I pressed the call button for my butler (ooh, how I like saying those words), John was knocking at the door within minutes.

"Here you go, Miss Ross," he said, handing me a shopping bag. Inside was a powder-pink velour running suit with the name "Tiffany Star" emblazoned across the back of the jacket. There was also a white T-shirt with the name "Tiffany Star" spelled out across the chest in rhinestones. What can I say about such an outfit? It was clean.

Another tissue-wrapped package revealed five pairs of cream-colored satin underwear. But yoinks! I'd never seen granny panties in size jack-o'-lantern before. I supposed they had to be extra large to accommodate those passengers using colostomy bags, but what about the rest of us? "Nothing smaller?"

"This was it," John said. "Women on this ship don't wear sexy *mutande*."

"Wow," I said, holding a pair up, imagining them on. If we were to get stranded on a desert island, I could build a boat and make a sail out of them. "Thank you, John. You're a dear to help me." I reached into my purse for a tip.

"Oh, no, Miss Ross. No gratuities along the way," he said. "If you're happy with the service you can tip at the end."

"Okay, but wait," I squealed. "Let me take your picture. I never had a butler before." John stood next to me and I held out my digital camera and snapped. I wanted to remember what it was like to live the good life in case it never happened again. Looking at the photo though, I cringed. What a mess—bed hair crushed into an asymmetrical Mohawk, raccoon under-eyes, glasses, and don't forget the headgear. I wished I knew how to delete it.

After John left, I headed to the bathroom to pull myself together. The room was marble from floor to ceiling and there was a switch to turn on the heated floor. Heated floors! The tub doubled as a Jacuzzi and there was a glass-enclosed steam shower. There was no soap or bubble bath because Pops had stolen it all. That was inconvenient. The hand towels were arranged to make perfect little swans and the end of the toilet paper was folded into the shape of a sunflower. Next door, there was a huge teak-paneled dressing room with double closets that I hoped to fill with the recovered costumes. Why did I take those stupid dresses? I wondered. I should have gone shopping for cheap new clothes at the City Opera Thrift Shop. That would have been easier—and safer. .

At eight thirty, I left for dinner, wearing my new pink running suit and the underwear I'd had on for the past forty-eight hours. I couldn't bring myself to put on the monster briefs—not yet, anyway—so I rinsed my old panties out, dried them with the blow-dryer, and freshened them with lemon-scented Endust I'd stolen off the maid's trolley.

I wandered down to the fifth-floor dining room, where the ship was most stable. Butterflies fluttered in my stomach at the thought of seeing Denis King. "You can do this," I chanted. "You *have* to do this."

The dining room was gorgeous with its round tables dressed in crisp pink linens graced with fresh red roses, Versace china, Riedel crystal, and Christofle silver (I knew only because it said so in the brochure). Dazzling hand-cut chandeliers hung like sparkling waterfalls from the ceiling. Off to the side, a Stradivarius string quartet played Mozart, and quite beautifully I might add. The convivial buzz of travel-weary passengers chatting away on nothing but adrenaline filled the air.

Enrico Derflingher, the world-famous Italian restaurateur, introduced himself. He was the guest chef on this leg of the cruise. Waiters in tuxedos were lined up at the door to escort guests to their table. A young man gallantly offered his arm and escorted me toward the center of the room. As we approached our destination, Lucille, the depressed dance-host killer, bolted out of her seat and cornered me. I was surprised at the old bird's energy.

"Holly, dear, you smell fabulous, simply *fabulous*. What's that you're wearing? Eau d'Hadrien?

Eau d'Endust, I thought, but didn't say. Instead, I just smiled. "How'd you guess?"

"Here, dear, the key to my closet. You can go after dinner and pick out whatever you like."

I looked at the card, which had a room number written on it with Magic Marker. "Is this your cabin key? I don't want to bother you."

"Oh, you won't," Lucille said. "It's for the suite next to mine. That's where I keep my clothes."

"You have a penthouse suite just for your clothes," I said. "Wow." *That's rich,* I thought.

"By the way, I want you to meet my family." Lucille gestured toward the others at the table. "Everyone, this is Holly, the girl I was telling you about."

Her son put down his BlackBerry, stood, and offered his hand. It was Denis King.

As we shook, Denis gave me a searching look. "Excuse me. We've met before, haven't we?"

Naturally, I froze under the pressure. So I just smiled.

Lucille continued her introduction. "Darlings, Holly's the one whose fiancé turned out to be a pedophile and who then had the audacity to dump her, can you believe it? Oh, and *then* she lost all her luggage; I'm going to lend her clothes *and* she was just passed over for a big promotion at work. Did I leave anything out?"

I could feel the blood rushing to my face. "No, you covered everything quite well."

Bewitched, Bothered, and Bewildered

SORRY TO HEAR ABOUT your troubles," Denis said.

"Thanks," I said, sorry that he had heard about them too.

Lucille introduced me to her son's fiancée, the exquisite blond-haired, blue-eyed Sydney Bass. She was stunning—more beautiful than any of her pictures. All her edges were soft, as if she were airbrushed by God.

"Hello," she said politely. There were two five-pound pink-crystal-encrusted dumbbells in front of her place setting. Dumbbells at the dinner table? Was she raised by wolves? Okay, I admit it. I can be judgmental to a fault. It's something I picked up at church as a kid.

Denis' ten-year-old, Annie, was too involved with her Game Boy to say hello. Her manny, Manuel, actually said, "Call me Manny," when we were introduced. Manny (who was indeed a man) was twentyish, thin like a distance runner, with thick black hair and heavy-lidded smoky-colored bedroom eyes. Why one would hire a manny with bedroom eyes, I'll never understand. Why one would hire a manny instead of a nanny for a little girl, I'll never understand that, either.

"Aren't you supposed to be in school?" I asked Annie.

"I'm getting to miss it for my dad's wedding. Whoo-hoo," she tooted.

"But you're keeping a trip diary and writing a report, right?" Denis said.

Annie rolled her eyes. "I guess."

"This is Sydney's mother, Bunny," Denis said, gesturing toward a blue-black-haired, patrician seventy-something woman attempting to pass herself off as late fiftyish (the crepey neck, smooth face mismatch was the giveaway). Nothing makes a woman look so old as desperately trying to look young. Coco Chanel said that and she should know. Bunny was impeccably dressed and coiffed, her skin tan and her lined lips like two perfect pincushions. With an icy smile and silken tone, she said, "So nice to make your acquaintance."

"You too," I said. Bunny frightened me.

A man seated to her left jumped up and took my hand, squeezing it. "Jolly good to meet you," he said breathlessly. "I'm Bunny's third and newest husband, Aston Martin. That's just like the car, only no relation." Aston was a tall, lanky chap with a shiny bald noggin. With his old-fashioned horn-rimmed glasses and skinny tie, he looked he'd stepped out of a black-and-white TV show from the 1950s.

I glanced at Pops, who was already seated, grinning amusedly and sipping a martini. He had relaxed considerably since last I saw him, no doubt after several cocktails. "Cheers," he said, raising his glass my way.

"Has everyone met my father?" I asked.

Pops raised his glass. "Sven Ross, man of the people," he said.

"Darlin', you never told me your father was such a fox," Carleen whispered.

"You think?"

"Hubba hubba," she said under her breath. "At my age, any man without stiff whiskers growin' out his ears is hot. Tell me, is there a Mrs. Ross?"

"Mama died when I was young; she's long gone. Speaking of gone, where's the captain?" I asked, sitting down next to Carleen. There was one more empty seat at the table. I assumed it belonged to him.

"He only comes on formal nights," she explained.

Denis King was staring at me. How could he not remember the girl who called him Penis in public? Frankly, I was hurt.

We studied our menus as the headwaiter, assistant headwaiter, and sommelier glided noiselessly about, delivering bread, pouring water, and popping open bottles of champagne.

I started with deep-fried zucchini flowers with shellfish and saffron consommé, then ordered lobster medallions with a puree of green apple and black truffle, and finally *millefoglie stracchin*, a delicate pastry filled with vanilla soufflé. Hopefully I'd put on a few pounds.

"Aren't you speaking tomorrow?" Carleen asked.

"Yes, at ten in the Galaxy Lounge. I hope you'll come."

"What's your topic?" Bunny asked.

"Hollywood legends as style makers."

"So you're what, some sort of fashion expert?" she asked.

Denis' eyes widened and his jaw dropped. Bingo! If this were What's My Line? he would have slammed the buzzer.

"Bugger," Aston said. "That's exactly when they're having the auction for French Impressionist paintings. I have my eye on the Degas."

"You mean the ballet dancer?" Pops said. "I was intent on acquiring that for my collection."

"Don't think you can outbid me, old chap," Aston said. "I'm a force of nature."

"If it's *that* important to you," Pops conceded, "then I shall refrain from bidding."

"You, sir, are a true gentleman," Aston said. "May I buy you a drink after dinner?"

"You may buy me several," Pops said, "plus a Cuban cigar."

I gave Pops a "Shut your trap; remember what we're here for" look.

"I want to do the scavenger hunt tomorrow," Annie said.

"Cool, I love scavenger hunts. I'll take you," Denis offered.

"No, I want to go with Maaaanny," she whined.

Denis gazed at his daughter with a pained expression and started to object.

"I don't mind," said Manny the manny.

Sydney rolled her eyes and turned to Denis. "Scavenger hunts. Do you see what I mean about public cruises? I told you we should have taken the yacht."

Denis turned to his young bride-to-be. "They do that sort of thing to entertain the kids on board. I think it's nice. And anyway, Mother loves the *Tiffany Star*. We're here for her."

"I thought we were here for our wedding," she said. "Thanks for taking my feelings into account."

"But you're here now," Carleen the peacekeeper said. "And you'll have a ball if you let yourself. Holly, darlin', *I'll* come to your lecture."

"Me too, dear. I think anything to do with fashion is simply fabulous," Lucille declared.

Nine waiters magically materialized at our table, all carrying covered plates on silver platters. Each waiter positioned himself behind someone's chair and then, in perfect lockstep, whisked off the domed top, set the plate on the table, and stepped back, retreating into the buzz of the dining room. It was a gastronomic ballet.

"*Bon appétit*," Aston said.

"Oh, waiter," Sydney said, catching hers by the tail of his tux. "In the future, bring me quarter portions. I just want to taste."

"Great idea," Pops said, setting down his drink a bit too hard. "In the future, would you bring me double portions of what I order?"

"*Pops*," I whispered.

"We don't have to pay. It's free," he blurted.

"That's not the point."

"If it's my weight you're worried about, don't. I'm working out. In fact, I'm meeting with Horace, my new trainer, tomorrow at ten," Pops said. "You don't mind if I miss your lecture, do you?"

"No, it's fine," I said, biting into my lobster, which was broiled to perfection.

He rubbed his ample belly. "Horace says I have the body of an Olympian covered in fat."

"Daddy," Annie said. "Did you know that Sydney is closer to my age than she is to yours? She's sixteen years older than me, but twenty-two years younger than you."

"What are you, the human calculator?" Sydney said.

Denis laughed. "No, but she's a whiz in math. You're right, Annie," he said. "Sydney *is* closer to your age than mine."

"So *I* should marry her, not *you*," Annie said. "But I can't."

"Oh, no, why not?" Denis asked.

Annie laughed. "Girls can't marry girls."

"Not yet," Denis explained. "But someday the laws will change."

"But how would we have babies?" Annie asked.

"Could we please talk about something else?" Sydney said, rolling her eyes.

"You could adopt," I suggested.

"Or have artificial insemination," Carleen said.

"The ol' turkey baster method," Pops added.

"Pops," I growled.

"See, Daddy," Annie giggled, "I'm not the only one who says inappropriate things at the table."

"This conversation is killing my appetite," Sydney said, throwing her napkin on the table.

"Forgive me," Pops said.

"Saves her having to stick her finger down her throat," Carleen whispered.

"Daddy, may I please be excused?" Annie said. "I need to go urinate."

"Yes, of course," Denis said, waving her away. "But next time . . . come here."

Annie walked over to her father, who whispered something in her ear. "Excuse me, everyone," she announced. "I'm going to go *powder my nose*."

After the plates were cleared, the waiter stopped by for coffee orders.

"You having dessert?" I asked Carleen.

She patted her nonexistent stomach. "No, darlin'. I'm just as full as a tick."

"So can anyone else come to my lecture tomorrow?" I asked.

"I just remembered," Bunny said, "there's a cooking demonstration with Enrico Derflingher at ten. I simply can't miss that."

"Maybe you should go, too, Syd," Denis said.

"Why?" Sydney said. "We have a private chef."

"I meant so you could be with your mother," Denis said. "You never have time together when you're working."

"Sorry," she said. "But when I'm not *working* working, I'm working out." She made a fist and showed off her biceps. "Gotta be a buff bride."

"There sure are lots of options," I said. "I hope *someone* comes to my talk."

"They will," Lucille said. "How about you, Denis dear? Join us for a lecture on Hollywood style. It'll be *fabulous*."

"I'd love to, Mother," Denis said.

Yay, I thought.

"Then maybe I *will* come," Sydney said.

Boo, I thought. A wide yawn escaped from my mouth. "Oh, excuse me. I'm exhausted. I think I'll say good night." It had been a long two days and I still needed to shop for clothes from Lucille's penthouse closet and catch some sleep before my lecture. Plus, I didn't want to have a conversation with Denis. Not yet, anyway.

Stormy Weather

THE RING OF THE phone jolted me awake. The cabin was pitch-black and the clock read 3:07 A.M.

"H-hello," I mumbled.

"Ship-to-shore call for Holly Ross," said an operator with a heavy Italian accent.

"Um, wait," I said, groggily unhooking my headgear so I could speak properly. I tried to remember. Who did I know from shore?

"Hello," I said.

"Holly, thank goodness you're there." It was Nigel, my colleague and best pal.

"Of course I'm here. It's the middle of the night. What is it?"

"There's been a crap development, simply crap," he said. "I was out today visiting Madonna, you know, for the Denis King show. You should see her apartment, luv. It's *huuuuuge*. And *soooo* opulent. She finally said yes on the nineteenth-century diamond tiara she wore for her wedding, the one from Asprey and Garrard? Seventy-eight karats of diamonds . . ."

"Nigel, what crap thing happened?"

"Right, well, while I was out, Sammie went through the Audrey exhibit boxes one last time. She realized the costumes were missing."

"Sammie? She had no business . . . this wasn't her project . . ." I sputtered. "You promised no one would find out."

"I know, and I'm bloody sorry. The show was packed to ship. Why she opened the trunks, I cannot fathom. I never thought . . ."

"What did she do?"

"Wait, I'm not finished. The thing is," he moaned and his voice trailed off.

"What? *What is the thing?*" I insisted.

"The thing is," he mumbled, "the Jennifer Love-Hewitt garments are *here*. The trunk containing *all* the *original* Givenchy evening gowns is missing."

"*What?*" I cried. "But that's impossible. You saw which case I took, didn't you?"

"Yes," he said. "And the packing slip said it held the reproductions. I even looked inside to verify. Someone must have switched the paperwork on the trunks at the last minute."

My heart sank. I was sure I knew who that someone was. "Sammie must have overheard us talking. She wants to ruin me. But to do *this*?"

"It's an act of fashion terrorism," Nigel professed.

"By someone who claims to love fashion," I snarled. "So what happened? Did she call the police?"

"No, it's worse," Nigel said. "She called Tanya. Then Tanya called the police *and* the FBI because they thought the dresses might end up on the black market somewhere. By the time I got to the office, everything was cordoned off with yellow tape. They were dusting for prints, questioning everyone, trying to sort it out. Elaina had to be medicated. Tanya insisted everyone take a lie detector test."

"Now I'll never get promoted," I groaned.

"That's the least of your problems."

"My problems," I said. "You're my coconspirator."

"I had to tell them everything, well *almost* everything. I left out my involvement because I'm sure you'll agree there's no point in us both getting sacked and going to jail. Orange jumpsuits do nothing for my silhouette."

"SACKED? JAIL?" I was standing now. "If you're trying to frighten me, you're doing a first-rate job."

"I'm just saying . . ." Nigel started.

My stomach was clenched tight. "Nigel, this was *your* idea. You *know* I didn't plan to steal anything."

"Yes, well, and I explained all that, except for the part about my making you courier for the reproductions and you taking the wrong trunk, but they didn't buy it. They think you acted alone."

"For the love of Pete! Of course that's what they think if you didn't tell them the truth." I was seething.

"The FBI called Interpol and now they're coming to arrest you, so you need to be prepared. Just give the dresses back and I'm sure they won't take you to jail."

"*I can't,*" I said. "They were lost in transit."

"*What?*" Nigel exclaimed. "How is that possible? Didn't you watch them load and unload the trunk?"

"I watched the loading but not the unloading."

"You *know* you're supposed to take custody of the goods at the gate."

"And you know you're supposed to tell the truth," I said, "so I guess we're even. But the dresses are insured, right? At least they're covered."

"Yes, for about eight million dollars," Nigel said. "But if you didn't follow security procedures transporting them—and you didn't—the insurance company will never pay the claim. If you don't find them, the museum will have to cover the loss."

"Oh, fuck," I said, crumpling into the bed. "When are the police coming?"

"Maybe at the next port or the one after that. Is there a lawyer on board?"

"There's a ship's doctor, but no lawyer. Well, maybe there's a passenger who's a lawyer. Oh, hell, I don't know." My breaths came in shallow, quick gasps. "How could you *do* this to me? You fed me to the sharks."

Nigel chuckled. "Oh, that's funny, the sharks. And you're on a ship."

"Nigel, I'm not laughing, not one bit. You go back to Tanya

and tell her what really happened, how this was *your* idea. How I thought I was carrying costumes worth eighty thousand dollars, not eight million, how I was planning to deliver them in Rome. I mean it. You *have* to tell her."

"Well, sure," Nigel said rather unconvincingly. "But *you* have to find the trunk. Those costumes are irreplaceable."

"I *know* they are and I'm working on it," I said, slamming down the phone.

Some best friend Nigel turned out to be, I thought. I finally get a wonderful, luxurious escape from my problems at home and look what happened. This trip was a disaster. How was I ever going to fix this mess? I closed my eyes and prayed that tomorrow would be a better day.

Let's Kiss and Make Up

MY TALK COULD NOT have gone worse, unless, perhaps, I had worn my clown underpants onstage.

I couldn't get those lost dresses out of my mind. What killed me was that I'd opened the trunk at the last minute to throw in my bras and panties. Why hadn't I checked the clothes inside just to be sure? How could I have assumed I was carrying the right costumes? All night, I tossed and turned, frustrated with myself, also worried that the baggage manager in Athens had been wrong, that Jorge didn't take the trunk to the *Golden Goddess*. If *he* didn't have it, who did? I needed a plan B. But what?

At sunrise, I gave up and did eight laps around the seventh-floor deck in the crisp morning air. The gray mist of the sea melted into the dawn sky. The only other person exercising at that ungodly hour was Sydney Bass, who was pumping her five-pound sparkly dumbbells as she did her roadwork. We said hello the first time we passed, but ignored each other after that.

Two miles later, I showered and put on a simple, navy-blue Armani shift I'd borrowed from Lucille's amazing Technicolor dream closet. The entire suite was filled with dress racks bursting with designer and hand-sewn couture outfits. Plus, there were drawers full of belts, scarves, hats, and jewels. Her shoe collection was as complete as Bergdorf's. Her bras and panties were exclusively La Perla, but I refrained from helping myself to those in the interest of sanitation.

I was grateful to have met such a generous, well-clothed passenger. Now her exquisite wardrobe filled my previously bare cabin closet. Lucille's taste reminded me of Corny's—impeccable. I wondered if Tanya would forgive me for taking the real Audrey dresses if I could convince Lucille to leave her collection to the museum. *I'll start planting seeds for that at dinner*, I thought.

Eventually, I made my way to the Galaxy Lounge and prepared for my speech. Exactly three-and-a-half passengers came—Denis, Lucille, Carleen, and Famous. When I read my *Tiffany Tattler* I could see why. Besides the celebrity-chef cooking demonstration, the French Impressionist painting auction, and the scavenger hunt, there was an archeologist talking about the treasures of Ephesus, a yoga class, an ice sculpture demonstration, a bridge tournament, a golf lesson, submarine rides (limit ten), and the ever-popular World War II veterans reunion. There were only three hundred passengers on board. You do the math.

I stepped off the stage and joined my meager audience. "Seriously, you don't have to stay," I said, not really meaning it. I'd have been delighted to give my speech to three people with such enormous donor potential.

"Oh, goody," Carleen said. "We'll just mosey over to the veteran's reunion and pick up some boys. C'mon, Lucille."

Lucille grabbed her gold walker and hustled behind Carleen to the World War II gathering. Those girls wasted no time hightailing it from my ill-fated talk.

That left Denis and me, which would have been thrilling if I weren't so nervous about being alone with him. How do I get him to forgive me? Do I come right out and ask or butter him up first?

"May I?" I said, pointing to the seat next to his.

"It's a free country," he said, turning on his BlackBerry and scrolling through his e-mails.

"Lots of messages, eh?" I said.

"Yes, lots."

My brain froze. *Why does it always do that in emergencies? Why? Think, think. Dazzle him with an anecdote. Impress him with your intellect.* I cleared my throat. "You know, on the flight over, I was reading this book on the history of the British royals. As a fashion historian, I . . . I'm intrigued by history, as you might imagine. Anyway, I cannot get over those English monarchs. They . . . why, they never cease to amaze."

"How so?" Denis asked as he typed an e-mail.

"Well . . . Oh! Did you know that King George II died while straining to relieve his constipation?" *Arrrrgh.*

"Fascinating," Denis said, shutting off his BlackBerry. "Excuse me. I'm going to join Annie at the scavenger hunt."

"Denis, wait!" I blurted. "I'm sorry I called you Penis King."

"Forget it," he said, averting his eyes.

"I can't. It was unforgivable. Especially in front of Annie."

Denis glared at me. "It's been years since anyone called me that."

"You mean I wasn't the first?"

"I was a chubby kid," he said, "with a name just begging to be made fun of."

"Ouch," I said. "So why didn't you go by your middle name?"

"My middle name is Evelyn."

You can't be serious, I thought.

"Like Evelyn Waugh, who wrote *Brideshead Revisited*," Denis said. "It's a family name."

"I'm sorry." I said. "About what I did, I mean, not your middle name."

"I should go look for Annie," he said, dismissing me.

"May I walk with you?"

"I suppose," Denis said. "Unless of course you want to . . ."

"Have breakfast with you in the Bistro? Yes, I'd love to."

"I was going to say, unless you wanted to let the activity director know how your talk went," he said.

"Why ever would I want to do that? Breakfast with you sounds much more pleasant."

Denis sighed. "Okay. Sure, why not?" The wall was coming down.

We strolled down the hall toward the small restaurant, passing a group of passengers looking at the photos that had been taken at the gangplank the day before. They were posted along the wall behind clear plastic holders.

"Excuse me," said a squat, gray-haired grandpa decked out in dark green Ralph Lauren shorts, shirt, and matching socks. He looked like an avocado. "How do you tell which picture is yours?"

"Oh, it's easy. You look for the one you're in," I said.

"Of course, thanks," he said thoughtfully.

Denis let out a laugh when we were out of the man's range. His eyes had softened.

The Bistro was a small restaurant full of shiny brass fixtures and frosted glass windows. It offered a buffet of bagels, smoked salmon, cream cheese, Danish, muffins, and fresh fruit. The air in the room was warm and thick with the scent of freshly baked bread. We each fixed a plate and took a seat. Denis' BlackBerry vibrated and he checked the message, then turned it off.

"Listen, don't feel bad that you didn't get a crowd," he said. "They offer so much on sea days, it's hard to choose."

"You're right," I said. "There's a lot going on. It's just that I want to do a good job so they'll ask me back. Plus, if I can rustle up a few donations, Tanya says she'll promote me to curator." I looked at Denis expectantly.

"Good luck with that," he said noncommittally.

"Do you like my outfit? It's your mom's."

"I do. You look very pretty. So what's your next speech about?"

"The style of Audrey Hepburn," I said. "It's based on our last exhibit."

"I don't know, after the showing this morning, you may need to spice up the topic to generate excitement," he said. "Add some sex appeal, why don't you?"

I dropped my bagel. "Denis! How can you say that? Talking about sex in the same breath as Audrey Hepburn. That's sacrilege. It insults her memory. The woman was a saint. Not only is the idea repugnant, but it devalues my entire fashion history education, which my ex-fiancé is still paying for, by the way."

"Hepburn *was* a real person," Denis said. "She smoked, she drank . . ."

"Oh . . . well . . . in that case, why not just call the talk Audrey Hepburn and the . . . the Thirty-Minute Orgasm for Seniors!" I proclaimed, waving my arms in the air.

"Good idea," he said with a chuckle. "But why not just call it The Thirty-Minute Orgasm for Seniors?"

"No. Whatever I talk about has to have a fashion angle," I said. "Gosh, I can't believe I just used the word 'orgasm' in the same sentence as 'Audrey Hepburn.' Anyway, I can't give that speech because what do I know about thirty-minute orgasms, even if they're physically possible."

"Especially among the elderly," Denis said.

"Exactly. And how would I make the connection between Audrey Hepburn and orgasms? She played a nun, for heaven's sake. You're right about one thing, though. To draw a crowd, I need to come up with a different topic, something more provocative than what I'd planned."

Denis smiled at me. "You know what you remind me of?"

"What?"

"Spring," he said.

"I beg your pardon?"

"You're a breath of fresh air."

I Get a Kick Out of You

A BREATH OF FRESH AIR! That was the nicest thing anyone had ever called me. I flashed my most adorable smile, in a modest and demure way.

Denis signaled for the waiter, who came right over. "More coffee?"

I nodded. "Thanks. With cream. So where are your peeps?"

"Syd's exercising. She works ungodly hours. That's her one release. And Annie's at the scavenger hunt with Manny."

I giggled. "Annie and Manny. Cute."

"Yes, they're a pair," he said. "Annie's mother got her a manny to take my place."

"I don't believe that," I said. "No one can take a father's place in a child's mind."

"That was the idea, anyway," Denis said. "One of the reasons I wanted to take this cruise was to spend time with Annie. She lives with my ex-wife during the school year. But Manny dotes on her. 'Course, that's fine with Sydney. She's not into children. And it gives me more time for Mother. She's been depressed."

"I heard."

"You did?"

"Oh, sure. There are no secrets on this ship. Her favorite dance host died doing the mattress mambo with her."

"No, it was the horizontal hora," he said with a wry smile.

"Your wedding will cheer her up," I said. "I hear you're getting married in Rome."

Denis nodded slowly. "Mother can die happy now. She and my father began orchestrating this match when my first marriage imploded. After Dad and Bunny's husband died, those two yentas made this union their life's mission. The Basses have the largest real estate portfolio in the city; we're the biggest developers. The Kings and the Basses, together at last."

"But you're marrying her for yourself, not because your mother wants you to, right?" I asked. It was none of my business, which was why I wanted to know.

"Do I seem like the kind of guy who does anything he doesn't want to do?"

I looked into Denis' eyes. "No, you don't."

"So were you really engaged to that Broadway Hound?"

"Ah, touché," I laughed. "You read about him, I see."

The waiter returned with our coffee, but brought skim milk instead of cream. I hate when that happens. Then I have to send the milk back and wait for the cream. I've always heard that waiters spit in your food when you send it back, but maybe they don't do that on such a fancy ship. Still, it wasn't worth the risk of infection.

"You know what I'd really like?" I said. "A glass of champagne."

"For breakfast?" Denis said.

"Absolutely," I declared. "I've never had champagne for breakfast and I want to commemorate my crushing defeat this morning in the Galaxy Lounge."

Denis raised his hand to get the waiter's attention. "Two glasses of champagne."

"Pink champagne," I said.

"Like Deborah Kerr drank with Cary Grant in *An Affair to Remember*?" Denis said.

"Well, cross my heart and kiss my elbow. You like old movies? So do I. You know what I've always wished? That my life would have been like a 1950s romantic comedy. Wouldn't that have been great?"

"Of all the words of tongue or pen, the saddest are these: it might have been," Denis said.

"Shakespeare?"

"It's from an old movie, *The Lavender Hill Mob*," he said. "Everyone has might have beens in their lives, things they wish had been different."

"Do *you*?" I said, moving my face a little closer to his. He smelled really good, like bath soap, only manlier. Never in my life had a man wearing black socks with brown leather sandals seemed so yummy. And that full face, those misty kohl eyes, those thick lashes—what I wouldn't give for a pair of those (thick ones, I mean; I do have lashes). I wanted to plant soft butterfly kisses on his eyelids right there in the Bistro. That would give those cruise passengers something to gossip about, but I reminded myself that I was here on a mission and he was engaged to someone else. So I maintained strict military discipline.

"I played baseball in college," he said. "After my senior year, I was drafted into the Columbus Clippers, the Yankees farm team. I'd just been accepted into Harvard Law. I suppose because I felt a sense of duty to the King family business, I chose law school. Bad move. My whole first year of Harvard, I was sick about it. I almost dropped out four times to get back to baseball. The next summer, though, I developed bursitis in my knees from the years of playing college ball. That would have killed my athletic career."

"So it was good that you chose law school."

"No, it was terrible. One year of baseball would have been a dream come true. Better to have played and lost . . ." he mused.

The waiter returned with two glasses of pink champagne. "Cheers," I said, clinking my glass with Denis'.

"Sometimes things happen that seem terrible, like me not playing ball or you falling for a creep, but later they turn out to be blessings."

I nodded. "That's exactly what Carleen said. My father too."

"It's nice that you brought your father with you," Denis said. "I like that."

I smiled. "Pops has a few might have beens in his life."

"Who doesn't? It's like that old Indian story."

"What's that?"

"I'm sure you've heard it. There was a brave who went riding one day and his horse fell on top of him, breaking his leg. The next day, all the young braves in his tribe went to fight in a battle. The young Indian was despondent that his injury kept him from joining his brothers. But then all the braves were killed in battle. So the Indian's bad break turned out to be a blessing. Just wait. That may be true for you."

"Well, if it is," I said, "I wish the blessing part would reveal itself."

"Patience, woman," Denis said, smiling.

"So did you finish law school?" I said. "It's always good to know a lawyer on a cruise."

"Why, you planning on getting arrested?"

"*No-oh*," I said, maybe a little too defensively.

"Even if someone *was* arrested, I couldn't help them," Denis said. "Local laws apply. 'Course, the last place you want to end up in jail are the countries we're cruising, like Turkey."

"Really," I said, my voice cracking. "Why?"

"Remember *Midnight Express*, that guy who was caught trafficking drugs in Istanbul? They strip-searched him, hung him naked upside down, and beat him, tortured him. Their prisons are barbaric. That's based on a true story."

"Whoo boy," I sighed.

"*There* you are," a woman's voice squealed.

I glanced up to see Sydney clacking toward us on the marble floor in a pair of stilettos and teeny white shorts that framed her annoyingly jiggle-free legs. "I've been looking everywhere." As she walked, she pumped her five-pound weights up and down, sculpting those already ripped arms.

Syd pulled up a chair, leaned over, and gave Denis a kiss on the lips. She handed him a stack of "while you were out" messages that the butler had put under their door. "What happened with the lecture?"

"It ended early," Denis said.

"Oh, word around the ship is no one came," Sydney said.

"Yes, it's true," I said. "Denis here was my audience of one."

Sydney looked at him and then at me, pumping her five-pound weight more furiously. "Well, I don't care what anyone else says, the lectures you're giving don't sound as dull as dishwater to me. Excuse me, waiter." Sydney snapped her fingers twice and a young man appeared to take her order. "Can I have six almonds, roasted, no salt?"

"I appreciate your support," I said. "See you guys at dinner." I needed to find John to see if he'd been able to reach Jorge, the butler on the *Golden Goddess*. He'd promised to call him while I was giving my lecture. If we didn't locate those clothes, I would surely get arrested. Lord have mercy, if I end up getting hung upside down and tortured in a Turkish prison over those missing costumes, I will be so pissed off.

"I heard you're judging the hat-making contest this afternoon. That's very cute." Sydney laughed.

"Well, I am the resident fashion expert. Hope you guys'll enter."

"Sorry," Sydney said, cuddling closer to her fiancé. "We have *real* work to do. Then I think we'll settle in for a little . . . *skyrockets in flight . . . afternoon delight*," she sang.

Denis turned bright red and looked the other way.

"Toodles." Sydney wiggled her fingers at me.

BACK AT OUR SUITE, Pops was partying with Carleen and two elder floozies I hadn't met before. One was wearing a Burberry plaid life vest that had been personalized with her initials (another perpetual cruiser, no doubt), and the other, a yellow bikini under a see-through orange muumuu. John was serving cocktails and finger sandwiches.

"Holly," Pops said, "join us. We're celebrating."

"What are you celebrating?"

"Life," Carleen said. "Ain't it grand?"

"It's all too marvelous," the Burberry lady exclaimed.

"Here, here," they all said, clinking their glasses together. Famous chased her tail at the *ping*.

"Here, here," I offered with limp enthusiasm. "John, can I see you in the bedroom for a minute?"

I took a deep breath, then came clean with him about the missing trunk, explaining how I'd accidentally taken costumes worth millions so he'd understand just how dire the situation had become, and how my very life and freedom were now at stake. He said he had called the *Golden Goddess* three times already, but was having trouble reaching either Jorge or the man whose name I had taken off the luggage tags in Athens. Apparently everyone was touring Kusadasi. John vowed to do everything humanly possible to find those clothes and keep me from getting arrested in Turkey. If he didn't reach Jorge today, he wouldn't stop calling until he connected with him tomorrow when the *Golden Goddess* was at sea. I promised to give him a generous tip at the end of the cruise, assuming I wasn't arrested first.

The Way You Look Tonight

DINNER THAT NIGHT WAS formal. I wore one of Lucille's smashing confections—a floor-length, strapless, nude tulle that glittered with clear iridescent sequins. Carleen lent me a pair of Christian Lacroix sparkly stilettos that were slightly loose until John added some Dr. Scholl's gels, which tightened them right up. Shoe inserts—just one more reason why I love having a butler. Also courtesy of Carleen was a ten-karat Christian Tse platinum and diamond necklace with matching earrings. Personally, I always thought it would be tacky to wear diamonds before I turned forty, but I made an exception.

On the way to dinner, everyone posed for pictures. The women were swathed in chiffon gowns peppered with beads or crystals, the men in sleek designer tuxedos. Never in my life have I seen so many jaw-dropping gems in one place. Wait, I take that back. Once we held an exhibit of the Russian crown jewels at the Fashion Museum. There were some serious rocks in that show, let me tell you. The ladies of the *Tiffany Star* sported dazzlers in the same league—no doubt having raided their safe-deposit boxes before coming on board. The men wore cuff links of gold or platinum, set with rainbows of precious stones. You'd never guess these were the same fellows in Bermuda shorts with black dress socks and sandals, or lizard-skinned women in teeny bikinis all buttered up and frying by the pool this afternoon.

Even though I preferred not to have my picture taken, the ship's photographer insisted. "But I never take a good one."

"That's because you've never been photographed by me," he said. "Allow me to be the first to capture your dangerous beauty."

How could I refuse? No one had ever called my beauty dangerous before. I had my portrait taken alone, then with Pops, then with Pops, Carleen, and Famous. The Yorkie now sported pink highlights, after having spent the afternoon at the beauty salon.

Our meal that night was divine. For appetizers, there were escargots, beluga caviar, and wild mushroom torte. For dinner, we could choose between tenderloin beef, crab-stuffed artichoke, duck with cherry sauce, or lobster prepared any way you wanted.

Personally, I went with the duck and ordered chocolate puss for dessert.

"That's chocolate *puss*," the waiter said.

"Yes, that's what I want," I repeated. "The chocolate puss."

"No, *puss*," he insisted, pointing to my evening bag.

"Oh, purse." I giggled. "Sorry, the accent threw me off."

Denis and his crew sat across the table. Tonight he was more involved with his BlackBerry than his fiancée, although he did stop to teach Annie the proper way to eat her artichoke.

"Pull off the leaf like this and pull it between your teeth like so." He demonstrated.

"Like this?" Annie tried it, but put the pointed end in her mouth.

"No, the other way," Denis said. "Then put the leaves on this little plate."

Annie dipped her leaf in dressing, tried it again, and got it right. "Yummy, it's good. I'm eating my whole dinner with my hands tonight."

"No, that would be bad manners," Denis explained. "Only certain foods can be eaten—"

"Hello, I'm Captain Paul Roffe." A tall man with thick strawberry-blond hair, a matching beard, and twinkling green eyes introduced himself. "But you can call me Captain."

I shook his hand as he took the seat next to mine. He wore his formal dinner uniform, which was like a sea-themed tuxedo in white with a short jacket and lots of navy, red, and gold stripes. Captain called the sommelier over and ordered wine for the table, which is apparently the custom when you sit with Captain—free booze, whoo-hoo!

"So I understand you're a speaker on the ship," Captain said. "What is your topic?"

"Bread?" I said, offering him the basket.

Steam poured from the loaf as he tore off a piece.

"I did Hollywood Legends as Style Makers earlier, but no one came. I *was* planning to do The Life and Times of Coco Chanel and Audrey Hepburn as a Fashion Icon, but I don't know, the other programs on the ship are so exciting I may need to spice up my topic."

"How would you do that?"

"Well, I've been thinking about doing my next talk on the history of undergarments, maybe give everyone a pair of edible panties."

Captain turned bright red and spit out the bread he had just put in his mouth.

"Captain, are you all right?"

"Please, call me Paul," he said, coughing. "So, are you an expert on the subject?"

"It's one of many speeches I've written for the Fashion Museum. Everyone gets a kick out of it. 'Course, we don't give away edible panties, but I thought perhaps you could ask the chef to make some."

"Darlin', if you're giving out edible undies," Carleen said, "I'll be there and so will a lot more people besides me."

"If you're going, I'm going," Pops said.

"Me too," Lucille said, grinning and raising her hand from across the table. "That sounds *fabulous*."

"So what do you think, Captain—I mean Paul. Should I do it?"

"By all means," he said. "I may even come."

Ten waiters magically appeared at our table, all carrying covered plates on silver platters. The waiters positioned themselves behind each chair and then, in precise lockstep, whisked off the domed tops, set the plates on the table, and stepped back in perfect harmony.

One returned to say, "Be careful. Your plate is hot."

"That's not all that's hot at that seat," Captain said, touching my shoulder and saying, "Tssss."

"Oh, Captain—I mean Paul," I purred, "it's just edible undies."

AFTER DINNER, WE GATHERED in front of the maître d' station. Captain—*I mean Paul*—invited me to the Saloon for a nightcap. Pops asked Carleen and Lucille to twirl the night away with him in the Milky Way Ballroom. Even though Lucille used a walker, Carleen insinuated it was mostly for sympathy. Apparently she did a mean tango. Bunny and Aston were off to see the Irving Berlin Extravaganza with the almost-ready-for-off-Broadway cast.

Captain Paul and I made our way to the Saloon. Everyone stopped to try to shake his hand, but when they did, he handed them a card saying he didn't shake hands or make skin contact in the interest of not spreading germs. It was very sanitary of him. Being on the captain's arm made me feel special, like I was a ship celebrity.

We sat down and Captain Paul ordered champagne. When the karaoke hostess asked for volunteers, the woman next to us who had to be one hundred—I was sure I'd seen Willard Scott wishing her happy birthday on the *Today* show—raised her gnarly wrist, which was weighted down with oversize diamonds. Her husband pushed her wheelchair center stage. He was at least thirty years her junior.

Next thing we knew, they were showing the Celine Dion video from the movie *Titanic* and the words to "My Heart Will Go On" were skipping along the bottom of the screen. The old lady held the mike in her hand, and sung the most beautiful rendition of the song you can imagine, looking straight into her lover's eyes:

Every night in my dreams I see you, I feel you . . .

Everyone in the bar was enraptured by her performance. She was incredible. When it ended, we all stood to applaud her. You couldn't help but be inspired by the passion she had for her husband and her will to go on, even after she was worm bait and he was spending her fortune. I noticed Denis and Sydney in the corner. They were sending messages on their his-and-hers BlackBerries.

"You are such a talented singer," I told the old lady when she finished.

"I performed in musicals in the forties. If I hadn't married my first husband, I would have pursued a professional career," she said modestly.

"Are you sorry you didn't?"

"Goddamn right I am," she said. "That man was a bastard. I'd pee on his grave if I wasn't stuck in this fucking wheelchair."

Check please, I thought.

The hostess was trolling for someone else to sing. I turned my attention to the peanut bowl so as not to get called on.

At the table behind ours, a woman in a magnificent peach chiffon Dolce & Gabbana gown tapped Paul on the shoulder. "Captain, I was just wondering, does the help live on board the ship?"

"Oh, no, madam," he said. "Haven't you seen the smaller boat that sails behind the *Tiffany Star*? Those are staff quarters."

"Really?" she said.

Captain laughed. "No . . ."

I glanced over at Denis, who had set down his BlackBerry. His arm was around Sydney and he was whispering into her ear. She laughed and then buried her face in his throat. My cheeks went hot.

"You look beautiful tonight, Holly. May I show you the bridge?" Captain said. "It's very romantic."

"Sure, Paul," I said. "I'd love to see it."

Isn't It Romantic?

FOR A GERMOPHOBE WHO couldn't shake anyone's hand, Paul didn't hesitate to tickle my tonsils with his flickering tongue. I suppose, as the ship's captain and number-one Romeo, that was part of the job. He took me to the bridge, which is like the cockpit of the ship. Three junior officers, engrossed in beeping radar monitors and online maps, sat behind a long console. There were jumbo-size windshield wipers on the front windows and an enormous mahogany steering wheel just for show.

For privacy, we snuck out on Paul's balcony. The salt-tinged air was quite chilly. He gave me his jacket and put his arm around my shoulder to keep me warm. The sky was sprinkled with stars. The ocean was as black as ink, with the silver reflection of the almost-full moon touching the ever-changing ripples of gentle waves. Every once in a while, we could see dolphins jumping out of the sea. I felt like we were in a movie.

Paul handed me a pair of binoculars and pointed to a brightly lit cruise ship in the distance. Looking through the glasses, I saw the tiny heads of passengers bobbing along the deck. I remember reading once that more binoculars were sold in New York City than any other place in the world. With its tall buildings and windows in such close proximity, Manhattanites are natural snoops. We get our jollies peeping into other people's apartments and seeing how beautiful they are, how well proportioned, and finely maintained (the apartments, not the people). Now, where was I? Ah, yes, sizing up the ship across the moonlit sea.

A young officer knocked on the sliding-glass door and handed Paul a silver ice bucket with a bottle of Krug Clos du Mesnil and two crystal flutes. I had no illusions that Paul was interested in me for the long term, maybe just for this leg of his journey. He struck me as one of those "if you can't be with the one you love, honey, love the one you're with" kind of sea captains. But that was okay. After what I'd been through with Alessandro, it felt good to know that another man found me attractive, even if he wasn't going to stick around.

Paul poured us each a glass, which I downed quickly. He took me in his arms and looked into my eyes for what felt like an intimately long time, then lifted my chin and covered my forehead and my eyes, and my cheeks, and my lips, and my neck with little soft kisses. When he bit my earlobes, butterflies fluttered inside my stomach. Soon his lips found their way back to mine. They were soft and moist, really lovely and sensual. He put his tongue in my mouth and flirted gently with mine. I encouraged him with the bedroom moan I had perfected while faking orgasms for Alessandro.

Paul slowly unzipped the back of my gown and let the top slip down. I wasn't wearing a bra. He bent down and sucked my nipples, which made my stomach flip all over again. Then he kissed my lips, running his hands through my hair, his hardness pressed against my groin, whispering, "Holly, I want to worship at the altar of your naked body." It sounds hokey, I know, but it *really* turned me on. Maybe you had to be there—the sea, the stars, the moon—it was all so seductive. We were approaching the point of no return when someone rapped at the door. I pulled the top of my gown up and turned so our uninvited guest couldn't see that my dress was unzipped.

"Captain, sorry to disturb, but we have a passenger who is threatening suicide on Deck Nine," said an Indian man in a turban wearing a blue "Security" windbreaker.

Was this person insane? I wondered. *What kind of sick passenger would kill himself on this magnificent ship with its gourmet food, synchronized waiters, and impeccable service? Hello-oh! Enjoy the cruise and then put a bullet in your brain.*

"I'll be right there," Captain said as the guy closed the door.

Paul sighed and readjusted his crotch. "So sorry. Duty calls. We'll have to resume this later," he said, zipping me back up, and even hooking the eye. What a gentleman he was.

"Of course," I said, secretly relieved that we'd been interrupted.

SNEAKING INTO OUR PENTHOUSE, I was surprised to see every light on. It was after 1:30 A.M. and Pops was still out. Well, good for him, I thought. Maybe one of us got lucky tonight.

A few hours later, the ring of the phone jolted me awake. The cabin was pitch-black. The clock read 4:12 A.M.

"H-hello," I mumbled.

"Ship-to-shore call for Holly Ross," said a heavily accented operator.

"Fine, fine," I said. "Put it through." I sat up and unhooked my headgear.

"Holly, thank goodness you're there."

It was Nigel calling with what I hoped would be good news.

"I have more crap news for you," he said.

"Great," I muttered. "Now what?"

"The story is all over the papers. The *Post* has a front-page picture of you taken at the Hepburn opening with the headline 'Roman Holiday.' And the *News* has a picture of you from the Geisha Costume Exhibit with the headline 'How to Steal a Million.'"

"Oh, swell," I said. "You can't be serious. Please tell me you told Tanya what really happened and that we think Sammie is behind this?"

"But we have no evidence," Nigel said, deftly evading my question. "There's more. They interviewed Alessandro and . . ."

"No!"

"Yes, and both papers printed a picture of him holding up a pawn shop receipt. He said you'd most likely *fenced* the dresses just like you had the diamond engagement ring he gave you. They quoted him saying that you'd hocked everything you owned to go on vacation to get over the heartbreak of him dumping you, the daft prick."

"The lying liar," I said.

"Isn't he just," Nigel said. "Now they're checking every pawn shop in town for the dresses."

"So you didn't come clean, did you?"

There was silence on the other end of the phone.

"Did you?"

"No," Nigel whined. "You know I'm too cute to go to jail. They'd sell me to some big, hairy prisoner for a candy bar and a pack of fags."

"I thought *I* was worthless in the face of danger, but *you* win the prize."

"Please, Holly," Nigel begged. "I'm doing everything I can to sort this out without implicating myself. Have you found the trunk yet?"

"No," I mumbled.

"Buggers," he said. "Are you looking?"

"Of *course* I'm looking."

"Well, look harder."

"If it's where I hope it is, we may find it tomorrow."

"Brilliant," Nigel said. "Oh, one more thing. I think she's got it."

"Who? Got what?"

"Sammie. The million-dollar donation, the curator job," Nigel said.

"How? So fast? Are you sure? Who's the donor?"

"I don't know," he said. "It may just be a rumor. Let me do some digging."

I slammed down the phone. What was I supposed to do now?

Blue Skies

When I awoke the next morning, the ship was still and land was visible out the window. We had docked in Kusadasi. The light on my phone was blinking. There were two messages. John rang to say that he hadn't been able to connect with Jorge on the *Golden Goddess*, but not to worry. That ship was at sea today and he was sure to reach him eventually. Carleen phoned as well, inviting me to join her, Pops, and a few others on a private tour of the ancient city of Ephesus.

Dare I leave the ship? I wondered. I wasn't sure, so I decided to get dressed and see what was what.

Pops was just coming out of the bathroom. "Holly, would you mind giving me a touch-up?" He handed me his black Magic Marker and sat on the edge of my bed.

"What time did you get home?" I asked, streaking his white-gray hair with touches of black.

"A few minutes ago," he said. "Carleen invited me to spend the night and we had quite a time." He did the Groucho Marx eyebrow thing.

"Carleen? Are you kidding me?" I said, shaking the Magic Marker at him.

"Hey, be careful with that," Pops said.

"No, you be careful. You're an unemployed cabdriver. She's Carleen frickin' kazillionaire. You're reaching for the moon."

"Nope," he said with a wink. "The moon's reaching for me."

"Puh-leeze." I rolled my eyes. "And what about Lucille? You've been spending time with her too. What if she finds out you've been courting Carleen? She could get upset."

"We're on vacation. Do you know how long it's been since a woman, *any woman*, found me attractive? But with these fancy clothes, and on this ship, I'm a babe magnet. Let me enjoy the fantasy before I go back to my doggie pillows at Muttropolis, okay?"

"All right, but please don't get Lucille or Carleen mad at you," I warned. "Between them and Denis, *someone* has to write a million-dollar check to the museum. That's our ticket out of the doghouse." I filled him in on the missing trunk, how I had inadvertently been carrying *original* costumes and not copies, how I was in a hundred times more trouble than I thought, and how we needed the donation now more than ever.

Pops was shocked and appalled at the news and promised to be on his best behavior. "We're leaving at ten," he said, checking his watch. "Meet us at the bottom of the gangplank if you're coming."

I ate breakfast alone in the main dining room—scrambled eggs, hash browns, bacon, coffee. I was on red alert for any unusual activity, namely police on board, but everything felt normal. John was calling the *Golden Goddess* in search of my trunk. There was nothing more I could do, so I decided to chance the outing.

There were twenty or more gray vans waiting for passengers in the parking lot, all headed to Ephesus and Sirince, where the Virgin Mary was said to have lived out her final days. We, on the other hand, would be ferried in a white stretch Hummer with a driver and private tour guide, the ultra-elite in a sea of the merely privileged, thanks to our host and perpetual cruiser, Carleen Panthollow.

As soon as I arrived, we took off. Pops, Carleen, Lucille, Denis, Annie, and Sydney (who was absentmindedly pumping her pink weights and staring out the window), were on board. In the searing sunlight, the limo was hot and stifling.

Carleen fanned herself with her hand. "Can we get some air in here? I'm sweating like a whore in church on Sunday."

As a bead of sweat trickled down my temple, I was relieved by the whir of the air conditioner. "You have nice definition in your arm muscles," I said to Sydney.

"Yes, thank you, it's true," she said.

Good answer, I thought, noting it for future use in my own bag of quips. "So where's Manny?"

"At the pool," said Denis, as he tapped out an e-mail with his BlackBerry.

"Where *I* should be," Annie declared.

"You got that right," Sydney mumbled.

"I *heard* that," Annie whined. "Dad, did you hear what she said?"

"Annie, I'm just saying that there's more to life than swimming all day in a cruise ship pool."

"Like what?" Annie said. "Learning about *culture*?"

"No," Sydney said, "like swimming at the Hotel du Cap. Now *they* have a pool *worth* spending the day by."

"Well, I'm not there now and I won't be until Christmas, will I?" Annie said.

"Not a moment too soon," Sydney muttered.

"Da-ad," Annie whined.

"C'mon, you two," Denis said. "Can we declare peace just for today?"

"What about your mom?" I asked Sydney. "They didn't want to come?"

"Aston's indigestion was acting up," she said. "He wanted to take it easy."

"With the food on this ship, I'm not surprised," Pops said, patting the blubber pad that protected his Olympian abs.

"Where's the captain?" Denis asked. "You two seemed awfully chummy last night."

I was surprised that he had noticed, and pleased too. "Oh, we're just friends," I said. "I'm sure he's busy doing ship things."

"The two of you left the bar awfully suddenly," he pressed. "First you were there, then you were gone."

"I was trying to escape the karaoke hostess," I kidded.

Our tour guide cleared her throat to get everyone's attention and began talking about the lovely landscape of the countryside as we glided along the mountainous terrain toward our first stop. I couldn't imagine a more perfect day to make this drive. Never had I seen a sky so blue (except in allergy pill ads, and those are Photoshopped). Our guide told us about Ephesus, which is one of the best-preserved ancient cities of the Mediterranean, having been founded in the tenth century BC. It was second only to Pompeii as a preserved Roman civilization tourists can visit today. Until this trip, I'd never heard of the place.

We arrived at the upper gate, the highest point, where the religious and state ruins were located. The sun was sizzling and there wasn't even a sliver of a breeze. Our guide explained that as we hiked down the main street to a lower elevation—twelve thousand years of history beneath our sneakers—we would see the public facilities such as baths, the library, theater, and whorehouse. I guess prostitution really is the world's oldest profession.

Speaking of sneakers, luckily I'd worn mine. The streets were made of marble. Yes, you heard right—Ephesus was the Beverly Hills of ancient civilizations. But marble streets make for slippery walking conditions. Sydney was in six-inch platform sandals that were ill suited to the terrain. Didn't they teach her anything at Harvard? Denis held her by the shoulders while she clung to him like a blood-sucking tick. Seriously, who wears heels to visit an archeological site? I mean, really.

As we descended a few blocks, we saw remnants of a town that was easy to imagine in its glory. Columns of porticos still standing, parts of fountains adorned with statues of the gods and headless torsos, the Gate of Hercules with two crumbly columns showing the hero wrapped in lion skin.

I tried to imagine what the women of Ephesus wore: Grecian chitons, himations, and peplos, most likely. *Wouldn't it be fun to mount an exhibit of ancient drapery wear and the couture it inspired?* I thought. Poiret reintroduced draping in the early twentieth century, freeing women from corsets forever (or at least until they came back in style). The Greek costumes Chanel designed for Cocteau's adaptation of *Antigone* informed her collections for years. I'll bet we could get our hands on one of those. Let's see, the silk chiffon evening dresses from Dolce & Gabbana's 2003 collection would be a perfect modern addition. And just this last season, gladiator sandals returned with a vengeance—*yes, we could absolutely create a show with this theme*, I thought. *That is, if I still have a job after this*.

Wandering down the gently sloping path past the remains of the Temple of Ephesus, our guide pointed out what was left of the Baths of Scholastic, including its original mosaic floor. My personal favorites were the Library of Celsus and the latrine. The library was amazingly intact, with three stories visible in a horseshoe-shaped gallery. That's where scrolls and books were stored for literate citizens who were allowed to check out reading material.

The public latrine was amusing. It consisted of an enormous U-shaped marble bench with lines of holes where men of yore would sit side by side to do their business and discuss current events. Pipes with running water ran through the trough and the whole city—who knew! Wealthy men would send their fatter slaves ahead to sit on the marble benches and warm them up—the first known incidence of heated toilet seats.

"Someone get a picture of me," Pops said, sitting on one of the toilets, pantomiming that he was doing number two.

"Pops, *stop*," I said, embarrassed for him.

"Oh, me too, me too," Annie said, taking the hole next to his.

"Annie, don't be vile!" Sydney yelled.

"Nobody strain too hard," Denis said. "That's how King George the Second died."

"Do you see how information like that comes in handy?" I giggled.

"Take our picture!" Annie yelled.

"Okay, you guys, say 'stink,'" I said, capturing for posterity Pops, Annie, and Carleen on the ancient cans, a photo they were sure to cherish. Sydney refused to pose in such a lewd manner. I swore to her I wouldn't e-mail the photo to gawker.com, but I don't think she believed me.

You Make Me Feel So Young

After Ephesus, our guide encouraged us to skip the home of the Virgin Mary, which she said was a modest house (if you've seen one, you've seen them all), in favor of shopping for Turkish carpets where (I was sure) she would secretly collect a commission on any rugs our party purchased.

She took us to a government-sponsored school and shop set in a luscious green oasis, where young women were taught how to make the traditional designs using natural vegetable dyes and hand looms—an attempt to maintain the ancient art for which Turkey has long been known. While everyone else shopped, I took Annie outside to see how the silk for the rugs was made. A girl named Khanti, not much older than Annie herself, walked us through the whole cycle. First she showed us a bucket of live silkworms they had extracted from the mulberry trees. They wiggled about, some as fat as my ring finger. Then she let us hold the creamy white cocoons the silkworms had spun. Finally we were taken to a special loom, where the cocoons were carefully un-spun to preserve the silk from which they were made. Later the silk would be dyed, and hand knotted into the gorgeous, intricate patterns that make Persian carpets so irresistible.

"This is really cool," I said to Annie. "You should take pictures and do a report on it for school."

"Good idea," she said, snapping shots with her digital camera. "I have to think of something to write about." She went back to the bucket of worms and peeked inside. "Khanti, I'll give you ten bucks for a bag of these."

Khanti shrugged, grabbed a sack from beneath the loom, and filled it with live, wiggling worms.

"C'mon," Annie said. "Follow me."

My eyes narrowed with suspicion. "What are you doing?"

"This'll be so much fun." She giggled.

As I watched, Annie went into the car, opened Sydney's Prada canvas bag, and poured the worms inside, zipping it behind her, then changing her mind and unzipping it. "Worms need air," she explained, slamming the limo door shut. "Don't tell anyone I did it, okay?"

"Did what?"

"Watch me do cartwheels," Annie said.

I clapped while Annie executed three perfect cartwheels in a row.

"Now you watch me," I said, as I did a wobbly headstand. It had been years since I'd even tried one.

Annie tickled my nose with a live worm she had stashed in her pocket, causing me to collapse in a fit of laughter. I sat next to her on the grass.

"You're cool. You should marry my dad."

"I can't," I told her. "He's marrying Sydney."

"Yeah, the queen of the pig people." Annie pushed the tip of her nose up and snorted a few times.

"Tell me how you really feel."

"It's obvious," Annie said. "Dad's got a daughter complex. He doesn't see enough of me, so he has to marry a daughter substitute. That's what Mom says."

"Nah," I said. "I'll let you in on something. Men don't need daughter complexes to marry younger women. They do it because, well, it's a reluctance to grow old. A young woman gives a man the illusion that youth is still his."

"You think?" Annie said. "C'mon, let's tell them it's time to leave. I want to go swimming."

When we stepped inside the shop, a man was serving our companions hot apple tea in clear mugs. Lucille and Carleen had bargained for rugs they would have shipped home. Denis and Sydney were choosing between six intricate silk pieces of varying size, no doubt for their new love nest.

"Let's just take them all," Sydney said. "I'm sure we can find a place for them at one of our homes, or on the yacht, maybe the jet."

Denis shrugged and handed over his black American Express card.

I was amazed at how expensive they were, especially the multicolored silks. A bathmat-size rug cost about ten thousand dollars.

The leather seat burned my leg when we got into the limo.

"Can we get some air back here?" Carleen said. "I'm hotter than a popcorn fart."

Annie snickered at that expression.

As we drove, Carleen surprised Pops by telling him that she would be giving him the intricate silk rug she had purchased for forty thousand dollars.

Lucille gasped. "But *I* was going to give you the rug *I* bought for *fifty* thousand dollars," she said.

Oh, dear. It was one thing for Pops to take ten- and twenty-dollar tips from Muttropolis customers convinced *their* dogs were getting special treatment, but taking forty- and fifty-thousand-dollar rugs from these lovely women who believed Pops liked *them* best was playing with fire.

"Mom," Denis said, "isn't that awfully extravagant? You've only just met."

"It's *my* money," she said, "and I want Sven to have something special to remember me by."

"I don't know what to say," Pops said, blowing each woman a kiss. "Thank you. These will look wonderful in my home, and I'll think of both of you every time I sleep, er, step on them."

I wondered how easily dog poop stains came out of Persian rugs.

"Ah ah ah—ohmigod!" Sydney was screaming and flicking

her hand wildly. An errant silkworm went flying into Lucille's lap.

"Aaaaaaa!" Lucille shouted. "Get that off of me." She flung it toward Carleen, who ducked.

Sydney turned her purse upside down and shook the contents out on the floor. "Denis, there are *worms* in my bag." She took off her seat belt and bolted to the other side of the limo.

"You little fiend," Sydney said, pointing her finger in Annie's face. "You did this, didn't you?"

"Why would I do that?" Annie said. "Daddy, she's unfairly accusing me."

"Denis, punish her," Sydney cried.

The car was just pulling up to the dock. Perfect timing for my exit.

I jumped out, removing myself from the fracas taking place in the limo. To be safe, I ducked into a carpet store in the strip mall across from the ship. I wanted to be sure there were no police cars or suspicious officials lurking around, but I didn't see anything. It seemed safe to get on board. Then, as soon as I flashed my ID and slipped through the metal detector, two Filipino security guys asked me to come with them. Apparently, the cops were waiting for me in the captain's office. I was about to be busted in the worst place possible—Turkey.

High Hopes

My feet felt like they were encased in concrete loafers as I trailed the security guards to the Lido Deck. We lumbered past the pool toward the stairs leading to the bridge where Captain Paul had his office. There was a knot in the pit of my stomach and my mouth was as dry as a silk cocoon. As we trudged past the guests who were lazing by the pool, soaking in the Jacuzzi, drinking frozen margaritas, and dancing to "Hot, Hot, Hot" (could someone please teach this band another song?), I wished I could turn back time. Why had I borrowed those dresses? Here I was on the ship doing just fine without them. What made me think I'd magically inherit Audrey's grace or luck by wearing knockoffs of her gowns? They were fabric and buttons and beads, nothing more.

Please God, don't let them drag me to some *Midnight Express* jail. I could see it now. The cops would carry me off the ship kicking and flailing. The band would *finally* play a different tune: *Holl-y, Holl-y, whatcha gonna do, whatcha gonna do when they come for you?*

Captain Paul stood politely when I entered his office. He flashed a wide smile, which gave me hope. In front of his desk were two cops sitting in visitor chairs. "Ah, Miss Ross," Captain said. "There seems to be some sort of misunderstanding. These officers insist that you're traveling with stolen costumes from a museum. Do you know what they're talking about?"

Breathe, breathe, I told myself. *Act innocent*. "*What?* I have no idea!" My eyes widened in feigned disbelief.

One of the officers, short, dark skinned with a massive, hairy cheek mole opened a manila folder. In it were photographs of twelve Givenchy gowns from our exhibit. "These dresses have gone missing."

I studied his face (well, mostly his mole). God help me if I end up going to prison in this dermatologically backward country. Then, perusing the photos, I took my time before speaking. "They're from a show we did at work. What happened to them?"

The officer paused and mopped his brow with a kerchief. "They are stolen and we have information that links them to you," he said in broken English.

I resented the insinuation even thought it was true. Throwing the folder on Captain's desk, I said, "Why, that's ridiculous. Search my cabin. They're not there." My luck, John had successfully retrieved them while I was out touring.

"That's what we plan to do," the taller officer said. His English was a bit better.

I shrugged. "Fine," I said, looking at my watch. "But can you hurry? I have a massage at five."

As Captain, the security guys, and the Turkish cops accompanied me to my cabin, we passed Pops, Lucille, and Carleen, who were enjoying Bloody Marys by the pool. Bunny was reading a novel under a large umbrella, and Aston, wearing only a red Speedo, was dancing the Macarena with a band of other lively (and amazingly limber) octogenarians.

Pops stood. "Is everything okay?"

"Fine," I said, shooing him away. "I'll see you at dinner."

I felt a rush of fear as we arrived at the cabin. John was just leaving. My stomach lurched at the thought that the costumes might somehow be waiting for me inside. But when we entered the room, the only clothes in my closet were those I'd borrowed from Lucille. The policemen searched everywhere and found nothing incriminating.

"We would like to have you into Kusadasi for questions," the mole cop said, furrowing his eyebrows. There was a fine sheen of sweat on his face.

Captain Paul spoke up. "Absolutely not. She is an American passenger on my ship. I will not leave her in a foreign country when I am responsible for her safety."

"Then we will come back with the papers of authority," the mole cop threatened.

"You do that." Captain asked the ship's security guards to escort the policemen out, which they did.

I wondered, if a guy saves you from going to a vermin-infested prison where daily rapes, beatings, and upside-down hangings are a virtual certainty, are you obligated to sleep with him? It had been so long since I dated, I didn't know the rules anymore.

"You're safe now," Captain said kindly.

"Thanks," I said. "But what if they come back with papers? You won't abandon me, will you?"

"Don't worry," he said. "By the time they return, we'll be long gone. But you'd better not get off the ship in Istanbul. If they arrest you there, I can't help. Turkish prisons are a nightmare. Did you ever see *Midnight Express*?"

"Yes, years ago. Thanks, Paul," I said, giving him a hug. "You're my hero."

He blushed. "Just doing my job. So, I'll look for you tonight in the bar?"

"You betcha," I said, winking.

As soon as Paul left, John came back in. "Is the coastline clear?"

I sat on the edge of the bed and then collapsed like my legs were made of quivering Jell-O. "That was so close."

"Yes, but you are safe now," John said. "I spoke to Jorge on the *Golden Goddess*."

My heart pounded like a tom-tom drum at the news. "What did he say?"

"He has the trunk and the bag," John said. "His passenger's luggage key wouldn't open the lock. So they looked at the tags and realized the mistake."

An enormous weight whooshed off my shoulders. "Thank God."

"Jorge said he would check them at the ship terminal in Istanbul, but we'll have to hide the trunk when we bring it on board. An investigator has joined the cruise."

"What?" I sat back up.

"His name is Frank Flannagan and he's with Interpol. I saw a man boarding with his luggage this morning, which was unusual. When he left the ship to visit Kusadasi, I asked the maid who services his room about him. He told her he was an orthodontist, but she thinks that's a cover story and he is with the authorities."

"Why?" I asked. "Does Captain know?"

"Captain thinks he's a passenger who joined us late," John said. "It happens sometimes. But I am certain the maid is right, because he was seated at your table at his request. I checked with Bradley. How else would you explain that?"

"I don't know," I said.

"I'd be careful if I were you," John said. "Tomorrow I'm going to pick up the trunk in Istanbul and hide it on the ship. When we dock in Civitavecchia, I'll deliver it to the museum in case you're being followed."

"Where?" I asked.

"Roma, that's the port for Roma."

I shook my head. "No, I can't let you get involved. You could be arrested." But of course, I could and I would if he absolutely insisted.

"I want to help," John said. "Roma's my home. I know my way around. By the time the museum realizes what is in the trunk I've left, I'll be gone. This will end your troubles."

"I hope you're right," I said. "It sounds like a smart plan."

John made his little butler bow. "I am at your service," he said in a humble tone. Then he backed out of the room with the deference of a royal subject.

How could I ever pay him back? I wondered. And why was he being so nice? From my experience, at least at the museum, people didn't offer to help without some kind of personal agenda. I shook my head. I was one jaded New Yorker.

The Man Who Got Away

THE RING OF THE telephone startled me. *Great*, I thought, *probably more good news from Nigel, my worthless-in-the-face-of-danger colleague*. But no, it was Carleen. She was in tears.

"What is it? Is it Famous?" *Please don't tell me she went overboard*.

"N-no, it's not her," she said. "It's Aston. He h-had a heart attack."

"Oh, my God, is he okay?" I asked. This was awful. Aston was the only likable member of Sydney's family, probably because he wasn't related by blood.

"N-no, he died," she said. "He had a massive heart attack by the pool. I'm with Lucille. She's a wreck. Denis' wedding to Sydney means the world to her, and now, with Aston's death, well, they can't possibly hold the ceremony."

Whoo-hoo, I thought. But then I felt terrible. Aston was dead. And he was a sweetheart. "Where are you guys?"

"Medical, Room 217."

"I'm on my way." As Aston's tablemate, it was my duty to be there.

Hustling down to the bowels of the ship, scurrying along an endless hallway, I finally found the doctor's office. Rushing inside, I asked for Aston Martin's family and was led to a small room. There was poor Aston lying on a blue, plastic-covered examination table. He was still wearing his red Speedo. His face and remarkably hairy chest were extremely sunburned. So were his ears. Dermatologists always tell you not to forget to put sunblock on the ears and this was why.

Bunny was holding Aston's head next to hers and crying. Sydney stood across from her mother, her eyes swollen like little mice eyes from weeping. It was the first time I'd ever seen her look bad, which was good. Denis comforted her with his arm around her shoulder, which was bad. *Why do even I care?* I wondered.

"How will I go o-o-o-on?" Bunny wailed, her face red, mascara streaks running down her cheeks. "He was my world."

My thoughts were interrupted. Bunny looked stricken. "Remind me how long they were married?"

"Two years," Carleen whispered.

Bunny heard that. "Two glorious years," she said. "The best twenty-four months of my life. Why me? Why now?"

"My condolences," I said, touching her arm lightly.

There was a knock at the door and Pops charged in. "I came as soon as I heard," he said. "Oh, Bunny." He attached himself to her like a leech. She sobbed into his shoulder.

Lucille and Carleen gave each other a look, their eyes wide. Since when was Pops friends with Bunny? Was something going on between these two, or had she been ogling him from afar? I needed to have a serious talk with him.

Another knock and Captain Paul entered.

Bunny looked up, her face streaming with tears. "We lost him, Captain. The love of my life."

"I'm so very sorry," he said, almost touching her, but then stopping and giving her his handkerchief, along with the card that said he doesn't shake hands or make skin contact with passengers for sanitary reasons. "We'll take care of the arrangements when we get to Istanbul. Our concierge will handle everything, including your air tickets home. You mustn't worry."

"What?" Bunny said. "I have to leave?"

"Well, Mother, under the circumstances . . ." Sydney started.

Bunny blotted her tears with Captain's handkerchief and put on her icy doyenne face. "I refuse to abandon my daughter on the eve of her betrothal. You'll put Aston in the morgue. We'll give him a proper burial after the wedding."

"I really think we should postpone," Denis said.

"Right," Sydney said. "It would be bad luck to marry now."

"Nonsense," Bunny said. "My ancestors hark back to England. We carry on."

"I agree," Lucille added. "Aston wouldn't have wanted to ruin your big day."

"Mrs. Martin," Captain said, "I'm afraid the refrigeration in our morgue isn't working properly."

"Surely you jest," Bunny said. "With all these elderly passengers, I should think this would happen every week."

"Yes, it occurs regularly," Captain said. "But on our last cruise, the cooling unit broke and we had to order a special part. We're picking it up in Rome. Truthfully, though, we rarely need a morgue. Normally, we ship remains home immediately. No passenger has ever asked to stay."

"Well, *this* passenger is asking," Bunny said. "No, she's *demanding*. You'll put him on ice in the ship's freezer. You do have a freezer, don't you?"

"Of course, but I'm not sure that's hygieni—"

"Not another word," Bunny commanded. "The wedding will go on as planned. Please, Captain, send your crew down immediately to retrieve my darling's body."

Captain bowed like John the butler and backed out of the room.

The nurse entered to help put Aston in a body bag. Silently, we waited outside. Soon the captain and the doctor were rolling his bagged remains on a gurney toward the kitchen.

We all accompanied Aston toward his temporary resting freezer, with Bunny sobbing buckets along the way. Pops bolstered her up with his arm around her shoulder. When we pushed the body into the kitchen, all activity stopped, and everyone took off his chef hat or hairnet as a show of respect. Inside, we passed a sink, where a life-size mermaid ice sculpture was melting and would soon exist only in memory and photos, just like Aston.

Captain spoke quietly to Donald, the manager (it said so on his name tag).

"Excuse me, Mrs. Martin," Captain said, "but would you mind if we store . . . er . . . place your husband's remains in the ice cream freezer? Donald feels he'd have more privacy there."

"What other accommodations are available?" Bunny asked.

"We have separate freezers for chicken, meat, and vegetables as well."

Bunny made a brave face. "Captain, I believe my Aston would have preferred the company of meat."

"Yes, I would agree," Lucille said. "He was very masculine."

"As you wish," Captain said.

Donald led our party into a walk-in freezer that was bigger than my cabin. He and the captain emptied a shelf of roasts, steaks, pork loins, legs of lamb, and other hunks of dead flesh. Donald, Captain, and some kitchen hands gently lifted Aston off the gurney and laid him in the shelf above the calves liver and beneath the veal cutlets.

"We'll clear this whole area of food as soon as you leave," Donald promised, "and put up a plastic curtain to give him privacy."

I didn't want to be the one to say it, but hello-oh! Wasn't this some kind of health code violation? Even if it wasn't, it couldn't be sanitary to store human remains with tonight's dinner. I was surprised that Captain didn't refuse, what with his no hand shaking policy and all.

"Shall I get a rabbi or priest?" Captain said. "Maybe someone should say a few words."

Bunny held up her hand as if to say stop. "Captain, please, let's not sully this man's memory by holding a religious service for him in the same place you store frankfurters."

"Forgive my insensitivity," Captain said.

Bunny knelt by his body and stroked the bag. "Aston was so looking forward to being in Istanbul. He's never been, you know. At least now his body will get there," she said bravely. "Come, let's prepare for dinner. Aston's death shall not cast a pall on our celebration of Sydney and Denis' nuptials."

Denis had an uneasy expression on his face. He was thinking, would Sydney continue *her* vacation if *I* died? At least, that was my interpretation. I *wouldn't go on with* my *vacation*, I thought. *I'd bury you right away, Denis, I promise.*

Captain stood at attention as we exited the freezer. When I passed him, I felt a distinct pinch on my bottom. Turning, I caught his eye, and he winked at me. *Has this man no shame?* I thought. *One of his passengers is dead and has been on ice for, what, two minutes, and he's already hitting on me. Oh, what the hell. I blew him a kiss.*

Tea for Two

THAT NIGHT, BEFORE DINNER, I asked Carleen to meet me for tea in the dimly illuminated Crystal Cove. The Tiffany Line, in an act of pure genius, lit its rooms with special pink-tinted bulbs that made anyone appearing in their soft glow look ten years younger—instant face-lift! Naturally, they sold the bulbs in the gift shop. That's what I love about the Tiffany Line. No detail is too small.

Carleen was on time, wearing a vintage black chiffon Poiret

with a skirt depicting the jungle designs of Henri Rousseau in white pearls, seed beads, rhinestones, and silk embroidery. It was the kind of important piece I would love to showcase in our museum if I didn't get fired. The Met had already done a Poiret exhibit, but we could show it as part of a different theme, maybe designers inspired by art of the twentieth century. If we did it in conjunction with MoMA, we could exhibit paintings right next to the dresses they inspired. Just last fall, I recalled, Marc Jacobs showed his line in Bloomingdale's windows with Jean Claude Wouters' photographs hung behind the mannequins. Yes, this was an idea with legs. But back to the business at hand—enlisting Carleen's help in getting the fuzz off my back.

"Carleen, you are chic, chic, chic," I marveled.

"Thanks, darlin'. Priceless gowns become me."

I leaned into her. "I have something *really* important to tell you," I whispered. "But it's a secret."

"You're a lesbian! I knew it."

"No, that's not it," I said. "Why would you say that?"

"Your short haircut."

I sighed. "Carleen, seriously, this is very important and you have to swear not to tell anyone. If you do, I could end up in big trouble, jail even."

A soft gasp escaped her lips. "Then, darlin', don't tell me," she said. "I can't be trusted. I'll forget and blurt it out at dinner or write about it in my memoirs."

"Carleen, please, I need your help."

She raised her hand and snapped her fingers twice. "Waiter, drinks."

"You don't want tea?" I said.

"I'll take something stronger."

I lowered my voice and leaned forward, explaining that there would be a new man at our table who was investigating me for a crime I didn't commit (it's true—I was hand delivering those costumes, not stealing them, and they were supposed to be knockoffs, not originals). I asked Carleen to get to know him and to distract him from watching me. "Do you think you can do that?"

"Holly, I may be old, but I'm not dead. Of course I can."

"I knew I could count on you. His name is Frank Flannagan. He claims to be an orthodontist, but he's really with Interpol."

"Interpol," Carleen said. "Sounds like James Bond."

A waiter in a tux offered us antipasti from a silver tray. I took a piece of shrimp wrapped in prosciutto.

"Flannagan's cute for a cop," I said. "My butler pointed him out before you came. Looks about sixty, olive skin, deep brown eyes, very dark hair—in fact, he seems hairy all over."

"Mmm, I like 'em hairy," Carleen mused. "Aston had the hairiest chest. Did you notice that when he was lying in state? Why is it always the hairy ones who die young?"

"Carleen, his heart gave out."

"Yes, darlin', but I read in *USA Today* that hairy men die earlier than their bald counterparts. It's because of progesterone."

The waiter came by and brought us each a glass of wine. We didn't specify what we wanted. The ship kept track of each passenger's preferences and served them before we even asked. Talk about service that delights and astonishes.

"To Aston," I said, clinking my glass with Carleen's. "A good man, a hairy man."

◆ ◆ ◆

OUR CELEBRITY CHEF, ENRICO Derflingher, prepared that night's feast. Naturally, the Tiffany Line spared no expense, flying in ten members of his staff to join the ship in Athens. The dining room had been transformed to resemble a romantic Italian palazzo illuminated by thousands of tall flickering candles, casting a mellow golden glow. We started with risotto served *alla pescatore* (with seafood), followed by fillet of turbot, lobster, or lamb. (I went with medium-rare leg of lamb, hoping it had been taken out of the freezer before Aston was interred.) Dessert was a mascarpone cheese tart with fresh whipped cream. It wasn't chocolate, but it was tasty. In deference to Aston's passing, Captain joined us even though it wasn't technically a formal night. Plus let's face it; no one wants to miss a meal prepared by Chef Derflingher. As was the custom, Captain sprang for the booze. *Whoo-hoo!*

Later, as we were meandering over to the Saloon, I sidled up to our newest tablemate. "Excuse me, Frank. I'm wondering if you can help me with something."

"Of course," he said.

I whipped my headgear out of my bag. "Do you know what this is?"

"Sure, it's a headgear."

"Yes, well, it got bent and I'm wondering if you could adjust it for me."

"Gee, I didn't bring my tools with me," Frank said. His left eyelid twitched as he spoke.

I *knew* it, I thought. First he called it a headgear instead of by its professional term, appliance. Then he came up with a likely excuse as to why he couldn't fix it. And then he called his instruments his "tools." Last but not least, his eyelid twitched when he lied. This man was no orthodontist. I would have to tread carefully around him.

We all gathered in the Saloon. Pops and Lucille brought Bunny, who was dressed in full widow's weeds (veil included). I wondered whether she traveled with funeral attire or bought it in the gift shop. With so many old passengers, they'd have to carry mourning clothes in the store. In fact, I think I recalled seeing them near the granny panties. Pops was plying her with gin so she was feeling no pain.

That gave me an idea. Why not hold an exhibit of widows' weeds through the ages! That would be fun. Well, maybe "fun" is not the operative term. We could show the dress Jackie donned at JFK's funeral, the outfit Audrey Hepburn (as Reggie Lampert) wore at her husband's viewing in *Charade*, the hoop-skirted widow's weeds Scarlett O'Hara donned as she danced with Rhett Butler, and . . . well, there have to be other famous mourning dresses we could feature. But I'll think about it tomorrow, I decided.

In front of the bar, two passengers were rolling out the Persian rugs they'd bought in Kusadasi, asking people what they thought of them, showing them from both sides so they could demonstrate how the colors went from light to dark depending on where you stood, telling anyone who would listen what they cost. I thought that was tacky, but the guests acted interested. By the time we finished our second round of drinks, the piano player ended his last set. So Pops approached the ivories and stopped the room with his music. Some of the songs were old favorites, others he improvised, blowing everyone away with his talent. I was awfully proud of him.

"Play 'Our Love Is Here to Stay,'" Bunny slurred. "It was our song."

Pops lifted his glass of whiskey. "To Aston and Bunny," he toasted.

It's very clear, our love is here to stay . . .

Captain joined our table and bought yet another round of drinks. It felt good that he wanted to be with me. He was the ship's Sting and I was his Trudie Styler, basking in the glow of his celebrity. I looked around the bar for Denis, hoping he'd see me with the captain, but he wasn't there. "Where's your son?" I asked Lucille.

"Oh, he took Annie to the outdoor movie tonight," she said. "Sydney didn't want to go. Something about those silly worms." She gestured with her head toward Sydney, who was at the back of the bar whispering into Manny's ear, a drink in one hand, a pink five-pound weight in the other.

"I thought you liked her," I said under my breath, lest Bunny hear.

Lucille hiccupped. "Excuse me," she whispered. "Don't get me wrong. The dynasty that will be created with this marriage will be fabulous, *fabulous*! My husband would have been proud of what I've engineered. I just wish the girl were more mature and less tiresome. I don't think she likes kids, and they'll have to produce an heir. Seeing how she is with Annie, I'm not sure what kind of mother she'll be."

"If she fails, they can always breed poodles," I joked.

"Excuse us," Frank said. "We're going to the bar by the pool."

Carleen gave me the thumbs-up signal as she followed Frank out the door. I could relax. The cop was off my tail.

How Long Has This Been Going On?

During Pops' second set, Bunny lay her head down on the table and simply deflated. When he and Lucille tried to rouse her, she mumbled something about throwing herself off the balcony and into the ocean. "Come," Pops said, helping her up. "You can use some fresh air and I could use a smoke."

"Good idea," Captain said to me. "How about a walk? There's nothing like sea air right before a storm."

"Did you say storm?" I said. "Do I need Dramamine?"

Captain laughed. "It'll be mild and gone by the morning. You'll sleep through most of it."

Lights from a town on the distant shore twinkled dimly. Captain took my hand and we strolled the Lido Deck, where I noticed we were having trouble walking straight. It was the weather, not the alcohol. "I should hire your father to perform on the ship," he said. "He's fantastic."

"Yes, he's a wonderful musician," I said. "I'm sure he'd say yes if you offered him a job. What's that noise?"

Captain pointed to the stairs leading to the Platinum Deck. "They're showing *An Affair to Remember* on the outdoor screen."

"That's one of my all-time favorites," I said. "Whoa." Captain caught me as I momentarily tipped sideways.

As we rounded the bow of the ship, which was swaying and rolling just enough to make me feel nauseous, we heard the moans and groans of a couple going at it in a secluded area where the chaise lounges were stored at night. Captain put on his official face and cleared his throat. "Excuse me," he said. "You'll have to take that inside."

"Oh, puh-lease," the woman said. "Mind your business." She threw something at him.

He jumped out of the way, but not before a loud *whump* sounded. "Yeow!" Captain shouted. "My toe!"

"I'm singin' in the rain, just singin' in the rain . . ." voices sang out.

I looked over. There was Pops linking arms with Lucille, Bunny, Carleen, and Frank Flannagan, just like Dorothy and her motley crew as they made their way to Oz. Only Pops and his pals were tipsy, tripping and laughing, stumbling as they sang—that is, until they ran into us.

"Captain, are you all right?" Pops said. "Did you fall?"

"No, I did not fall," Captain said, limping over to retrieve a pink, jewel-encrusted five-pound weight. "Someone threw *this* at me." Captain hopped on one foot to the dark corner and switched on a light. Oops. There were Sydney and Manny in all their natural glory.

"Hhhhuuuuuh!" Lucille gasped, her eyes boinging from their sockets.

I couldn't believe it. This was no random act of sex we had stumbled upon. *Au contraire*, it was Sydney, and she'd been caught in flagrante delicto by her future mother-in-law. Sodom and Gomorrah on the Lido Deck. Yikes! Let the fireworks begin!

Sydney tried to cover herself, but what could she do with two hands and three private parts. It was impossible not to stare at her *nuda* (that's Italian for naked) bits. I'm talking boiled-chicken naked, not a pube on her vajayjay. Her full, round breasts defied gravity. She obviously worked her tushy off to achieve that level of perfection. Sydney was a Greek goddess, a Girl Next Door, and a Victoria's Secret model all rolled into one. Seeing Sydney Bass and her perfect ass(ets) helped me understand why men who had everything always wanted one of those for their very own.

"Promise you won't tell Denis," Sydney begged Lucille. "He'll call off the wedding. You don't want that."

Tee-hee, I laughed (on the inside).

"What's wrong with you?" Bunny said, sounding surprisingly lucid considering how liquored up she was. "You don't fool around until you have a ring on your finger. How many times have I told you that?"

"I have to say something," Carleen said.

"Don't," Lucille admonished. "This is *our* family business."

"That's what I mean, it's *business*," Carleen said. "The boy should marry for love."

"A union with infidelity can never work," I declared.

"Holly, hush," Pops said. "Just because that was true for you doesn't mean it's true for everyone. C'mon, let's give the lovers their privacy." He gathered up his posse and moved them along. *I'm singin' in the rain, just singin' in the rain . . .*" The group skipped off with Lucille looking back nervously.

"Goddamn you, Manny," Sydney said, retrieving her clothes, which were scattered about. "This is all your fault. Where's my BlackBerry? I can't find my BlackBerry."

"You're the one who likes to do it in public places," Manny whined.

Captain sat on a deck chair and rubbed his foot. "I think you broke my toe."

"Well, I'm sorry about that. If I'd known it was you, I wouldn't have thrown it," Sydney said. "Holly, you'll cover for me if Lucille says anything, right?"

I gaped at Sydney and thought, *Why would I want to help you? Why?* But as I prided myself on not being impolite, I didn't say that.

"Will you?" she pressed.

"You want me to lie for you?" I said. "Tell me, do you love him?"

"Who? Manny?"

"No. *Denis*," I said.

Sydney rolled her eyes. "Why would you ask me such a ridiculous question?"

Thank you. I had my answer.

THAT NIGHT, I BARELY slept as the "little" storm Captain predicted raged, raged, raged against the dying of the night. The wind howled and the ship pitched and groaned like it was about to break in half. One of the tenders that hadn't been tightly secured banged against the hull—*boom, boom, boom*. I peeked out the window and watched the lighting make the sea appear and disappear in gray ghostly flashes. Little storm? I think not. Oh, how I wished I'd never seen the remake of *The Poseidon Adventure*. I kept imagining a rogue wave whooshing out of nowhere and swamping the ship. Why hadn't I mustered for the safety drill? Why? Of course, if we were to find ourselves capsized and upside down, it would be impossible for me to swim to safety, not with my terrible sense of direction. It felt like the night that wouldn't end. Eventually, I must have passed out because next thing I knew, the sun was sifting through the part in my curtains and the ship had docked in Istanbul.

Just in Time

SINCE I WAS EXHAUSTED (and in deference to the *Midnight Express* prison), I turned over and went back to sleep. Sadly, I would miss the spice market, the grand bazaar, the Blue Mosque, and the Topkapi Palace, all of which I had been looking forward to seeing. I would just have to read about them in Fodor's and pretend I'd actually visited for my friends back home if they asked. Could I be any sorrier about borrowing those Audrey costumes? Losing them was ten times worse than losing Alessandro, which, by the way, didn't seem quite so *tragique* anymore.

A knock on my door interrupted my drowsy contemplation.

"Just a minute," I said, thinking I must have forgotten to put out the Do not Disturb sign. Donning the luscious Frette bathrobe that came with the suite, I opened the door.

"May I come in?" John looked both ways.

"Of course," I said, pointing toward my balcony. I slid open the glass door, stepped outside, and gestured for John to sit in one of my teak chairs.

"I have the trunk and your suitcase," he said under his breath.

"Hhhhhh," I gasped. "Already?" I said. "What time is it?"

"It is after ten o'clock. I retrieved them as soon as we docked. The trunk, it is hidden away in the ship where no one will find it. You needn't give it another thought," he said. "The bellman will bring your suitcase within the hour."

A feeling of such enormous relief swept over me that I practically swooned. "Thank you," I said, hugging him. "You have no idea how worried I was."

"No, I could see you were concerned, but now you must relax and enjoy the rest of your trip," he said. "I will deliver the trunk in Roma. Tell me, which museum is hosting the exhibit?"

"It's the Istituto di Moda," I said. "That's in the Galleria Borghese."

"I know it well."

"Wait," I said, "don't you think we should inspect the trunk, make sure nothing's missing?"

"I don't believe it's necessary," John said. "Jorge said they realized the mistake when his passenger's key wouldn't open the lock. Nothing has been touched."

I sighed with relief. "Let me pay you something extra for all your trouble," I said, stepping inside to get my wallet out of the safe.

"No, no, no," John said, shaking his finger as though insulted. "Pleasing you is what pleases me."

"Well, you're my hero," I said. "You have delighted and astonished me."

As soon as John left, I remembered that my bras and panties had been thrown in the trunk at the last minute. I wondered, would it be too much to ask him to get those for me so I could be liberated from the underpants-for-two I'd been wearing? I decided to leave well enough alone. Surely I could pick up new panties in Santorini, our next port.

I celebrated the safe return of the Audrey costumes with a Pilates class, followed by a Lomi Lomi massage and then an antiaging facial (where they dipped my hands and feet in paraffin just for good measure). The spa was practically empty, since most people were touring Istanbul.

After lunch, I went to see the Whirling Dervishes of Rumi, who were performing on board for the passengers who hadn't gotten off the ship. For some odd reason, I had always thought whirling dervishes were twirling birds. But no, they were men who took vows of poverty and danced as a way of worshipping God. Wearing dramatic, flowy white robes and tall black hats, they raised their arms, with one palm facing heaven, one facing earth, and spun counterclockwise so fast and furiously that you couldn't believe they didn't fall over when they were done, and yet they did not. The costumes were beautiful and the music hypnotic, but I finally left because I was feeling dizzy. As I exited the theater, I caught Frank Flannagan's eye and he smiled. What was *he* doing here? Why wasn't he touring with everyone else?

I spent the rest of the afternoon lolling by the pool in the sizzling heat enjoying Annie, the lone swimmer. She was going down the slide over and over again, laughing and giggling with delight each time. It looked like so much fun that I finally joined her. It was a saltwater pool, which the facialist told me was great for the skin.

After a cool dip, I returned to the chaise lounge, from where I could see that Manny was drinking a Bloody Mary across the pool. I gave him a friendly wave, but he avoided my gaze. Thinking about him and Sydney last night, I wondered why smart, educated people behave like guests on *The Jerry Springer Show*. Here Sydney had this great fiancé and amazing future ahead of her and she risked it all for what? Manny the manny. Not that there's anything wrong with being a manny. It's as respectable as being an airline steward or a male nurse. But Denis King is a five-star catch. I've done some pretty dumb things in my life, but playing with the affections of a man as attractive as Denis was something I would never do.

"May I sit?"

I looked up, using my hand to block the sun. There was Denis dressed for a day at the office.

"Of course," I said.

"Da-deee!" Annie yelled, jumping into his lap, thoroughly soaking him with salt water. "Ha-ha, I got your suit all wet."

Denis laughed. "That's all right. It's drip-dry."

"Daddy, will you swim with me?"

"Sure," he said, "but you have to run back to the cabin and get my trunks. Here, take the key."

"Why're you so dressed up?" I asked, as Annie skipped off.

"Sydney and I went to Athens today. Her family owns a ten-acre parcel downtown that I'm going to develop. We met with some government ministers."

"How synergistic," I muttered, as the horn from the ship sounded. From below, the vague thrumming of engines could be felt.

"What?"

"Nothing," I said. "So you didn't get to tour Istanbul?"

"Not this time," he said. "We'll have to come back."

The ship started to move and the voice of Louis Armstrong came over the loudspeaker.

I see trees of green . . . red roses too . . .

They always played "It's a Wonderful World" when we pulled out of a port. It was a lovely ship tradition.

"How'd you get to Athens?"

"My jet. I keep it close by in case I need to get somewhere fast."

"That's handy," I said.

"Waiter," Denis said. "Would you like something to drink?"

"Lemonade, thanks," I said.

"Two lemonades," he said.

"Did you enjoy Istanbul?" Denis asked.

"Loved it," I lied. "Especially the Topkapi Palace."

"Here, Dad," Annie said, holding up a blue swimsuit.

"I'll go change," Denis said, standing. "Want to join us?"

"Sure. But where's Sydney? Doesn't she like to swim?"

"She's having a massage. The negotiations in Athens left her all tense."

That and the fact that seven people saw her screwing Manny the manny last night, I thought.

Peel Me a Grape

On reading that evening's *Tiffany Tattler*, I saw that the competition would be fierce among tomorrow's eleven o'clock activities. Besides attending my provocatively titled lecture, A Peek Inside Panties from Past to Present, passengers could partake in a talent show, cha-cha lessons, a Chagall auction, outdoor yoga, a lecture on Santorini and the Legend of Atlantis, a submarine ride (limit ten), and a cooking class with Enrico Derflingher. I realized I needed to hustle to avoid a repeat of my ill-attended first talk.

In the computer room, the Apple expert slash deckhand slash waiter helped me create a flyer advertising my program. I thought I'd post them throughout the ship, but that seemed lame. I decided to chuck the flyers and make a more dramatic appeal that night.

As passengers enjoyed their dinner, I arrived in the kitchen wearing nothing but my Frette robe. In the rear of the stainless-steel series of rooms, pastry chef Guy Saint Martin gestured for me to make myself comfortable on a silver platter the size of a bathmat. Shedding the robe, I lay on the cold tray, positioning my nude self on its side in as voluptuous a pose as I could.

"Fold your knee over your crotch," Guy said. "Our dining room is rated G." With the precision and artistry for which he was widely admired, Guy painted my body with a coat of dark Godiva chocolate in the shape of a sexy corset. The chocolate was warm as he slathered it on and the scent was sweet and rich. The spatula tickled as he applied a thick coat.

"Can you add extra to my breasts?" I asked.

"Ah, so you are modest," Guy said.

"No, I always wanted bigger breasts."

"Of course, madam. Consider it done."

I loved the way they were so customer-service oriented on this ship.

Guy decorated my edible underpinnings with marzipan lace, pink and red roses made from sugar frosting, thin stripes of icing applied in artistic swirls, and strategically placed swathes of fresh whipped cream. He drew chocolate fishnet stockings on my legs and for the final touch, filled the empty parts of the tray with piles of freshly cut strawberries and bananas. After inserting a single peeled grape into my navel, Guy dusted his creation with powdered sugar. Two waiters carefully lowered a vast silver cover over me.

I couldn't stop giggling when I felt the tray being lifted by the four waiters assigned to carry me to the dining room. As the platter moved through the kitchen doors and into the dining room, my heart pounded madly. It was pitch-black and stuffy inside the serving dish.

The tray came to a halt and was placed on top of a table. I heard the muffled voice of Chef Saint Martin saying, "Ladies and gentlemen, tonight we bring you a very special dessert made possible for your dining pleasure by the lovely Holly Ross, who will be lecturing tomorrow morning at eleven in the Galaxy Lounge. Her talk is called A Peek Inside Panties from Past to Present. She invites you all to attend. But tonight she wished to give *you* a peek at what you would see should you decide to join her. And voilà!" The cover was whisked off and there I was in my naughty chocolate corset glory.

There were gasps and shrieks and giggles and half-open mouths all around. Four waiters lifted the tray and paraded me through the dining room so that everyone could take a closer look or a photograph.

After visiting all the passengers, I was placed on top of a table in the center of the room. The chef spoke. "And now, my dear friends, you are all invited to partake in Holly's delectable unmentionable confection." Every man in the room (including Denis) made a beeline toward me, lining up to dip a strawberry or banana or bare finger in my corset. A few curious women even joined the fray and asked if the tasty undergarment was sold in the gift shop.

"So, will I see you tomorrow?" I'd purr, as each guest partook in the thick, rich sweetness slathered over my body. Every single person said "yes" (married people did too). Surrounded by so many chocolate lovers dipping fruit into my corset until little was left but my sticky bare skin, I felt like a star. Tonight, *I* was the Sting of the *Tiffany Star*! And I didn't even need a Trudie Styler. The entire ship had fallen under my spell. It was a new and heady feeling, one I enjoyed shamelessly and desired to feel again.

Puttin' on the Ritz

The next day we were at sea, and what a breathtaking day it was. As far as the eye could take in, there was nothing but ocean, miles and miles of azure water that melted into the crisp cobalt-blue sky. Every once in a while, a school of flying fish could be seen swimming along with us.

As eleven approached, the ship was buzzing with activities. By popular demand, my talk had to be moved to the Emerald Auditorium, the largest lecture space on the ship. It seemed that everyone, even those who hadn't attended dinner last night, had heard about my bold stunt. Gossip travels through this ship faster than a gastrointestinal virus. There was not a soul on board who didn't want to know what I would do next.

Naturally, I could not disappoint them. As I made my entrance, the crowd giggled and hooted. I took the mic and gestured to my costume, a pair of the giant silk underpants pulled all the way up to cover my breasts. "Like my bloomers? Cute, huh? Can you believe these are the only panties they sell on this ship? It's true. Frankly, ladies, I think this calls for a mutiny. Wouldn't you rather go commando than wear these?" As I stripped off the underwear and tossed them aside, the audience gasped.

Beneath the clown underpants, I revealed my secret weapon. Assistant Chef Dubois had picked up some large fresh fig leaves at the spice market in Istanbul, which I had sewn into a pair of G-string panties and a bra. Being as skinny and daintily proportioned as I was, it didn't take much to cover my girly bits.

"In spite of last night, let me assure you, I'm *not* an exhibitionist," I explained. "No, this is an example of the first pair of underwear ever created, straight from the Garden of Eden." Never in the history of the Tiffany Cruise Line had a lecturer presented to so packed an audience wearing so little clothing (the speaker, not the audience). It was a pivotal moment in the life and times of Holly Ross.

At my request, Assistant Chef Dubois had created two hundred pairs of mouth-watering panties by sculpting pink and blue cotton candy into the shape of bowls and punching out leg holes. The pants were so thick that they resembled edible adult diapers, but that made them all the more attractive to this crowd. Pops had two pairs in his hands and Carleen had three. I didn't want to think about how they would put them to use. The important thing was, the talk was standing-room only. Even Captain Paul came for a while. Denis accompanied Lucille. Sydney wasn't there, probably honing her heinie at the gym.

The audience was surprised by my deep knowledge of all things panty. For example, I asked them, "Did you know there is evidence of underpants existing over five thousand years ago in Egypt?" It's true.

"But even before that," I explained, "a frozen body of a man from 5300 BC was found in the Tyrolean Alps and he was wearing an animal-skin loincloth." The visuals from my laptop accompanied the presentation, although most of the old codgers stared unapologetically at my fig-leaf bra and panties, no doubt hoping they would fall off.

"In early Rome, Egypt, and Greece, the lower you were on the social strata, the less you wore under your clothes," I explained. "So your slaves usually went commando, while your kings might wear as many as twelve undergarments. In 1352 BC, King Tut, being at the top of the social pyramid—get it, *pyramid*," I said, inspiring a few polite coughs, "was buried with one hundred and forty-five pairs of underpants for the afterlife."

"My wife brought more than that for the world cruise," a heckler yelled. I laughed to show how good-natured I was.

The audience was intrigued to learn that in Victorian times, open-crotched bloomers were de rigueur (for hygiene purposes, naturally). The style came to an abrupt end after Parisian cancan dancers wore them in the cabaret. One octogenarian even claimed to remember that, and I played along. I discussed the freeballer movement, dedicated to protecting the rights of people who dare to wear nothing but air. The women oohed and ahed and the men sat slack-jawed as I showed my slides of today's lingerie, from frumpy to latex to thongs to G-strings to fetish undergarments to nasty va-va-voom designs.

"What about men?" a shriveled woman with liver-spotted skin shouted. "Got something to turn on us ladies?"

"I believe I do," I said, cutting to a photograph of a bare-chested Clark Gable with Claudette Colbert in *It Happened One Night*. "When Gable took his shirt off in this scene and he was bare-chested, men across America decided, 'Well, if Clark Gable doesn't have to wear an undershirt, neither do I!' Sales of men's undershirts dropped seventy-five percent after that. Of course, later, when James Dean was photographed wearing a cotton undershirt in *Rebel Without a Cause*, sales zoomed back up. It's really quite astounding how underwear fashion in the movies impacts what people wear in real life."

Hmm, that would make a great theme for a show at the museum, I thought. We could get Elizabeth Taylor's silk and lace slip from *Cat on a Hot Tin Roof*, Mae West's sequined corset from *Diamond Lil*, and Madonna's Jean Paul Gaultier–designed corselet with cone-shaped cups that started the underwear as outerwear trend. This was an excellent idea, one I would definitely propose when I returned to work. With the original Hepburn costumes safely on board, my future at the museum seemed secure.

After my titillating talk, the audience rewarded me with a shower of applause and a standing (yes, standing!) ovation. I could see Pops telling everyone who would listen that I was his daughter. Then my adoring fans clamored for a piece of me, saying I had given the best speech they'd ever heard (okay, it was a crowd of dirty old men, but still). I've never felt so appreciated. Denis King waited until everyone left to congratulate me.

"That was impressive," he said. "You had them eating out of the palm of your hand."

I giggled as I slipped on one of Lucille's bathing suit cover-ups. "I did, didn't I?"

"Your father was sure proud of you," he said. "That must have felt good."

I thought it odd that Denis would notice something like that, but then he was awfully devoted to his own daughter, so maybe not. "It felt wonderful," I said.

"You are a connoisseur when it comes to fashion history, and an extraordinary showman . . . show-woman."

"Yes, thank you, it's true," I said, taking a page out of Sydney's book. "Do you still think I work at a two-bit museum?"

"I shouldn't have said that. I was angry at the time," Denis said.

"Soooo . . . maybe you'd reconsider your decision to never give us another dime?"

"Maybe," Denis said, smiling, "if you're really nice to me."

"Why, you flirt," I teased. "*You'd* better be nice to me or I'll tell your fiancée you're trying to seduce all the pretty girls."

"Not *all* the pretty girls," he said, "just one in particular."

"You bad boy, you."

"Please don't tell the old ball and chain."

"All right, it'll be our secret," I said. "Hey, are those edible undies I see sticking out of your bag?"

"I took them for Annie."

"Yeah, sure you did," I said, giving him a playful swat. Denis and I were friends now, maybe even a little more than friends. It was as though I'd never called him Penis in front of a roomful of reporters. The Audrey costumes were safe. Life was good.

Who Can I Turn To?

I AWOKE THE NEXT MORNING to the buzz of Pops' electric shaver. That's the problem with these penthouse suites. Even the largest ones are tight for two people. *The perks of the rich can be such a mixed blessing,* I thought, stretching my arms and yawning. For a moment I felt there was something wrong, something I should be worried about. Then I remembered that, no, everything was fine. Finally, I could relax and enjoy the trip.

Smiling, I stumbled toward the balcony and opened the curtains, blinded by diamonds of sunlight glistening on the crystalline blue water. Grabbing a pair of sunglasses and my robe, I went outside and took in the sparkling sea air. We had stopped in a glorious bay broken by the crescent rim of an ancient volcano. The island in front of us seemed to erupt from the ocean to the sky. I had seen this place in every Greek island tourist brochure I'd ever laid eyes on and in at least one American Express commercial. Perched on top of Santorini's dramatic limestone cliffs were dots of whitewashed houses, cafés, and churches that resembled sugar cubes from where I stood.

"I'm meeting Bunny and Lucille for breakfast," Pops said, sticking his head outside. "What are you doing?"

"Carleen, Frank, and I are going to ride donkeys to the town," I said. "You guys taking the tram?"

"Oh, yeah," Pops said. "I can't see Bunny or Lucille on a donkey, can you?"

I laughed. "No. But, Pops, seriously, please don't lead all these women on. It's bound to end badly."

"I know," Pops said, "and that's why I've settled on my one special lady. I decided I'm too old to play the field anymore."

"Really? Which one have you settled on?"

Pops pretended to zip his lips. "I can't tell *you* before I tell *her*, can I?" He leaned over and kissed the top of my head. "We'll look for you in town."

After Pops left, I ordered room service and jumped in the shower. If I was going to meet Carleen and Frank at eleven, I had to hurry. The ship was docked in the middle of the bay, so we'd have to catch a tender to shore and hike up to the donkey rental hut. The only way to get to the town of Santorini from the dock was to traverse a steep cliff by tram, donkey, or foot. Frank was dying to ride up the hill even though Carleen warned us that last time the ship docked in Santorini, a passenger had broken her leg when her animal fell on top of her. But that was unusual, she admitted, having seen it only twice on her many Greek island stops.

There was a knock. "Room service."

I opened the door to a gaunt blond-haired waiter with bright blue eyes and a rather large head. He set my breakfast down on the table and lifted off the silver cover. "Hash browns, bacon, a soft-boiled egg just as you like it. Allow me to introduce myself," he said with a bow. "I'm Darwin and I'll be your butler for the rest of the cruise."

"Excuse me," I said. "Where . . . what about John?"

"He had a family emergency and had to leave the ship this morning. I believe someone died. It was all very sudden," Darwin said.

"*What?*" I shrieked. "You can't be serious. John wouldn't leave without telling me first. That's impossible." I started to pace. The blood drained from my head so fast I saw stars. How could he abandon me like this? He didn't tell me where he'd hidden my trunk. I'd *never* find it now. I felt so betrayed. "Did he leave a note or a message for me?"

"Not that I know of," Darwin said, "but I can check."

"Yes, please," I said. "Would you, right now? It's *very* important."

After Darwin left, I sat down at the desk. *This* cannot *be happening,* I thought. *Everything was fixed and now it's broken again. What do I do?* Think. *Think.* I picked up the phone and dialed Carleen.

"I was just on my way out the door," she said. "Shall we meet at the tender, darlin'? It's leaving from Deck Three."

"I'm afraid I can't go," I said, my voice shaky. "Something's come up."

"Well, hay-ell," she said. "Frank will be disappointed. I think he was counting on tailing you today."

"I—I'll meet up with you in town," I said. "There's something I need to take care of first."

"It doesn't involve edible panties, now, does it?" Carleen teased.

"No, nothing like that," I said.

As soon as we hung up, the phone rang. It was Darwin calling to say that there were no messages for me from John. It appeared that something must have happened in the middle of the night, because nobody knew he was leaving until today, not even his girlfriend, a tour guide slash librarian slash karaoke hostess. His roommate said that he gave notice this morning and disembarked carrying his tan suitcase and a large brown trunk he had picked up in Istanbul. He left no forwarding address. With a dead thud in my pit of my gut, I realized that I had been had.

Too Darn Hot

I THREW ON A PAIR of jeans and a tight black T-shirt that said, "Liv'n Out Loud" in rhinestones. Then I put on my cherry tree Choos, which had been packed in the bag that was returned the day before. When that city bus decimated my wardrobe, these were the only surviving pieces. Maybe they would bring me luck.

Grabbing the elevator to the Lido Deck, I walked past the pool and made a beeline for the stairs leading to the bridge, and

Captain Paul's office. If there was information that would help me find John, Captain would have it. But when I arrived at his office, the door was closed and I was asked to wait.

Ten minutes later, Denis King emerged with Annie and Manny. Annie looked red-faced and contrite, as did Manny.

"Can I go swimming now?" Annie said.

"No," Denis said. "There will be no swimming for you today and there'll be no donkey ride in Santorini, either."

"Fine," she said. "I didn't want to swim and I didn't want to ride on a stupid ass, anyway. C'mon, Manny, let's go to the game room."

"No," Denis said. "You're to stay in all day. And you know that Prada backpack I bought you in Athens? You can use it only on weekends until further notice. Manny, take her to the cabin, please."

"No problem, sir," Manny said, taking Annie's elbow. As they left the office, Manny winked at Annie. Yup, she'd be swimming today, just as soon as Dad was out of sight.

"Is everything okay?" I asked.

Denis shook his head and sighed. "Annie was caught in the meat freezer with a bunch of children she'd snuck out of the Kid'z Club. Apparently she was charging five dollars for a peek at Aston's body, ten dollars to take a picture with him. What am I gonna do with that child?"

I stifled a giggle because Denis looked so worried. "Look at the bright side," I said. "She's an entrepreneur like her dad."

"Obviously," Denis said. "She'd already made forty-five dollars when we caught her. It's just, it's so disrespectful to Aston. Raising a child is the hardest thing I've ever done. And I only have her for summer and Christmas."

I looked at Denis, who seemed down to earth and wise, and made a split-second decision. "Denis," I said slowly, "I need to see Captain about something important. Would you come with me, you having gone to law school and all?"

"Did someone threaten to sue you over the edible underwear?" he said, smiling. "Was there patent infringement?"

I returned the smile, but nervously. "If only it were that simple, but no. I'm in this awful trouble."

I hated for Denis to know how badly I'd screwed up. But I needed help, so I let go of my pride and asked for it.

" . . . so you see, I didn't know the costumes were real and I certainly never meant to *steal* them. Only now John the butler seems to have stolen them, so I'm totally screwed, aren't I?"

Captain and Denis nodded their heads.

Captain picked up the phone and asked the hotel manager to bring him John's file.

A pair of metal crutches leaned against Captain's back wall. Sydney had broken his big toe when she threw that dumbbell at him. I wondered if Denis knew what havoc his fiancée had wreaked. Probably not.

"We'll check John's paperwork," Captain said. "Maybe we have an address or phone number that'll help locate him."

"Oh, oh, oh," I said excitedly, "there's a cop from Interpol on board. His name is Frank Flannagan. Do you think we should get him involved? He's investigating me."

"Frank Flannagan?" Captain said. "He's not with the police. He's a Tiffany Star Society Member and an orthodontist from Niagara Falls. Who said he was a cop?"

"John," I said. "The maid told him. That's why he said he had to hide the trunk. He was sure Mr. Flannagan was following me. He specifically asked to be seated at my table."

"He *always* requests the captain's table," Paul said.

"You *are* gullible, aren't you?" Denis said sadly.

I sunk down in my chair, wanting to melt.

There was a knock on the door. An officer in a starched white navy-looking uniform stuck his head in and handed over John's file. After perusing it, Captain said, "There's *some* information here. His family's address. We require it so we can reach our staff when they're on holiday."

"Oh, I just remembered," I cried. "He's Italian royalty; he *told* me."

Both Captain and Denis regarded me with dubious expressions.

"What?" I said. "You think he was lying?"

"I wouldn't put it past him if he would steal the dresses," Denis said.

"But he had such good manners," I said. "And he really cared about his job. Did you know he shared best practices with butlers from other ships so he could delight and astonish his guests?"

Captain seemed unimpressed. "I'm calling Interpol, the real Interpol. Let's let the professionals track him down."

"They're already on the case," I said. "I'm told my boss notified them, naming *me* as the prime suspect."

"So that's why those Turkish police came looking for you," Captain said.

I nodded. "Please don't call them yet. Let me go to Santorini and see if I can learn anything. Someone may have seen him boarding a ferry or something. I'll dig around. If I can fish up some good leads, maybe Interpol won't arrest me."

"I wish you'd let me help," Denis said. "This doesn't sound like the kind of thing a young woman should try to handle alone."

"Oh, I couldn't ask you to do that," I said modestly, but of course I totally wanted his help.

"What else am I gonna do today?" he said. "Supervise Annie in her cabin? Manny can do that."

"And very well, I'm sure," I lied.

Denis reached over and touched my hand. "Besides," he said, "it's in my nature to rescue damsels in distress."

He is so sexist, I thought. *Okay, I can live with that.* "So, have you rescued any recently?"

Denis smiled. "No, but I never shy away from the opportunity."

Either he didn't remember saving a drenched damsel in the rain or he didn't want to toot his own horn. I liked to think it was the latter. "Sydney won't mind if you spend the day with me?"

He checked his watch. "She's with a trainer right now and has a conference call that'll go on all afternoon. I think she was happy to get Annie and me out of her hair. Syd's a great girl, but she doesn't have the maternal gene. Not yet, anyway."

I do. I have the maternal gene, I thought; *I have lots and lots of them.*

Captain held up John's file. "I'll copy this for you," he said, "but let's call the police as soon as you get back. Learn what you can. Then we'll turn this over to the professionals."

"Thanks, captain—I mean, Paul."

As we said goodbye, Denis offered Captain his hand, but Paul handed him his "I don't shake hands for sanitary reasons" card.

I, on the other hand, tried to give him a breezy one-armed hug. But Paul planted a wet one right on my kisser. It seemed unfair to Denis.

"For this one," Captain said, pointing at me, "I'd do anything."

Oh, well, it was good to have friends in high places.

I'll Be Seeing You

THE WATER WAS SURPRISINGLY rough as the tender vroomed toward Santorini. This was starting to feel like a fool's errand. John was probably long gone. Who would remember him anyway? Thousands of day-trippers get on and off the cruise ships and ferries in Santorini every week. On the plus side, I'd get to spend the afternoon with Denis. Maybe we'd get lucky and have a madcap Mediterranean adventure like Cary Grant and Grace Kelly in *To Catch a Thief*. Come to think of it, we *were* trying to catch a thief.

At the dock, we could go one way and check out the ferries or the other way and catch the tram. We started with the ferry pier, which was packed tight with tourists. That would be the most logical way to leave quickly. There were two clerks selling tickets for all the lines. Neither remembered seeing John. Nor did any of the ticket takers recognize him. Lucky for me I'd never had a butler before, because I'd taken a picture of us together in case I never had one again. With no success at the ferries, we made our way to the tram.

"Oh, shoot," Denis said.

"What?"

"I forgot my BlackBerry. Do you mind if we go back to the ship?"

"We'll only be a few hours," I said. "It might do you good to take a break from work."

He considered my suggestion, radical as it seemed. "I have the kind of job where people have to be able to reach me," he said. "It's like being a doctor. I'm on call day and night."

"Do you like that?"

"Well, life isn't always what one likes, is it?"

"No, it often isn't."

"But I suppose I *could* take a few hours off," Denis decided, "and enjoy a little freedom."

"Good for you," I said, leading the way to the tram ticket window.

"Have you seen this man?" I asked the agent, a leather-skinned fellow with hairy patches on his elbows and neck. I showed the photo, covering my face with my thumb so Denis wouldn't see it. When I took the picture, my hair was a mess,

I wore my glasses, had raccoon under-eyes, and sported lovely headgear. It was not the image I wanted to publicize.

"Let me see the picture," Denis said playfully.

"No," I said. "I look terrible."

He snatched the camera from my grasp. "It can't be that bad. Ooh, that is one ugly picture," he laughed. Then he examined it more closely. His eyes went from the camera to my body, to my face, then back down to my cherry tree Choos. A flash of recognition crossed his eyes. His body stiffened.

Oh, no, I thought. *He remembers. Do I fess up or clam up?*

"I don't have all day," the ticket agent said.

Denis appeared puzzled, but handed the camera back to the agent.

"Yes, yes, he was here this morning," the man said eagerly. "I remember because he was carrying a *megalos* trunk." He held his arms far apart to show how big it was. "It took up a lot of room in the car and I made him buy a ticket for it."

"A ticket for a trunk?" I said. "That's bold."

"If it would take a donkey to carry something up the cliff, you have to buy a seat for it. That's the rule. Why do you complain? You should be happy because now I remember him."

"Oh, yes, I am happy, thank you," I said. "Can you tell us anything else? Was he traveling alone? What was he wearing?"

"I can do better than that," the agent said. He left his partner in the booth and invited us to follow him to a cramped office. Turning on an old Dell computer, he clicked on a file of photographs. "Our security camera takes a picture of everyone as they enter the building. Let's see, he was here at least two hours ago, maybe more." He started to scroll through the photos until he came to a guy with an oversize brown case. "Is this your man?"

"Great Scott, it is," Denis said.

"Look, he's alone," I added, clapping enthusiastically.

"Can we get a copy?" Denis said.

"I'm afraid that would be impossible without the proper papers."

Denis reached into his wallet and pulled out a wad of bills. "Will these do?"

Silently, the man clicked the print button and handed us the photo. "This never happened," he said like we were in a James Bond movie. "Follow me."

After escorting us into a tramcar, he slammed the door and said, "Good luck and Godspeed."

The tram rose so rapidly it felt like I'd left my stomach back at the station. We were being carried up the mountain at what seemed to be a ninety-degree angle, but that's probably an exaggeration. They say it takes only two minutes to get to the top, and I could believe it. We were moving like a fierce trade wind.

"Let's keep this for evidence," Denis said, filing the photo in his backpack.

I was busy snapping pictures of the bay, the volcano, the terraced hills, and the ship, which looked like a white cigar from this height. Finally, I set the camera down and took in the breathtaking view myself.

That's when I saw her.

It was quick, but there was no mistaking the face. Sitting opposite me on the tramcar speeding down the mountain, Tanya

Johnson, the devil herself, whizzed past my line of sight. Sammie was with her. Tanya was boldly staring out the window. When she saw me, her eyes bugged out and she leaped up, whomping her head on the top of the car. There were suitcases on the seat. She yelled to me, but by then the car was too far below us to see or hear anything.

"Who was that?" Denis asked.

"It was Tanya and Sammie," I gulped.

"You mean Witchy and Dopey are here? Now?" he said.

"I am so dead."

Prelude to a Kiss

My first instinct when we stepped off the tram was to run, just in case Tanya and Sammie decided to ride the tram back up. But then I realized they would never chase me. Tanya was too lazy. She'd board the ship and wait while sipping expensive champagne and tapping her designer-clad foot.

"Come," Denis said, taking my hand. "There's no time to sightsee."

Right, I thought. *We need evidence*.

We hiked past the small boutiques and elegant cafés until we found a brick road. Denis approached a convertible taxi that was waiting at the corner and then beckoned me to get inside. "There's an airport on the other side of the island."

The cab took off toward the back side of town, zipping down winding paved roads that led toward the sea. I was surprised at the immensity of the island, the lushness of the meticulously tended vineyards, the olive, pine, and cypress trees that dotted the landscape. A half hour later, we stopped at a surprisingly large, modern airport. It was teeming with casually dressed, deeply tanned tourists who were leaving the Greek paradise, and bleary-eyed, lighter-skinned visitors who were arriving.

We made our way inside and checked to see if there was a flight to Rome. That was where John was from, at least according to his file. Indeed, there was and it was leaving within the hour. We ran toward the gate, but were stopped by security. No ticket, no entry. Two men in combat fatigues stood near the metal detectors, both carrying large machine guns.

"Quick," Denis said, "we'll buy tickets."

Rushing to the counter, we stood in a long line that moved agonizingly slowly. By the time we got to the front, the departure time for the flight to Rome had come and gone.

"What do you think?" Denis asked. "Should we buy tickets just to get to the gate area? Maybe he's going somewhere else?"

"Why not?" I said. "Let's do it."

Unfortunately, without our passports, they wouldn't sell us tickets.

Looking out the window as we made our way back in the taxi,

my eyes welled. *Is this it? Is this the end of the story? How could I have trusted John? Am I that bad a judge of character?* It felt like Alessandro's betrayal all over again. I burst into tears.

Denis took my hand. "It's not your fault," he said. "John stole the trunk. *He's* the bad guy."

"Yes, but if I hadn't taken the dresses in the first place," I started. "I'm responsible."

"When we get back to the ship, we'll call Interpol," Denis said.

"Sure," I said, wiping my wet cheeks.

"At least we got the picture of John with the stolen trunk," Denis added.

"True," I said, "but there's no proof the costumes are in it. For all anyone knows, I could have sold the dresses on the black market. I didn't, but the police could think I did. I don't want to go to jail," I said, blubbering all over again.

"Look," Denis said gently. "I'll come with you to talk to the authorities. You won't be alone."

"Thanks," I mumbled. Checking my watch, I realized we had four hours before we had to board.

"Do you mind if we don't go right back to the ship?" I asked. I was in no hurry to return, knowing that Interpol would be waiting to interrogate me, Tanya would be waiting to skewer me, and Sammie would be waiting to taunt me. "How 'bout we go to the beach for lunch or a swim?" I suggested. "Carleen said it was beautiful."

The cabdriver took us to Koloumbos, a volcanic black-sand beach with a smattering of restaurants and shops across the road. He explained that buses left from the general store every hour and that the one to Fira would take us back to the tram. I was listening carefully to his instructions as Denis handed him one hundred euros and asked him to wait. It must be nice to be rich, I thought. You never have to take public transportation.

We bought Greek salad wraps and beer at an outdoor snack bar, and then wandered into a small surf shop, where we picked up towels and a few bottles of water. By the time we found our way to the sand (which was so hot you could hardly walk on it), I had cheered up a bit. Being at this beautiful beach, I could forget my troubles, at least for a few hours.

Then it dawned on me that everyone on the beach was nude—it was a veritable sea of exposed breasts, mushy tushies, jiggly stomachs, and bare derrières. There were mothers, fathers, and children of every shape, size, and shade of scrotum—I mean, brown. It was disconcerting, mainly because they were all naked. On the other hand, I secretly wouldn't have minded seeing Denis au natural.

"What do you think?" I said, wondering if he would suggest we go native.

He blushed and then flashed his dimples. "I can swim in my boxers."

Rats, I thought, making my way to the ladies' room, which was nothing but a primitively constructed hut up by the road. I undressed, and then pulled the elastic waistband of my satin granny panties up over my boobs and (voilà!) instant strapless bathing suit. It wasn't very shape-flattering. Why was I such a wispy little thing? I wondered. I wished my breasts were bigger. How could I ever hope to attract a good man with peanut-size boobs (*my* boobs, not his)? In the bedroom with Alessandro, my body never bothered me. That's because we always did it in the dark and I could squeeze my arms against my body to make my breasts appear bigger when I was on top. But out in the hot sunlight, I couldn't think of a logical reason to squeeze.

"Come on," I said, motioning toward the water. "Let's cool off." Denis was putting our towels down in the sand, so I ran ahead, wondering what my butt looked like to him, wishing I had been more diligent at the gym. I tried running in a sensual gait to make a good impression from the back, but ended up jumping up and down all the way to the shore saying, "Ooh, ooh," because the sand was like a sizzling pancake griddle.

By the time I made it into the cool water and dodged a few light waves, Denis (in blue plaid boxers) was goose-stepping across the blistering sand in my direction.

The water was chilly and refreshing. We swam away from the shore until our feet didn't touch the bottom and splashed each other like children. The elastic waist of my underwear kept slipping down under my breasts because they weren't large enough to create a natural rack. "Over there," Denis said, pointing to an area behind an improbably empty formation of corrugated lava jutting out of the sea. We paddled over to it and climbed on a big flat rock that shielded us from the beach crowd. Lying on my back, I soaked in the Mediterranean sun. The elastic from the panties barely covered my nipples, which showed through the wet cream silk panties.

"Do you like my bathing suit?" I teased.

"Are those the giant underpants from your talk?" he said. "It's amazing how many uses you find for them."

I giggled. "It's all they sell on the ship."

Denis looked me up and down. "Nice eggs," he said.

I touched my stomach near my ovaries. "You like my eggs?"

"No, nice *legs*."

I looked around for the long-legged creature he was talking about. "Where?"

"You," Denis laughed. "You make granny panties look sexy."

"Aw, that's the second nicest thing anyone has ever said to me."

"The second nicest?" Denis said. "What was the nicest?"

"When you told me I reminded you of spring," I whispered. "That I was a breath of fresh air."

Denis blushed, or maybe he was getting sunburned.

"Thank you for helping me," I said. "I don't know why you are."

To my surprise, Denis brought his face to mine, and our lips met for an exquisitely slow kiss that tingled and tasted sweet.

"Oh, that's why," I said when we parted. "I'm so stupid." I turned to face him. "Explain it to me again."

This time, he pressed his lips to mine more urgently, sending my stomach into a wild ride. Then, very slowly, he kissed the tip of my nose, my eyelids, my temples, my neck. He rested on his side, reached over, and caressed my ribs with his fingertips, soft as a whisper, tracing them down toward my belly button.

Desire radiated through my body. My nipples hardened. "You're giving me goose bumps."

He stopped.

"No, it's okay, I love goose bumps."

Denis turned on his side and nestled next to me. Our bodies were close enough that I felt the light tickle of his arm hairs brushing my skin. It was pure torture.

"Doesn't the heat feel fantastic?" he said.

I was breathless and hot, hoping he would take me right there on the lava rock, no matter how painful and scratchy that might be. Sadly, he didn't because we both dozed off.

When I woke up, I realized we must have slept for quite some time. Denis' face had turned the color of rare meat.

"Denis, wake up. You're really sunburned."

His eyes blinked open and he sat up. "Look at you," he said. "You're as red as Rudolph's ass."

"You mean nose?"

"Right, that's what I meant."

I lowered the elastic band of the giant underpants I was wearing and saw the difference between my milky-white breasts and my newly fried décolleté.

Then, from far away, I heard the long and low horn of a ship. My head turned. "Did you hear that?"

"What?"

It sounded again.

"That," I said. "It sounds like a ship is pulling out."

Denis sat up and checked his watch. "Maybe it's a different ship," he said. "What time were we supposed to leave?"

"At five, I think," I said. "What time is it now?"

"It's five."

I'm Just a Lucky So and So

By the time we made our way back to the tram station, which overlooked the bay, our ship had sailed.

"I can't believe they didn't wait for us," I said. "Especially since you're the captain's pet," Denis added.

"Are you jealous?" I teased.

"No, I'm just stating the obvious . . . Captain's pet, captain's pet," he sang.

"Would you stop it?" I said, swatting him playfully.

"May I borrow your cell phone?"

Denis called the Tiffany Cruise office in California to find out what we were supposed to do.

While he talked, I took in the setting. The town of Santorini clung to the sculpted volcanic cliffs against the bluest sky imaginable. There were white buildings, many with deep azure roofs that melted into the sky, donkeys carrying visitors up the steep cobble road with their bells ringing and horseshoes clacking, rows and rows of descending terraces with stone-paved courtyards decorated with pots of red, purple, and pink azaleas, and clusters of bougainvillea spilling over the walls like magical fuchsia waterfalls. The fragrant breeze blowing up from the water felt like a buttery caress against my skin.

"Here's the deal," he explained. "Tomorrow's a sea day, so we're stuck. The ship'll be in Livorno, the port for Florence, on Thursday. They said to get a ferry there because they won't let us buy air tickets without our passports. But I can arrange for my jet to take us. I'll call Sydney and ask her to watch Annie."

Soon Denis was on the phone having harsh words with someone. Sydney, I guessed. Edging closer to where he stood, I heard bits and pieces. "Give her a chance . . . I'm counting on you . . . I don't care if it's Manny's job, someone needs to be the parent . . ." Denis was combing his hands through his thick brown hair. I stood at the ancient stone wall, staring out at the bay, feeling the warm afternoon sun cook my freshly fried skin. I decided I'd best find some shade.

"I have to call my mother," Denis said. "Do you mind?"

"Lucille? No. Is there a problem?"

Denis nodded. "Sydney doesn't want to watch Annie when there's staff to do it."

"But why?" I said. "That's silly." *Note that I would never be so selfish.*

Denis talked to his mother for quite a while. His face was sensationally flushed (or maybe it was the sunburn, hard to tell) and he was waving his hands about. I wondered if she blew the whistle on Sydney and Manny, but doubted it. Lucille wanted that wedding to happen even if it cost her son's happiness. Then Denis called his office, arranging for his jet to pick us up. When he was finished, I phoned Pops and let him know I was safe with Denis and not to worry.

"Holly, you listen to me. Don't get involved with him," Pops said. "You're from two different worlds. It can never work out. Believe me, I know."

"It seems to me I gave you the same advice concerning your lady friends onboard," I whispered.

"I just don't want you to get hurt, that's all."

"Don't worry about me, Pops."

"Your boss is on the ship with someone named Sammie," he said. "They've been by twice demanding to know about the Audrey Hepburn gowns."

My stomach lurched. "What'd you tell them?"

"I told them I didn't know what they were talking about and let them search your closet," he said. "But they didn't believe me. How dare they question my veracity! My word is all I have in this life."

"Well, you *are* lying," I said.

"Yes, but they don't know that."

"Do me a favor?" I asked. "Tell Tanya I was supposed to give the speech on Coco Chanel tomorrow, but I missed the boat. Tell her Sammie should take my place."

"I don't think your boss is in the mood to help you out," Pops said. "She was loaded for bear."

"It's not for me," I said. "Explain that I've befriended some big potential donors on the trip. If we don't do the speech, it'll reflect badly on the museum. Give her my laptop. All my presentations are on it."

"You'd better find the dresses," Pops said. "Losing those will *really* reflect badly on the museum."

If I Had You

DENIS TOOK MY HAND and led me down a cobble road. We stopped at a general store, and picked up some aloe vera gel to soothe our sunburns, then made our way to a table at a small café overlooking the emerald bay.

I took a deep breath, surrendering to the pleasure of the jasmine- and oleander-scented air and cool sea breeze on my face. As the sun fell, the sky lit up a bank of pink and golden clouds on the horizon. A yacht floated beneath us on the glasslike surface of the water. On the bow, a trim blond woman wearing a blue bikini stood and sang "Vissi d'arte," an aria from Puccini's *Tosca*, her rich voice reverberating throughout the bay. The American man at the table next to ours said that the soprano was Julie Nelson, one of the leads from the Metropolitan Opera. I don't know how he knew, but judging by her magnificent sound, I believed him. When the song ended, the audience that had gathered to watch from the Santorini cliffs clapped wildly, their applause and "bravas" falling like raindrops from the sky. I have never seen anything like it and probably never will again.

Denis ordered espresso and I had cappuccino and fruit. For most people, missing their ship would be a huge upset, but I wanted to dance like a Whirling Dervish over it. That gave me thirty-six hours more to look for the missing dresses, and time alone with Denis, whom I was growing fonder of by the minute.

"May I ask you a personal question?" I started.

"I've been hoping you would."

"Why are you with Sydney? I know why your mother wants you to marry her, but why do *you*?"

He started to speak.

"No, I'm sorry," I said, holding up my hands. "It's brazen of me to ask. I'm sure she has many lovely qualities."

"It's hard to explain . . ." he began.

"It's just, she's so much younger than you, and she's . . ."

"What? She's what?"

A thumping bore, I thought. Then I realized I had said that out loud. "Oh, my gosh," I said, slapping my hand to my mouth. "I'm sorry. Forgive me. This is *none* of my business."

"This marriage means everything to my mother," he said,

"and when you're born into a family like mine, there are certain obligations . . ."

"Yes, but you have to sleep with her. Your mother doesn't."

Denis grew thoughtful for a moment. "By marrying Sydney, my mother will be happy and I'm glad, but I'm not doing it for her. This is *my* choice. With my first wife, I followed my heart. That turned into a bloody mess. This time, I'm following my head," he said, tapping his temple. "Syd's clever, beautiful, accomplished. She works in Manhattan real estate, like me. She knows that my first love will always be the business. Marrying her makes perfect sense."

"I used to tell myself that marrying Alessandro made sense."

"At least we aren't going into it with stars in our eyes."

I put my hand over Denis'. "Call me a dreamer, but next time I fall in love, I don't just want stars, I want 'The Star-Spangled Banner.' Sydney's not going to make you happy, Denis. You deserve someone who will adore you *and* Annie."

Denis took a sip of his espresso and gazed out on the harbor. Instead of saying, "Would that someone be you?" as I expected after those sweet kisses we'd shared, he changed the subject. "Santorini's the most beautiful island in Greece, don't you think?"

"I don't know. It's the only one I've ever seen." I used my fingers to pick up a strawberry, and slowly bit into its deliciously sweet and tart flesh. "Mmmm," I murmured, using my tongue to lick the pink juice that dribbled down my chin.

Denis cleared his throat. "This harbor was formed about thirty-five hundred years ago when the volcano blew out the island's center," he said. "Some people think that was the incident that gave rise to the myth of the lost continent of Atlantis."

"So under the water, there might be the remains of an ancient civilization?" I said.

"Could be."

"Cool beans," I said, offering him a cube of watermelon.

Denis smiled at me. "You should see your face right now."

"What's the matter with it?" I asked, worried I must look like a ripe tomato after that nap in the sun.

"It's lovely," he said. "Here, give me the camera. May I take a picture of you."

"Oh, sure." I handed it over and smiled alluringly.

He fiddled with the buttons until he brought up the picture of John and me.

"Hey," I said, grabbing for it.

Denis held his arm too high for me to reach it. Then he showed me the photo. "It's you, isn't it? You're the woman I picked up in the rain a few weeks ago."

"Guilty," I said, my face burning even more than it was already.

"Why didn't you say anything?"

"That day, in the rain, I was such a mess, just like I am in that picture. I didn't want you to know that was me."

"How did you come to be on the ship?"

"To meet someone as charming as you, of course."

Denis stared at the photo again, then at me. "When you were in my car, I told you I was coming on this cruise."

This man didn't miss a trick. I suppose that's how one gets to be the ninth-richest guy in America under fifty. "Yes, so?"

He cocked his head. "You're not here because of me, are you?"

Busted, I thought, my heart thumping with fear. "Those speeches on the *Tiffany Star* were booked months ago." That was all I could think of to say.

"You wouldn't lie to me, would you?" Denis said. "Because I could tell."

"You could?" I said. "How?"

"There's an old tale about two tribes of Indians—the Whitefeet always tell the truth and the Blackfeet always lie. So let's say one day you meet an Indian, and you ask him if he's a truthful Whitefoot or a lying Blackfoot. He tells you he's a truthful Whitefoot, but which one is he?"

"What is it with you and Indian stories?"

"Which are *you,* Holly?"

"Me? I'm a truthful Whitefoot, of course."

Denis smiled. "That's what I thought. I have to be careful because I don't always know who I can believe." He tapped my nose. "But I have a funny feeling that you might be entirely trustworthy."

This would have been the perfect time to admit what I had really come on the trip to do. But I couldn't get the words out. I reached my hand across the table and put it on top of his. "Thank you for rescuing me that day. You were my knight in shining armor."

Denis flashed a modest smile. "You sure clean up well."

"You know," I said, "we'd met a few times before that day. At the museum."

Denis looked puzzled. "How is that possible? You're unforgettable."

"Yes, it's true, but inexplicably you didn't notice me until I humiliated you in front of a room full of reporters."

"So that was just a ploy to get my attention," Denis teased.

"It worked, didn't it?"

Denis laughed. "My Gulfstream's on its way. What would you like to do?" he asked. "Stay here tonight, fly to Florence tomorrow?"

My. Gulfstream's. On. Its. Way. *The five best words in the English language*, I thought. "You know," I mused, "since we can't meet the ship till day after tomorrow, we may as well go to Rome, look up John's address, see what we can learn."

"Of course! You're right," Denis said. "We could. We should. We will!"

I jumped up and gave him a hug. "Oh, thank you, thank you," I said, relieved to be back on the trail of the costumes, grateful that Denis had the means to arrange it. "This'll be amazing. Maybe we'll find him. Do you think we will? Do you think he'll still have the dresses?"

Denis laughed. "I hope so. Hey, in this case, we can honestly say that the butler did it."

"I've always wanted to say that," I said. I don't know why I said that. When have I ever wanted to say the butler did it? Never, that's when.

Denis took my hand and led me to the street, where he hailed a cab. "Come, *bella*, the Eternal City awaits us."

Roma, Italy

Fly Me to the Moon

NOTHING STARTS A TRIP off on the right foot like a private jet.

There are three reasons for this. First, you don't have to deal with security checkpoints, pat downs, liquid carry-on restrictions—all the indignities that make flying so torturous; second, the food is even better than in first class (not that I've flown first class, but hello! We had our *own* chef); and third, you can have sex at thirty-six thousand feet and they won't arrest you. Denis and I did not join the mile-high club on this flight, but we could have and that's my point.

When we landed in *Roma* (that's how they say it in Italian), a uniformed driver was waiting with a stretch limo right on the tarmac to whisk us to our hotel. It was almost nine P.M. Denis (or his staff, I suppose) arranged for us to stay in a two-bedroom suite at the Hassler Villa Medici, a small, old-world, five-star hotel located at the top of the Spanish Steps. Everyone who is anyone has stayed there, including Audrey Hepburn when she made *Roman Holiday*. How do I know? Let's just say there is very little about Miss Hepburn that I don't know.

The king-sized beds in each room were made with 1,020-thread-count sheets and topped by feather duvets so thick that you could disappear right into them. Believe it or not, there were real antiquities in a display case in the living room of our suite. I wondered if anyone would notice if I took a really small one for a souvenir (tee-hee!). The bathrooms were enormous, finished in pink marble and twenty-three-karat gold-plated faucets. Near the tub, fresh cucumber slices were set in a bowl of ice. I could barely tolerate all that luxury at once, but somehow I managed.

The first order of business was to draw a cool bath to soothe my burned skin. With the water running, I poured in the orange-scented oil the hotel provided and the room became humid and smelled of citrus. I lit a candle, lay cucumber slices over my face and eyes, then relaxed in the tub until the bubbles disappeared. It was heavenly to just soak and feel fresh again, but then I remembered that I had no clean clothes. So I dried off and put on the thick terry-cloth robe that had been warming on the heated rack.

When I stepped into the oak-paneled living room, Denis was wearing his robe and standing on the balcony that overlooked the city. He had ordered room service. A tuxedo-clad waiter was setting up the table while another lit candles. There was an open bottle of Brunello di Montalcino. A few stars peeked out from behind a curtain of gray clouds in the night sky. I could smell the aloe vera gel on Denis' skin. "Want some?" he asked, offering me the bottle.

I squirted out a dollop and rubbed it on my face and chest. It was just what the doctor ordered.

Then I noticed all the food on the table. "What did you do?" I said. After the rich meal we'd had flying over, I wasn't very hungry (did I mention the private chef? Oh, yes, I believe I did). Still, a glass of wine would be perfect.

Denis turned and smiled. "It's only a snack. See, there's stuffed mussels, fried anchovies, some gnocchi, cheese."

"Ooh, goody," I said, taking a seat while the waiter politely bowed out.

Denis raised one eyebrow. Pouring us each a glass of wine, he made a toast. "To finding what we're missing," he said, as we clinked our glasses together.

"You mean the dresses?"

"That and anything else we might be missing," he said mysteriously.

"What are *you* missing?" I asked, ever the sleuth.

"You said it before. The affections of a good woman." He gazed into my eyes in loverlike fashion. "You know something? I wish to make a statement," Denis declared. "I adore you."

I choked, and coughed out the fried anchovy I'd just popped in my mouth. "Excuse me. Cheese?" I said, cutting him a slice and offering it. He took it out of my fingers with his mouth, chewing it slowly. Exotic-dancer slowly, if you know what I mean. I was starting to see where this was going and for reasons I can't possibly explain, I panicked.

"You know, cheese is one of my favorite foods, always has been," I said. "When I was growing up, we didn't have much money and I always put cheese on my Christmas list. Goat cheese, very unusual in those days, but Pops was something of a gourmet. I asked for a pony too, a miniature one so I could keep it in the apartment. Never got that either. When we moved to Queens, I put Canadian ice wine on my list. I'd tasted it at a bar Pops played at and it was so delicious. But I was underage so he wouldn't give it to me for Christmas. Do you think children should be allowed—"

Mercifully, the phone rang, interrupting my holiday rant.

"Wait, slow down," Denis said. "You woke up and he was gone? Did you check the whole suite? Are you sure?"

He listened for a while, the furrow between his eyebrows deepening. "Annie, don't be scared. You're safe on the ship," he said. "But I want you to go to Grandma's cabin."

"She's not? Where is she?" he said evenly. "Okay, fine; put me on hold, call Sydney on the other line, and tell her I said you *have* to stay with her."

Denis ran his fingers through his thick brown hair. "She didn't answer? Where could she be?"

Oh, dear, I thought. Doesn't Denis realize the ship is a veritable Peyton Place? I waved my arm like a nerdy schoolgirl. "If she can't find Lucille, tell her to call Carleen. I'll bet she can stay with her."

Denis told her to ring Carleen, and if she wasn't available, to call him back. "Jeez," he said, "she woke up and Manny was gone. Syd's not answering. Neither is my mother. Where is everyone?"

I checked my watch and realized it was after eleven. For some intuitive reason, I said, "Maybe they're at the bar."

"You're right."

I backed up my chair and yawned. "You know, I'm beat. Do you mind if I go to bed?"

"Sure, of course," Denis said, standing like a gentleman. "I want to call the bar anyway."

"Well, good night," I said, giving him a friendly wave. "Sleep tight. Don't let the bedbugs bite." *Oh, you are lame*, I thought miserably, toddling off to my room. Alone.

Mad About the Boy

When I woke up the next morning, my first thought was not of the possibility that I had blown it with Denis the night before, not of the luxurious hotel room or luscious feather bed in which I found myself, not of the fact that for the first time in six months, I hadn't slept with my headgear and it felt great. No, the first thing that came to my mind was the missing trunk and the very real possibility I would go to jail if it wasn't found. This did not feel liberating in the least. So I put all thoughts of incarceration out of my head and told myself that we'd find the dresses today.

Making my way to the bathroom, I took a shower and got back into the soft, fluffy robe. My stomach was making little noises that I hoped Denis would find cute, if not adorable. Poking my head into the living room, I spotted him reading a coral-colored newspaper.

"Morning," he said, looking up, smiling. "Hungry?"

"Starved."

"I want to take you out to breakfast, but in keeping with our tradition, here's some pink champagne to tide you over."

"Ooh, yummy, how nice of you," I said. Our first tradition, I marveled, and what better tradition than champagne for breakfast! Looking at that sweet face, those earnest brown eyes, the cleft in his chin, the dimples when he smiled, even that teddy-bear frame, I realized what a good heart he had and how much I wanted him. That was why I couldn't be with him last night. I needed him to care. A casual fling would kill me after what happened with Alessandro. Well, maybe not kill me, but it would seriously wound me.

"Was everything okay with Annie?"

Denis took a sip of bubbly. "Yes, Mom was in the bar like you thought. She took care of her."

I held out my flute and Denis filled it with champagne.

"I ordered us some clothes," Denis said. "They were delivered this morning."

"I could get used to this kind of service."

Denis laughed. "Wait'll you see the clothes."

The two of us made quite the pair with our bright sunburned

faces, matching Nike trainers, and Adidas running suits (in red and green like the Italian flag) with white T-shirts that said "Roma."

"I hope nobody thinks we did this on purpose," I said.

"Oh, but I specifically asked for matching outfits in the national colors," Denis said. "You don't like?"

"You did?" I said. "That's so sweet. I—I love it."

Denis burst out laughing.

I am so gullible.

"There's a Prada boutique a block away, but it doesn't open till ten thirty," he said. "We can shop later."

"If we have time," I said. "These are fine."

The hot sun made for lazy weather. We meandered down the Spanish Steps, which was flooded with tourists, locals, lovers, backpackers, and the like, to the Piazza di Spagna, where we found a quaint English teahouse called Babington's. Outside a jeans-clad musician strummed a guitar, his case open and filled with coins. The place was buzzing (with tourists mostly), but we snagged a table in the back room where the air-conditioning was blowing the hardest. The place looked just like a quaint English cottage. I ordered a Blushing Bunny, which was grilled tomato, creamy Italian cheese, and mushrooms on toast. Denis had Canarino, a poached egg on rice pilaf with cheese sauce. Plus, we ordered tea. "Maybe we should go for Italian food tonight," I suggested. "We *are* in Roma."

Denis agreed, then pulled out a map, which he studied. "According to this, John's family lives right off via Boncompagna, which doesn't look like it's too far from here. We can rent a Vespa at the hotel."

"You just want to show up at his house? Unannounced?" I said. "Do you think that's wise? Mmm, this Blushing Bunny is delicious."

Denis reached over with his fork and took a bite, smacking his lips in approval. "If it's his parents' house and we tell them what their son did, maybe they can pressure him into doing the right thing," Denis said. "Kids want their mother's and father's approval."

"You mean like you," I said. "The way you chose law school over baseball, the way you're marrying Sydney? Can I try yours?"

Denis cut me a bite of his poached egg with rice and put it on my plate. "Here," he said. "What can I say? Where I come from, duty trumps pleasure. Nothing was more important to my parents than seeing me run the family business, make the right marriage, that sort of thing."

"Mmm, yummy," I said, tasting his Canarino. "*You* are a good son. But a lowlife like John doesn't care what his parents think. Haven't you ever watched *Law & Order: Criminal Intent*?"

"And *I* disagree," Denis said, standing, putting some cash down on the table. "That's why we're going to talk to his mother. No boy wants to disappoint his mother."

To get to via Boncompagna, we hiked back up the Spanish Steps, beyond the throng of tourists, toward the Trinità dei Monti (the ancient church at the top of the Steps), and swung behind the hotel, where we rented a Vespa. Denis almost backed out when he found out the vendor didn't have helmets. But I talked him into living on the wild side.

I had no idea how wild until we started driving on the uneven streets with all that crazy loud traffic. The city was chaotic, proud, and utterly beguiling. We drove off, weaving through tourists as we sped down narrow cobbled roads. There were crumbling buildings, ancient walls, choppy brick streets, charming boutiques, greengrocers, fish markets, and baroque fountains on every block. Cars were honking, taxi drivers were shouting, Vespas were shooting in and out of traffic—the pace was more frenetic than New York City when the president was in town.

"Hold on," Denis yelled as we careened around a sharp corner.

I grabbed his waist for dear life. We hit a bump and I squeezed him even tighter to stay on the Vespa.

As we traversed a crooked side street, an old lady snoozed on a park bench with a basket of daisies by her head, a black cat sunned himself on a stone wall, a hunched-over man begged for change, a fruit vendor gave an apple to a little boy who was holding hands with his young, stylish mother. Each living tableau we passed made me feel like I was watching a movie about a place I'd been to a thousand times, yet had never seen at all.

Denis kept pulling over so I could take pictures. This was a trip I never wanted to forget. Plus, I was stalling. What if John became violent when we showed up at his house? I've never known a butler to be violent before, but there's always a first time. Come to think of it, John was my first butler ever. How sad that my impression of butlers would forever be marred because my first one turned out to be a criminal.

We whizzed around the corner of via Boncompagna to via Piave and finally came to a stop at an ochre-stained home bearing the name Villa Savoy.

"That's it," I said. "John's last name is Savoy. He told me."

Denis checked the paper. "Yep. It must be his family's home."

We parked the Vespa in front, opened the creaking gate latch, and entered a courtyard. The little square was dotted with cherry trees. Vines of sweet-smelling honeysuckle climbed along the stone walls. A chipped mosaic floor surrounded a once-elegant (but now crumbling) fountain. The water bubbled out of a carved fish's mouth in the center, sounding just like the brook from Alessandro's sleep machine. There were coins on the bottom of the fountain.

"Wait," I said, lollygagging. "Do you have any more change?"

Denis reached into his pocket and pulled out a handful of coins. I closed my eyes and thought real hard before wishing that I'd get the guy, but not the prison term. Then I tossed them into the water.

"Stand by the fountain," I said. "Let me take your picture."

Denis smiled at the camera, looking adorably dorky in his Italian tourista tracksuit.

"Say *grazie*," I said, snapping the picture.

Suddenly, the gate swung open. A bald grandfather, all stooped over, wearing a heavy black suit, his arm around the shoulders of a younger man, appeared in the doorway.

My stomach dropped like a bungee jumper. "John," I said. "We've been looking for you."

I Got a Right to Sing the Blues

JOHN GRINNED WHEN HE spotted me. "*Ciao*, Miss Ross," he said. "What are you doing here?" He escorted the old man to a wrought-iron bench by the side of the fountain and helped him sit down. "Look how ripe your skin is," he said, taking us in. "You must put vinegar on your burns."

The gate opened again and a tiny, gray-haired woman in black orthopedic shoes, wooly tights, and a dark kerchief ambled through carrying a white cake box tied with red-and-white string.

Behind her came a procession of men, women, and children all dressed in their Sunday best, many holding covered dishes of food or fresh baguettes from the *panetteria*. John spoke to them in Italian, pointing to Denis and me. "Blah blah blah blah blah blah blah *pedophilo* blah blah blah blah blah" was all I heard him say. People gasped and shook their heads. He gestured toward the house. Two gangly teenage boys helped the old man go inside.

"Did you just tell them my pedophile boyfriend dumped me?" I asked, my voice higher by an octave.

"Oh, yes, do you mind?" John said. "I was explaining who you were."

"How did you even know?" Denis asked.

"There are no secrets on the ship. I know that the woman you are to marry has taken a lover."

Denis' face grew redder than it already was and his jaw flapped open.

"That's right," John said gently, "the caregiver for your daughter. I saw them together with my own eyes. And I know that your father has taken a lover."

"What!" I said.

"Yes," he said, "Miss Carl—"

"That's okay, I can guess," I said, sticking my fingers in my ears.

"A luxury cruise ship is like a small village," John said. "Everyone knows everyone else's business. So what brings you to my neck of the forest?" John said.

"The woods," I said. "My neck of the woods."

"Is your mother home?" Denis asked. "We'd like to speak to her." If John was going to shock Denis with his revelations, Denis would return the favor.

The butler's face fell. "She has passed away. We've just come from her funeral. That is why I left the ship."

Denis and I looked at each other.

"I'm sorry," I said. "We didn't realize."

John's eyes filled. "It was too soon. She was young."

"My condolences," Denis said. "But why did you take Holly's trunk with you?"

John cocked his head and appeared puzzled. "I promised Miss Ross that I would deliver it to the Istituto di Moda."

"So you were still planning to do that?" I asked.

"Of course," John said.

"Can we see it?" Denis asked.

John hesitated and bit his lip. "There is one small matter I must confess." He sat on the iron bench and looked at his feet. "Please forgive me. I borrowed one of the dresses for my mother to wear at her viewing. It was the beautiful white shiny gown with the red sash and tiara. You see, we are descendants of Italian royalty and I wanted her to look regal in her casket."

My heart was racing. "*What?*" I said. "You *borrowed* the *Roman Holiday* gown? But the trunk was locked."

"I broke the lock," he said. "But I never intended to steal the dress. Just like you."

"How small was your mother? That dress is tiny."

"It was too little. We had to cut it, I fear," John said.

"*WHAT*? You *cut* the dress? How *could* you? It's irreplaceable!"

"Not the material. The seams," John said in a pleading voice. "My sister let them out."

"You didn't cremate her in it, did you?" Denis asked.

I gasped. That thought had not occurred to me.

Think Pink

"Cremate?" John's face flushed with indignation. "No, we are good Catholics. We bury our people whole. We bought Mama an extrawide coffin to fit all the skirt inside the box."

"Tell me you didn't bury her wearing it," I said, on my knees before John, my hands clasped in front of my heart.

The front door opened. A young woman with a black net veil over her hair stuck out her head. She spoke urgently in Italian.

"Caroline, no!" John leaped up and bolted into the house. We followed.

The bald old man had fainted and was lying on the floor. "Papa," John said. "Papa." He tapped his father's cheek firmly until the man's eyes fluttered open. John and two other guests helped him to his feet and made him comfortable on a flowery sofa. The girl with the veil brought him a glass of water.

When things calmed down, John approached me, head bowed. "I am sorry, Miss Ross. My meaning was to ask Mr. Delani—he is the mortician—to take her out of the dress before they sealed the mausoleum, but in my grief I forgot."

Now *I* was going to faint and I don't mean that metaphorically. I became dizzy and Denis had to help me into a chair. "John, please," I said. "You have to change her clothes."

His eyes widened as though horrified. "No, that is impossible. How could I do that to my mother, who has only but for a few hours been planted in her resting place?"

"But she's not underground. She's in a mausoleum, right?" I said.

"Yes, a vault."

"We're not asking you to dig her up, just to do a quick above-ground costume change," I pleaded.

Denis intervened. "John, you took something that didn't belong to you. Even though you meant to give it back, you could go to jail for not returning it, just like Holly could."

"It isn't *any* dress," I added. "Audrey Hepburn wore it in the ball scene at the beginning of *Roman Holiday*. It's the centerpiece for the exhibit celebrating the fiftieth anniversary of that movie. If it's not in the show, your countrymen will be crushed." I tried to appeal to his sense of national pride.

"But to disturb my mother," John said, "that is a sacrilege."

"It'll be fast," Denis said.

"She won't even notice," I added. "Besides, no woman wants to spend eternity in a dress that's too tight."

"Please, can you pick another outfit for her?" Denis said, ever the deal closer. "We'll go see the mortician and make the arrangements."

John's eyes glittered with unshed tears. I felt like a heel for what we were asking him to do.

He nodded. "I suppose."

I embraced him. "Thank you."

Later that afternoon, John drove us to the Istituto di Moda, where we delivered the trunk full of costumes, with a note attached from me explaining that the last remaining gown from *Roman Holiday* would be dropped off shortly, and at that point I would be available to help them dress the mannequins for the show. Then we headed to the cemetery where John's mother had been interred. It was built on the side of a hill. White marble vaults were stacked one on top of another, sometimes twenty high. It was like a high-rise condo building for corpses. In the side of the marble were carved names and epitaphs, glassed-in photos of the deceased, and built-in urns filled with artificial flowers.

Mr. Delani, the mortician, had arranged for the vault to be opened, the casket to be removed and then taken to a private area where Mrs. Savoy's clothes could be changed. The family priest was with the body. He was there to repeat the required prayers when the remains were reconsigned to the mausoleum.

"Here," John said, handing the mortician a shopping bag containing a powder-pink silk suit. "She wore this to my sister Caroline's wedding. It holds happy memories."

Mr. Delani, a tall man with enormous pockets under his eyes, excused himself in order to make the switch. Forty minutes later, he emerged with the shopping bag that now held the priceless gown. Words cannot describe the relief I felt. But let me try. It was as though I had been carrying the weight of the *Tiffany Star* cruise ship on my shoulders and I could finally let it go. Now all I had to do was find a spool of matching thread from the 1950s (which I doubted Paramount had kept in its costume archives), repair the dress, and deliver it to the Istituto.

My biggest concern was maintaining the value of the piece. If it became known that the dress had suffered a serious breach and was restored, its worth could plummet dramatically. On the other hand, if I lined the seams up and hand stitched them together in the original holes made by the studio's seamstresses using vintage thread (if I couldn't locate the actual spool), the repair might not affect the gown's value.

"Here," Mr. Delani said, bringing me the bag. "I am sorry for the confusion."

"It's not your fault," John said. "I forgot to tell you to change her clothes."

"Yes, but when you asked me to remove her false teeth, I should have inquired if there was more," Mr. Delani said.

"You remembered to ask for her dentures, but not the dress?" Denis asked.

"Her sister, my aunt, is in need of a new set, and in my grief—" John started.

As soon as I grasped the bag, I knew there was a problem. It was too light. "Oh, my God," I shrieked, looking inside. Instead of the *Roman Holiday* gown, it contained a polyester dusty-pink nightie, nothing more.

With a Little Bit o' Luck

"THIS IS NOT THE dress you wanted?" Mr. Delani said.

"*No*," I screamed. "It's a cheap piece of yecch."

Mr. Delani pulled the nightgown out of the shopping bag. "I gave my wife something just like it for her birthday."

"Oh. Sorry. But this isn't the dress your mother wore at her viewing, right, John?"

"No, it isn't," he said, his brow puckered with worry.

"Someone pulled a switch," Denis said. "Who had access to the body after the service, before she was buried?"

"Only my son," Mr. Delani said. "But he is honest as the day is strong, like me. And what would he want with a fancy gown?"

"I don't know," I said. "Maybe he's a cross-dresser."

Denis kicked my foot, to shut me up, I suppose. "Where is he? Can we speak to him?" he said calmly.

The man shrugged. "He is back at the *camera ardente*.

"Where?" I said.

"The mortuary," John explained.

I looked up to heaven. "Why is this happening? Why?"

"It's challenging, I'll admit," Denis said. "But doesn't that make it more interesting? C'mon."

After a ten-minute nail-biting ride from the cemetery to the mortuary, I collapsed on a wooden bench outside the office as we waited for Mr. Delani to find his son. "My luck, the kid sold it on the black market."

"Or put it on eBay," John added.

"That would be better," Denis said. "Then we could bid on it ourselves."

"Not so fast," I said. "The sleeveless black satin Givenchy that Audrey wore in *Breakfast at Tiffany's* sold at auction for a million dollars after commissions. This could be worth as much. We couldn't afford to bid on it."

"Speak for yourself, woman," Denis teased.

"Oh, so you'd buy it back for me? Aren't you the generous one," I kidded (sort of).

Denis checked his watch. "It's only been gone a few hours. If he took it, there's a good chance we'll get it back."

Mr. Delani marched back into the room, holding a contrite-looking green-eyed, black-haired Adonis by the collar of his dress shirt.

"This is my son, Mario. He has a confession." He jerked the boy twice.

"I—I took the dress. I couldn't stand for something so breathtaking to be hidden in a vault for eternity. It wasn't right. I'm sorry," he mumbled.

Thank God! I thought. *We found our thief.* "That's okay. I won't press charges. The important thing is that we can get it back. Where is it?"

Mario's face took on a deepening hue of shame. "My fiancée has it," he said. "She is recutting it into a wedding dress."

"*What!* She's cutting it? With scissors?" I said, horrified.

"Magda is a fine seamstress," Mr. Delani said.

"No, she is a *designer,* like Miuccia Prada, but not as famous," Mario explained.

"She has won many awards," Mr. Delani added.

"Look," Mario said, twirling around, modeling. "She made my shirt by hand."

My heart was racing. We had to stop her. "Has she already begun?"

Mario nodded. "We're getting married Saturday," he said. "She was to wear her mother's dress, but this was much more beautiful. And she didn't mind it had been on a dead woman first."

The mortician spoke to Mario in Italian, accompanied by passionately gesticulating hands. John involved himself in the conversation just as loudly and as physically as the two of them. Finally Mario wrote down an address on a piece of paper and gave it to us. "Here is where Magda took the gown," he said. "It is her shop. I will call and tell her to stop what she is doing. But she has been sewing for hours. You are most probably too late."

I'm Getting Married in the Morning

Denis parked the Vespa on the sidewalk in front of a small storefront marked "Sarta" just south of Piazza Navona. From the painting of a spool of thread and needle on the sign, I figured that meant "tailor." Call it instinct.

Bells jangled as we opened the door.

A woman appeared from behind a brocade gold curtain. Her round face was doll-like with bright blue eyes, a turned-up nose, and thin lips. She wore the tiara that went with the *Roman Holiday* costume in her mound of wavy auburn hair. Her top half was slight and waiflike, while her buttocks and hips were anything but. The overall effect was that of a small torso resting on top of an end table. I'm not being catty; I'm just pointing out that from a physics standpoint, there was no way that she was going to fit into that a gown made for Audrey Hepburn.

"Magda San Giovanni?" I said.

"Are you the couple who have come for the dress?"

I nodded.

Magda fell to her knees and clasped her hands in front of her face. "Please, please," she begged. "Do not make me give it back until after the wedding. My mother's dress makes me look like pork."

This was Mario's fiancée? How could such a classically handsome boy marry such an oddly shaped girl? Was their love so strong it transcended the physical? Did the brilliance of Magda's sewing skills blind Mario to her thunder hips? Was Magda a tigress in bed? Could I be any more superficial? All these questions whirled through my mind as Magda hugged my green pant leg with her head and quivering arms. I gave her a gentle kick so she'd let go.

"Magda, this dress was worn by Audrey Hepburn in *Roman Holiday*," I explained. "It has to be delivered to the Istituto di Moda for a show."

"But the show will not start until Monday," Magda said. "Someday I plan to be a great designer and I never miss their exhibits. If you'll allow me to wear it at my wedding, I'll sew it back together for the Istituto. No one will ever know it was dismantled."

"Dismantled? Completely?" I said, feeling light-headed. "You're kidding, right?"

"I removed the seam stitching so I could change the shape of the gown to fit my figure," Magda said.

We followed her into the workroom. Pinned onto a mannequin of what appeared to be Magda's unique bottom-heavy form was the princess-styled bodice of Audrey's dress. The seams had been opened to just above the waist. In each of these original seams, Magda had created six narrow gussets by stitching triangular pieces of delicate, cream-colored silk, expanding the lower bodice to accommodate her ample hips. The heavily gathered folds of the skirt had been loosened and reattached to the newly expanded bodice. The hem had been turned up by about ten inches, but it had not yet been stitched. The red sash that Princess Ann wore in the movie had been removed and carelessly tossed on the table. Seeing such an iconic gown desecrated like that was almost too much to bear.

"When is your wedding?" Denis asked.

"Saturday at ten," she said, "at the chapel at Mario's *padre's camera ardente*."

"You're getting married at the morgue?" I said. "Isn't that bad luck?"

"Yes," Magda said, "of course it is. How can a couple start their life at the house of death? But it is, ah, how do you say, free, so Mario insisted. He is as cheap as he is handsome. If I have to wear a pork dress for a wedding in a *camera ardente*, what chance does our marriage have?"

"She has a point," Denis said. "The ship docks here on Sunday. Maybe we should stay till then, and get the dress fixed after the wedding."

Can this dress be repaired in a day? I wondered. Conservators would take months to undertake such a job.

"Our wedding is Saturday morning, unless there is a funeral, in which case it will be delayed," Magda said. "I'll stay up all night to make alterations."

"On your wedding night?" Denis said.

"It's all right," Magda said. "Mario is, how do you say, like thunder in the bedroom, ten minutes and *finito*." She clapped her hands together to emphasize the point.

"You mean lightning, right?" I said. "The electrical bolts from the sky." I pantomimed lightning for her.

"Yes," Magda said. "He is *rapido* like lightning."

"I don't know, Magda. What if you sweat? What if something spills on it? What if it can't be fixed in time? The dress has to be returned to its original state and I'm not sure that's even possible now that you've added those gussets."

"It's your call," Denis said.

I bit my lip. "You're on the museum board. What do *you* think?"

"I think you're . . ."

"Really something," I said hopefully.

"Yes, the way you've relentlessly pursued the gown. It's impressive."

"Oh," I said, disappointed. I had hoped he meant that personally.

"Please, I beg you . . ." Magda was on her hands and knees.

"I'll put plastic shields under my arms. I won't wear the gown to dinner. I'm a *fantastico* seamstress, everyone will tell you that. And look at what I'd have to wear instead."

Magda sprung to her feet, scrambled to a closet, and pulled out the most gruesome wedding gown ever. The bright white top was covered in large satin roses that would make Magda's one pleasing feature (her small top) blend right in with her problem area (her wide arse). Enormous midlength sleeves resembling satin helium balloons were stuck on each side. The skirt was poufy, like Cinderella's ball gown. It looked more like a wedding cake than a wedding gown. You would expect to see a getup like this at uglyweddingdress.com (if there was such a site) so people could come from far and wide just to laugh and post mean comments. Come to think of it, that might be a really fun idea for an exhibit at the museum—Ugly Wedding Gowns through the Ages.

Denis turned to me. "If Magda's willing to stay up all night to fix the dress, she could get it to you Sunday morning."

I shook my head. "Only a trained conservator can repair it," I explained. "If I could get Nigel Calderwood here, then *maybe* the two of us could put it back together. He'd have to contact Paramount to see if he could get his hands on the thread from the spool that was used to make the garment in the first place."

"They would have that?" Denis asked.

"A couturier would," I said. "They'd have the original needles too. I'm not so sure about Paramount. Movie studios are notoriously bad about archiving that sort of thing. But if we *could* find it, we might be able to preserve the gown."

"I could arrange transportation for Nigel to fly to L.A. and then Rome," Denis said.

"You'd do that?" I asked.

"It's business. I *am* on the board of the museum. The two of you can fix the gown on Saturday, and drop it at the Istituto Sunday morning."

"The two of *us* can drop it? Does that mean you're leaving me in Rome?"

"I'd stay, but I have to get to Annie," Denis said. "We'll be back Sunday. You'll be fine. There's so much to see in Rome anyway."

Yeah, all by my lonesome, I pouted to myself.

If I stayed in Rome, I'd miss the stop in Florence. Michelangelo was one of my favorite artists and I'd waited a lifetime to see David's penis.

On the other hand, Tanya and Sammie were waiting for me on the ship. How could I face them before the dress was fixed and delivered? The damage was already done. The gussets had been added to the bodice. *Let's see. If the wedding is over by noon, we'd have that day and night to repair the garment, deliver it the next day, then get back on the ship to tell Tanya the clothes were ready for exhibit. I could stop by the Istituto on Friday to help them dress the mannequins in the costumes we'd already delivered.*

"You would need to get the gown back to me as soon as you're married, *capeesh?*" I said. That's a word I learned from watching *The Sopranos*.

"*Capisco,*" Magda said.

"And you must wear underarm pads, no deodorant or perfume, and don't eat or drink anything while you have it on," I said. "And tape the hem; do not sew it. In fact, do not put one more stitch in the dress or even a pin through the fabric."

"I promise," Magda said. "And you must come to our wedding."

"All right, I guess."

Magda threw her arms around my shoulders, squeezing so hard that she practically knocked me to the ground. "*Grazie*, *grazie*, *grazie*," she said.

"It's okay," I said, laughing. "You're going to be a beautiful bride."

He Loves and She Loves

Denis and I stopped for an espresso at Caffè Greco, where the air smelled of fresh cinnamon pastries too warm and tempting to resist. Later, we returned to the hotel to make a few calls. I needed to reach Nigel and tell him the plan. Denis wanted to check on Annie and then have his "people" arrange transportation to Florence as well as a jet for Nigel's use.

"Oh, no," I said. "Nigel can fly commercial. This mess was

as much his making as it was mine. Let him suffer like I have." *That wasn't very Buddhist of me*, I thought. *Oh, well. Enlightenment takes time*.

I decided to take a bubble bath. Drawing the water, I added the thick liquid soap from Claus Porto, which soon filled the room with a sweet rose scent. I lit two candles floating in gold holders on the tub, turned off the light, and submerged myself in the warm, velvety liquid. It felt divine after the crazy day we'd had. I wanted to forget about John's dead mother, the mortician's crooked son, Magda the big-butted bride, and most of all, I wanted to forget about Audrey's costumes and how sorry I was for taking them in the first place. Although I supposed I wouldn't be in this luxurious suite with Denis King if not for Audrey and her elusive dresses, so *grazie*, Miss Hepburn.

I opened my eyes and took in the bathroom, so utterly resplendent with its gold faucet, oversized pink marble tub, and flickering yellow lights. What a treat it was. *Enjoy it while you have it*, I thought, closing my eyes for a spell and breathing in the rose-scented foam. That made me sneeze. Twice.

"God bless you," Denis said.

My eyes popped open and I repositioned the bubbles to cover myself. "Is everything okay on the ship?"

Denis moseyed over to the toilet, closed the lid, and sat down. "Better than okay," he said. "I've arranged to have Manny put off. He won't be there when we get back."

"That was decisive of you."

"I'm a decisive guy."

"Who's watching Annie?"

"Mom's hiring a twenty-year-old who works in the dress shop

to take over as babysitter. She's supposedly great with kids. Annie sounded happy as a clam."

"That's wonderful," I said. "Sydney doesn't want to help?"

"No," he said. "She'll be too busy supervising the butler, who'll be moving her things to another cabin."

"Oh," I peeped. "Supervising a butler is a lot of work. Not that I ever had a butler before. Well, I had John until he quit on me. And then there was Darwin . . ."

Denis stood and unzipped his green running suit jacket.

"I suppose you grew up with your own butler, like Mr. French on *Family Affair*. Did yours have an English accent like Mr. Fr—"

Denis bent down and felt the water. "Do you mind if I heat this up?" he asked, his hand on the gold faucet.

"Not too hot," I said. "The cool water feels good on my sunburn."

Denis adjusted the water so it ran warm, slipped off his shoes, and then climbed into the tub, fully clothed, opposite me. It was highly unorthodox. My fingers and toes had grown all shriveled from spending so long in the water and I should have gotten out to de-wrinkle, but I didn't dare.

"What are you doing?" I said, giggling. "You're all dressed."

He reached into the jacket and looked for a tag. "Don't worry. It says 'wearing this suit during washing will help protect its shape.'"

"Very funny!" I said. "This isn't fair. I'm naked and you're not."

"Oh, it's not fair, is it?" Denis said as he masterfully slid the lemon-scented soap up my legs, inch by inch, slow like a Brahms concerto. It felt sublime.

"Do you want me to stop, *bella?*" he whispered. "Since it's not fair, I mean."

My eyes rolled back in my head. "No, that's all right. Life's not fair, you know."

"So I've heard," he said, stroking the inside of my thigh with soap. Every once in a while, his hand grazed my crotch, which sent my stomach into orbit. Then he switched over to my side and lay next to me, gently rubbing my arms and breasts with slippery suds. It was all very erotic, especially when accompanied by the light ear nibbling and deep neck sucking. I reached over to take off his jacket, but he whispered, "No, no, I want to pleasure you."

Oh, my dear God, a man wanted to pleasure *me* before himself. I wasn't sure what to do with that piece of news.

Denis took my hand and kissed each of my wrinkled fingertips. "You're turning into a prune," he teased. "But I love prunes; I always have." He helped me out of the tub and covered me with a thick terry-cloth towel. I made myself comfortable on the feather duvet as he removed his dripping-wet running suit in the bathroom.

I would describe his body, but in the interest of his privacy, I won't go into detail. Okay, I will. Let's just say Michelangelo's David with about thirty extra pounds comes to mind. Though he wasn't sporting a six-pack, there was no gut to speak of. His upper body was muscular and defined. His penis was perfect. He had the ideal level of hairiness, enough to run your hands through and feel a tingle but not enough to smother you in if he rolled on top.

Denis joined me and we immediately entwined ourselves

in each other's bodies, sharing a thousand exquisite kisses. In time, he turned away from the lips and began to lick and kiss and suck me—my neck, my breasts, my belly—leaving wet trails on my skin and sending shivers through my body. He soon ventured to the insides of my thighs, where he teased me with his quick tongue alternating between light and deep flickering until I was half out of my mind with pleasure. I had to bite my lip to keep from screaming, but finally I couldn't contain myself. "Ohh . . . ohhh . . . ohhhhh . . . YES!"

Denis looked up, satiated. "No applause, please. Wait until you see what I do for an encore."

Ooh la la. Denis' tongue would be illegal in fourteen states. Eventually, he came back up for air. "I could do this for hours."

Oh. My. God. That was music to my clitoris, I thought, but no, I learned in kindergarten that it was important to take turns.

"And you can, but first . . ." I said, pulling him toward me so I could kiss those lips, nibble on that ear, bite his neck, but mostly so I could love every part of him and most especially his warm heart. I felt his hardness pressed against me and kissed my way down his chest and stomach to his penis, devouring it like a dripping ice cream cone on a steamy hot day. We fumbled a bit with a condom and I guided him inside of me until I could feel that delicious ache of two becoming one. Surrendering to my pleasure, I reveled in the smells and tastes and sensations of our passion. As we made love, Denis looked in my eyes and I saw such honest yearning, which made our connection all the more exciting. He was masterful, touching me exactly where I longed to be touched, igniting fires I didn't know I had. He came in a shudder, and we crawled under the thick duvet, cuddling and caressing each other until we could not resist each other's touch and fell back into making love.

"Do you know what you are?" I said after.

"What?" he murmured.

"You are the da Vinci of cunnilingus."

"Thank you, it's true," he said, his face flushed with pride.

"Now can I call you Penis King?"

"You are something else." He laughed. "I've never met a woman quite like you."

"To be irreplaceable, you have to be different," I said, quoting Coco Chanel.

"That would make you irreplaceable then."

"I wish you didn't have to leave."

"I don't. Annie's in good hands now," he said, gently pushing a patch of hair off my forehead. "She won't even notice I'm gone."

Thank you, thank you, I thought. Smiling, I snuggled my head into the crook of his arm, looking up at his face, touching the cleft in his chin. "Hey, how do you shave in there?"

"Very carefully," he whispered. "Your sunburn's looking better. Shall I put some gel on it?"

"Oh, yes," I said. He opened the bottle and carefully applied the aloe vera to my face, neck, arms, and legs.

Then I took the cooling gel and rubbed it on his sunburn, which was already starting to heal. "Denis," I started, "there's something I have to get off my chest . . ." I glanced at him and his eyelids were closing. Soon his rhythmic breathing said he was out, so I watched him sleep. My confession would have to wait. He looked like a little boy, so perfectly at peace. A faint whistling sound came out of his nose each time he exhaled. Oh, how I loved that sound. *Tonight you're mine completely*, I sang to myself. *But will you love me tomorrow?* Look at me, I sighed. I'm just like the woman in the Carole King song. I tried to recall what happened at the end, but couldn't. Did he love her when the night met the morning sun? Damned if I could remember. The last thing I recall before drifting to sleep was wishing that I could stay in this bed with Denis forever.

Let's Do It (Let's Fall in Love)

I WOKE UP CURLED AGAINST this warm, sleeping bear of a man and for a moment thought he was Alessandro. Then I remembered the feel of his rough cheek against my skin, the smell of his breath as we kissed, and the slow, sweet shudder of orgasms we'd shared. My heart filled with joy and gratitude. Something wonderful had happened to me and it hadn't been a dream. I glanced at the clock. It was ten. The room was so dark,

I wasn't sure if that meant ten in the morning or evening. Surely we hadn't slept through the night? It would be so unlike me to skip a meal. I slipped out of bed and crept over to the window and peeked out. The sun blinded me for a moment and I realized that we had indeed slept all night.

In the bathroom, I brushed my teeth and played with my hair. I have one of those messy haircuts that's supposed to make me look like I just rolled out of bed, but it never looks like I just got out of bed when I really did. It takes a lot of work and careful arranging to create that careless tousled look. So I spent about five minutes working to achieve perfect bed head.

Sneaking under the covers, I cuddled up to Denis, who slowly opened his eyes and smiled when he saw me. "You just wake up?" he said dreamily.

That's what I mean about the haircut.

Denis reached over and drew me to him, holding my face in his hands, then kissing my lips urgently, hungry for my tongue. Alessandro would never have pressed his lips to mine if either of us had overnight bacteria buildup, but Denis didn't care and neither did I. His beard scratched my cheek as we kissed. He regarded my body with satisfaction, then slowly nibbled my breasts, caressed my belly, licked my thighs. I loved how he didn't rush the way Alessandro always did. Moments later, I sensed Denis' desire to enter me, to merge our hearts and bodies. "Yes, yes," I said, and we were making love again. All thoughts of Alessandro flitted into oblivion. Afterward, we spooned in bed, and with Denis's warm body cuddled close, he ran his fingertips up and down my belly, softly like a feather. It felt divine, but my stomach started to rumble, which reminded me that I was hungry, which reminded me that we couldn't go out to eat in our dirty green running suits. We'd just have to order in breakfast along with two new sets of clothes, preferably not matching.

"WHAT WOULD YOU LIKE to see?" Denis asked, pouring coffee. We were enjoying room service in bed. "The Colosseum? The Vatican? The Forum? There's so much history in Rome. I could hire a guide."

"Why don't we just walk around and let the city surprise us?" I said. "I've never been here before, except yesterday, and that doesn't really count."

Denis slathered strawberry jam on a steamy croissant and held it to my lips. I opened my mouth and took a bite, trying to eat it in the slowest, most sensuous way, but jam dribbled down my chin and crumbs spilled all over the sheets. He laughed at me.

"Oh, you think that's funny, do you?" I said. I stuck my finger in the crystal jar of orange marmalade and removed a dollop, which I promptly smeared on his chest.

"Hey," he said. "Are you trying to start a food fight?"

"Not exactly," I said, moving onto my knees and licking the sticky sweetness off his nipple.

"Ooh, I like that," he said, leaning back and surrendering to his bliss.

"Well, if you like that, here's something you'll like even more," I said. This time, I took a generous helping of strawberry jam (which I personally prefer over orange marmalade) and rubbed it on his belly, chest, and rapidly rising erection. After licking the jam off each finger with my tongue (oh so slowly), I tore the bill for our breakfast into little scraps and stuck them on all his sticky places.

"Why, you kinky thing," he said. "Whatever are you doing?"

"Well," I purred, "I dripped jam on you, so I marked the spots where I'm going to have to lick it up. You just lie back while I eat you." My tongue flickered across his belly and chest while he moaned with ecstasy. Once that was squeaky clean, I moved down to his penis and hungrily took it into my mouth. You'd have thought I hadn't eaten in a week.

Honestly, I don't know what came over me. I'd never been inspired to engage in such gustatory pleasures with Alessandro. Come to think of it, Alessandro and I really had only two techniques in our bag of sex tricks—him on top, me on top, repeat if necessary (usually not). Then I put Alessandro out of my mind because I wanted to live in the moment and devour Denis' strawberry-jam-slathered penis, which was really quite yummy. *Be in the now*, I thought. *It's the Buddhist way*. Not that I know so much about Buddhism, because I don't. But I do know that sucking Denis' sweet cock was as close to a religious experience as I'd had in years.

Denis thrust the breakfast tray aside. It plunged to the floor, breaking plates, splattering hot coffee and water everywhere. *Mama mia*, I thought, gasping at his audacity. He took me in his arms as though he could not wait another second to have his way with me and we made love with a reckless fury I hadn't experienced with any man, not even Alessandro (*especially* not Alessandro).

I never did get to tour Rome that day.

◆ ◆ ◆

By the end of our *dolce amore* (that's Italian for sweet love), we were famished. Since we'd been too distracted to order new clothes, we were back in our matching green running suits, which weren't terribly sexy, although I wouldn't have traded the day for all the shopping on the via Condotti.

"You ready?" I said, turning off the light by the bed.

Denis nodded, then hesitated, as though he had forgotten something. I started to ask him if he wanted it back on. "Do you want—"

"To eat your pussy again?" he said. "Why, yes, I'd love to."

You could have scraped me off the floor. We had been making love all day long—in the shower, on the bed, the sofa, the balcony—and now he wanted *more*? (Naturally) I said, "Yes, please. How can I resist that gifted tongue of yours? This time, would you try something new while you're down there?"

"Anything," he said.

"Would you hum 'The Star-Spangled Banner'? I know it sounds silly, but a girlfriend once told me that felt good."

Dennis laughed. "Well, let's find out."

I just adored the way Denis was open to researching his sexual pleasure (or mine, as the case may be). And yes, YES, *YES*, his humming felt divine. Denis King not only gave me stars, he gave me "The Star-Spangled Banner" (tee-hee!).

We left the hotel around ten that evening, bound for Il Palazzetto, a nearby outdoor restaurant overlooking the Spanish Steps. The concierge recommended it when I asked for something romantic and utterly Italian.

"Before we go," Denis said, "I want to show you something." We took a horse and carriage to the elaborate Trevi Fountain, where we dutifully threw in three coins each to ensure a return visit. Then Denis took me over to a rectangular basin on the far left side. "They call this 'the small fountain of lovers,'" he said. "Legend has it that couples who drink from its waters will forever be faithful to each other." He cupped his palms together, collected some water, and drank it.

I must be dreaming, I thought. *This man is too good to be true*. Silently, I took water in my hands and sipped it. Hopefully it wasn't teeming with amoebas and microbes. Even if it was, it would be worth the gastrointestinal illness.

Denis grinned as I drank the water. How I loved the crow's feet that formed when he smiled. They were beyond adorable. "Do you know what's wrong with you?" I said.

"What?"

"Nothing."

"Denis, I—I want to thank you for what was the loveliest day I've ever known." I don't think I'd ever felt so happy.

We grabbed a cab to go to Il Palazzetto, which was too far to walk. By the time we arrived, my appetite was roaring. The waiter immediately brought us a plate of deep-fried zucchini flowers, which Denis fed me and I ate with such languorous relish that it felt like we were still making love. I ordered *spaghetti alla carbonara*, and Denis had roasted *capretto* (that's "kid" in Italian) with rosemary. We toasted each other with the yummiest champagne I'd ever tasted, Veuve Clicquot's La Grande Dame. The sky was bright with stars and colored lights that had been strung around the patio where we dined.

At midnight, a jazz quartet started to play, and Denis and I took to the small dance floor. Soon the music slowed, and Denis held me in his arms for a waltz. I closed my eyes and smiled. Denis was so practiced a dancer, all I had to do was surrender to his lead as we floated across the floor. Oh, how I wished I could do that in real life. But that would be a fairy tale, and one thing life has taught me is that there are no happy endings, at least not for me.

I looked into his eyes. "Hello."

Denis smiled at me. "Hello."

I rested my head on his shoulder and felt his heart beating as we moved to the rhythm. When the music ended, we took our seats, quenching our thirst with more champagne.

Denis reached over and kissed me lightly on the lips, touching my cheek with the tips of his fingers. "*Signorina*, are you having a good time?"

"The best," I said.

"What's been your favorite thing we've done so far?"

"Gosh, everything in its own way was . . . unforgettable. It would be difficult to . . . this morning, breakfast in bed, of course," I said. "I will cherish the meal we shared in memory as long as I live." It was my very own Princess Ann moment.

Denis gave a smile of recognition and then touched his lips to mine like a gentle whisper.

"Denis," someone called.

It felt like someone threw a bucket of cold water on our heads. *Who knew we were here?* I wondered, looking around. That's when I saw them. A pair of pink-rhinestone-studded weights furiously moving up and down. They could only belong to one person.

The Shadow of Your Smile

DENIS GLARED AT THE sight of his fiancée with the Satan Twins in tow. He reached for my hand under the table and squeezed it. "How does she know we're here?"

"The concierge?" I said. "Did you tell your mother where we were staying?"

"I gave her the number."

"That must be how they found us."

"Darling," Sydney said, setting her weights on the table and giving her fiancé a peck on the forehead. "Don't get up. We'll join *you.*" She pulled up a seat, wedging herself between Denis and me.

"Hello, Holly," Tanya said. "How are you? Oh, never mind. I don't care."

"Yoo-hoo, waiter," Sydney said, summoning the uniformed man over to take her order for a glass of club soda with a splash of chardonnay.

"Oh, and a sloe gin fizz for me," Sammie said.

"Now, Denis," Sydney said. "What is all this nonsense about putting me out of our suite? Have you gone mad?"

Denis' face reddened. "I know you had an affair with Manny."

"I did no such thing," Syd lied, shooting me the hairy eyeball.

What? Like your screwing the manny is my *fault? I don't think so.*

"A witness saw you," Denis said.

Sydney turned to me. "You *had* to tell him, didn't you?"

"I didn't tell him," I said. "John did. But I should have."

"Denis," Sydney said. "Oh, thank you," she added as the waiter delivered her drink and Sammie's sloe gin fizz. "Even if I had a dally, so what? Your own father took lovers. He slept with my mother. She told me. They never *meant* anything."

Sydney looked right at me when she said those words. And for the record, I resented that. "Maybe you had a fling with Holly here," she continued. "If you did, consider us even. Have your giggles with girls like Holly; don't *marry* them."

Denis shot her a withering look. *Bitch*, it said. *How dare you talk like that about the woman I love and in whose womb I desire to plant my seed* (at least, that was my interpretation).

Sammie was oblivious to Denis' angry reaction. "You see, Holly," she said, "that's what Tanya means about you never being able to fit in our world. Our men fuck girls like you; they don't marry them."

"Why, you heartless guttersnipe . . ." I picked up her ridiculous pink drink and threw it right up her fat nostrils.

Sammie sprang out of her chair. "Ha," she squealed, spraying gin-laced snot from her pug nose. "You just proved my point. No one in our circle would do that."

A *pox on your circle*, I thought miserably.

Sydney ignored the brouhaha and gently stroked Denis' arm. "The important thing," she said, "is that the Basses and the Kings are *finally* coming together to create a force that is impenetrable. Darling, it's up to us. Other things being equal, I'm not sure I'd marry you either, but our families, our employees, and our shareholders are depending on us."

Denis shook his head. "No, Sydney, forget it . . ." he said firmly.

I raised my hand like the class nerd, straight up like a missile, not all floppy at the end like a bunny ear. It wasn't effective. No one called on me. "Excuse me, but last I checked this was the twenty-first century. Who in God's name marries to create a dynasty anymore?"

"There you go again, Holly," Sammie said as she blotted the sticky drink off her face. "That's another thing you'll never understand. Denis comes from a rarefied milieu. The right union is expected. The Denis Kings of the world align themselves with women of consequence and hardly ever for love."

"*Love*," Tanya said, practically vomiting out the word.

"Sammie, I am so sick of you and Tanya telling me I'm not *of* your world," I started. "The difference between a woman of consequence and a nobody has nothing to do with where she is brought up, but how she's treated. I'll forever be a nobody to you because you treat me as a nobody and always will. But to Denis I'm a woman of consequence because he treats me as one and always will."

"That's right," Denis said, touching my cheek. "Holly has more substance than any woman I've ever known."

Sydney grabbed Denis' hand possessively. "Darling," she said. "You may think you have something special with Holly here, but trust me, you don't. The only reason she's with you is because she bet her boss that she could fleece you out of a million-dollar donation."

Denis looked at me with suspicious bewilderment. "That's not true, is it?"

Blood drained from my face. "I . . . I never said fleece."

"You knew I would be on the ship," he said in a sad but gentle tone. "You *followed* me?"

I grabbed his arm. "Please, I may not have started out with the purest intentions but *everything* changed. You have to believe me."

"Holly," Tanya said, all gloaty and superior-like, "you'll be interested to know that Sammie won our little bet. She arranged for Sydney and her mother to make that million-dollar donation *before* you got your check from Denis. Sammie and Sydney went to Spence together. Naturally she was able to convince them. So she gets the curator position. And as for your assistantship, well, your services are no longer needed. You're fired."

"Don't bother. I quit. And you'd better watch your ass," I hissed, "because I just might decide to write one of those *Devil Wears Prada* books about you."

Tanya laughed. "What a marvelous idea. You'll need something to keep busy in jail."

"The dresses will all be returned; no one's going to jail, no thanks to *you*, Sammie," I said, giving her a bitter stare.

"I don't know *what* you're talking about," Sammie lied.

"Denis," Sydney said, checking her watch. "It's time to go. The ship leaves at sunrise. Tomorrow's a sea day and you have to talk with that daughter of yours."

This got Denis' attention. "Why? What happened?"

Sydney's smile became smirky. "Apparently she posted pictures of Aston's body on her Kidspace page. Angela, that's the new babysitter, caught her in the computer room. She told *me*. I don't know what she thought *I* would do about it. I'm not the child's mother, as she so often reminds me."

"Jesus Christ," Denis said. "What am I going to do with her?"

"Boarding school," Sydney suggested.

"I think he meant that rhetorically," I said.

"Holly, do you need a ride back?" Sydney offered. "Our jet's at the airport."

"She can't leave," Denis said. He turned to me. "I have to take care of Annie. Will you be all right?"

"I'll be fine," I said, mustering my special brave face. *Just abandon me for your daughter*, I thought. But, of course, I couldn't say that without sounding cold and selfish like Sydney, which I suppose I was because that's how I felt.

Sydney flashed a triumphant smile my way.

"Annie needs you. It's all right," I said. "But first, hear me out. I did come on board to convince you to make a donation to the museum. It was business. You, who agreed to marry Sydney to create a real estate empire, should be the first person to understand that. I *never* planned to fall in love with you."

"Yes," he whispered, "but at least Sydney was honest about why she was with me."

"I didn't lie to you about how I felt. Everything that happened between us was real," I implored.

Denis shook his head in confusion. He reached in his wallet and pulled out a wad of euros. "Here's some cash in case you run short. The hotel is yours until the ship docks on Sunday. I'll have my people make the arrangements, okay?"

"Sure, why not," I said, waving him away. "You guys go on to the airport. I'll stay and have another drink." *Maybe dance by myself*, I thought glumly.

"*Ciao, ciao*," Sydney said, grabbing her pink weights, heading off with Denis and her two henchwomen, Tanya and Sammie. As I watched them disappear, I knew Denis was lost to me. He was a good son who honored his family duty. That's why he chose fancy Harvard over blue-collar baseball. When it came to a marriage, no matter how well he had treated me, he would choose the heiress over the nobody.

Love and Marriage

When I opened my eyes the next morning, my hand reached over to the other side of the bed. The sheets were tucked in perfectly and they were cold. Then I remembered the tragic ending to my affair—Denis had gone back with Sydney and the Satan Twins. I sighed. It was the story of my life. I rolled over, pulled the covers over my head, and wept until I'd left a fat black mascara stain on the crisp white linen. Wasn't it Coco Chanel who said that great love must be endured? Yes, I believe it was.

Well, I wasn't going to feel sorry for myself, I decided. I was getting the Hepburn gown repaired and then delivering it to the Istituto in time for the exhibit. So Tanya fired me. There are other fashion museums out there that would be lucky to have me.

Hmmm, I thought, *maybe I could convince Lucille to make a million-dollar donation to the Metropolitan Museum's Fashion Institute as a sort of consolation prize since I didn't come between Denis and the marriage she so desperately wanted for him.* Carleen could write a big check too. She was trying to spend all her money. What better way than to help me? I could show up at the Met with two huge donations that are theirs if they make me curator. My gloom started to lift. I could still end up with a good job and a way to take care of Pops, I told myself.

I noticed my message light on the other side of the bed blinking. Was it Denis? It had to be. He was the only person who knew where I was. Oh, happy day. He *does* care! I leaped over to the phone. But no, it wasn't Denis. It was one of his people, a Miss McCardle, calling to say that there would be a car and driver at my disposal until Sunday when the ship docked in Rome. She assured me I could charge all my expenses to the room, including clothes, which Denis told her I would need. I sighed. It's good to have people.

After breakfast, I called the Prada boutique and arranged for a saleswoman to bring me several choices. I might as well enjoy the perks of the rich, since I was unlikely to experience them again. After choosing a new skirt, top, shoes, and some clean Prada underwear (yes, Prada makes underwear *and it's small*!). I was ready to take on the world, or at least Magda to get the *Roman Holiday* gown back. The car and driver were waiting for me outside the hotel. I thought it best to attend the wedding just to protect my interest in the dress.

On my way out, I stopped at the front desk. "Has Nigel Calderwood arrived?"

The desk clerk checked his computer. "Not yet, but we are expecting him."

"When he gets here, will you tell him not to leave the hotel, but to wait for me in my suite?" We would need every minute to repair that gown.

THE FUNERAL HOME WAS teeming with mourners wearing various outfits in every imaginable shade of black. I snuck a peek in the chapel and saw an open casket with a shrunken old lady fast asleep—er, dead—inside.

"Where is Magda?" I asked Mario's father, who was escorting the bereaved to their seats.

"Ah, she is in the embalming room," he said. "But she is not in a good way. Mario is trying calm her."

I went looking for Magda, praying she wouldn't get embalming fluid on Audrey's dress. *That stuff had better be clear,* I thought. The air in the back of the mortuary was arctic and smelled like formaldehyde. After checking a few empty rooms, I came upon Mario working on a male corpse in his tuxedo (Mario wore the tux, not the corpse). Behind him, Magda sat in a green plastic chair in her modified Audrey Hepburn wedding gown, bawling like someone had died. Oh, right, someone did.

"Why the tears?" I asked. "On your wedding day?"

Magda wailed louder. Her heavy makeup was smearing and

I was concerned that she might get mascara stains on the dress. Grabbing a rag off the table, I dried her eyes. I hoped there weren't dead leftovers on it.

"Magda is upset because we are fully scheduled with funerals all day," Mario explained. "There is no time for a wedding. And see how beautiful she looks in the dress."

Magda stood and twirled around, sniveling as she spun. The white and silver off-the-shoulder brocade ball gown that had so elegantly adorned Audrey Hepburn in *Roman Holiday* now sported silk gussets to accommodate Magda's unusual figure. The skirt had been taped up by a third. When I was little, I had a troll doll in a wedding dress that looked like Magda. Her name was Bubbles. She was one of my favorites.

"You're a vision," I said, "like a princess bride."

"But I won't be walking down the aisle," Magda said, sniffing back tears. "Too many *corpi* to bury." She turned to Mario. "I *told* you we shouldn't marry here. This is exactly what I was afraid would happen."

"Magda, my love, we can marry tomorrow," Mario said. "There are no funerals on Sunday."

"No-no-no-no-no-no," I interjected. "I *must* have the dress back today. The Hepburn exhibit starts Monday. It's now or never, my friend. Come. I'll need you to translate."

Mario followed me to the lobby outside the chapel, where the mourners were gathering. "Take me to the family of the woman who died."

He directed me to the front row, where two middle-aged women sat drying their tears with freshly ironed handkerchiefs. "Twin daughters," Mario whispered. "The Romano sisters."

I knelt in front of them and offered my condolences. Then I asked if they wouldn't mind if, before their mother was eulogized, we held a quick wedding ceremony. "It would be life affirming," I explained.

Mario translated.

The women gasped in perfect unison. As twins, that probably happened a lot. "No, no," they both said, vehemently shaking their heads.

"But if you say 'yes,'" I added, "Mario's family will *give* you this funeral for free."

Mario gasped. "No, that's impossible. It is too much money for my family to lose."

"Listen to me, Mario," I said, "if you want to marry Magda, I suggest you do it now and stop being such a cheapskate. That girl could change her mind at any moment. She already thinks you're a dud in the bedroom."

Mario raised his eyebrow in question. "She told you this?"

"You think I'd make it up? She says you are too quick on the trigger, that you don't take time to pleasure her. If this wedding doesn't take place today, well, there's a chance it may never happen."

Mario spoke rapidly in Italian to the Romano sisters.

They spoke back.

"What are they saying?" I asked.

"They want to know if the casket will be free. They chose one of our most expensive models. And they wondered if they would be charged for the plot and for eternal upkeep. I don't see how—"

"YES! Give 'em everything. You want to marry Magda, don't you? Let's get this show on the road."

Five minutes later, Magda's and Mario's families were scattered among the mourners. The organist began to play a bridal march, which sounded funereal to me, but it would have to do. Magda started down the aisle. Half an hour ago she was a blubbering troll doll, but now she was radiant. A halo of light followed her as she floated down the aisle in that sumptuous cream silk dress. Mario's eyes sparkled at the sight of his bride. The funeral guests rose, and Mario broke into a wide grin. He and the priest stood in front of the open casket. Even the corpse seemed to be smiling.

In the presence of so much love, you hardly noticed the dead body lying in the open casket behind the happy couple. Someone really should have thought to close it. Just as the idea crossed my mind, Magda turned, took hold of the casket lid, and pulled it down. It must have been awfully heavy because it slammed right on the bride's finger or hand (it was hard to tell from where I was sitting). Magda shrieked, grabbed herself, as blood spewed forth.

"NOOOOOOO!" I screamed, diving out of my seat, hoping to heave my body between the dress and the scarlet liquid, knowing I would never get there in time.

I've Been Down for So Long (It Looks Like Up to Me)

Mario, God bless his soul, grabbed the wound with the sleeve of his jacket. The color drained from Magda's face until it was as pale as her gown. Mario spoke to her in rapid Italian (is there any other kind?) and she nodded, biting her lower lip. There were no obvious bloodstains, at least none that I spotted from twenty feet away.

The priest resumed the ceremony as Mario continued to compress Magda's wound. The Romano sisters stopped weeping, which made me think that combining weddings with funerals wasn't such a bad idea.

After Mario kissed the bride and the two made their way up the aisle, the priest opened the casket up, the Romano sisters went back to bawling, and everyone settled into funeral mode. I skipped out because I wanted to congratulate the happy dress . . . er, couple. It was almost noon.

By the time I caught up with Magda in the embalming room, she had changed outfits. Mario's father was stitching up her hand. How handy to have a father-in-law who could both stitch you and bury you. Magda's father was passing out canapés, while her mom popped the cork on a bottle of champagne. She poured glasses for the rest of the family, who were gathered around the body Mario was back to embalming. In my opinion, the whole scene wasn't very hygienic.

"*Grazie*," Magda said, beaming. "You saved me from being a, how do you say it, bridezilla."

"Did you get blood on the dress?" I asked, my voice quivering.

She shook her head and crossed herself with her good hand.

Magda's mother folded the wedding gown into a box, lay the red sash on top, and closed the lid. The tiara and earrings were in a separate jewelry case. "*Grazie*," she said. "*Ciao*."

I left the wedding party to their canapés and corpses, and headed for the hotel, where the promise of an all-nighter lay ahead.

NIGEL WAS WAITING FOR me in the suite. The instruments of his trade (needles, large spools of thread, two Singer sewing machines circa 1950, magnifying glasses, dressmaker's shears, thread nippers, pin cushions, and OTT-LITES) were assembled on the table.

"Show me the patient," he said.

I lay the dress out on the couch. "It was only deconstructed. You see? The seam stitching was removed," I said, "but no fabric was cut."

Nigel gasped at the sight of it. Then he sat down and put his head between his legs.

"Nigel, there's no time for tears. Give it to me straight. Can this dress be saved?"

Nigel lifted his head. Then he put on his magnifying glasses and examined the garment. "Can you give me a bit more light?"

I switched on another of the lights.

Finally Nigel spoke. "We can put it back together so that it looks like it did before. The average bloke will never be able to tell the difference. But it's depreciated by at least ninety percent."

"Oh, dear God, no," I said, sinking into the sofa. "Do we have to tell anyone?" It's not that I wanted to be dishonest and hide the truth; it's just that I wanted to know if it was possible to get away with it in case I did want to hide the truth (which, of course, I did not).

Nigel shook his head. "It will be thoroughly inspected when it's returned to the Hollywood Motion Picture Museum."

"And they'll definitely be able to tell?"

"Look at the fabric along the seam line," Nigel said, showing me the inside of the bodice. "See this fine row of holes left from the original sewing machine needle as it passed through the silk?

Each machine, combined with the needle used and particular seamstress, leaves its own signature. The stitch length, needle size, speed, and guidance of the material through the machine creates a unique fingerprint. We can try to stitch it back together in the holes made by the seamstresses at Paramount, but it won't be a perfect match. Plus, there are new holes from where the dress was altered. And no one at Paramount could find the original thread, although I did bring some that's pretty close from the early 1950s."

"I am so fired," I said. Then I remembered that I *was* fired. "You know what? I'll take the blame. There's no point in us both losing our jobs. But you may have to support me for the rest of my life."

Nigel smiled. "For you, luv, anything."

"Come, let's get started on the repair."

Carefully we dismantled the altered dress. It was then that we realized the enormous skirt was filled with horsehair stuffing and small lead weights to make it pouf and fall just the right way for the movie. *Arrrgh*, I thought, *why does this have to be so difficult?* Working with the 1950s Singers, we did our best to line up the seams as they had been previously and painstakingly sew the garment back together, stitch by stitch, coming as close to the original holes made in 1953 as we could. It was slow going, but there were two of us and we had all afternoon and night.

As we worked, I caught Nigel up on everything that had happened. How I had fallen hard for Denis King and then lost him to Sydney. *Poor Denis*, I thought. *His life will be misery if he marries that icy heiress. I'll bet she'd never lick strawberry jam off his private parts*. I giggled at the memory.

As I told Nigel the story, it hit me. "You know," I said, "I don't have to roll over and take it. I *could* fight for him. *I could.* In fact I think I will."

"Bravo," Nigel cheered. "She may be prettier and younger and wealthier and better connected, but you're somebody too."

"Thank you, it's true. I mesmerized a whole boatload of passengers with my chocolate corset and my fig-leaf bathing suit. I couldn't have done that unless I had *something* to recommend me."

Nigel regarded me with affection. "I still can't believe you did that, you naughty girl."

"Do you really think Sydney's prettier than me?"

Nigel threw an empty spool of thread at me.

"Careful, you could poke my eye out with that. So was that a yes or a no?"

"It was a no, by all means no."

"Thank you, it's true," I said.

Three Coins in the Fountain

NIGEL AND I ARRIVED at the Istituto Sunday morning with the *Roman Holiday* ball gown in hand. From the outside, the gown looked like perfection. But alas, that was not so. On close inspection, its defects were glaring.

"Signor Barbaro," I said to the Istituto's director, a gray-haired, impeccably dressed gentleman who smelled of musk the way European men often do, "Allow me to introduce my colleague, Nigel Calderwood, who is here to help you dress the mannequins." I handed him the gown. "I believe this is what you've been waiting for?"

"Ah, signorina, *grazie*," he said, kissing me on both cheeks and shaking Nigel's hand. Then he launched into a rapid Italian soliloquy that I couldn't understand, not that I could have if he'd spoken slower.

A tall, slender woman with perfect posture approached us. She had fine features, jade eyes, and a heart-shaped face haloed by an upsweep of dark brown hair. It was Rosa Di Giacinto, the curator I had spoken with many times. "*Grazie, grazie*," she said in her smoky voice. "We were so worried. What is the fiftieth anniversary of *Roman Holiday* without the famous ball gown worn by Miss Hepburn?"

Signor Barbaro chimed in, sounding angry, but thankfully I couldn't understand him.

"How do I tell him I'm sorry in Italian?" I asked.

"*Mi dispiace*," Rosa said.

"*Mi* so, so, so, so *dispiace*," I said.

"I was planning to help you dress the mannequins," Nigel said, "but I see you beat me to it." He gestured to the exhibit in an effort to change the subject. It had been set up just as we had done at the Fashion Museum, with costumed Hepburn mannequins placed in front of a series of small black box theaters showing movie clips (with Italian subtitles).

"*Sì*," Rosa said. "We could not wait. Now all that is left is for us to make the condition report and display this gown."

My stomach dropped. I had forgotten that the receiving museum's conservator had to inspect the garments.

Nigel whipped a piece of paper out of his bag. "There is no

need. I knew we would be pressed for time so I made the report this morning."

"Ah, *grazie*," Rosa said.

"You've done the most beautiful job with the show," I said, taking in the exhibit. I noticed the clip from *My Fair Lady* was playing the scene where Eliza Doolittle made her famous entry at the embassy ball in one of the theaters. But the mannequin in front of the screen was clad only in a cream silk and lace slip. "You haven't received the *My Fair Lady* gown yet?"

"It is being repaired," Rosa said.

"Yes, it was torn, but I thought it would be ready by now."

"Jacques Doucet is shipping it any day now," Nigel explained. "You can't rush these kinds of repairs, you know."

"Are you coming to the opening tomorrow? We just learned that Tanya will be here," Rosa said.

"I have a flight this evening," Nigel said.

"Sorry," I said. "I can't either."

"Then I hope you will return someday and spend more time with us," Rosa said.

"I will," I said. "I threw three coins in the Trevi Fountain just to be sure. I wish you great success." I kissed Signor Barbaro and Rosa on both cheeks and bid my *ciaos*. The ship had already docked and I needed to get on board. Denis' wedding to Sydney was scheduled for that afternoon. If I was going to fight for my man, I had no time to lose.

Thanks for the Memory

"POPS, I'M BACK," I said, exploding into the suite.

Not a cool move. There, in my bed, was my naked father with an equally naked woman, who was completely and utterly *nude*. They were going at it like Irving the humping poodle and Bartholomew the submissive bulldog. It was a horrific sight for any child to see. Making it all worse, Famous was fast asleep on the bed, oblivious to the human fornication taking place in her midst.

Carleen's voice rang out from beneath the covers. "It's okay, darlin'. We're all adults here."

My *eyes, my precious eyes*, I thought, retreating for cover.

Pops and Carleen donned their robes and joined me in the living room.

"Sorry I walked in on you," I said, my face burning.

"That's okay," Pops said. "We didn't know when you were coming back. Did you find the dresses?"

I nodded. "Yes, it's all handled, although I've been fired from the museum."

"Did that bitch can you?" Pops asked. "She was up here at least five times accusing me of lying. Can you imagine?"

"I told her to go to hay-ell," Carleen added. "Why would you want to work for someone like that? She did you a favor."

I sighed and crumpled into the couch. "It's not that I *want* to. Pops and I need the money."

Pops' face lit up. "I forgot to tell you. I got a job. The captain offered me a contract to sing and play piano in the Saloon for the next six months."

A feeling of pride mixed with relief washed over me. "That's wonderful. I'm so happy for you."

"Me too, darlin'," Carleen added. "I'm thrilled to have him onboard."

"I'll bet you are." I laughed.

There was a knock at the door. Darwin drifted in with a tray of hors d'oeuvres and a bottle of Krug Clos du Mesnil. "I saw you come in and thought you might like a snack," he said, setting up the table, popping the cork, and pouring three flutes.

Pops started to spread caviar, egg, and onion on the little toasts. "Ain't this the life?"

I gulped down my champagne and started toward the bedroom. "I need to freshen up," I said. "Darwin, can you find out where Denis King is right now?"

Darwin's eyes darted between me, Pops, and Carleen. "I'm sorry, but he and his family left the ship this morning. I believe he's marrying Miss Bass today. Then they're flying back to New York to bury Mr. Martin."

Darwin's words hit me like a sucker punch. "Are you sure?" I said. "Did you see them leave? With your own eyes?"

"I . . . I was told to remove Mrs. King's clothes from your closet last night. The King party was picked up hours ago, right after breakfast," he said. "I'm sorry." Then he bowed and backed out of the room the way John used to do.

I stood motionless for a moment, staring into the abyss, wondering if I could possibly look as tragic as I felt. Then I erupted into tears and fled to the bathroom, locking the door. Falling to the cold floor, I sobbed.

Pops was knocking. "Holly, what is it? What are you doing in there?"

"I'm having a nervous breakdown," I gulped out, then continued blubbering.

"I told you not to get involved with him," Pops said.

"In hindsight, you have perfect foresight . . . huh . . . huh," I cried. It felt as if my heart had been ripped in half. This was just like *Roman Holiday*, the *one* Audrey Hepburn movie whose ending I didn't want for myself, only Denis was the dutiful princess and I was the reporter left behind.

"Let me in," Pops begged. "Please."

My chest shook with sobs as I gasped for air. Hot tears came, sheets and sheets of them, salty to the taste as I blubbered, wailed, and choked until finally I was spent. Denis had moved on and there was nothing I could do.

"SO THAT'S MY PROPOSITION, Carleen. A million dollars would go a long way in making you an important donor at the Met's Costume Institute, *and* they'd take me seriously as a rainmaking curator if I brought you to them," I explained.

"Can you pass me the toast, Holly," Pops asked, "and the strawberry jam?"

I handed him the basket. "No more for me," I said to the waiter pouring coffee.

Carleen opened her pocketbook, ripped out a check, and started writing. "You sure one million's enough?" she asked. "It doesn't even put a ding in what I need to spend to keep Tex's money-grubbing tit-sucking children from getting their sticky little paws on it."

"Well, I . . ."

"Let's make it two, just to be safe," she said. "Here. Now, you listen to me, Holly, there's way more where this comes from. Not just from me, but from all my girlfriends back home. They'd love to be involved in a big important New York charity. I'm writing the check out to you as my agent. If the Met won't hire you, then find another fashion museum that will and give them my donation, got it? Now, you go out there and get yourself a new job so your daddy doesn't have to worry about you."

My eyes welled at her generosity. "I don't know how to thank you."

Carleen smiled and waved away her kind act. "Puh-lease, you deserve it. If that boss of yours with her thumpin' gizzard heart can't see how valuable you are, well, someone else will. In fact . . ." Carleen grabbed the check from my hand and ripped it in half. She turned over one of the halves and jotted down a name and number.

"What are you doing?" I asked.

Carleen gave me a sly smile. "How much would it take to endow my own museum in New York, one that knocks the teeth down the throat of that two-bit fashion house you work for and spits 'em out in single file?"

"Wait. You want to start a *new* museum?" I asked.

Carleen nodded. "Yes, and *you're* going to run it for me. What'll it take? Fifty million? A hundred million? I got more money than sense and I'd just as soon spend it as leave it."

I stared at her, too stunned to speak.

"Darlin', when I saw you being carried through the dining room in that chocolate corset, I knew you were a fashion superstar. And that fig-leaf bikini just sealed the deal for me. It was pure genius, something I might have done in my youth." She pointed to the name she'd written on the back of the check. "When you get home, you call this man. He's my lawyer. Work with him to put the whole shebang together. I'll be on your board. Sven'll be on your board, and pick whoever else you like. And pay yourself a nice fat salary from the get-go. You hear?"

"Carleen, I can't take that from you. What about your

stepchildren? Not to mention world hunger? AIDS? Cancer? That kind of thing . . ."

"Bless your heart, darlin'," Carleen said. "It's sweet of you to be concerned, but you needn't be. Tex was richer than a hound dog with two sets of balls. He left his family billions with a capital B. Those evil children of his will be swimming in dough no matter how many times I book the penthouse on this ship. Our foundation gives buttloads of money to all those five-hankie charities. I think it'd be a hoot to start my own museum. Tex always wanted me to have fun with his money. You gonna begrudge me that?"

"Far be it from me . . ." I said. "Can we name the museum after you?"

"After me and Tex," Carleen said. "It'll be another tribute to his legacy, not that he cared for dresses much. In point of fact, he mainly liked to remove my clothes to enjoy my womanly charms."

I reached over and hugged her tight. "*You* are my fairy godmother."

"And don't you forget it," Carleen said. "Now, get on off to the ball. You're about to be busier than a one-legged man at a butt-kicking contest."

I turned to my father. "I'll miss you, Pops," I said, hugging him goodbye one last time.

"Give my love to BL," Pops said, putting his napkin on the table. "Tell her I'm sorry, she'll have to find another dog walker."

"She'll understand when I explain what you're doing." I was carrying an extra bag—Pops' tuxedos and suits. The borrowed finery had to go back to Armani, but Svenderella had finally found his happy ending. Queen Carleen had taken him shopping on via Borgognona the morning before and now he was fully outfitted and moving into the floating castle.

Pops and Carleen escorted me down the long hallway to the opulent two-story marble lobby where the staff was bidding everyone *arrivederci*. It was changeover day and they needed to get us off the ship so it could be cleaned and readied for the next lucky group of passengers.

"Now, you be good," I whispered to Pops. "Don't get into trouble."

"Me? Trouble? Are you kidding? I'm going to be on my best behavior. This is the finest gig I've ever had. Room, gourmet food, a steady paycheck, hot women, I mean woman—I won't mess up; I promise."

As I journeyed down the gangplank to the waiting bus, I turned and saw Pops smiling at me. Carleen stood behind him holding Famous, waving me off. Okay, so I didn't get the prince. Thanks to my fairy godmother, I still had a shot at happily ever after.

New York City

The Boulevard of Broken Dreams

As soon as I returned to New York, I dug up the business card Denis had given me the day his car nailed my Versace suit in the rain. I wanted to apologize and let him know that while I'd deceived him about the donation, the rest had been real, at least for me. It was too late for the two of us, but I didn't want him to go through life thinking I was a no-good conniving skunk. Each time I called him, I'd get his assistant, Elvira. She said she was giving him the messages, but he never called back.

"Here you go, luv." Nigel handed me the framed photograph of Pops and me that I'd kept at my desk.

"Thanks," I said, slipping it into my bag. We were tucked into a booth in Jackson Hole (the restaurant, not the ski resort). Nigel and I were back on good terms. He'd agreed to share the blame with me over the *Roman Holiday* gown, not that we'd come clean about it yet, but soon we would have to. I promised Nigel a job at my new museum. How could I start such a project without him, Elaina, and Cosima by my side? I couldn't. It was still very hush-hush, but all three had agreed to join me as soon as I found a building to house the Tex and Carleen Panthollow Institute of Fashion. I wondered what Tanya would say when her staff did a mass exodus. At least she'd still have Sammie. That would be a comfort (to me).

"Thanks for the stuff," I said. "It would have been tough to go back for it." Nigel had cleaned off my desk and brought me my Rolodex and a few personal items.

"I hate to tell you, luv, but you're going back," Nigel said, "at least for one night."

"Methinks you're mistaken," I said. "Tanya would call the police if I showed up."

"*Au contraire*. Apparently Denis King pitched a fit when he found out you weren't coming to his opening tomorrow."

"What? I've been trying to reach him for days. He won't return my calls. Now he wants me at his opening. Why?"

"You know your little mistake at the press conference?" Nigel said. "It was the typo heard round the world. The film from *Extra* was posted on YouTube. It's been played a couple of million times. His company has gotten more attention in the past two weeks than it got in the past two years. The stock's up ten percent from all the publicity. Where have you been?"

"On a cruise, remember?" I said. "*With* Denis King, I might add." I wondered why he hadn't told me what a boon my little mistake had been to his business. How dare he let me feel awful about it and grovel for forgiveness!

"Hot plate," the waiter said, putting my hamburger and fries in front of me. Nigel was having a salad, as usual. Me? I needed to put on weight.

"Mr. King has you to thank for his sudden increase in fortune. I'm sure that's why he asked Phinnaeus to invite you. Phinn called me personally to make sure you'd be there." Phinnaeus Milch was the chairman of the Fashion Museum's board. I'd spoken to his secretary before, but never to the man himself.

"What did you say?"

"Well," he said conspiratorially, "I told him you wouldn't come because you had absolutely nothing to wear. Then I asked for special permission to let you borrow something from the museum."

"And?"

Nigel shrugged. "He said fine, borrow anything you like just as long as you come."

My stomach was filled with butterflies at the thought of seeing Denis again. I wanted to say I was sorry, but not to his face. Why had I made that stupid bet? Of course he went back to Sydney. Her motives may not have been pure, but they were out in the open.

"So? Will you come?" Nigel said. "Everyone who'll be there is a potential donor to your new museum."

"Tanya won't like it," I mumbled, sucking the salt off a hot French fry.

"What choice does she have? Phinn's her boss," Nigel said. "I'd stay out of her way, though. Here's the best part. Denis is making a big announcement at the party, but nobody knows what it is. Cosima thinks he's giving a huge gift to the institute in appreciation of *your* fortuitous error."

"Oh, that's rich. Sydney gets Denis. Tanya gets a big donation. I get fired, not that I care because I don't. French fry?"

"I'm sorry for what happened between you and Denis," Nigel said, taking a handful of fries. "What was he like, anyway?"

I considered the question. "He was like no billionaire I've ever known."

"How many have you known?"

"Do you mean personally?"

Nigel nodded.

"Two. Him and Carleen. But trust me, Denis is unusual. He was kind, handsome like a teddy bear, generous, fun, loyal to his family, a good father. But as soon as he thought he couldn't trust me, he put up this wall. Polite but unforgiving, you know?" I shook my head sadly. "He was falling in love with me, but I blew it. It doesn't matter. I deserved it."

"Don't say that," Nigel said. "You were going to tell him the truth."

"Of course. Eventually," I said. "Don't you think he should have forgiven me? Princess Ann forgave Joe Bradley when she found out he was a journalist trying to get a story in *Roman Holiday*."

"Life isn't like the movies, luv."

I sighed. "I know. But I wish it was. For a while, I was hoping

Denis would be my prince—you know, rescue me from my godforsaken life. At least now I know there's only one person I can depend on when I need to be rescued."

"Me, right?" Nigel said.

"No! You are the *antithesis* of dependable. It's *me*. I'm the only safety net I have."

"Well, I'm glad I helped you realize that," Nigel said. "But I'm sorry I let you down."

"And well you should be."

"Let me make it up to you. Tell me you'll be my date to the opening tomorrow night."

"But what would I wear?"

"Funny you should ask," Nigel said. "Look what I just picked up from Jacques Doucet." He reached into the shopping bag he had set in the booth and unwrapped the tissue paper covering a cream embroidered and beaded silk organza sheath that was—

"WHAT! That's the ball gown from *My Fair Lady*. Are you kidding me? I'm not wearing that, not after . . ."

"Not after what?" Nigel said. "After all you went through, you deserve to wear a real Hepburn costume. What's Tanya going to do? Fire you? Phinn said you could borrow anything as long as you came."

"He must not know it's against the rules."

"Take advantage of his ignorance. I'm not the only one who wants to see you in it. Cosima and Elaina do too. In fact, we insist." Nigel was shaking his finger at me to make his point when he hit his glass and knocked it over.

I watched, as though it were in slow motion, as the liquid began cascading over the rim, sloshing on the table, and flowing toward the unprotected priceless gown. At the last second, Nigel whipped the garment out of the path of the oncoming vegetable juice. It was a brilliant save.

I patted the spill with my napkin and grabbed several more from the empty table next to us.

"The dress is unharmed," Nigel said, his voice shaking. "You see; it's a sign. This is something you *must* do because . . . you must do it."

"Okay, fine, I'll come and I'll wear the gown," I said, after cleaning up the spill. "There are things I want to say to Mr. Penis King."

"You're not going to embarrass yourself, are you?" Nigel asked. "Or the Fashion Museum?"

I gave Nigel a sly look. "Have you ever known me to do anything like that?"

Let's Face the Music and Dance

"Tiaras through Time at the National Fashion Museum is a magnificent exhibit, epitomizing majesty, romance, and glamour, while showing that all that glitters is indeed gold, and diamonds, and rubies, and sapphires . . ." —VOGUE

THE OPENING GALA FOR Denis King Presents: Tiaras through Time was the hottest invitation in town. Everyone was dying to see the stunning creations that had decorated the heads of the most celebrated women ever to walk the face of the earth. The Fashion Museum had invited all their major donors and board members, along with the socialite A-list as determined by the blue-haired old guard—those self-appointed society Nazis who have taken on the vital task of determining who matters in the worlds of fashion, philanthropy, arts, and the social whirl. Of course, there were the newer, younger "celebutants," including Sydney and her privileged posse.

The exhibit had been set up in our ballroom, which always felt to me like a royal palace, with its gilded mirrors, looming faux masterpieces, and over-the-top crystal chandeliers. Glass cases with special lights designed to make gems sparkle at their brightest intensity lined the walls. Each display contained priceless tiaras—a gold-wreath crown from ancient Greece, a ruby garland of roses adorned with diamonds and emeralds from Rome, a crystal-engraved crown decorated with rows of brilliant-cut diamonds made by Cartier, a Russian tiara comb set with emeralds and sapphires with matching necklace and earrings—each piece more breathtaking than the last. This show was a jewelry lover's wet dream. Okay, that was crass. But it was true.

I was proud of the understated elegance of our event. Too often, society fetes resembled over-the-top vomitzvahs as a result of party planners run amuck. We had avoided that pitfall by allowing the elegant venue and majestic treasures of our exhibit to speak for themselves.

Arriving fashionably late, I entered the room slowly, holding my head high. The gown I had borrowed, a cream embroidered and beaded silk organza sheath covering a matching crepe de chine slip, fit as though it were tailor made. The scoop neckline with its cap sleeves sparkled with crystal and gold beads that had been featured throughout the dress, most generously around the shoulders, sleeves, neck, and hemline. The empire silhouette did wonders for my bustline, which had been pushed up and amplified with the help of a new high-tech patented Victoria's Secret bra. Wearing fabric that had once adorned Audrey Hepburn was everything I could have ever imagined and more—the exquisite detail of the embroidery, the sensual sheen of the organza sheath, the bright sparkle of the tiny crystals. What intoxicating bliss! In this gown, nothing bad could happen to you.

The replica starburst tiara from the movie graced my head. Diamond waterfalls spilled from my earlobes. The Edwardian choker that Edith Head had designed to hide Hepburn's prominent collarbones and gazelle-like neck worked its magic on mine. I felt like Eliza Doolittle entering the embassy ball, having just been transformed from a Cockney flower girl to a duchess. Heads turned when I floated in, and I imagined guests asking, "Who *is* that spellbinding creature?"

Who is she indeed!

A waiter in tails offered me a crystal flute of champagne, which I downed in three gulps.

Out of the corner of my eye, I spotted Sammie, who was having an impassioned conversation with Sydney. Even from here, I could see Sammie was engaged in some serious sucking-up.

"There you are, luv. Mwaa-mwaa." Nigel said, air-kissing me. He stood back and gave me the once-over. "You are *radiant* tonight. That dress is positively sublime."

"Thank you," I murmured.

Cosima with her cloud of flame-colored curls was right behind him with more air kisses. "Look at you! You're dazzling."

"I feel like a princess," I admitted. "And you look amazing too." Cosima was wearing a black Behnaz Sarafpour lingerie-inspired cocktail slip dress that she must have borrowed from the designer.

"It's so lonely without you here," Cosima whispered. "We can't wait until we're working together again."

"It won't be long. You've done a wonderful job with the room."

"Do you like it?" Cosima asked. "You should. You arranged it and it's perfect."

I smiled modestly and took another glass of champagne from a waitress. Glancing over Cosima's shoulder, I saw Denis standing with Lucille. He was watching me from across the room.

"Would you excuse me?" I said, starting to make my way to the Kings. I was not going to hide from them. Plus, I looked *très magnifique* and wanted Denis to see what he had foolishly cast aside.

By the time I reached them, Lucille had moved over to the sushi station and was deep in conversation with Muffie Rockefeller.

Denis lit up when he saw me. If I didn't know he was married, I would have thought he wanted to kiss me. Considering whom he married, it made perfect sense that he would want to kiss me, but that was not in the cards.

"You are stunning," he marveled.

"It's the dress," I demurred.

"What dress?" Denis said. "The only thing I see is you. There's a magnificence that comes out in your eyes and voice, in the way you stand, in the way you walk. It's like you're lit from within, Holly."

"Stop, you're making me self-conscious."

"Will you forgive me for not saying goodbye on the ship?"

I held up my hand to stop him. "I'm the one who is sorry. I should have been honest with you from the beginning. Did you get the message that I called?"

"Yes, I . . . I did, but I didn't have a chance—"

"It doesn't matter. Here," I said, reaching into my evening bag and handing him a note and a personal check.

"What's this?" he asked.

"Read it," I said, as he opened the letter.

Dear Mr. King,

Enclosed is an itemized statement of all expenses incurred by you on my behalf. This includes the use of your private jet, hotel meals, clothing, Vespa rental, and tips, which comes to a total of $10,411.35. It is only an estimate. If your figure amount differs, please let me know. Enclosed is a check covering such amount.

With best wishes for your continued success,
Holly J. Ross

"Ten thousand, four hundred eleven dollars and thirty-five cents? How did you figure that?" Denis suppressed a smile.

"It was my best guess."

Denis tore the check in half. "I can't accept this."

A feeling of relief washed over me. My ship was in the harbor, but it hadn't quite come in. Carleen's lawyer couldn't meet with me until next week. Kitty and I were still sleeping on the AeroBed in the basement of Muttropolis. If Denis had cashed the darn thing, it would have bounced. But at least now he could see I was an honorable person who paid her debts rather than the despicable schemer he thought I was. Not that giving someone a hot check was honorable. I was doing the best I could with what little I had.

"Well, then I thank you for—" I said.

"Excuse me," Tanya said, interrupting our conversation. "Oh, hello, Holly. Borrowed another dress, I see. We're starting the presentation, Denis. I can't *wait* to find out what all the mystery is about." Tanya took Denis' elbow and guided him toward the dais.

Denis glanced back at me. "Stay, please," he said.

It Had to Be You

NIGEL APPEARED AS IF by magic. "Is everything all right, luv?"

Cosima was behind him. "Ignore Tanya. Someday she'll get hers."

Phinnaeus Milch took the mike. "Ladies and gentlemen, tonight is a most auspicious occasion. This party marks the opening of Denis King Presents: Tiaras through Time, which we at the Fashion Museum are honored to present. It is also a very special night because of the exciting announcement we are about to make. As you know, when our patron, Cornelia Von Aston LeClaire Peabody, died, she bequeathed twenty million dollars, this elegant mansion, and a stunning collection of her own couture wardrobe to be used to establish our museum. But no one knew better than Corny that it takes much more than that to endow an organization such as this in perpetuity. It was Corny's express wish that we not name the museum for her, but that we wait for an even bigger gift, a gift of at least one hundred million dollars, and that we allow *that* donor to name our museum. Ladies and gentlemen, we have received such a gift tonight."

The room buzzed with excitement. A one-hundred-million-dollar donation was gasp-worthy, even for this jaded crowd. It would take "the Little Fashion Museum That Could" into a whole new league.

"Ladies and gentlemen, Denis King," Phinnaeus said, gesturing toward the biggest man in town.

Denis approached the microphone, grinning like a kid who just found a train set under his Christmas tree. "Fashion Museum, friends, my chest swells with pride as I stand before you tonight. This exhibit is spectacular, don't you agree?"

Everyone clapped and a few less civilized guests hooted. Lucille stood near the front, beaming at her son like he just won the Academy Award. Annie, who must have gone back to her mother, wasn't there. That was too bad. It would have meant a lot to Denis to share the moment.

"New York City is one of the world's most important cultural capitals," Denis said. "We have the best in art museums, theaters, dance companies—you name it. And while this city hosts spectacular costume museums that are affiliated with larger institutions like the Met and the Fashion Institute of Technology, there is enough interest in the subject to warrant a stand-alone, equally important museum. So I have decided to make a gift of ten million dollars a year over the next ten years to the National Museum of Fashion; that's one hundred million dollars in total."

There was gasping, applause, and squealing from the crowd. I glanced at Tanya, whose mouth was agape. How would she spend one hundred million dollars? I wondered for a nanosecond. Oh, let me count the ways. This was going to get interesting, I thought. Our two museums would be on equal footing. Let the games begin.

Tanya rushed the dais. "Thank you. *Thank you*, Mr. King," she said. Shaking Denis' hand and grabbing the mike, she went on. "You have no idea what this will mean to us. There is so much work to be done and now, with my leadership and your capital, we can make this the finest fashion institute in all the world!"

Denis touched Tanya's shoulder and whispered in her ear.

"Oh, sorry. Mr. King has more to say." She stepped away from the mike, but stood on the dais.

Denis gave Tanya an annoyed look; at least that was my interpretation. "Thank you," he said. "As is customary with donors of large gifts, the board of directors has allowed me to have a limited hand in the direction the museum will take in the future. And our first order of business was to name the institute for a woman I care deeply about." Denis gestured to a large sign on an easel that had been covered with black velvet draping.

I glanced at Lucille, who was smiling demurely, and Sydney, who looked like she had pickle juice running through her veins. *Guess we know who's getting the museum named after her*, I thought.

Phinnaeus whipped off the cloth to reveal the new name of the museum: The Holly Boss Institute of Fashion.

Everyone looked around, confused. *Who in tarnation was Holly Boss?* they had to be wondering. That was odd, I thought. They're giving the directorship to someone with a name similar to mine . . .

"Well, what do you know?" Denis said, his eyes twinkling with mischief. "There's a typo." He was staring right at me.

"Oh, dear, sorry about that," Phinnaeus said. "As you mentioned, when you give an institution one hundred million dollars, you have a say in its future direction. And Mr. King has been most effective in persuading our board members that our museum is ready for a different kind of leader, a new boss, if you will. And that new leader is our own Holly Boss—I mean Ross." Phinnaeus gestured my way and the crowd began chattering. Everyone stared at me. I would have reacted if I could have found my jaw. It was somewhere on the floor.

"Now, wait just a moment," Tanya started. "As the director, I have some say in this matter . . ."

"Now, don't you worry, Tanya," Phinnaeus said. "You're a talented girl. I'm sure Holly will find a role for you."

"But—but," she stammered, "why?"

Phinnaeus spoke under his breath, but it was loud enough for those of us in the front to hear. "She brings more to the table than you. It's that simple."

"What does *she* bring that I don't?" Tanya said.

"One hundred million dollars, you fool," Phinnaeus said through clenched teeth.

Rags to Riches

OKAY, LET ME GET this straight. Last week I was fired. Today my cup runneth over with two fashion museums to run. It was eerily reminiscent of the last time all my dreams converged into one perfect storm—when I was on the brink of being married and promoted. We all know how that turned out.

I could not believe this was happening. My mouth was drier than happy hour at the Betty Ford Clinic. I gulped down half an abandoned, lipstick-stained flute of champagne, which was teeming with someone else's microorganisms.

Denis held up his hands to stop the chatter. "Holly Ross, our new director, why don't you come up here so everyone can meet you?"

I floated up the steps to the stage, stood next to Denis, and faced the crowd. "I'm smiling and pretending to be joking with you," I whispered, "but I'm going to kill you. How could you surprise me with this?"

"Now we're even," he said, laughing at his lame typo joke. Let's face it: typo jokes are only rarely funny.

Nigel, Cosima, and Elaina were holding on to each other, their mouths open so wide I could count their fillings. Gus, my favorite security guard, was standing in the back of the room giving me the thumbs-up signal. He looked ten years younger. Sammie and Tanya were fuming in the corner next to Sydney—the three scrooges. I wondered why Sydney wasn't up here and what she must think about Denis naming the museum for me and not her. *She's got to be pissed,* I thought.

"Ladies and gentlemen," Denis said, "Holly Ross is a hidden gem at this museum. She came here after earning her master's at the Fashion Institute of Technology. I had the opportunity to see Holly in action recently while in Italy. First she bewitched a ship full of cruisers who have seen and heard it all with her mesmerizing lecture on the history of underwear. Then some valuable costumes went missing while in transit to another museum in Rome. Holly was relentless in getting those pieces returned to where they belonged. I've never seen such dogged determination in one person, and when I had the opportunity, through my wallet, to influence the leadership of this institution, I knew Holly was the one. This woman is the da Vinci of fashion historians." Denis caught my eye and smiled, flashing those irresistible dimples.

Oh, stop, please, I thought modestly. *'Twas I who lost those dresses in the first place . . .*

"Holly," Denis said, "I'm sure everyone would love to hear from you."

This was awkward.

I stepped up to the mike. A hush fell over the crowd. "Ladies and gentlemen, I'm honored. I'm flattered. I'm shocked. I don't know what to say, really, other than thank you for this show of confidence. But I'm . . . I'm going to have to . . . Denis, could I have a word with you in private?"

(I Did It) My Way

S THE CROWD BUZZED with speculation, I led Denis to a walnut-paneled anteroom behind the dais.

"You should see yourself right now," Denis said.

"What?"

"You are the most magnetic woman I've ever seen," he said, brushing my cheek with his hand. "There's something about you that makes me have to look at you, listen to you. My God, there's no escaping you."

A week he's married and he already has a roving eye. I kicked him in the shin. "Shame on you."

"Aaaaah," he cried. "What did you do that for?"

"The answer's no. You can't name the museum for me and I won't run it for you."

"But why?" he asked, looking deflated and in pain. "I thought you'd be thrilled."

"Thrilled? What? To win second place?" I said. "I get the job but not the man. How could I work with you after what happened between us? Don't you think Sydney would have something to say about that?"

"Sydney? Why would I care what she says?"

I knocked on his head. "Hello. Anyone home? She's your *wife*."

"Ooooh, you think I married her," Denis said, his eyebrows arched mischievously. "I called it off."

My body stiffened in shock. "You did? Then what is she doing here?"

"She's here because she and Bunny are million-dollar donors. And I called it off because I'm in love with *you*," he said, smoothing a wayward tuft of my hair.

I crossed my arms and shot him a cold look. "You have a funny way of showing it, leaving the ship without saying goodbye, not calling me back."

His expression grew serious. "I'm sorry. I was worried Sydney would cause a scene. And I wanted to get back to arrange all this," he said, gesturing toward the ballroom, "to surprise you. I told you I had a thing about rescuing damsels."

I met his gaze. "Denis, I don't need rescuing."

"Of course you don't. What I meant was—"

I shook my head and held my palms up to stop him. "Forget it. You see, the point is. Denis, here's the thing . . ."

"What is the thing?"

A slow smile spread across my face. "The thing is, Carleen is donating one hundred million dollars so I can start a fashion museum in *her* name. Can you believe it? I'm thrilled. I'll get to do *everything*—find the building, build a permanent collection, put on shows. It's *all* going to be my vision. That's why I couldn't possibly let you name this place for me. It wouldn't look right if I was running a competing institute across the street."

"Ah, I see," Denis said. He stroked his chin as though he had a beard. "This does complicate things."

"It doesn't have to," I said. "You can name *your* museum for Lucille or Annie . . ."

"I have a better idea," Denis said.

"I'm listening."

"How about a merger?"

"A merger?"

"Yes," Denis said. "Take Carleen's money, along with my donation, and run *this* museum according to your vision. Name it whatever you like. That way, you don't have to start from scratch. It'll be up and running much faster. You would control the most highly endowed fashion museum in the world."

"That's certainly tempting," I said thoughtfully. "So what you're proposing is a business merger between our two museums?"

Denis lifted my chin with his hand. "*And* a personal merger between the two of us."

"And you're proposing this why?"

Denis took me in his arms and pressed his lips to mine, softly caressing my mouth more than kissing it, teasing me with his lips and tongue until we finally parted.

"Oh, that's why," I murmured. "I can be so stupid."

It occurred to me that if the film of my life were *An Affair to Remember,* this would be the part where Cary Grant comes back to give Deborah Kerr his grandmother's shawl and then he realizes she's in a wheelchair and that's why she never met him at the top of the Empire State Building and then they fall into each other's arms and . . . *shut up*! This isn't *An Affair to Remember.* This is my real, honest-to-goodness life, so go live it for crying out loud . . .

"Excuse me, Denis, but could you explain that to me again?"

He looked at me, his eyes moist with affection, then reclaimed my lips, ravishing them with his deep, warm kiss, sending my stomach into orbit.

"And again . . ." I said.

I've Grown Accustomed to Her Face

One year later . . .

"I DIDN'T BRING YOU all the way to Los Angeles so you could go swimming," Denis said to Annie. "You'll love Disneyland, I promise."

"But, Daddy, Poppy said it's an hour-and-a-half drive. That's boring," Annie whined. "And aren't you proud of how I'm not complaining that you dragged me to this stinky, grown-up restaurant."

"The Ivy isn't a grown-up restaurant, Annie," I said. "Didn't you see Hilary Duff walk out when you were coming in?"

"Yeah, but she's so yesterday," Annie protested.

I playfully lobbed my buttered roll her way, and watched it bounce off her arm and fall to the ground. Two bluebirds landed to partake in the feast. We were sitting outside, under a large white umbrella, inside the picket fence enclosing the Ivy's brick patio. The space was utterly charming with hanging baskets of flowers and wooden boxes of blooming red roses.

"I'll hear none of that, young lady," Lucille said. "You're going and that's that. You're going by *helicopter*!"

"A helicopter. Grandma, you are so cool."

"Yes, aren't I fabulous?" Lucille said. "You don't mind if I spoil her, do you? I only have one grandchild . . . that is, unless you have something you want to tell me."

Denis laughed and looked at me. "What do you think, Holly?"

"Nothing to report, but spoil her all you like," I said. "It's a grandmother's right."

Denis and I were going to Sotheby's while Annie and Lucille went to Disneyland. There were a few pieces we had our eyes on, most especially a 1958 Balenciaga blue silk-taffeta gown, a conical bra Jean Paul Gaultier designed for Madonna's Blond Ambition tour, and the black dress Audrey Hepburn wore in *Breakfast at Tiffany's*.

Few people know it, but they made three black dresses for the movie (in case one was damaged) and now a second one was up for sale. I just love having my own fashion museum. It's so much fun to shop for. Naturally, the first piece we bought for our permanent collection was the 1953 Edith Head ball gown from *Roman Holiday* (acquired at full price even though it had mysteriously been damaged—tee hee!). Over the next few years, we hoped to acquire one costume from every movie Audrey ever made. That was my idea, but everyone thought it was brilliant. Did I mention how much I loved having my own fashion museum? Oh, yes, I believe I did.

"Don't forget, Annie, we're taking you to Universal Studios tomorrow," Carleen said.

"Thank you so much," I said. "She'd be bored stiff with us." The next day, Pops and Carleen were entertaining Annie while Denis and I attended the wedding of Sammie Kittenplatt to Brewster Budgeon (of the Beverly Hills Budgeons). After Sammie's fashion career crashed and burned (which coincided with the day I became her boss), her mother underwrote her new line of evening bags (called Simply Sammie) and arranged to marry her off to a model-actor-socialite who was very much *of* her world. We were invited, of course, since Denis and Sammie's mother both served on the Carleen and Tex Panthollow Fashion Museum board. Rich people are very civilized that way.

"It's our pleasure to take her," Pops said. "We can't get enough of the little pipsqueak."

"Don't call me a pipsqueak," Annie said.

"Pipsqueak," he whispered, with a twinkle in his eye.

The waiter came over to take our order. Pops insisted that the Ivy had "the best fried chicken anywhere, better even than Popeyes," so everyone followed his recommendation.

"Will you want a leg or a breast?" I asked Denis.

He leaned over to kiss me. "I'll have both."

I giggled. "Oh, stop!"

"Holly, is that *you*?" someone said.

I looked up and saw a familiar face, but I wasn't sure.

"Suzy. *Suzy Hendrix*," she said.

"Oh, my God!" I shrieked. "Give me a hug. Suzy, this is my husband, Denis King. Denis, this is Suzy Hendrix. She represented my old boyfriend in entertainment matters and when he was arrested for, well . . . you remember."

"I just moved to L.A.," Suzy said. "I'm working for CAA."

"Do you ever see Alessandro?"

"Yes, I just negotiated his appearance this fall on *The Surreal Life* with Carrot Top, the Snapple lady, and Robert Blake. It's all he's been able to get since the 'incident,'" she said, making air quotes. "Such a pity."

"Life isn't always what one wants," I mused.

Suzy waved at her friends, who were almost at the patio door. "Well, gotta run. Great to see you, Holly. Let's do lunch sometime."

I fell back into my seat, my eyes wide with disbelief. "Poor Alessandro, doing reality TV was his worst nightmare. Between the two of us, I got the happy ending."

Denis leaned over and kissed my lips. "Honey, our happiness is only just beginning."

My cell phone vibrated and I looked to see if it was the call I had been waiting for. It was Tanya. You'd think I would have fired her after all that happened between us, but I didn't. The woman was a master fund-raiser and we needed someone with that talent. I made her assistant director of the museum and paid her the same salary as before (as long as she met her donation quotas). Over the past year, she'd lost her superiority complex and the Anna Wintour sunglasses. It was progress.

"Holly, I think we got it," Tanya started. "Victoria's Secret says they're in for eight hundred thousand."

"Good work," I said. "This'll be huge. And remember what I said about selling cotton candy underwear and chocolate corsets at the museum store. People love them."

"Got it," Tanya said. "Gus wants to talk with you. Something about the consultant's report." As soon as I took over the museum, I promoted Gus to head of security. Since taking the job, he had grown younger by the day. The violations I had gotten away with—borrowing clothes, traveling with inventory—highlighted just how vulnerable our collection was. We needed to tighten our procedures so that no one could ever commit the kinds of transgressions I had, at least not under my watch.

"Tell him to send an e-mail and I'll get back to him later."

"What did Tanya say?" Denis asked.

"It seems she got full funding for the History of Underwear show."

Denis cocked his head thoughtfully. "So you were smart to keep her. I admit . . ."

I interrupted him mid-cock. " . . . That you married a brilliant museum directress," I teased.

He leaned over and gave me kiss. I just love Denis' scent. Kind of musky but slightly sweet—it's his deodorant, very sexy and masculine.

"You should see yourself right now," he whispered.

"What?"

"You've never looked lovelier."

As I playfully tapped the cleft in his chin, I closed my eyes and gave thanks for the blessings I'd been given, for the wringers I'd endured, and for the dreams that had come true.

The End

Did you spot the Audrey Hepburn and Cary Grant movie references?

THERE ARE MORE THAN 125 hidden (and not so hidden) references to Audrey Hepburn and Cary Grant movies in this novel. How many did you notice? If you want to see what they are, e-mail your request to the author at hollywoulddream@aol.com and she will be happy to send you the list.

Holly Would Dream

About This Guide

The suggested questions are intended to help your reading group find new and interesting angles and topics for your discussion of *Holly Would Dream*. We hope that these ideas will enrich your conversation and increase your enjoyment of the book. Many fine books from Simon & Schuster feature reading group guides. For a complete listing, or to read the guides online, visit www.BookClubReader.com.

Questions for Discussion

1. The novel opens with the fairy tale beginning of "Once upon a time . . ." How is this story a fairy tale? What Audrey Hepburn movie does this opening pay homage to?

2. Holly Ross is a bright, ambitious career woman who seems to have it all. What do you think the attraction was between her and Alessandro? Their breakup turned into a tabloid

nightmare and he ends their engagement in a text message. When she asks him to help cancel the wedding arrangements, he refuses like a petulant child. "At that moment, I saw Alessandro, *really* saw him. He was appearing in the movie of his life and it was about to bomb. Why would I want to costar with such a loser? Was I *that* afraid to be alone?" What attracted Holly to Alessandro in the first place? Did she really love him? How does this action show Holly who Alessandro truly is? How did Holly miss this before?

3. Real estate mogul Denis King makes quite an impression after he rescues a rain-soaked Holly in true Prince Charming fashion: "A woman could live happily ever after with a man like that. Any guy who would return to help the stranger his car splashed could be counted on to hold your hand when you walked down the street or your hair back when you puked." Why doesn't Holly completely trust Denis? Why do you think she doesn't let on who she is?

4. Conniving Sammie Kittenplatt is a girl who, in Holly's words, was "born with a Kmart exterior that had been attended to by the right dermatologists, hairdressers, trainers, and stylists. Now she was all Bergdorf's." Why is Holly so furious at losing the job to Sammie? After being passed over for the promotion that was rightfully hers, why didn't Holly quit?

5. Holly makes a deal with her boss, Tanya: If she can land a million-dollar benefactor for the museum, she can have the

position she wanted. Tanya decides to make it a contest between Holly and Sammie. How does this make both women feel? Who do you think is more qualified for the job?

6. Holly's father laments: "I never should have let you watch those old films. They ruined you for real life." What does he mean by this statement? How are Holly and her father different? How are they alike?

7. When the Hepburn collection is found to be missing from the museum, why doesn't Nigel tell Tanya that Holly is the courier for the clothes?

8. On board the luxurious Tiffany liner, Holly meets wealthy Texas widow Carleen Panthollow. How is Carleen like a fairy godmother to Holly? The oceanic adventure takes Holly to some beautiful ports of call. Which one was your favorite and why?

9. Denis King's engagement to the beautiful Sydney Bass is a merger of two families. Do you think Denis has any real feelings for Sydney, or is he marrying her to please his mother? How does Holly feel about this engagement?

10. *Holly Would Dream* is filled with hidden secrets and people who aren't what they seem. What did you think of Sydney's behavior on the cruise? Why is the truth kept from Denis? Who is Frank Flannagan?

11. In an effort to create interest in her lectures aboard the ship, Holly chucks her clothes and has the ship's pastry chef decorate her as a live dessert. What was the result? What is it about Holly's personality that allows her to do this? What does this experience show Holly about herself?

12. Holly finally gets to give the "Satan Twins" (Sammie and Tanya) a piece of her mind when she says: "Sammie, I am so sick of you and Tanya telling me I'm not of your world. . . . The difference between a woman of consequence and a nobody has nothing to do with where she is brought up, but how's she's treated. I'll forever be a nobody to you because you treat me as a nobody and always will. But to Denis I'm a woman of consequence because he treats me as one and always will." Which Audrey Hepburn movie does this speech remind you of? What do you think prompted Holly to make this declaration now?

13. When Holly returns to New York, she's invited to attend Denis' opening and does so wearing the ball gown from *My Fair Lady*. "Wearing fabric that had once adorned Audrey Hepburn was everything I'd imagined and more—the exquisite detail of the embroidery, the sensual sheen of the organza sheath, the bright sparkle of the thousand tiny crystals. What intoxicating bliss! In this gown, nothing bad could happen to you." Is Holly being herself or playing a part? Does wearing the dress empower Holly?

14. Discuss Holly's transformation and the other characters' development including her father, Tanya, and Denis. How

is the ending like an Audrey Hepburn film? Did then ending surprise you?

15. Do you ever wish your life could be like a romantic comedy from the 1950s? What is it about those stories that you find appealing? What does not appeal to you?

16. There are several plot parallels between *Holly Would Dream* and some old Hollywood classics. In what way is *Holly Would Dream* like *Sabrina*, *Roman Holiday*, *How to Steal a Million*, *Charade*, *My Fair Lady*, *An Affair to Remember*, or *That Touch of Mink*?

17. Which movie stars of today come close to having the style and class of Audrey Hepburn and Cary Grant?

18. Do women today still wish for a prince to rescue them and a fairy tale ending or are we too liberated for that kind of thinking?

19. Have you ever encountered people like Tanya and Sammie in a work environment? If so, what was the worst thing a Tanya or Sammie has ever done to you? How do you fight back against snakes like that in the workplace?

A Conversation with Karen Quinn

The romantic locations of Holly Would Dream *are wonderful. What sort of research process did you undergo for this novel?*

My husband, Mark, and I took several cruises over the last few years and I took copious notes. We sailed to many of the same ports as the *Tiffany Star*. Ephesus was one of my favorite cities, and I set an important scene there. We also went to Santorini, a gorgeous Greek island that you can only get around on via donkey or tram. That is where Holly and Denis were stranded when they missed the ship. On one of our cruises, there really was a woman who walked around pumping five-pound pink free weights all the time. That's where I got that idea to have Sydney do that. On another cruise, there was a passenger who wore stilettos when she went to Pompeii (another silly thing I had Sydney do). On the day we visited Ephesus, a passenger brought the rugs she had purchased to the bar that night to show them off. She told people what she had spent on them. Details like that found their way into the story. Finally, Mark and I went to Rome last summer so that I could check out all the places I'd written about in the story. We stayed at the Hassler, where Holly and Denis stayed (and where Audrey Hepburn stayed when making *Roman Holiday*), ate at the restaurants, and visited the same sites as the characters. Researching this book was as much fun as writing it.

What made you choose Audrey Hepburn as Holly's touchstone in the story?

I have always adored her movies, especially her early romantic comedies. They never fail to make me happy. I admire her because she was such a talented actress, devoted mother, and great humanitarian. Plus, she had her own unique style that has stood the test of time. You can go on youtube.com today and get advice on how to do your makeup like Audrey Hepburn. People still style their hair as she did. Every year, new books come out about her. There are scores of sites on myspace.com and facebook .com devoted to her. From the bios I've read, is seems like she was a lovely, authentic person. I felt it would be fun to create a character like Holly, who was completely enamored with Audrey Hepburn.

Now that you are a full-time novelist, what are some of the differences between writing part-time and writing full-time? What would you say is the best part about writing novels? What is the most stressful aspect of this career?

When you write full-time, you have no excuses for not producing. So that keeps me working hard. The thing I love most about writing novels is creating a world and filling it with characters I really get to know and love over the course of a project. I'm always sad to say goodbye to my characters at the end of the story. They feel very real to me. The most stressful part of a full-time writing career is that you live and die by your own work. For many years, I was a VP at American Express. If I missed a few weeks of work, I still got paid and the company never missed a beat. But now if I took a month off writing, nothing would happen. Also, at Amex (as is the case with many jobs), every project I worked on had twenty people's handprints on it. As a writer, it's my editor and me. So I feel total ownership of my writing. On the flip side, there is no one to blame if the critics don't like my work (except my editor, of course).

Each of the chapter titles are song titles, such as "Isn't It Romantic" or "Let's Call the Whole Thing Off." What made you choose this device?

I'm a sucker for these old songs, and I thought they would make good chapter titles. It was such fun to choose the titles that seemed connected to each chapter. I made a playlist for my iPod of all the songs that I used as chapter titles. It's a great list—you can easily make your own.

The Ivy Chronicles *has been optioned for a film and there's film interest in* Wife in the Fast Lane. *If* Holly Would Dream *were to be a movie, who would you like to see in the role of Holly?*

It would have to be someone thin, because she would have to fit into the Hepburn costumes. One person I can see in the role is Heather Graham because she is beautiful and so talented at comedy. I could also imagine Jessica Alba, Anne Hathaway, or Renée Zellweger. I would love to see *Holly Would Dream* turned into a movie in the same style as the 1950s films that inspired it.

You open the novel with a very inspirational line from Audrey Hepburn. What made you choose this particular quote?

It is a line that reflects the journey of a woman who seemed to have had it all but in fact lived a very difficult life at times. Still, she always saw herself as getting the prize in the end. It is such a positive statement about Hepburn's outlook on life. Also, *Holly Would Dream* is a bit of a fairy tale and I thought that line would tell the reader a bit of what was coming.

Strong family ties are evident in all your books, and Holly Would Dream *is no exception. Holly and her father share a very close relationship. Does their relationship mirror any of your own?*

I was very close to my own father who died about ten years ago. I wish he had lived long enough to see me publish my first book. My mother and I talk daily on the phone since we don't live in the same city. We take a trip together—just the two of us—every year. So, yes, I come from a close family.

How much did you know about fashion and fashion history before starting this book?

Very little. All I knew was how much I adored going to fashion exhibits at the Met or the FIT Museum. I thought that writing about a fashion museum would give me a great excuse to learn what life is like working in one. Dr. Valerie Steele, who is the director of the Museum at the Fashion Institute of Technology, talked to me about how they come up with ideas for exhibits, what it takes to put a show together, the security measures in place to ensure the safety of their costumes, how delicate gowns are restored, what might be a giveaway that a gown had been altered, and much more. It was fascinating stuff. I tried to build much of what I learned from her into the story. When I told Dr. Steele what I had in mind for the costumes at Holly's museum, she was horrified. Still, she was a great sport in helping me devise fictional ways that Holly might have slipped those dresses out of the museum.

Even though you deal with some serious subjects—including work, love, and family—there is always a strong sense of humor and fun in your novels. How important is it to you to incorporate humor?

I love reading novels or watching shows that make me laugh out loud. So I purposefully aim for that when writing my books. The world is a pretty tough place, isn't it? We can all use a good laugh. I hear it's as good for your health as working out.

Denis and Holly share some steamy scenes while they are in Rome. Are loves scenes difficult to write?

They used to be very hard for me to write. When I had to write my first sex scenes, I bought several books on how to write sex scenes and followed their advice. I remember writing my first steamy scenes and e-mailing them to my mother who told me they were not hot enough. Over the last few years, I've studied at Mama Gena's School of Womanly Arts. There is a lively sexual component to the classes. That has really helped me write about sex in a more playful way.

Holly lives every girl's dream when she dons the ball gown Audrey Hepburn wore for the embassy ball in My Fair Lady*. If you could wear one of her iconic ensembles, which one would you choose?*

Of course, the black dress in *Breakfast at Tiffany's* comes to mind. That would still be in style today. I also love the red gown with the matching scarf that she wore in *Funny Face*. The dress that Princess Ann wore in the last scene of *Roman Holiday* is one of my all-time favorites. It reminds me of my mother's wedding gown from 1953. That was the same year *Roman Holiday* was released.

What are you working on now?

My books tend to start out as one thing and turn into something else entirely. So if I told you the plot of my newest novel, it will probably have nothing to do with the book that is actually published.

Enhance Your Book Club

1. To find out more about author Karen Quinn, check out her official site, www.karenquinn.net, which includes information about her other titles as well as Karen's personal blog.

2. You can learn more about screen legend Audrey Hepburn at www.audreyhepburn.com, which has information about her life, her career, and her charity, the Audrey Hepburn Children's Fund.

3. Make your book club night a book-and-a-movie night by screening some of the many great films mentioned in *Holly Would Dream*. The author recommends *Roman Holiday* and *An Affair to Remember*.